A
Stark
and
Wormy
Knight

A $\mathcal{S}$TARK *and* $\mathcal{W}$ORMY $\mathcal{K}$NIGHT

*Tales of Fantasy,
Science Fiction and Suspense*

TAD WILLIAMS
EDITED BY DEBORAH BEALE

Subterranean Press 2012

First Edition

ISBN
978-1-59606-461-4

Subterranean Press
PO Box 190106
Burton, MI 48519

www.subterraneanpress.com

Contents

Introduction by Tad Williams—*11*

And Ministers of Grace—*19*

A Stark And Wormy Knight—*57*

The Storm Door—*69*

The Stranger's Hands—*89*

Bad Guy Factory—*115*

The Thursday Men—*165*

The Tenth Muse—*199*

The Lamentably Comical Tragedy
(or the Laughably Tragic Comedy)
of Lixal Laqavee—*229*

The Terrible Conflagration
at The Quiller's Mint—*263*

Black Sunshine—*273*

Ants—*427*

TO LISA TVEIT, WHO OVER MANY YEARS HAS
PROVIDED INCALCULABLE SUPPORT AND FRIENDSHIP.
WITH SMARTS, STYLE, HARD WORK AND GENEROSITY
SHE HAS KEPT MY WORK VERY PRESENT ON THE
INTERNET. WE THANK HER EVERY DAY AT MY
HOUSE, BUT NOT OFTEN ENOUGH IN PUBLIC.
FOR ALL YOU DO, LISA, THIS BOOK'S FOR YOU.

INTRODUCTION

I'M KNOWN PRIMARILY AS A writer of novels, but there's something truly special about short stories, especially in my field (which we usually lumber with the unwieldy handle of "Science Fiction and Fantasy" or the puzzling-to-outsiders "SF&F.") Much of the history of our artform is contained in short stories, including classic works by people like Bradbury, Theodore Sturgeon, Lord Dunsany, Lovecraft, Poe, Asimov, Ursula Le Guin and Arthur C. Clarke, just to name a few. Even some of the best novels in our genre started out as shorter pieces, which were then combined with other stories to make famous collections (like Bradbury's *Martian Chronicles* or Asimov's *I, Robot*) or were expanded from earlier short works, like Zelazny's prize-winning *The Dream Master.*

For me, though, the greatest lure of writing short stories is the chance to experiment, to find new ways (new to me, at least) to tell tales. I love to bring in elements of my work that I tend to play down (or at least try to control) in longer works, like my sense of humor and my love of fiddling around with language.

TAD WILLIAMS

The title story of this collection, for instance, *A Stark and Wormy Knight*, is told in a very unusual, very playful and punning style that might wear out its welcome over a full-size novel, but is just another fascinating flavor of storytelling at shorter length.

All of these stories come from a stretch of 2007-2008 when, because of invitations to write for a bunch of anthologies (all of which attracted me because of the subject matter, the other participants, or both) I turned into a bit of a short-story machine. Not in the sense that any of it came easily—I should be so lucky!—but because I wrote something like half a dozen or more substantial short works in a stretch of less than a year's time. This was very unusual for me—especially because, as always, I was also writing a novel at the time. (Probably two! I can't quite remember.)

The first story, *And Ministers of Grace*, is either a stand-alone story or the opening gun in a large project—a sweeping epic about the eventual interplanetary war between Archimedes and Covenant, bastions of Science and Belief respectively. I've been thinking about this project for years but haven't decided if or when I'd write it, so when a chance to write a story for Gardner Dozois' and George R. R. Martin's *Warriors* anthology presented itself, I thought it might be a good time to meet Lamentation Kane, who (if such an epic ever comes to be) would be one of the major players. He's also a serious bad-ass, with all meanings of the word "serious" most definitely intended.

The second tale, *A Stark and Wormy Knight*, just sort of happened. I was thinking about a story idea for a dragon anthology and wondered, "How do dragons feel about these knights who are always trying to slay them?" But I couldn't just stop there—it was going to be an entire anthology of dragon stories, so a simple reversal of the norm might not even blip the reader's radar. But as I played with it I began to hear the voice of the story's telling as sort of a cross between Dr. Seuss and James Joyce, and once I got that it pretty much wrote itself from there. I don't believe stories ever "write themselves", but this was about as close as I get to that inspired-by-the-muses kind of thing.

The Storm Door was for a *New Dead* anthology edited by Christopher Golden, and although this too reads like the first chapter of a novel (at least until the end!) it was meant to be just what it is, a meditation on dying and death and the things one might meet on the way from one to the other. It's also about zombies, but not the stupid, clumsy kind. And I apologize for any gross errors in interpretation of the Tibetan Buddhist philosophy and faith—any mistakes are mine. Please do not write letters to the Dalai Lama. He already told me he's tired of hearing from me and my readers.

I wrote *The Stranger's Hands* for the *Wizards* anthology edited by Jack Dann and Gardner Dozois. It's about magic and magicians, but not in the normal way. Don't worry! It has spells and trickery and danger and all that, but in the end it's about how good and evil are not always as clear as the old stories lead us to believe—especially when sorcerors are involved. As Tolkien once said (or had a character say for him), "Do not meddle in the affairs of wizards, for they are subtle and quick to anger." You'll see how true that is in this one.

I was also inspired by the idea that the personal relationships in fantasy stories are often under-examined, especially when it comes down to matters of Good versus Evil—and let's face it, that's what most fantasy stories come down to, often in a rather pedestrian way. The bad guy capers on, usually explaining how he's risen from the dead after X-thousand years and now will bring on an age of horror, because...well, because that's what undead villains always do. And then the good guys reluctantly beat their plowshares into swords and go out to do the right thing, for the sake of free people (or at least happy feudal peasants) everywhere.

To which I always asked myself: Really? All conflict is that simple?

Anyway, this story raises a few questions about that traditional good vs. bad approach.

Bad Guy Factory is the kind of project you only get to see in collections like this. When I was writing *Aquaman* for DC Comics I proposed a series based on the idea that all those supervillains had to get their training and their equipment somewhere—I don't think even the Joker can just call up Monster.Com and order a bunch of disposable henchmen at clerical staff wages. I wanted to get into the whole thing, the training, the economics, how a lifelong career in crime could seem like a good idea when you knew you were eventually going to get pounded on by Batman or the Flash.

Sadly, it never came to be. At the time I proposed it DC was in the middle of one of their all-inclusive "Crisis" events and it would have been immediately dragged into the service of that storyline, which wouldn't have worked out for what I envisioned. I never really tried very hard to sell it after that, but I still think it would make a cool series. I also had a lot of help from Dietrich Smith and Walden Wong doing presentation artwork to go with it, and I've never properly thanked them. Thanks, guys. The Factory, especially with your help, deserved better, but at least now some actual readers will finally get to see it.

The Thursday Men was originally written for a Hellboy anthology edited by Christopher Golden, based (of course) on Mike Mignola's now-famous creation. Being a comic book geek practically since birth, I've been a fan of Mike Mignola's big red guy for a long time, and I jumped at the chance to write a story about him. Those who've read the comics know that Hellboy's been around a long time (in his fictional world, anyway), born in 1944 when an attempt at supernaturally grabbing victory from the jaws of defeat by the Nazis went awry, and the only thing summoned from the nether regions was Hellboy himself, at the time a little red horned baby. Because of his long life, he's had lots of time for adventures, so there's lots of room to play with him, both in geography and history.

My wife Deborah Beale was contemplating a ghost story set on the California coast north of San Francisco at the time, so the place was in my thoughts. If you haven't been there, some of it is pretty much ideal supernatural fiction territory, windswept and sparsely populated. It was a pretty easy choice of location to make, and since Deb hasn't written that story yet, I didn't feel like I was poaching on her territory.

Everything else was straightforward, which is another great thing about Hellboy—he'll deal with subtlety if he has to, but he prefers punching evil in the face. Hard. And repeatedly. When your hero is a giant guy who looks like a demon and likes to smash things, but also loves cats and beer, it's hard to go wrong.

In other words, I think it's basically a fun story, the interesting science-fictional/supernatural ideas notwithstanding. I hope you'll think so too.

I love anthologies because they give me a chance to try things much different than what I usually do in my books, and this is definitely the case with *The Tenth Muse*, originally written for the Dozois-edited *The New Space Opera 2* anthology. This is perhaps the closest thing to a classic, old-fashioned science fiction story I've ever written—I think it wouldn't seem badly out of place in one of the magazines like Galaxy or Astounding. Even better, it's one of the few space opera stories to feature actual opera. Like most of the best science-fiction tales of an earlier era, it's not so much about technology or the future as it's about solving a dangerous, perhaps fatal problem. And like all good problem stories, I struggled to make the plot fair to the reader so that he or she could try to solve the terrible mystery right alongside the characters.

TAD WILLIAMS

The longest piece, *The Lamentably*...no, bugger that, let's just call it *Lixal*...was part of a very good anthology inspired by the work of Jack Vance. In most cases this would be called a "pastiche", which is a term meaning a friendly send-up of someone's style. However, I know for a fact that most of the writers in our field have always been in awe of Jack's style and would never dream of making fun of it. Rather, I think many of us tried to imitate it as purely as we could, because it seems like the only authentic way of telling a story set in his "Dying Earth" universe. And the style itself, with its elegance and sly sense of humor, has its own rewards for both the writer and the reader. I'm proud of *Lixal*, but I would never pretend that it exceeds the work of the master. I do, however, believe that it greatly exceeds mere imitative flattery and is about as good a fantasy story as I'm capable of writing in anybody's style.

The Terrible Conflagration at the Quiller's Mint is a story I wrote when we launched my *Shadowmarch* story as an online serial. I was doing stuff for the website and wrote one *Shadowmarch*-related story (you can find it in *Rite*, my first short story collection) about the early meetings between humans and Qar (the magical folk of Eion), but this one is a bit more subtle, especially if you haven't read the *Shadowmarch* books. If you have, you may find some entertaining clues to the larger story and its history here. However, I think it works just as a tale, the kind that people tell and re-tell for generations.

Black Sunshine is another one with a strange history. This idea has bounced around in my head for decades, and at one point near the turn of the millenium it was going to be my next novel, but for various reasons that didn't happen. I eventually wrote it in the form of a screenplay, because it was the best way to explain the music (mostly of the 70s) that I heard in my head with the various scenes. It would still make a cool, scary movie, and maybe it will happen someday—who knows? But it also has bits of autobiographical stuff in it from my own cool, scary teenage years, so even if it never gets filmed it will still hold a place in my heart.

The last story, *Ants*, is something I'd written in my head a long time before I wrote it down on paper. I did it for a commemorative Twilight Zone anthology edited by Carol Serling (wife of the show's famous creator, Rod Serling.) But to be perfectly honest, it's more of a Roald Dahl story than a Serling story in the way it juxtaposes horror with the ordinary. Those of you who've read Dahl's short fiction will recognize that pretty quickly. Those who haven't—what are you waiting for?

But one thing that definitely fits in that Twilight Zone universe is that it's a story about how human beings are never quite as clever as they think they are. Either that, or the gods do indeed have a very dry sense of humor.

I hope you'll enjoy the range of these stories. I hope they'll make you smile (where appropriate) and recoil in horror (also where appropriate—please don't confuse the two.) I had a wonderful time writing all of them and I think you'll feel that when you read them.

Tad Williams, Woodside, CA. April 6th, 2011

And Ministers of Grace

T HE SEED WHISPERS, SINGS, OFFERS, instructs.

A wise man of the homeworld once said, "Human beings can alter their lives by altering their attitudes of mind." Everything is possible for a committed man or woman. The universe is in our reach.

Visit the Orgasmium—now open 24 hours. We take Senior Credits. The Orgasmium—where YOU come first!

Your body temperature is normal. Your stress levels are normal, tending toward higher than normal. If this trend continues, you are recommended to see a physician.

I'm almost alive! And I'm your perfect companion—I'm entirely portable. I want to love you. Come try me. Trade my personality with friends. Join the fun!

Comb properties now available. Consult your local environment node. Brand new multi-family and single-family dwellings, low down payment with government entry loans...!

Commodity prices are up slightly on the Sackler Index at this hour, despite a morning of sluggish trading. The Prime Minister will detail her plans to reinvigorate the economy in her speech to Parliament...

A wise woman of the homeworld once said, "Keep your face to the sunshine and you cannot see the shadow."

His name is Lamentation Kane and he is a Guardian of Covenant—a holy assassin. His masters have placed a seed of blasphemy in his head. It itches like unredeemed sin and fills his skull with foul pagan noise.

The faces of his fellow travelers on the landing shuttle are bored and vacuous. How can these infidels live with this constant murmur in their heads? How can they survive and stay sane with the constant pinpoint flashing of attention signals at the edge of vision, the raw, sharp pulse of a world bristling and burbling with information?

It is like being stuck in a hive of insects, Kane thinks— insects doing their best to imitate human existence without understanding it. He longs for the sweet, singular voice of Spirit, soothing as cool water on inflamed skin. Always before, no matter the terrors of his mission, that voice has been with him, soothing him, reminding him of his holy purpose. All his life, Spirit has been with him. All his life until now.

Humble yourselves therefore under the strong hand of God, so that He may raise you up in due time.

Sweet and gentle like spring rain. Unlike this unending drizzle of filth, each word Spirit has ever spoken has been precious, bright like silver.

Cast all your burdens on Him, for He cares for you. Be in control of yourself and alert. Your enemy, the devil, prowls around like a roaring lion, looking for someone to devour.

Those were the last words Spirit spoke to him before the military scientists silenced the Word of God and replaced it with the endless, godless prattle of the infidel world, Archimedes.

For the good of all mankind, they assured him: Lamentation Kane must sin again so that one day all men would be free to worship God. Besides, the elders pointed out, what was there for him to fear? If he succeeds and escapes Archimedes the pagan seed will be removed and Spirit will speak in his thoughts again. If he does not escape—well, Kane will hear the true voice of God at the foot of His mighty throne. *Well done, my good and faithful servant...*

Beginning descent. Please return to pods, the pagan voices chirp in his head, prickling like nettles. *Thank you for traveling with us. Put all food and packaging in the receptacle and close it. This is your last chance to purchase duty-free drugs and alcohol. Cabin temperature is 20 degrees centigrade. Pull the harness snug. Beginning descent. Cabin pressure stable. Lander will detach in twenty seconds. Ten seconds. Nine seconds. Eight seconds...*

It never ends, and each godless word burns, prickles, itches.

Who needs to know so much about nothing?

A child of one of the Christian cooperative farms on Covenant's flat and empty plains, he was brought to New Jerusalem as a candidate for the elite Guardian unit. When he saw for the first time the white towers and golden domes of his planet's greatest city, Kane had been certain that Heaven would look just that way. Now, as Hellas City rises up to meet him, capital of great Archimedes and stronghold of his people's enemies, it is bigger than even his grandest, most exaggerated memories of New Jerusalem—an immense sprawl with no visible ending, a lumpy white and gray and green patchwork of complex structures and orderly parks and lacy polyceramic web skyscrapers that bend gently in the cloudy upper skies like an oceanic kelp forest. The scale is astounding. For the first time ever in his life, Lamentation Kane has a moment of doubt—not in the rightness of his cause, but in the certainty of its victory.

But he reminds himself of what the Lord told Joshua: *Behold I have given into thy hands Jericho, and the king thereof, and all the valiant men…*

Have you had a Creemy Crunch today? It blares through his thoughts like a klaxon. *You want it! You need it! Available at any food outlet. Creemy Crunch makes cream crunchy! Don't be a bitch, Mom! Snag me a CC—or three!*

The devil owns the Kingdom of Earth. A favorite saying of one of his favorite teachers. *But even from his high throne he cannot see the City of Heaven.*

Now with a subdermal glow-tattoo in every package! Just squeeze it in under the skin—and start shining!

Lord Jesus, protect me in this dark place and give me strength to do your work once more, Kane prays. *I serve You. I serve Covenant.*

It never stops, and only gets more strident after the lander touches down and they are ushered through the locks into the port complex. *Remember the wise words, air quality is in the low thirties on the Teng Fuo scale today. First OK? time visitors to Archimedes go here, returning go there,* where to stand, what to say, what to have ready. Restaurants, news feeds, information for transportation services, overnight accommodations, immigration law, emergency services, yammer yammer yammer until Kane wants to scream. He stares at the smug citizens of Archimedes around him and loathes every one of them.

How can they walk and smile and talk to each other with this Babel in their heads, without God in their hearts?

Left. Follow the green tiles. Left. Follow the green tiles. They aren't even people, they can't be—just crude imitations. And the variety of voices with which the seed bedevils him! High-pitched, low-pitched, fast and persuasive, moderately slow and persuasive, adult voices, children's voices, accents of a dozen sorts, most of which he can't even identify and can barely understand. His blessed Spirit is one voice and one voice only and he longs for her desperately. He always thinks of Spirit as "her", although it could just as easily be the calm, sweet voice of a male child. It doesn't matter. Nothing as crass as earthly sexual distinctions matter, any more than with God's holy angels. Spirit has been his constant companion since childhood, his advisor, his inseparable friend. But now he has a pagan seed in his brain and he may never hear her blessed voice again.

I will never leave thee, nor forsake thee. That's what Spirit told him the night he was baptized, the night she first spoke to him. Six years old. *I will never leave thee, nor forsake thee.*

He cannot think of that. He will not think of anything that might undermine his courage for the mission, of course, but there is a greater danger: some types of thoughts, if strong enough, can trigger the port's security E-Grams, which can perceive certain telltale patterns, especially if they are repeated.

A wise man of the homeworld once said, "Man is the measure of all things..." The foreign seed doesn't want him thinking of anything else, anyway.

Have you considered living in Holyoake Harbor? another voice asks, cutting through the first. *Only a twenty-minute commute to the business district, but a different world of ease and comfort.*

...And of things which are not, that they are not, the first voice finishes, swimming back to the top. *Another wise fellow made the case more directly: "The world holds two classes*

of men—intelligent men without religion, and religious men without intelligence."

Kane almost shivers despite the climate controls. *Blur your thoughts,* he reminds himself. He does his best to let the chatter of voices and the swirl of passing faces numb and stupefy him, making himself a beast instead of a man, the better to hide from God's enemies.

He passes the various mechanical sentries and the first two human guard posts as easily as he hoped he would—his military brethren have prepared his disguise well. He is in line at the final human checkpoint when he catches a glimpse of her, or at least he thinks it must be her—a small, brown-skinned woman sagging between two heavily armored port security guards who clutch her elbows in a parody of assistance. For a moment their eyes meet and her dark stare is frank before she hangs her head again in a convincing imitation of shame. The words from the briefing wash up in his head through the fog of Archimedean voices—*Martyrdom Sister*—but he does his best to blur them again just as quickly. He can't imagine any word that will set off the E-Grams as quickly as "Martyrdom".

The final guard post is more difficult, as it is meant to be. The sentry, almost faceless behind an array of enhanced light scanners and lenses, does not like to see Arjuna on Kane's itinerary, his last port of call before Archimedes. Arjuna is not a treaty world for either Archhimedes or Covenant, although both hope to make it so, and is not officially policed by either side.

The official runs one of his scanners over Kane's itinerary again. "Can you tell me why you stopped at Arjuna, Citizen McNally?"

Kane repeats the story of staying there with his cousin who works in the mining industry. Arjuna is rich with platinum and other minerals, another reason both sides want it. At the moment, though, neither the Rationalists of Archimedes or the Abramites of Covenant can get any traction there: the majority of Arjuna's settlers, colonists originally from the homeworld's Indian sub-continent, are comfortable with both sides—a fact that makes both Archimedes and Covenant quite uncomfortable indeed.

The guard-post official doesn't seem entirely happy with Lamentation Kane's explanation and is beginning to investigate the false personality a little more closely. Kane wonders how much longer until the window of distraction is opened. He turns casually, looking up and down the transparent u-glass cells along the far wall until he locates the one in which the brown-skinned woman is being questioned. Is she a Muslim? A Copt? Or perhaps something entirely different—there are Australian Aboriginal Jews on Covenant, remnants of the Lost Tribes movement back on the homeworld. But whoever or whatever she is doesn't matter, he reminds himself: she is a sister in God and she has volunteered to sacrifice herself for the sake of the mission—*his* mission.

She turns for a moment and their eyes meet again through the warping glass. She has acne scars on her cheeks but she's pretty, surprisingly young to be given such a task. He wonders what her name is. When he returns—if he returns—he will go to the Great Tabernacle in New Jerusalem and light a candle for her.

Brown eyes. She seems sad as she looks at him before turning back to the guards. Could that be true? The Martyrs are the most privileged of all during their time in the training center. And she must know she will be looking on the face of God Himself very soon. How can she not be joyful? Does she fear the pain of giving up her earthly body?

As the sentry in front of him seems to stare out at nothing, reading the information that marches across his vision,

TAD WILLIAMS

Lamentation Kane opens his mouth to say something—to make small-talk the way a real returning citizen of Archimedes would after a long time abroad, a citizen guilty of nothing worse than maybe having watched a few religious broadcasts on Arjuna—when he sees movement out of the corner of his eye. Inside the u-glass holding cell the young, brown-skinned woman lifts her arms. One of the armored guards lurches back from the table, half-falling, the other reaches out his gloved hand as though to restrain her, but his face has the hopeless, slack expression of a man who sees his own death. A moment later bluish flames run up her arms, blackening the sleeves of her loose dress, and then she vanishes in a flare of magnesium white light.

People are shrieking and diving away from the glass wall, which is now spiderwebbed with cracks. The light burns and flickers and the insides of the walls blacken with a crust of what Kane guesses must be human fat turning to ash.

A human explosion—nanobiotic thermal flare—that partially failed. That will be their conclusion. But of course, the architects of Kane's mission didn't want an actual explosion. They want a distraction.

The sentry in the guard post polarizes the windows and locks up his booth. Before hurrying off to help the emergency personnel fight the blaze that is already leaking clouds of black smoke into the concourse, he thrusts Kane's itinerary into his hand and waves him through, then locks off the transit point.

Lamentation Kane would be happy to move on, even if he were the innocent traveler he pretends to be. The smoke is terrible, with the disturbing, sweet smell of cooked meat. What had her last expression been like? It is hard to remember anything except those endlessly deep, dark eyes. Had that been a little smile or is he trying to convince himself? And if it had been fear, why should that be surprising? Even the saints must have feared to burn to death.

Yea, though I walk through the valley of the shadow of death, I will fear no evil...

Welcome back to Hellas, Citizen McNally! a voice in his head proclaims, and then the other voices swim up beneath it, a crowd, a buzz, an itch.

He does his best not to stare as the cab hurtles across the metroscape, but he cannot help being impressed by the sheer size of Archimedes' first city. It is one thing to be told how many millions live there and to try to understand that it is several times the size of New Jerusalem, but another entirely to see the hordes of people crowding the sidewalks and skyways. Covenant's population is mostly dispersed on pastoral settlements like the one on which Kane was raised, agrarian cooperatives that, as his teachers explained to him, keep God's children close to the earth that nurtures them. Sometimes it is hard to realize that the deep, reddish soil he had spent his childhood digging and turning and nurturing was not the same soil as the Bible described. Once he even asked a teacher why if God made Earth, the People of the Book had left it behind.

"God made all the worlds to be earth for His children," the woman explained. "Just as he made all the lands of the old Earth, then gave them to different folk to have for their homes. But he always kept the sweetest lands, the lands of milk and honey, for the children of Abraham, and that's why when we left Earth he gave us Covenant."

As he thinks about it now Kane feels a surge of warmth and loneliness commingled. It's true that the hardest thing to do for love is to give up the beloved. At this moment, he misses Covenant so badly it is all he can do not to cry out. It is astounding in one as experienced as himself. *God's warriors don't sigh,* he tells himself sternly. *They make others sigh instead. They bring lamentation to God's enemies. Lamentation.*

He exits the cab some distance from the safe house and walks the rest of the way, floating in smells both familiar and exotic. He rounds the neighborhood twice to make sure he is not followed, then enters the flatblock, takes the slow but quiet elevator up to the eighteenth floor, and lets himself in with the key code. It looks like any other Covenant safe house on any of the other colony worlds, cupboards well stocked with nourishment and medical supplies, little in the way of furniture but a bed and a single chair and a small table. These are not places of rest and relaxation, these are way stations on the road to Jericho.

It is time for him to change.

Kane fills the bathtub with water. He finds the chemical ice, activates a dozen packs and tosses them in. Then he goes to the kitchen and locates the necessary mineral and chemical supplements. He pours enough water into the mixture to make himself a thick, bitter milkshake and drinks it down while he waits for the water in the tub to cool. When the temperature has dropped far enough he strips naked and climbs in.

"You see, Kane," one of the military scientists had explained, "we've reached a point where we can't smuggle even a small hand-weapon onto Archimedes, let alone something useful, and they regulate their own citizens' possession of weapons so thoroughly that we cannot chance trying to obtain one there. So we have gone another direction. We have created Guardians—human weapons. That is what you are, praise the lord. It started in your childhood. That's why you've always been different from your peers—faster, stronger, smarter. But we've come to the limit of what we can do with genetics and training. We need to give you what you need to make yourself into the true instrument of God's justice. May He bless this and all our endeavors in His name. Amen."

"Amen," the Spirit in his head told him. "You are now going to fall asleep."

"Amen," said Lamentation Kane.

And then they gave him the first injection.

When he woke up that first time he was sore, but nowhere near as sore as he was the first time he activated the nanobiotes or "notes" as the scientists liked to call them. When the notes went to work, it was like a terrible sunburn on the outside and the inside both, and like being pounded with a roundball bat for at least an hour, and like lying in the road while a good-sized squadron of full-dress Holy Warriors marched over him.

In other words, it hurt.

Now, in the safe house, he closes his eyes, turns down the babble of the Archimedes seed as far as it will let him, and begins to work.

It is easier now than it used to be, certainly easier than that terrible first time when he was so clumsy that he almost tore his own muscles loose from tendon and bone.

He doesn't just *flex*, he thinks about where the muscles are that would flex if he wanted to flex them, then how he would just begin to move them if he were going to move them extremely slowly, and with that first thought comes the little tug of the cells unraveling their connections and re-knitting in different, more useful configurations, slow as a plant reaching toward the sun. Even with all this delicacy, his temperature rises and his muscles spasm and cramp, but not like the first time. That was like being born—no, like being judged and found wanting, as though the very meat of his earthly body was trying to tear itself free, as though devils pierced his joints with hot iron pitchforks. Agony.

Had the sister felt something like this at the end? Was there any way to open the door to God's house without terrible, holy pain? She had brown eyes. He thinks they were sad. Had she been frightened? Why would Jesus let her be frightened, when even He had cried out on the cross?

TAD WILLIAMS

Lamentation Kane tells the pain, *This is Your way of reminding me to pay attention. I am Your servant, and I am proud to put on Your holy, I praise You Lord, armor.*

It takes him at least two hours to finish changing at the best of times. Tonight, with the fatigue of his journey and long entry process and the curiously troubling effect of the woman's martyrdom tugging at his thoughts, it takes him over three.

Kane gets out of the tub shivering, most of the heat dispersed and his skin almost blue-white with cold. Before wrapping the towel around himself he looks at the results of all his work. It's hard to see any differences except for a certain broadness to his chest that was not there before, but he runs his fingers along the hard shell of his stomach and the sheath of gristle that now protects his windpipe and is satisfied. The thickening beneath the skin will not stop high-speed projectiles from close up, but they should help shed the energy of any more distant shot and will allow him to take a bullet or two from nearer and still manage to do his job. Trellises of springy cartilage strengthen his ankles and wrists. His muscles are augmented, his lungs and circulation improved mightily. He is a Guardian, and with every movement he can feel the holy modifications that have been given to him. Beneath the appearance of normality he is strong as Goliath, scaly and supple as a serpent.

He is starving, of course. The cupboards are full of powdered nutritional supplement drinks. He adds water and ice from the kitchen unit, mixes the first one up and downs it in a long swallow. He drinks five before he begins to feel full.

Kane props himself up on the bed—things are still sliding and grinding a little inside him, the last work of change just finishing—and turns the wall on. The images jump into life and the seed in his head speaks for them. He wills his way past sports and fashion and drama, all the unimportant gibberish with which these creatures fill their empty hours, until he finds a stream of current events. Because it is Archimedes, hive of Rationalist pagans, even the news is corrupted with filth, gossip and whoremongering, but he manages to squint his way through the offending material to find a report on what the New Hellas authorities are calling a failed terrorist explosion at the port. A picture of the Martyrdom Sister flashes onto the screen—taken from her travel documents, obviously, anything personal in her face well hidden by her training—but seeing her again gives him a strange jolt, as though the notes that tune his body have suddenly begun one last, forgotten operation.

Nefise Erim, they call her. Not her real name, that's almost certain, any more than Keenan McNally is his. *Outcast*, that's her true name. *Scorned*—that could be her name too, as it could be his. Scorned by the unbelievers, scorned by the smug, faithless creatures who, like Christ's ancient tormentors, fear the word of God so much they try to ban Him from their lives, from their entire planet! But God can't be banned, not as long as one human heart remains alive to His voice. As long as the Covenant system survives, Kane knows, God will wield his mighty sword and the unbelievers will learn real fear.

Oh, please, Lord, grant that I may serve you well. Give us victory over our enemies. Help us to punish those who would deny You.

And just as he lifts this silent prayer, he sees *her* face on the screen. Not his sister in martyrdom, with her wide, deep eyes and dark skin. No, it is her—the devil's mistress, Keeta Januari, Prime Minister of Archimedes.

His target.

Januari is herself rather dark skinned, he cannot help noticing. It is disconcerting. He has seen her before, of course, her image replayed before him dozens upon dozens of times, but this is the first time he has noticed a shade to her skin that is darker than any mere suntan, a hint of something else in her background beside the pale, Scandinavian forebears so obvious in her bone structure. It is as if the martyred sister Nefise has somehow suffused everything, even his target. Or is it that the dead woman has somehow crept into his thoughts so deeply that he is witnessing her everywhere?

If you can see it, you can eat it! He has mostly learned to ignore the horrifying chatter in his head, but sometimes it still reaches up and slaps his thoughts away. *Barnstorm Buffet! We don't care if they have to roll you out the door afterward— you'll get your money's worth!*

It doesn't matter what he sees in the Prime Minister, or thinks he sees. A shade lighter or darker means nothing. If the devil's work out here among the stars has a face, it is the handsome, narrow-chinned visage of Keeta Januari, leader of the Rationalists. And if God ever wanted someone dead, she is that person.

She won't be his first: Kane has sent eighteen souls to judgment already. Eleven of them were pagan spies or dangerous rabble-rousers on Covenant. One of those was the leader of a crypto-rationalist cult in the Crescent—the death was a favor to the Islamic partners in Covenant's ruling coalition, Kane found out later. Politics. He doesn't know how he feels about that, although he knows the late Doctor Hamoud was a doubter and a liar and had been corrupting good Muslims. Still...politics.

Five were infiltrators among the Holy Warriors of Covenant, his people's army. Most of these had half-expected to be discovered, and several of them had resisted desperately.

The last two were a politician and his wife on the unaffiliated world of Arjuna, important Rationalist sympathizers. At his masters' bidding Kane made it look like a robbery gone wrong instead of an assassination: this was not the time to make the Lord's hand obvious in Arjuna's affairs. Still, there were rumors and accusations across Arjuna's public networks. The gossipers and speculators had even given the unknown murderer a nickname—the Angel of Death.

Dr. Prishrahan and his wife had fought him. Neither of them had wanted to die. Kane had let them resist even though he could have killed them both in a moment. It gave credence to the robbery scenario. But he hadn't enjoyed it. Neither had the Prishrahans, of course.

He will avenge the blood of His servants, and will render vengeance to His adversaries, Spirit reminded him when he had finished with the doctor and his wife, and he understood. Kane's duty is not to judge. He is not one of the flock, but closer to the wolves he destroys. Lamentation Kane is God's executioner.

He is now cold enough from his long submersion that he puts on clothes. He is still tender in his joints as well. He goes out onto the balcony, high in the canyons of flatblocks pinpricked with illuminated windows, thousands upon thousands of squares of light. The immensity of the place still unnerves him a little. It's strange to think that what is happening behind one little lighted window in this immensity of sparkling urban night is going to rock this massive world to its foundations.

It is hard to remember the prayers as he should. Ordinarily Spirit is there with the words before he has a moment to feel lonely. *I will not leave you comfortless: I will come to you.*

But he does not feel comforted at this moment. He is alone.

Looking for love? The voice in his head whispers this time, throaty and exciting. A bright twinkle of coordinates flicker at the edge of his vision. *I'm looking for you...and you can have me for almost nothing...*

He closes his eyes tight against the immensity of the pagan city.

TAD WILLIAMS

Fear thou not; for I am with thee: be not dismayed; for I am thy God.

He walks to the auditorium just to see the place where the prime minister will speak. He does not approach very closely. It looms against the grid of light, a vast rectangle like an axe head smashed into the central plaza of Hellas City. He does not linger.

As he slides through the crowds it is hard not to look at the people around him as though he has already accomplished his task. What would they think if they knew who he was? Would they shrink back from the terror of the Lord God's wrath? Or would a deed of such power and piety speak to them even through their fears?

I am ablaze with the light of the Lord, he wants to tell them. *I have let God make me His instrument—I am full of glory!* But he says nothing, of course, only walks amid the multitudes with his heart grown silent and turned inward.

Kane eats in a restaurant. The food is so over-spiced as to be tasteless, and he yearns for the simple meals of the farm on which he was raised. Even military manna is better than this! The customers twitter and laugh just like the Archimedes seed in their heads, as if it is that babbling obscenity that has programmed them instead of the other way around. How these people surrounded themselves with distraction and glare and noise to obscure the emptiness of their souls!

He goes to a place where women dance. It is strange to watch them, because they smile and smile and they are all as beautiful and naked as a dark dream, but they seem to him like damned souls, doomed to act out this empty farce of love and attraction throughout eternity. He cannot get the thought of martyred Nefise Erim out of his head. At last he chooses one of the women—she does not look much like the martyred one, but she is darker than the others—and lets her lead him to her room behind the place where they dance. She feels the hardened tissues beneath his skin and tells him he is very muscular. He empties himself inside her and then, afterward, she asks him why he is crying. He tells her she is mistaken. When she asks again he slaps her. Although he holds back his strength he still knocks her off the bed. The room adds a small surcharge to his bill.

He lets her go back to her work. She is an innocent, of sorts: she has been listening to the godless voices in her head all her life and knows nothing else. No wonder she dances like a damned thing.

Kane is soiled now as he walks the streets again, but his great deed will wipe the taint from him as it always does. He is a Guardian of Covenant, and soon he will be annealed by holy fire.

His masters want the deed done while the crowd is gathered to see the prime minister, and so the question seems simple: before or after? He thinks at first that he will do it when she arrives, as she steps from the car and is hurried into the corridor leading to the great hall. That seems safest. After she has spoken it will be much more difficult, with her security fully deployed and the hall's own security acting with them. Still, the more he thinks about it the more he feels sure that it must be inside the hall. Only a few thousand would be gathered there to see her speak, but millions more will be watching on the screens surrounding the massive building. If he strikes quickly his deed will be witnessed by this whole world—and other worlds, too.

Surely God wants it that way. Surely He wants the unbeliever destroyed in full view of the public waiting to be instructed.

Kane does not have time or resources to counterfeit permission to be in the building—the politicians and hall security will be checked and re-checked, and will be in place long before Prime Minister Januari arrives. Which means that the only people allowed to enter without going through careful screening will be the prime minister's own party. That is a possibility, but he will need help with it.

Making contact with local assets is usually a bad sign—it means something has gone wrong with the original plan—but Kane knows that with a task this important he cannot afford to be superstitious. He leaves a signal in the established place. The local assets come to the safe house after sunset. When he opens the door he finds two men, one young and one old, both disconcertingly ordinary-looking, the kind of men who might come to tow your car or fumigate your flat. The middle-aged one introduces himself as Heinrich Sartorius, his companion just as Carl. Sartorius motions Kane not to speak while Carl sweeps the room with a small object about the size of a toothbrush.

"Clear," the youth announces. He is bony and homely, but he moves with a certain grace, especially while using his hands.

"Praise the Lord," Sartorius says. "And blessings on you, brother. What can we do to help you with Christ's work?"

"Are you really the one from Arjuna?" young Carl askes suddenly.

"Quiet, boy. This is serious." Sartorius turns back to Kane with an expectant look on his face. "He's a good lad. It's just—that meant a lot to the community, what happened there on Arjuna."

Kane ignores this. He is wary of the Death Angel nonsense. "I need to know what the prime minister's security detail wears. Details. And I want the layout of the auditorium, with a focus on air and water ducts."

The older man frowns. "They'll have that all checked out, won't they?"

"I'm sure. Can you get it for me without attracting attention?"

"'Course." Sartorius nods. "Carl'll find it for you right now. He's a whiz. Ain't that right, boy?" The man turns back to Kane. "We're not backward, you know. The unbelievers always say it's because we're backward, but Carl here was up near the top of his class in mathematics. We just kept Jesus in our hearts when the rest of these people gave Him up, that's the difference."

"Praise Him," says Carl, already working the safe house wall, images flooding past so quickly that even with his augmented vision Kane can barely make out a tenth of them.

"Yes, *praise* Him," Sartorius agrees, nodding his head as though there has been a long and occasionally heated discussion about how best to deal with Jesus.

Kane is beginning to feel the ache in his joints again, which usually means he needs more protein. He heads for the small kitchen to fix himself another nutrition drink. "Can I get you two anything?" he asks.

"We're good," says the older man. "Just happy doing the Lord's work."

They make too much noise, he decides. Not that most people would have heard them, but Kane isn't most people.

I am the sword of the Lord, he tells himself silently. He can scarcely hear himself think it over the murmur of the Archimedes seed, which although turned down low is still spouting meteorological information, news, tags of philosophy and other trivia like a madman on a street corner. Below the spot where Kane hangs the three men of the go-suited security detail communicate among themselves with hand-signs as they investigate the place he has entered the building. He has altered the evidence of his incursion to look like someone has tried and failed to get into the auditorium through the intake duct.

TAD WILLIAMS

The guards seem to draw the desired conclusion: after another flurry of hand-signals, and presumably after relaying the all-clear to the other half of the security squad, who are doubtless inspecting the outside of the same intake duct, the three turn and begin to walk back up the steep conduit, the flow of air making their movements unstable, headlamps splashing unpredictably over the walls. But Kane is waiting above them like a spider, in the shadows of a high place where the massive conduit bends around one of the building's pillars, his hardened fingertips dug into the concrete, his augmented muscles tensed and locked. He waits until all three pass below him then drops down silently behind them and crushes the throat of the last man so he can't alert the others. He then snaps the guard's neck and tosses the body over his shoulder, then scrambles back up the walls into the place he has prepared, a hammock of canvas much the same color as the inside of the duct. In a matter of seconds he strips the body, praying fervently that other two will not have noticed that their comrade is missing. He pulls on the man's go-suit, which is still warm, then leaves the guard's body in the hammock and springs down to the ground just as the second guard realizes there is no one behind him.

As the man turns toward him Kane sees his lips moving behind the face shield and knows the guard must be talking to him by seed. The imposture is broken, or will be in a moment. Can he pretend his own communications machinery is malfunctioning? Not if these guards are any good. If they work for the prime minister of Archimedes, they probably are. He has a moment before the news is broadcast to all the other security people in the building.

Kane strides forward making nonsensical hand-signs. The other guard's eyes widen: he does not recognize either the signs or the face behind the polymer shield. Kane shatters the man's neck with a two-handed strike even as the guard struggles to pull his side arm. Then Kane leaps at the last guard just as he turns.

Except it isn't a he. It's a woman and she's fast. She actually has her gun out of the holster before he kills her.

He has only moments, he knows: the guards will have a regular check-in to their squad leader. He sprints for the side-shaft that should take him to the area above the ceiling of the main hall.

Women as leaders. Women as soldiers. Women dancing naked in public before strangers. Is there anything these Archimedeans will not do to debase the daughters of Eve? Force them all into whoredom, as the Babylonians did?

The massive space above the ceiling is full of riggers and technicians and heavily armed guards. A dozen of those, at least. Most of them are sharpshooters keeping an eye on the crowd through the scopes on their high-powered guns, which is lucky. Some of them might not even see him until he's on his way down.

Two of the heavily armored troopers turn as he steps out into the open. He is being queried for identification, but even if they think he is one of their own they will not let him get more than a few yards across the floor. He throws his hands in the air and takes a few casual steps toward them, shaking his head and pointing at his helmet. Then he leaps forward, praying they do not understand how quickly he can move.

He covers the twenty yards or so in just a little more than a second. To confound their surprise, he does not attack but dives past the two who have already seen him and the third just turning to find out what the conversation is about. He reaches the edge of the flies and launches himself out into space, tucked and spinning to make himself a more difficult target. Still, he feels a high-speed projectile hit his leg and penetrate a little way, slowed by the guard's go-suit and stopped by his own hardened flesh.

He lands so hard that the stolen guard helmet pops off his head and bounces away. The first screams and shouts of surprise are beginning to rise from the crowd of parliamentarians, but Kane can hardly hear them. The shock of his fifty-foot fall swirls through the enhanced cartilage of his knees and ankles and wrists, painful but manageable. His heart is beating so fast it almost buzzes, and he is so accelerated that the noise of the audience seemed like the sound of something completely inhuman, the deep scrape of a glacier, the tectonic rumbling of a mountain's roots. Two more bullets snap into the floor beside him, chips of concrete and fragments of carpet spinning slowly in the air, hovering like ashes in a fiery updraft. The woman at the lectern turns toward him in molasses-time and it is indeed her, Keeta Januari, the Whore of Babylon. As he reaches toward her he can see the individual muscles of her face react—eyebrows pulled up, forehead wrinkling, surprised...but not frightened.

How can that be?

He is already leaping toward her, curving the fingers of each hand into hardened claws for the killing strike. A fraction of a second to cross the space between them as bullets snap by from above and either side, the noise scything past a long instant later, *wow, wow, wow.* Time hanging, disconnected from history. God's hand. He *is* God's hand, and this is what it must feel like to be in the presence of God Himself, this shimmering, endless, bright NOW...

And then pain explodes through him and sets his nerves on fire and everything goes suddenly and irrevocably

black.

Lamentation Kane wakes in a white room, the light from everywhere and nowhere. He is being watched, of course. Soon, the torture will begin.

Beloved, think it not strange concerning the fiery trial which is to try you, as though some strange thing happened unto you... Those were the holy words Spirit whispered to him when he lay badly wounded in the hospital after capturing the last of the Holy Warrior infiltrators, another augmented soldier like himself, a bigger, stronger man who almost killed him before Kane managed to put a stiffened finger through his eyeball into his brain. Spirit recited the words to him again and again during his recuperation: *But rejoice, inasmuch as ye are partakers of Christ's sufferings; that, when his glory...when his glory....*

To his horror, he cannot remember the rest of the passage from Peter.

He cannot help thinking of the martyred young woman who gave her life so that he could fail so utterly. He will see her soon. Will he be able to meet her eye? Is there shame in Heaven?

I will be strong, Kane promises her shade, *no matter what they do to me.*

One of the cell's walls turns from white to transparent. The room beyond is full of people, most of them in military uniforms or white medical smocks. Only two wear civilian clothing, a pale man and...her. Keeta Januari.

"You may throw yourself against the glass if you want." Her voice seems to come out of the air on all sides. "It is very, very thick and very, very strong."

He only stares. He will not make himself a beast, struggling to escape while they laugh. These people are the ones who think themselves related to animals. Animals! Kane knows that the Lord God has given his people dominion.

"Over all the beasts and fowls of the earth," he says out loud.

"So," says Prime Minister Januari. "So, this is the Angel of Death."

"That is not my name."

"We know your name, Kane. We have been watching you since you reached Archimedes."

A lie, surely. They would never have let him get so close.

She narrows her eyes. "I would have expected an angel to look more...angelic."

"I'm no angel, as you almost found out."

"Ah, if you're not, then you must be one of the ministers of grace." She sees the look on his face. "How sad. I forgot that Shakespeare was banned by your mullahs. 'Angels and ministers of grace defend us!' From Macbeth. It precedes a murder."

"We Christians do not have mullahs," he says as evenly as he can. He does not care about the rest of the nonsense she speaks. "Those are the people of the Crescent, our brothers of the Book."

She laughed. "I thought you would be smarter than the rest of your sort, Kane, but you parrot the same nonsense. Do you know that only a few generations back your 'brothers' as you call them set off a thermonuclear device, trying to kill your grandparents and the rest of the Christian and Zionist 'brothers'?"

"In the early days, before the Covenant, there was confusion." Everyone knew the story. Did she think to shame him with old history, ancient quotations, banned playwrights from the wicked old days of Earth? If so, then both of them had underestimated each other as adversaries.

Of course, at the moment she did hold a somewhat better position.

"So, then, not an angel but a minister. But you don't pray to be protected from death, but to be able to cause it."

"I do the Lord's will."

"Bullshit, to use a venerable old term. You are a murderer many times over, Kane. You tried to murder me." But Januari does not look at him as though at an enemy. Nor is there kindness in her gaze, either. She looks at him as though he is a poisonous insect in a jar—an object to be careful with, yes, but mostly a thing to be studied. "What shall we do with you?"

"Kill me. If you have any of the humanity you claim, you will release me and send me to Heaven. But I know you will torture me."

She raises an eyebrow. "Why would we do that?"

"For information. Our nations are at war, even though the politicians have not yet admitted it to their peoples. You know it, woman. I know it. Everyone in this room knows it."

Keeta Januari smiles. "You will get no argument from me or anyone here about the state of affairs between Archimedes and the Covenant system. But why would we torture you for information we already have? We are not barbarians. We are not primitives—like some others. We do not force our citizens to worship savage old myths..."

"You force them to be silent! You punish those who would worship the God of their fathers. You have persecuted the People of the Book wherever you have found them!"

"We have kept our planet free from the mania of religious warfare and extremism. We have never interfered in the choices of Covenant."

"You have tried to keep us from gaining converts."

The prime minister shakes her head. "Gaining converts? Trying to hijack entire cultures, you mean. Stealing the right of colonies to be free of Earth's old tribal ghosts. We are the same people that let your predecessors worship the way they wished to—we fought to protect their freedom, and were repaid when they tried to force their beliefs on us at gunpoint." Her laugh is harsh. "'Christian tolerance'—two words that do not belong together no matter how often they've been coupled. And we all know what your Islamist and Zionist brothers are like. Even if you destroy all of the Archimedean alliance and every single one of us unbelievers, you'll only find yourself fighting your allies instead. The madness won't stop until the last living psychopath winds up all alone on a hill of ashes, shouting praise to his god."

Kane feels his anger rising and closes his mouth. He suffuses his blood with calming chemicals. It confuses him, arguing with her. She is a woman and she should give comfort, but she is speaking only lies—cruel, dangerous lies. This is what happens when the natural order of things is upset. "You are a devil. I will speak to you no more. Do whatever it is you're going to do."

"Here's another bit of Shakespeare," she says. "If your masters hadn't banned him, you could have quoted it at me. *'But man, proud man, dressed in a little brief authority, most ignorant of what he's most assured'*—that's nicely put, isn't it? *'His glassy essence, like an angry ape, plays such fantastic tricks before high heaven as make the angels weep.'*" She puts her hands together in a gesture disturbingly reminiscent of prayer. He cannot turn away from her gaze. "So—what *are* we going to do with you? We could execute you quietly, of course. A polite fiction—died from injuries sustained in the arrest—and no one would make too much fuss."

The man behind her clears his throat. "Madame Prime Minister, I respectfully suggest we take this conversation elsewhere. The doctors are waiting to see the prisoner..."

"Shut up, Healy." She turns to look at Kane again, really look, her blue eyes sharp as scalpels. She is older than the Martyrdom Sister by a good twenty years, and despite the dark tint her skin is much paler, but somehow, for a dizzying second, they are the same.

Why do you allow me to become confused, Lord, between the murderer and the martyr?

"Kane comma Lamentation," she says. "Quite a name. Is that your enemies lamenting, or is it you, crying out helplessly before the power of your God?" She holds up her hand. "Don't bother to answer. In parts of the Covenant system you're a hero, you know—a sort of superhero. Were you aware of that? Or have you been traveling too much?"

He does his best to ignore her. He knows he will be lied to, manipulated, that the psychological torments will be more subtle and more important than the physical torture. The only thing he does not understand is: Why her—why the prime minister herself? Surely he isn't so important. The fact that she stands in front of him at this moment instead of in front of God is, after all, a demonstration that he is a failure.

As if in answer to this thought, a voice murmurs in the back of his skull, *Arjuna's Angel of Death captured in attempt on PM Januari.* Another inquires, *Have you smelled yourself lately? Even members of parliament can lose freshness—just ask one!* Even here, in the heart of the beast, the voices in his head will not be silenced.

"We need to study you," the prime minister says at last. "We haven't caught a Guardian-class agent before—not one of the new ones, like you. We didn't know if we could do it—the scrambler field was only recently developed." She smiles again, a quick icy flash like a first glimpse of snow in high mountains. "It wouldn't have meant anything if you'd succeeded, you know. There are at least a dozen more in my party who can take my place and keep this system safe against you and your masters. But I made good bait—and you leaped into the trap. Now we're going to find out what makes you such a nasty instrument, little Death Angel."

He hopes that now the charade is over they will at least shut off the seed in his head. Instead, they leave it in place but disable his controls so that he can't affect it at all. Children's voices sing to him about the value of starting each day with a healthy breakfast and he grinds his teeth. The mad chorus yammers and sings to him nonstop. The pagan seed shows him pictures he does not want to see, gives him information about which he does not care, and always, always, it denies that Kane's God exists.

The Archimedeans claim they have no death penalty. Is this what they do instead? Drive their prisoners to suicide?

If so, he will not do their work for them. He has internal resources they cannot disable without killing him and he was prepared to survive torture of a more obvious sort—why not this? He dilutes the waves of despair that wash through him at night when the lights go out and he is alone with the idiot babble of their idiot planet.

No, Kane will not do their job for him. He will not murder himself. But it gives him an idea.

If he had done it in his cell they might have been more suspicious, but when his heart stops in the course of a rather invasive procedure to learn how the note biotech has grown into his nervous system, they are caught by surprise.

"It must be a failsafe!" one of the doctors cries. Kane hears him as though from a great distance—already his higher systems are shutting down. "Some kind of auto-destruct!"

"Maybe it's just cardiac arrest..." says another, but it's only a whisper and he is falling down a long tunnel. He almost thinks he can hear Spirit calling after him...

And God shall wipe away all tears from their eyes; and there shall be no more death, neither sorrow, nor crying, neither shall there be any more pain: for the former things are passed away.

His heart starts pumping again twenty minutes later. The doctors, unaware of the sophistication of his autonomic control, are trying to shock his system back to life. Kane hoped he would be down longer and that they would give him up for dead but that was overly optimistic: instead he has to roll off the table, naked but for trailing wires and tubes, and kill the startled guards before they can draw their weapons. He must also break the neck of one of the doctors who has been trying to save him but now makes the mistake of attacking him. Even after he leaves the rest of the terrified medical staff cowering on the emergency room floor and escapes the surgical wing, he is still in a prison.

Tired of the same old atmosphere? Holyoake Harbor, the little village under the bubble—we make our own air and it's guaranteed fresh!

His internal modifications are healing the surgical damage as quickly as possible but he is staggering, starved of nutrients and burning energy at brushfire speed. God has given him this chance and he must not fail, but if he does not replenish his reserves he *will* fail.

Kane drops down from an overhead air duct into a hallway and kills a two-man patrol team. He tears the uniform off one of them and then, with stiffened, clawlike fingers, pulls gobbets of meat off the man's bones and swallows them. The blood is salty and hot. His stomach convulses at what he is doing—the old, terrible sin—but he forces himself to chew and swallow. He has no choice.

Addiction a problem? Not with a NeoBlood transfusion! We also feature the finest life-tested and artificial organs…

He can tell by the sputtering messages on the guards' communicators that the security personnel are spreading out from the main guardroom. They seem to have an idea of where he has been and where he now is. When he has finished his terrible meal he leaves the residue on the floor of the closet and then makes his way toward the central security office, leaving red footprints behind him. He looks, he feels sure, like a demon from the deepest floors of Hell.

The guards make the mistake of coming out of their hardened room, thinking numbers and weaponry are on their side.

Kane takes several bullet wounds but they have nothing as terrible as the scrambling device which captured him in the first place and he moves through his enemies like a whirlwind, snapping out blows of such strength that one guard's head is knocked from his shoulders and tumbles down the hall.

Once he has waded through the bodies into the main communication room, he throws open as many of the prison cells as he can and turns on the escape and fire alarms, which howl like the damned. He waits until the chaos is ripe, then pulls on a guard's uniform and heads for the exercise yard. He hurries through the shrieking, bloody confusion of the yard, then climbs over the three sets of razor-wire fencing. Several bullets smack into his hardened flesh, burning like hot rivets. A beam weapon scythes across the last fence with a hiss and pop of snapping wire, but Kane has already dropped to the ground outside.

He can run about fifty miles an hour under most circumstances, but fueled with adrenaline he can go almost half again that fast for short bursts. The only problem is that he is traveling over open, wild ground and has to watch for obstacles—even he can badly injure an ankle at this speed because he cannot armor his joints too much without losing flexibility. Also, he is so exhausted and empty even after consuming the guard's flesh that black spots caper in front of his eyes: he will not be able to keep up this pace very long.

Here are some wise words from an ancient statesman to consider: "You can do what you have to do, and sometimes you can do it even better than you think you can."

Kids, all parents can make mistakes. How about yours? Report religious paraphernalia or overly superstitious behavior on your local Freedom Council tip node...

Your body temperature is far above normal. Your stress levels are far above normal. We recommend you see a physician immediately.

Yes, Kane thinks. *I believe I'll do just that.*

He finds an empty house within five miles of the prison and breaks in. He eats everything he can find, including several pounds of frozen meat, which helps him compensate for a little of the heat he is generating. He then rummages through the upstairs bedrooms until he finds some new clothes to wear, scrubs off the blood that marks him out, and leaves.

He finds another place some miles away to hide for the night. The residents are home—he even hears them listening to news of his escape, although it is a grossly inaccurate version that concentrates breathlessly on his cannibalism and his terrifying nickname. He lays curled in a box in their attic like a mummy, nearly comatose. When they leave in the morning, so does Kane, reshaping the bones of his face and withdrawing color from his hair. The pagan seed still chirps in his head. Every few minutes it reminds him to keep an eye open for himself, but not to approach himself, because he is undoubtedly very, very dangerous.

"Didn't know anything about it." Sartorius looks worriedly up and down the road to make sure they are alone, as if Kane hadn't already done that better, faster, and more carefully long before the two locals had arrived at the rendezvous. "What can I say? We didn't have any idea they had that scrambler thing. Of course we would have let you know if we'd heard."

"I need a doctor—somebody you'd trust with your life, because I'll be trusting him with mine."

"Cannibal Christian," says young Carl in an awed voice. "That's what they're calling you now."

"That's crap." He is not ashamed because he was doing God's will, but he does not want to be reminded, either.

"Or the Angel of Death, they still like that one, too. Either way, they're sure talking about you."

The doctor is a woman too, a decade or so past her child-bearing years. They wake her up in her small cottage on the edge of a blighted park that looks like it was manufacturing space before a halfway attempt to redeem it. She has alcohol on her breath and her hands shake, but her eyes, although a little bloodshot, are intelligent and alert.

"Don't bore me with your story and I won't bore you with mine," she says when Carl begins to introduce them. A moment later her pupils dilate. "Hang on—I already know yours. You're the Angel everyone's talking about."

"Some people call him the Cannibal Christian," says young Carl helpfully.

"Are you a believer?" Kane asks her.

"I'm too flawed to be anything else. Who else but Jesus would keep forgiving me?"

She lays him out on a bed sheet on her kitchen table. He waves away both the anesthetic inhaler and the bottle of liquor.

"They won't work on me unless I let them, and I can't afford to let them work. I have to stay alert. Now please, cut that godless thing out of my head. Do you have a Spirit you can put in?"

"Beg pardon?" She straightens up, the scalpel already bloody from the incision he is doing his best to ignore.

"What do you call it here? My kind of seed, a seed of Covenant. So I can hear the voice of Spirit again..."

As if to protest its own pending removal, the Archimedes seed abruptly fills his skull with a crackle of interference.

A bad sign, Kane thinks. He must be overworking his internal systems. When he finishes here he'll need several days rest before he decides what to do next.

"Sorry," he tells the doctor. "I didn't hear you. What did you say?"

She shrugs. "I said I'd have to see what I have. One of your people died on this very table a few years ago, I'm sad to say, despite everything I did to save him. I think I kept his communication seed." She waves her hand a little, as though such things happen or fail to happen every day. "Who knows? I'll have a look."

He cannot let himself hope too much. Even if she has it, what are the odds that it will work, and even more unlikely, that it will work here on Archimedes? There are booster stations on all the other colony worlds like Arjuna where the Word is allowed to compete freely with the lies of the Godless.

The latest crackle in his head resolves into a calm, sweetly reasonable voice. ...*No less a philosopher than Aristotle himself said, "Men create gods after their own image, not only with regard to their form, but with regard to their mode of life."*

Kane forces himself to open his eyes. The room is blurry, the doctor a faint shadowy shape bending over him. Something sharp probes in his neck.

"There it is," she says. "It's going to hurt a bit coming out. What's your name? Your real name?"

"Lamentation."

"Ah." She doesn't smile, at least he doesn't think she does—it's hard for him to make out her features—but she sounds amused. "'*She weepeth sore in the night, and her tears are on her cheeks: among all her lovers she hath none to comfort her: all her friends have dealt treacherously with her, they are become her enemies.*' That's Jerusalem they're talking about," the doctor adds. "The original one."

"Book of Lamentations," he says quietly. The pain is so fierce that it's all he can do not to reach up and grab the hand that holds the probing, insupportable instrument. At times like this, when he most needs to restrain himself, he can most clearly feel his strength. If he were to lose control and loose that unfettered power, he feels that he could blaze like one of the stellar torches in heaven's great vault, that he could destroy an entire world.

"Hey," says a voice in the darkness beyond the pool of light on the kitchen table—young Carl. "Hey. Something's going on."

"What are you talking about?" demands Sartorius. A moment later the window explodes in a shower of sparkling glass and the room fills with smoke.

Not smoke, gas. Kane springs off the table, accidentally knocking the doctor back against the wall. He gulps in enough breath to last him a quarter of an hour and flares the tissues of his pharynx to seal his air passages. If it's a nerve gas there is nothing much he can do, though—too much skin exposed.

In the corner the doctor struggles to her feet, emerging from the billows on the floor with her mouth wide and working but nothing coming out. It isn't just her. Carl and Sartorius are holding their breath as they shove furniture against the door as a make-shift barricade. The bigger, older man already has a gun in his hand. Why is it so quiet outside? What are they doing out there?

The answer comes with a stuttering roar. Small arms fire suddenly fills the kitchen wall with holes. The doctor throws up her hands and begins a terrible jig, as though she is being stitched by an invisible sewing machine. When she falls to the ground it is in pieces.

Young Carl stretches motionless on the floor in a pool of his own spreading blood and brains. Sartorius is still standing unsteadily, but red bubbles through his clothing in several places.

Kane is on the ground—he has dropped without realizing it. He does not stop to consider near-certainty of failure, but instead springs to the ceiling and digs his fingers in long enough to smash his way through with the other hand, then hunkers in the crawlspace until the first team of troopers come in to check the damage, flashlights darting through the fog of gas fumes. How did they find him so quickly? More importantly, what have they brought to use against him?

Speed is his best weapon. He climbs out through the vent. He has to widen it, and the splintering brings a fusillade from below. When he reaches the roof dozens of shots crack past him and two actually hit him, one in the arm and one in the back, these from the parked security vehicles where the rest of the invasion team are waiting for the first wave to signal them inside. The shock waves travel through him so that he shakes like a wet dog. A moment later, as he suspected, they deploy the scrambler. This time, though, he is ready: he saturates his neurons with calcium to deaden the electromagnetic surge, and although his own brain activity ceases for a moment and he drops bonelessly across the roofcrest, there is no damage. A few seconds later he is up again. Their best weapon spent, the soldiers have three seconds to shoot at a dark figure scrambling with incredible speed along the roofline, then Lamentation Kane jumps down into the hot tracery of their fire, sprints forward and leaps off the hood of their own vehicle and over them before they can change firing positions.

He can't make it to full speed this time—not enough rest and not enough refueling—but he can go fast enough that he has vanished into the Hellas City sewers by time the strike team can re-mobilize.

The Archimedes seed, which has been telling his enemies exactly where he is, lies behind him now, wrapped in bloody gauze somewhere in the ruins of the doctor's kitchen. Keeta Januari and her Rationalists will learn much about the ability of the Covenant scientists to manufacture imitations of Archimedes technology, but they will not learn anything more about Kane. Not from the seed. He is free of it now.

He emerges almost a full day later from a pumping station on the outskirts of one of Hellas City's suburbs, but now he is a different Kane entirely, a Kane never before seen. Although the doctor removed the Archimedes seed, she had no time to locate, let alone implant, a Spirit device in its place: for the first time in as long as he can remember his thoughts are entirely his own, his head empty of any other voices.

The solitude is terrifying.

He makes his way up into the hills west of the great city, hiding in the daytime, moving cautiously by night because so many of the rural residents have elaborate security systems or animals who can smell Kane even before he can smell them. At last he finds an untended property. He could break in easily, but instead extrudes one of his fingernails and hardens it to pick the lock. He wants to minimize his presence whenever possible—he needs time to think, to plan. The ceiling has been lifted off his world and he is confused.

For safety's sake, he spends the first two days exploring his new hiding place only at night, with the lights out and his pupils dilated so far that even the sudden appearance of a white piece of paper in front of him is painful. From what he can tell, the small, modern house belongs to a man traveling for a month on the eastern side of the continent. The owner has been gone only a week, which gives Kane ample time to rest and think about what he is going to do next.

The first thing he has to get used to is the silence in his head. All his life since he was a tiny, unknowing child, Spirit has spoken to him. Now he cannot not hear her calm, inspiring voice. The godless prattle of Archimedes is silenced, too. There is nothing and no one to share Kane's thoughts.

He cries that first night as he cried in the whore's room, like a lost child. He is a ghost. He is no longer human. He has lost his inner guide, he has botched his mission, he has failed his God and his people. He has eaten the flesh of his own kind, and for nothing.

Lamentation Kane is alone with his great sin.

He moves on before the owner of the house returns. He knows he could kill the man and stay for many more months, but it seems time to do things differently, although Kane can't say precisely why. He can't even say for certain what things he is going to do. He still owes God the death of Prime Minister Januari, but something seems to have changed inside him and he is in no hurry to fulfill that promise. The silence in his head, at first so frightening, has begun to seem something more. Holy, perhaps, but certainly different than anything he has experienced before, as though every moment is a waking dream.

No, it is more like waking up from a dream. But what kind of dream has he escaped, a good one or a bad one? And what will replace it?

Even without Spirit's prompting, he remembers Christ's words: *You shall know the truth, and the truth shall set you free.* In his new inner silence, the ancient promise seems to have many meanings. Does Kane really want the truth? Could he stand to be truly free?

Before he leaves the house he takes the owner's second-best camping equipment, the things the man left behind. Kane will live in the wild areas in the highest parts of the hills for as long as seems right. He will think. It is possible that he will leave Lamentation Kane there behind him when he comes out again. He may leave the Angel of Death behind as well.

What will remain? And who will such a new sort of creature serve? The angels, the devils...or just itself?

Kane will be interested to find out.

A STARK AND
WORMY KNIGHT

"MAM! MAM!" SQUEED ALEXANDRAX FROM the damps of his strawstooned nesty. "Us can't sleep! Tail us a tell of Ye Elder Days!"

"Child, stop that howlering or you'll be the deaf of me," scowled his scaly forebearer. "Count sheeps and go to sleep!"

"Been counting shepherds instead, have us," her eggling rejoined. "But too too toothsome they each look. Us are hungry, Mam."

"Hungry? Told you not to swallow that farm tot so swift. A soiled and feisty little thing it was, but would you stop to chew carefulish? Oh, no, no. You're not hungry, child, you've simpledy gobbled too fast and dazzled your eatpipes. Be grateful that you've only got one head to sleepify, unbelike some of your knobful ancestors, and go back and shove yourself snorewise."

"But us *can't* sleep, Mam. Us feels all grizzled in the gut and wiggly in the wings. Preach us some storying, pleases—

something sightful but sleepable. Back from the days when there were long dark knights!"

"Knights, knights—you'll scare yourself sleepless with such! No knights there are anymore—just wicked little winglings who will not wooze when they should."

"Just one short storying, Mam! Tale us somewhat of Great-Grandpap, the one that were named Alexandrax just like us! He were alive in the bad old days of bad old knights."

"Yes, that he was, but far too sensible and caveproud to go truckling with such clanking mostrositors—although, hist, my dragonlet, my eggling, it's true there *was* one time..."

"Tell! Tell!"

His mam sighed a sparking sigh. "Right, then, but curl yourself tight and orouborate that tale, my lad—that'll keep you quelled and quiet whilst I storify.

"Well, as often I've told with pride, your Great-Grandpap were known far-flown and wide-spanned for his good sense. Not for him the errors of others, especkledy not the promiscuous plucking of princesses, since your Great-grandy reckoned full well how likely that was to draw some clumbering, lanking knight in a shiny suit with a fist filled of sharp steel wormsbane.

"Oh, those were frightsome days, with knights lurking beneath every scone and round every bent, ready to spring out and spear some mother's son for scarce no cause at all! So did your wisdominical Great-Grandpap confine himself to plowhards and peasant girls and the plumpcasional parish priest tumbled down drunk in the churchyard of a Sunday evening, shagged out from 'cessive sermonizing. Princesses and such got noticed, do you see, but the primate proletariat were held cheap in those days—a dozen or so could be harvested in one area before a dragon had to wing on to pastors new. And your Grand-Greatpap, he knew that. Made no mistakes, did he—could tell an overdressed merchant missus from a true damager duchess even by the shallowest starlight, plucked the former but shunned the latter every time. Still, like all of us he wondered what it was that made a human princess so very tasty and tractive. Why did they need to be so punishingly, paladinishly protected? Was it the creaminess of their savor or the crispiness of their crunch? Perhaps they bore the 'boo-kwet', as those fancy French wyverns has it, of flowery flavors to which no peat-smoked peasant could ever respire? Or were it something entire different, he pondered, inexplicable except by the truthiest dint of personal mastication?

"Still, even in these moments of weakness your Grandpap's Pap knew that he were happily protected from his own greeding nature by the scarcity of princessly portions, owing to their all being firmly pantried in castles and other stony such. He was free to specklate, because foolish, droolish chance would never come to a cautious fellow like him.

"Ah, but he should have quashed all that quandering, my little lizarding, 'stead of letting it simmer in his brain-boiler, because there came a day when Luck and Lust met and bred and brooded a litter named Lamentable.

"That is to say, your Pap's Grandpap stumbled on an unsupervised princess.

"This royal hairless was a bony and brainless thing, it goes without saying, and overfond of her clear complexion, which was her downfalling (although the actual was more of an uplifting, as you'll see). It was her witless wont at night to sneak out of her bed betimes and wiggle her skinny shanks out the window, then ascend to the roof of the castle to moonbathe, which this princess was convinced was the secret of smoothering skin. (Which it may well have been, but who in the name of Clawed Almighty wants smoothered skin? No wonder that humans have grown so scarce these days—they wanted wit.)

"In any case, on this particularly odd even she had just stretched herself out there in her nightgown to indulge this lunar tic when your Great-Grandpap happened to flap by overhead, on his way back from a failed attempt at tavernkeeper tartare in a nearby town. He took one look at this princess stretched out like the toothsomest treat on a butcher's table and his better sense deskirted him. He swooped scoopishly down and snatched her up, then wung his way back toward his cavern home, already menu-rizing a stuffing of baker's crumbs and coddle of toddler as side dish when the princess suddenfully managed to get a leg free and, in the midst of her struggling and unladylike cursing, kicked your Great-Grandpap directedly in the vent as hard as she could, causing him unhappiness (and almost unhemipenes). Yes, dragons had such things even way back then, foolish fledgling. No, your Great-Grandpap's wasn't pranged for permanent—where do you think your Grandpap came from?

"In any case, so shocked and hemipained was he by this attack on his ventral sanctity that he dropped the foolish princess most sudden and vertical—one hundred sky-fathoms or more, into a grove of pine trees, which left her rather careworn. Also fairly conclusively dead.

"Still, even cold princess seemed toothsome to your Great-Grandpap, though, so he gathered her up and went on home to his cavern. He was lone and batchelorn in those days—your Great-Grandmammy still in his distinct future—so there was none to greet him there and none to share with, which was how he liked it, selfish old mizard that he was even in those dewy-clawed days. He had just settled in, 'ceedingly slobberful at the teeth and tongue and about to have his first princesstual bite ever, when your Grandpap's Pap heard a most fearsomeful clatternacious clanking and baying outside his door. Then someone called the following in a rumbling voice that made your G-G's already bruised ventrality try to shrink up further into his interior.

" 'Ho, vile beast! Stealer of maiden princesses, despoiler of virgins, curse of the kingdom—come ye out! Come ye out and face Sir Libogran the Undeflectable!'

"It were a knight. It were a big one.

"Well, when he heard this hewing cry your Great-Grandpap flished cold as a snowdrake's bottom all over. See, even your cautious Great-Grandy had heard tell of this Libogran, a terrible, stark and wormy knight—perhaps the greatest dragonsbane of his age and a dreadsome bore on top of it.

" 'Yes, it is I, Libogran,' the knight bellows on while your G's G. got more and more trembful: 'Slayer of Alasalax the Iron-Scaled and bat-winged Beerbung, destroyer of the infamous Black Worm of Flimpsey Meadow and scuttler of all the noisome plans of Fubarg the Flameful...'

"On and on he went, declaiming such a drawed-out dracologue of death that your Great-Grandpap was pulled almost equal by impatience as terror. But what could he do to make it stop? A sudden idea crept upon him then, catching him quite by surprise. (He was a young dragon, after all, and unused to thinking, which in those days were held dangerous for the inexperienced.) He snicked quietly into the back of his cave and fetched the princess, who was a bit worse for wear but still respectable enough for a dead human, and took her to the front of the cavern, himself hidebound in shadows as he held her out in the light and dangled her puppetwise where the knight could see.

" 'Princess!' cried Libogran. 'Your father has sent me to save you from this irksome worm! Has he harmed you?'

" 'Oh, no!' shrilled your Great-Grandpap in his most high-pitchful, princessly voice, 'not at all! This noble dragon has been naught but gentlemanifold, and I am come of my own freed will. I live here now, do you see? So you may go home without killing anything and tell my papa that I am as happy as a well-burrowed scale mite.'

"The knight, who had a face as broad and untroubled by subtle as a porky haunch, stared at her. 'Are you truly certain you are well, Princess?' quoth he. 'Because you look a bit battered and dirtsome, as if you had perhaps fallen through several branches of several pine trees.'

" 'How nosy and nonsensical you are, Sir Silly Knight!' piped your Great-Grandpap a bit nervous-like. 'I was climbing in the tops of a few trees, yes, as I love to do. That is how I met my friend this courtinuous dragon—we were both birdnesting in the same tree, la and ha ha! And then he kindly unvited me to his home toward whence I incompulsedly came, and where I am so happily visiting...!'

"Things went on in this conversational vain for some little time as your Great-Grandpap labored to satisfy the questioning of the dreaded dragonslayer. He might even have eventually empacted that bold knight's withdrawal, except that in a moment of particularly violent puppeteering your great-grandsire, having let invention get the best of him while describing the joyful plans of the putative princess, managed to dislodge her head.

"She had not been the most manageable marionette to begin with, and now your Great-Grandpap was particular difficulted trying to get her to pick up and re-neck her lost knob with her own hands while still disguising his clawed handiwork at the back, controlling the action.

" 'Oops and girlish giggle!' he cried in his best mock-princessable tones, scrabbling panicked after her rolling tiara-stand, 'silly me, I always said it would fall off if it weren't attached to me and now look at this, hopped right off its stem! Oh, la, I suppose I should be a bit more rigormortous about my grooming and attaching.'

"Sir Libogran the Undeflectable stared at what must clearful have been a somewhat extraordinate sight. 'Highness,' quoth he, 'I cannot help feeling that someone here is not being entirely honest with me.'

" 'What?' lied your Great-Grandpap most quickly and dragonfully. 'Can a princess not lose her head in a minor way occasional without being held up left and right to odiumfoundment and remonstrance?'

" 'This, I see now,' rumbled Sir Libogran in the tone of one who has been cut to his quink, 'is not the living article I came to deliver at all, but rather an ex-princess in expressly poor condition. I shall enter immediately, exterminate the responsible worm, and remove the carcasework for respectful burial.'

"Your Great-Grandpap, realizing that this particular deceptivation had run its curse, dropped the bony remnants on the stony stoop and raised his voice in high-pitched and apparently remorsive and ruthful squizzling: 'Oh, good sir knight, don't harm us! It's true, your princess is a wee bit dead, but through no fault of us! It was a terrible diseasement that termilated her, of which dragon caves are highlishly prone. She caught the sickness and was rendered lifeless and near decapitate by it within tragical moments. I attempted to convenience you otherwise only to prevent a fine felon like you from suckling at the same deadly treat.'

"After the knight had puddled out your grandsire's sire's words with his poor primate thinker, he said, 'I do not believe there are diseases which render a princess headless and also cover her with sap and pine needles. It is my counter-suggestion, dragon, that you thrashed her to death with an evergreen of some sort and now seek to confuse me with fear for my own person. But your downfall, dragon, is that even 'twere so, I cannot do less than march into the mouth of death to honor my quest and the memory of this poor pine-battered morsel. So regardless of personal danger, I come forthwith to execute you, scaly sirrah. Prepare yourself to meet my blameless blade...' And sewed on.

"*Clawed the Flyest*, thought your Great-Grandpap, *but he is deedly a noisome bore for true.* Still, he dubited not that Sir Libogran, for all his slathering self-regard, would quickly carry through on his executive intent. Thus, to protect his own beloved and familiar hide for a few moments langorous, your Pap's pap's pap proceeded to confect another tongue-forker on the spot.

" 'All right, thou hast me dart to tripes,' he told the knight. 'The realio trulio reason I cannot permit you into my cavernous cavern is that so caught, I must performeat give up to you three wishes of immense valuable. For I am that rare and amnesial creature, a Magical Wishing Dragon. Indeed, it was in attempting to claw her way toward my presence and demand wishes from me that your princess gained the preponderosa of these pine-burns, for it was with suchlike furniture of evergreenwood that I attempted pitifullaciously to block my door, and through which she cranched an smushed her way with fearsome strength. Her head was damaged when, after I told her I was fluttered out after long flight and too weary for wish-wafting, she yanked off her crown and tried to beat me indispensable with it. She was a pittance too rough, though—a girl whose strength belied her scrawnymous looks—and detached her headbone from its neckly couchment in the crown-detaching process, leading to this lamentable lifelessness.

" 'However,' went on your Great-Grandpap, warming now to his self-sufficed subject, 'although I resisted the wish-besieging princess for the honor of all my wormishly magical brethren, since you have caught me fairy and scary, Sir Libogran, larded me in my barren, as it were, I will grant the foremansioned troika of wishes to *you*. But the magic necessitudes that after you tell them unto my ear you must go quickly askance as far as possible—another country would be idealistic—and trouble me no more so that I can perforce the slow magics of their granting (which sometimes takes years betwixt wishing and true-coming.)'

"Libogran stood a long time, thinking uffishly, then lastly said, 'Let me make sure I have apprehended you carefully, worm. You state that you are a Magic Wishing Dragon, that it was her greed for this quality of yours which cost the unfortunate princess her life, and that I should tell you my three wishes and then leave, preferably to a distant land, so that you may grant them to me in the most efficacious manner.'

" 'Your astutity is matched only by the stately turn of your greave and the general handfulness of your fizzick, good sir knight,' your Great-Grandpap eagerly responded, seeing that perhaps he might escape puncturing at the hands of this remorseless rider after all. 'Just bename those wishes and I will make them factive, both pre- and post-haste.'

"Sir Libogran slowly shook his massive and broadly head. 'Do you take me for a fool, creature?"

" 'Not a fool creature as sort,' replinked your grandpap's daddy, trying to maintain a chirrupful tone. 'After all, you and your elk might be a lesser species than us *Draco Pulcher*, but still, as I would be the first to argue, a vally-hooed part of Clawed the Flyest's great creation...'

" 'Come here, dragon, and let me show you my wish.'

"Your Great-Grandpap hesitated. 'Come there?' he asked. 'Whyso?'

" 'Because I cannot explain as well as I can demonstrate, sirrah,' quoth the bulky and clanksome human.

"So your forebear slithered out from the cavernous depths, anxious to end his night out by sending this knight out. He was also hoping that, though disappointed of his foreplanned feast, he might at least locate some princessly bits fallen off in the cave, which could be served chippingly on toast. But momentarily after your Great-Grandpap emerged into the lightsome day, the cruel Sir Libogran snatched your ancestor's throat in a gauntleted ham and cut off that poor, innosensitive dragon's head with his vicious blade.

"Snick! No snack.

"This treacherness done, the knight gathered up the princess' tree-tattered torso and emancive pate, then went galumphing back toward the castle of her mourning, soon-to-mourn-more Mammy and Daddums."

"But how can that be, Mam?" shrimped wee Alexandrax. "He killed Great-Grandpap? Then how did Grandpap, Pap, and Yours Contumely come to be?"

"Fie, fie, shut that o-shaped fishmouth, my breamish boy. Did I say aught about killing? He did not kill your Great-Grandpap, he cut off his head. Do you not dismember that your great-grandcestor was dragon of the two-headed vermiety?

"As it happened, one of his heads had been feeling poorly, and he had kept it tucked severely under one wing all that day and aftermoon so it could recupertate. Thus, Libogran the Undeflectable was not aware of the existence of this auxiliary knob, which he would doubtless of otherwise liberated from its neckbones along with the other. As it was, the sickened head soon recovered and was good as new. (With time the severed one also grew back, although it was ever after small and prone to foolish smiles and the uttering of platitudinous speech—phrases like, 'I'm sure everything will work off in the end' and 'It is honorous just to be nominated,' and suchlike.)

"In times ahead—a phrase which was sorely painful to your Great-Great-Pap during his invalidated re-knobbing—your G.-G. would go back to his old, happy ways, horrorizing harrowers and slurping shepherds but never again letting himself even veer toward rooftopping virgins or in fact anything that bore the remotest rumor of the poisonous perfume of princessity. He became a pillar of his community, married your Great-Grandmammy in a famously fabulous ceremony—just catering the event purged three surrounding counties of their peasantly population—and lived a long and harpy life."

"But Mam, Mam, what about that stark and wormy Sir Libogran, that...dragocidal maniac? Did he really live hoppishly ever after as well, unhaunted by his bloodful crime?"

"In those days, there was no justice for our kind except what we made ourselves, my serpentine son. No court or king would ever have victed him."

"So he died unpunwiched?"

"Not exactly. One day your Great-Grandpap was on his way back from courting your Grandest-Greatmam-to-be, and happened to realize by the banners on its battlements that he was passing over Libogran's castle, so he stooped to the rooftop and squatted on the chimbley pot, warming his hindermost for a moment (a fire was burning in the hearth down below and it was most pleasantly blazeful) before voiding himself down the chimbley hole into the great fireplace."

"He couped the flue!"

"He did, my boy, he did. The whole of Libogran's household came staggering out into the cold night waving and weeping and coughing out the stinking smoke as your Grand's Grandpap flew chortling away into the night, unseen. Libogran's castle had to be emptied and aired for weeks during the most freezingly worstful weather of the year, and on this account the knight spent the rest of his life at war with the castle pigeons, on whom he blamed your Great-Grandpap's secret chimbley-discharge—he thought the birds had united for a concerted, guanotated attempt on his life. Thus, stalking a dove across the roof with his bird-net and boarspear a few years later, Sir Libogran slipped and fell to his death in the castle garden, spiking himself on his own great sticker and dangling thereby for several days, mistaken by his kin and servants as a new scarecrow."

"Halloo and hooray, Mam! Was he the last of the dragon-hunters, then? Was him skewerting on his own sharpitude the reason we no longer fear them?"

"No, dearest honey-sonny, we no longer fear them because *they* no longer see *us*. During the hunders of yearses since your Greatest Grandpap's day, a plague called Civilization came over them, a diseaseful misery that blinded them to half the creatures of the world and dumbfounded their memories of much that is true and ancient. Let me tell you a dreadsome secret." She leaned close to whisper in his tender earhole. "Even when we snatch a plump merchant or a lean yet flavorful spinster from their midst these days, the humans never know that one of us dragons has doomfully done for the disappeared. They blame it instead on a monster they fear even more."

"What is that, Mam?" Alexandrax whimpspered. "It fears me to hear, but I want to know. What do they think slaughters them? An odious ogre? A man-munching manticore?"

"Some even more frightfulling creature. No dragon has ever seen it, but they call it...Statistics."

"Clawed Hitself save us from such a horridly horror!" squeeped the small one in fright.

"It is only a man-fancy, like all the rest of their nonned sense," murmed his Mam. "Empty as the armor of a cracked and slurped knight—so fear it not. Now, my tale is coiled, so sleepish for you, my tender-winged bundle."

"I will," he said, curling up like a sleepy hoop, most yawnful. "I s'pose no knights is good nights, huh, Mam?"

"Examply, my brooded boy. Fear not clanking men nor else. Sleep. All is safe and I am watching all over you."

And indeed, as she gazed yellow-eyed and loving on her eggling, the cave soon grew fulfilled with the thumberous rundle of wormsnore.

THE STORM DOOR

NIGHTINGALE DID NOT TAKE THE first cab he saw when he stepped out into the rainy San Francisco streets. He never did. Some might call it superstition, but in his profession the line between "superstitions" and "rules of survival" was rather slender. He stepped back onto the curb to avoid the spray of water as the second cab pulled up in response to his wave. Paranormal investigators didn't make enough money to ruin a pair of good shoes for no reason.

Somebody should have warned me that saving the world from unspeakable horrors is like being a teacher—lots of job satisfaction, but the money's crap.

"Thirty-three Gilman Street," he told the driver, an ex-hippie on the edge of retirement age, shoulder-length gray hair draggling out from under his Kangol hat and several silver rings on the fingers holding the wheel. "It's off Jones."

"You got it." The driver pulled back into traffic, wipers squeaking as city lights smeared and dribbled across the glass beside Nightingale's head. "Helluva night," he said. "I know we need the rain and everything, but...shit, man."

Nathan Nightingale had spent so much of the past week in a small, overheated and nearly airless room that he would have happily run through this downpour naked, but he only nodded and said, "Yeah. Helluva night."

"Gonna be a lot more before it's over, too. That's what they said. The storm door's open." The driver turned down the music a notch. "Kind of a weird expression, huh? Makes it sound like they're..." he lifted his fingers in twitching monster-movie talons, "*coming to get us*. Whooo! I mean, it's just clouds, right? It's nature."

"This? Yeah, it's just nature," agreed Nightingale, his thoughts already drawn back to that small room, those clear, calm, terrifying eyes. "But sometimes even nature can be unnatural."

"Huh? Oh, yeah, I guess so. Good one." But it was clear by his tone that the driver feared he'd missed the point.

"That's it—the tall house there."

The driver peered out the window. "Whoa, that's a spooky one, man. You sure you gonna be okay, man? This is kind of a tough neighborhood..."

"I'll be fine, thanks," said Nightingale. "I've been here before—it was kind of my second home."

"If you say so." The driver called just before Nightingale slammed the door, "Hey, remember about that storm door. Better get an umbrella!"

Nightingale raised his hand as the man drove off. *An umbrella.* He almost smiled, but the wet night was getting to him. *If only all problems were that easy to solve.*

As he pressed the button beside the mailbox lightning blazed overhead, making it seem as though one had caused the other. A moment later the thunder crashed down, so near that he did not hear the sound of the door being buzzed open but felt the handle vibrating under his hand.

The light was out in the first floor stairwell, and no lights were on at all on the second floor, what Uncle Edward called "the showroom", although no one ever saw it but a few old, trusted collector friends. Enough of the streetlight's glow leaked in that Nightingale could see the strange silhouettes of some of the old man's prize possessions, fetish dolls and funerary votives and terra cotta tomb statuettes, a vast audience of silent, wide-eyed shapes watching Nightingale climb the stairs. It was an excellent collection, but what made it truly astounding were the stories behind the pieces, most of them dark, many of them horrifying. In fact, it had been his godfather's arcane tales and bizarre trophies that had first lured Nightingale onto his odd career path: at an age when most boys wanted to be football players or firemen, young Nate had decided he wanted to hunt ghosts and fight demons. Later, when others were celebrating their first college beer-busts, Nightingale had already attended strange ceremonies on high English moors and deep in Thai jungles and Louisiana bayous. He had heard languages never shaped for the use of human tongues, had seen men die for no reason, and others live when they should have been dead. But through the years, when the unnatural things he saw and felt and learned overwhelmed him, he always came back here for his godfather's advice and support. This was one of those times. In fact, this was probably the worst time he could remember.

Strangely, the third floor of the house was dark, too.

"Edward? Uncle Edward? It's me, Nathan. Are you here?" Had the old man forgotten he was coming and gone out with his caretaker Jenkins somewhere? God forbid, a medical emergency... Nightingale stopped to listen. Was that the quiet murmuring of the old man's breathing machine?

Something stirred on the far side of the room and his hackles rose; his hand strayed to his inside coat pocket. A moment later the desk lamp clicked on, revealing the thin, lined face of his godfather squinting against the sudden light. "Oh," Edward said, taking a moment to find the air to speak. "Guh-goodness! Nate, is that you? I must have dozed off. When did it get so dark?"

Relieved, Nightingale went to the old man and gave him a quick hug, being careful not to disturb the tracheotomy cannula or the ventilator tubes. As always, Edward Arvedson felt like little more than a suit full of bones, but somehow he had survived in this failing condition for almost a decade. "Where's Jenkins?" Nightingale asked. "It gave me a start when I came up and the whole house was dark."

"Oh, I had him the night off, poor fellow. Working himself to death. Pour me a small sherry, will you, there's a good man, and sit down and tell me what you've learned. There should be a bottle of Manzanilla already open. No, don't turn all those other lights on. I find I'm very sensitive at the moment. This is enough light for you to find your way to the wet bar, isn't it?"

Nightingale smiled. "I could find it without any light at all, Uncle Edward."

When he'd poured a half glass for the old man and a little for himself as well, Nightingale settled into the chair facing the desk and looked his mentor up and down. "How are you feeling?"

Arvedson waved a dismissive hand. "Fine, fine. Never felt better. And now that we're done with that nonsense, tell me your news, Nate. What happened? I've been worrying ever since you told me what you thought was happening."

"Well, it took me a while to find a volunteer. Mostly because I was trying to avoid publicity—you know, all that 'Nightingale—Exorcist to the Stars' nonsense."

"You shouldn't have changed your name—it sounds like a Hollywood actor now. Your parents wouldn't have approved, anyway. What was wrong with Natan Näktergal? It was good enough for your father."

He smiled. "Too old country, Uncle Edward. Remember, being well-known gets me into a lot of places. It also leads people to misjudge me."

Arvedson made a face. He still hadn't touched his sherry. "Fine. I'm also old country, I suppose. I should be grateful you even visit. Tell me what happened."

"I'm trying to. As I said, it wouldn't do to recruit just anyone. Ideally, I needed someone with special training...but who gets trained for something like this? I figured that my best bet was through my Tibetan contacts. Tibetan Buddhists spend years studying the Bardo Thodol, preparing to take the journey of dying, which gave me a much larger group to choose from. I finally settled on a man in Seattle named Geshe, who had pancreatic cancer. He'd refused pain relief and the doctors felt certain he only had a few days left when I met him, but he was remarkably calm and thoughtful. I told him what I wanted, and why, and he said yes."

"So you had found your...what was your word? Your 'necronaut'."

Nightingale nodded. "That's what I called it before I met Geshe—it sounded better than 'mineshaft canary'. But after I got to know him it...it seemed a little glib. But he was precisely the sort of person I was looking for—a man trained almost since childhood to die with his eyes and mind open."

Lightning flashed and a peal of thunder shivered the windows. In the wake, another wash of rain splattered against the glass. "Filthy weather," said Arvedson. "Do you want another drink before you start? You'll have to get it yourself, of course, since we don't have Jenkins."

"No, I'm fine." Nightingale stared at his glass. "I'm just thinking." Lightning flashed again and so he waited for the thunder before continuing. "You remember how this started, of course. Those earliest reports of spontaneous recovery by dying patients...well, it didn't seem like anything I needed to pay attention to. But then that one family whose daughter went into sudden remission from leukemia after the last rites had already been said..."

"I remember. Very young, wasn't she? Nine?"

"Yes, a few weeks before her tenth birthday. But of course what caught my attention was when the parents started claiming it wasn't their daughter at all, that she'd changed in ways that no illness could explain. But when I got in to see the child she was asleep, and although she looked surprisingly healthy compared to my general experience with possession cases, I couldn't get any kind of feeling from her one way or another. When I tried to contact the family a few days later they'd moved and no one could find them.

"There were others, too—too many to be coincidence, most of them unknown to the general public. The greatest hindrance in these situations is the gutter press, of course—any real study, let alone any chance to help the victims and their families, is destroyed by the sort of circus they create. These days, with television and the internet, it's even worse. If I don't strenuously keep my comings and goings a secret, I wind up with cameras in my face and following me everywhere and looking over my shoulder."

"They are vermin," said Edward Arvedson with feeling.

"In any case, when I talked to you I had just learned of an accident victim in Minnesota who had recovered from a coma and, like the girl in Southern California, seemed to have undergone a complete personality shift. He had been a mild and soft-spoken churchgoer, but now he was a violent, alcoholic bully. His wife of twenty-four years had divorced him, his children no longer saw him. The front yard of his house in Bloomington was a wreck, and when he opened the door the stink of rot and filth just rolled out. I only saw him for a few seconds through the chain on his front door, but what

I witnessed was definitely madness, a sort of...emotionless focus that I've only seen in the criminally insane. That doesn't prove anything, of course. Brain damage can do that, and he'd certainly been badly injured. But he *recognized* me."

"You told me when you called," said Arvedson. "I could tell it upset you."

"Because it wasn't like he'd seen my picture in *The Enquirer*, but like he *knew* me. Knew me and hated me. I didn't stay there long, but it wasn't just seeing the Minnesota victim that threw me. I'd never heard of possessions happening at this rate, or to people so close to death. It didn't make sense!"

"It has my attention, too," Edward said. "But what I want to hear now is what happened with your Buddhist gentleman."

Nightingale let out a breath. He swallowed the last of his sherry. "Right. Well, Geshe was a very interesting man, an artist and a teacher. I wish I could have met him at a different time, but even in our short acquaintance he impressed me and I liked him. That's why what happened was so disturbing.

"He had checked out of the hospital to die at home. He'd lost his wife a few years earlier and they'd had no children, so although some of his students and colleagues came by to sit with him from time to time, at the end there was only his friend Joseph, an American Buddhist, and the hospice nurse who checked in on him once a day. And me, of course. Geshe and I didn't speak much—he had to work too hard to manage the pain—but as I said, he impressed me. During the long days in his apartment I spent a great deal of time looking at his books and other possessions, which is as good a way to get to know someone as talking with them. Also, I saw many of his own works of art, which may be an even better way to learn about another human being—he made beautiful Buddhist Thangkas, meditation paintings.

"As Geshe began to slip away Joseph read the Bardo Thodol to him. I've never spent much time studying it, myself—I think that hippie-ish, "Tibetan Book of the Dead" reputation put me off when I was younger, and these days I don't really need to know the nuts and bolts of any particular religious dogma to work with the universal truths behind them all—but I have to say that hearing it and living with it, even as Geshe was *dying* with it, opened my eyes."

"There is great truth at the heart of all the great faiths," Arvedson said solemnly.

"Yes, but what I truly came to admire was the calmness of the people who wrote the bardos—the practicality, I suppose is the best word. It's a very practical book, the Bardo Thodol. A road map. A set of travel tips. 'Here's what's going to happen now that you're dead. Do this. Don't do that. Everything will be okay.' Except that this time it wasn't.

"The famous teacher Trungpa Rinpoche said the best thing we can do for the dying and the newly dead is maintain an atmosphere of calmness, and that's certainly what Geshe seemed to have around him at the end. It was raining outside most of that week, but quietly. Joseph read the bardos over and over while he and I took turns holding Geshe's hand. With my special sensitivities, I was beginning to sense something of what he was sensing—the approach of the Great Mystery, the crossing, whatever you want to call it—and of course it troubled me deep down in my bones and guts, but Geshe wasn't frightened in the least. All those years of training and meditation had prepared him.

"It was fascinating to see how the dying soul colors the experience, Uncle Edward. As I said, I have never delved too deeply into Tibetan Buddhism, yet the version of dying I experienced through Geshe was shaped so strongly by that tradition that I could not feel it any other way—it was as real as you and I sitting here in the dark, listening to the wind and the rain." Nightingale paused for a moment while the storm rattled the windows of the old house. "The thousands of gods, which are one god, which is the light of the universe...I can't explain. But touching Geshe's thoughts as he began his journey, although I felt only the barest hint of what he felt, was like riding a roller-coaster through a kaleidoscope, but simultaneously falling through an endless, dark, silent void."

" '...*When your body and mind separate, the dharmata will appear, pure and clear yet hard to discern, luminous and brilliant, with terrifying brightness, shimmering like a mirage on a plain*', " Arvedson quoted. "At least, that's what the bardo says."

"Yes." Nightingale nodded. "I remember hearing it then and understanding it clearly, even though the words I heard were Tibetan. Joseph had begun the Chikkhai Bardo, you see—the bardo of dying. In the real world, as we sometimes think of it, Geshe had sunk so far into himself he was no longer visibly breathing. But I was not really beside him in that little room in Seattle, although I could still hear Joseph's voice. Most of me was *inside*—deep in the experience of death with Geshe.

"I could feel him, Uncle Edward, and in a way I could see what he saw, hear what he heard, although those aren't quite the right words. As the voices of people I did not know echoed around us—mostly Geshe's friends and relations and loved ones, I suspect, for I do not think he had many enemies—he and I traveled together through a misty forest. It seemed to me a bit like some of the wild lands of the Pacific Northwest, but more mountainous, as if some of Geshe's Tibetan heritage was seeping through as well."

"*Climbing*," said Edward Arvedson quietly.

"Yes, the part of the afterlife journey the Egyptians called 'the Ladder' and the Aztecs thought of as the beginning of the soul's four-year journey to Mictlan. I've never dared hold a connection with a dying soul as long as I did with Geshe, and going so deep frightened me, but his calm strength made it possible. We did not speak, of course—his journey, his encounters, were his alone, as all ours will be someday—but I felt him there beside me as the dark drew in.

"I won't tell you everything I experienced now, but I will tell you someday soon, because it was a researcher's dream come true—the death experience almost firsthand. To make the story short, we passed through the first darkness and saw the first light, which the bardos call the soft light of the gods and which they counsel the dead soul to avoid. It was very attractive, like a warm fire to someone lost in the night, and I was feeling very cold, very far from comfort and familiar things—and remember, *I* had a body to go back to! I can only imagine what it seemed like to Geshe, who was on a one-way journey, but he resisted it. The same with what the bardo calls the 'soft light of the hell-beings.' I could feel him yearning toward it, and even to me it seemed soothing, alluring. In the oldest Tibetan tradition the hot hells are full of terrors—forests of razor-leaved trees, swamps bobbing with decomposing corpses—but these aspects are never seen until it's too late, until the attractions of one's own greed and anger have pulled the dying soul off the path.

"But Geshe overcame these temptations and kept on moving toward the harsher light of truth. He was brave, Edward, so brave! But then we reached the smoky yellow light, the realm of what the bardo calls *pretas*..."

"The hungry ghosts.".

"Yes, the hungry ghosts. Found in almost every human tradition. Those who did not go on. Those who can't let go of anger, hatred, obsession..."

"Perhaps simply those who want more life," Arvedson suggested.

Nightingale shook his head. "That makes them sound innocent, but they're far from that. Corpse-eating *jikininki*, ancient Rome's Lemures, the *grigori* of the Book of Enoch—almost every human tradition has them. Hell, I've *met* them, although never in their own backyard like this. You remember that thing that almost killed me in Freiberg?"

"I certainly do."

"That was one of them, hitchhiking a ride in a living body. Nearly ripped my head off before I got away. I still have the scars..."

The night-time city waited now between waves of the storm. For a moment it was quiet enough in the room for Nightingale to hear the fan of his godfather's ventilator.

"In any case, that smoky yellow light terrified me. The bardo says it's temptation itself, that light, but maybe it didn't tempt me because I wasn't dying—instead it just made me feel frightened and sick, if you can be sick without a body. I could barely sense Geshe but I knew he was there and experiencing something very different. Instead of continuing toward the brilliant white light of compassion, as the bardo instructed, this very compassionate man seemed to hesitate. The yellow light was spreading around us like something toxic diffusing through water. Geshe seemed confused, stuck, as though he fought against a call much stronger than anything I could sense. I could feel something else, too, something alien to both of us, cold and strong and...yes, and *hungry*. God, I've never sensed hunger like that, a bottomless need like the empty chill of space sucking away all living warmth..."

Nightingale sat quietly for a long moment before he spoke again. "But then, just when I was fighting hardest to hang onto my connection to Geshe, it dissolved and he was gone. I'd lost touch with him. The yellow light was all around me, strange and greasy...repulsive, but also overwhelming...

"I fell out. No, it was more like I was shoved. I tumbled back into the real world, back into my body. I couldn't feel Geshe any more. Joseph had stopped reading the Chakkhai Bardo and was staring in alarm. Geshe's body, which hadn't moved or showed any signs of life in some time, was suddenly in full-on Cheyne-Stokes respiration, chest hitching, body jerking—he almost looked like he was convulsing. But Joseph swore to me later on that Geshe had stopped breathing half an hour earlier and I believe him.

"A moment later Geshe's eyes popped open. I've seen stranger things, but it still startled me. He had been dead, Uncle Edward, really dead, I swear he had. Now he was looking at me—but it wasn't Geshe any more. I couldn't prove it of course, but I had touched this man's soul, traveled with him as he passed over, the most intimate thing imaginable, and this just wasn't him.

"'*No, I will not die yet,*' he said. The voice sounded like his, but strong, far too strong for someone who had been in periodic breathing only a minute earlier. '*There are still things for me to do on this earth.*' It was the eyes, though. That same cold, flat stare that I'd seen through the doorway in Minnesota, the one I've seen before in other possession cases, but there was none of the struggle I'd seen in classic possession, no sense of the soul and body fighting against an interloper. One moment it was Geshe, a spiritual man, an artist, the next moment it was...someone else. Someone as cold and detached as a textbook sociopath.

"He closed his eyes then and slept, or pretended to, but already he looked healthier than he had since I met him. I couldn't tell Joseph that I thought his friend was possessed— what a horrible thing to say to someone already dealing with several kinds of trauma!—and I didn't know what else to do, what to think. I sat there for most of an hour, unable to think of anything to do. At last, when the nurse came and began dealing with this incredible turn of medical events, I went out to get a drink. All right, I had a few, then went home and slept like a dead man myself.

"I should never have left them, Edward. When I went back the next day, the apartment was empty. A few weeks later I received an email from Joseph—or at least from Joseph's address—saying that after his miraculous recovery Geshe wanted to travel to Tibet, the place of his heritage. I've never heard from either of them since…"

The lightning, absent for almost a quarter of an hour, suddenly flared, turning the room into a flat tableau of black and white shapes; the thunder that followed seemed to rock the entire building. The light on Edward Arvedson's desk flickered once, then went out, as did the lights on his ventilator. Through the windows Nightingale could see the houses across the street had gone black as well. He jumped up, suddenly cold all over. His father's oldest friend and his own most trusted advisor was about to die of asphyxiation while he watched helplessly.

"Good God, Edward, the electricity…!"

"Don't…worry…" Arvedson wheezed. "I have a…standby… generator."

A moment later Nightingale felt rather than heard something begin to rumble somewhere in the house below and the desk light flickered back on, although the houses across the street remained dark. "There," said his godfather. "You see, young Natan? Not such an old-fashioned fool after all, eh? I am prepared for things like this. Power for the street will be back on soon—it happens a lot in this ancient neighborhood. Now, tell me what you think is happening."

Nightingale sat back, trying to regain his train of thought. If only the old man wasn't so stubborn about living on his own with only Jenkins—no spring lamb himself—for company.

"Right," he said at last. "Well, I'm sure you're thinking the same thing as me, Uncle Edward. Somehow these predatory souls or spirits have found a way to possess the bodies of the dying. Which would be bad enough, but it's the incredible frequency with which it seems to be happening. I can't possibly investigate them all, of course, but if even half the reports that reach me are real it's happening all over the world, several times a day."

The rain was back now, lashing the windows and tattooing the roof of Edward's Victorian house. When the old man spoke, there was an unfamiliar tone in his voice. "You are... frightened, my dear Natan."

"Yes, Uncle Edward, I am. I've never been this frightened, and I've seen a lot. It's as if something fundamental has broken down, some wall between us and the other side, and now the living are under attack. What did the cab driver say to me on the way over, babbling about the weather—'the storm door is open'...? And I'm afraid the storms are just going to keep coming thicker and faster until all our houses are blown down."

"But why? And why now?"

"Why? Because they've always been there—the hungry ones, the envious things that hate us because we can still breathe and sing and love. Do they want that back, or do they just want to keep us from having it? I don't know. And why now? I don't know that either. Perhaps some universal safeguard has stopped working, or these entities have learned something they didn't know before."

"Then here is the most important question, Nate. What are you going to do about it, now you know? What can one person do?"

"Well, make sure it isn't just one person trying to deal with it, to begin with. You and I know lots of people who don't think I'm a charlatan—brave people who study this sort of thing, who fight the good fight and know the true danger. More than a few of us have dedicated our lives to keep the rest of humanity safe, without reward or thanks. Now I have to alert them all, if they haven't discovered this already." He stood and began to pace back and forth before the desk. "And to make sure the word gets out, I'll use the very same tabloid vultures that you and I despise so much. They'll do good without knowing it. Because for every thousand people who'll read headlines that say things like 'So-Called Demon Hunter Claims Dead *are* Invading the Living World' and laugh at it as nonsense, one or two will understand...and will heed the warning." He moved to the window, looked out into the darkness. "We can only hope to hold these hungry ghosts at bay if every real paranormal researcher, exorcist, and sympathetic priest we can reach will join us—every collector you know, every student of the arcane, every adventurer behind the occult lines, all of those soldiers of the light that the rest of society dismisses as crazy. This will be our great war."

Nightingale turned and walked back to his chair. "So there you have it, Uncle Edward. I'll spread the word. You spread the word, too. Call in old favors. If enough of us hear the truth, we may still be able to get the storm door shut again."

The old man was silent for a long time as thunder rolled away into the distance.

"You're a brave young man, Nate," he said at last. "Your parents would be proud of you. I'm going to have to think for a while about the best way to help you, and though it embarrasses me to admit it, I also need some rest. You'll forgive me—I get tired so quickly. I'll be all right until Jenkins comes back in a few hours. You can let yourself out, can't you?"

"Of course, Uncle Edward." He went to the old man and gave him a quick hug, then kissed his cool, dry cheek. He carried his empty sherry glass to the sideboard. "Now that I'm back in town, I'll be by to see you again tomorrow. Good night." On his way to the door Nightingale stopped and held his fingers up to catch the light from the desk lamp and saw that the darkness there was only dust.

"Tell Jenkins he's getting sloppy," he said. "I can't imagine you giving him a night off in the old days without finishing the cleaning. Looks like he hasn't dusted in weeks."

"I'll tell him," said his godfather. "Go on, go on. I'll see you very soon."

But Nightingale did not go through the doorway. Instead, he turned and slowly walked back into the room. "Uncle Edward," he said. "Are you certain you're going to be all right? I mean, the power's still off. You can't breathe without your ventilator."

"The generator can run for hours and hours. It'll shut itself off when the regular power comes back." He waved his hand testily. "Go on, Nate. I'm fine."

"But the strange thing," said Nightingale, "is that when the generator came on half an hour ago, the ventilator didn't. There must be something wrong with it."

Arvedson went very still. "What...what are you talking about?"

"Here. Look, the little lights on it never came back on, either. Your ventilator's off." The room suddenly seemed very quiet, nothing but the distant sound of cars splashing along out on Jones Street, distant as the moon. "What happened to Edward?"

The old man looked surprised. "I don't...Nate, what are you saying...?"

The gun was out of Nightingale's coat and into his hand so quickly it might have simply appeared there. He leveled it at a spot between the old man's two bushy white eyebrows. "I asked you what happened to Edward—the real Edward Arvedson. I'm only going to ask this once more. I swear I'll kill him before I let you have his body, and I'm betting you can't pull your little possession trick again on a full-grown, healthy man like me— especially not before I can pull the trigger."

Even in the half-light of the desk lamp, the change was a fearful one: Edward Arvedson's wrinkled features did not alter in any great way, but something moved beneath the muscles and skin like a light-shunning creature burrowing through the dark earth. The eyes fixed his. Although the face was still Edward's, somehow it no longer looked much like him. "You're a clever boy, Nightingale," said the stranger in his godfather's body. "I should have noticed the ventilator never came back on, but as you've guessed, this sack of meat no longer has a breathing problem. In fact, it no longer needs to breathe at all."

"What's happened to him?" The gun stayed trained on the spot between the old man's eyes. "Talk fast."

A slow, cold smile stretched the lips. "That is not for me to say, but rather it is between him and his god. Perhaps he is strumming a harp with the other angels now...or writhing and shrieking in the deepest pits..."

"Bastard!" Nightingale pulled back the trigger with his thumb. "You lie! He's in there with you. And I know a dozen people who can make you jump right the hell back out..."

The thing shook its head. "Oh, Mr. Nightingale, you've been playing the occult detective so long you've come to believe you're really in a story—and that it will have a happy ending. We didn't learn new ways to possess the living." The smile returned, mocking and triumphant. "We have learned how to move into the bodies of the recently dead. Quite a breakthrough. It's much, much easier than possession, and we cannot be evicted because the prior tenant...is gone. Your 'Uncle Edward' had a stroke, you see. We waited all around him as he died—oh, and believe me, we told him over and over what we would do, including this moment. Like you, he caused us a great deal of trouble over the years—and as you know, we dead have long memories. And when he was beyond our torments at last, well, this body was ours. Already my essence has strengthened it. It does not need to breathe, and as you can see..." The thing rose from the wheelchair with imperial calm and stood without wavering. Nightingale backed off a few steps, keeping the gun high. "...it no longer needs assistance to get around, either," the thing finished. "I feel certain I'll get years of use out of it before I have to seek another—time enough to contact and betray all of the rest of Edward Arvedson's old friends."

"Who are you?" Nightingale fought against a despair that buffeted him like a cold wind. "Oh, for the love of God, what do you monsters want?"

"Who am I? Just one of the hungry ones. One of the unforgiving." It sat down again, making the wheelchair creak. "What do we want? Not to go quietly, as you would have us go—to disappear into the shadows of nonexistence and leave the rest of you to enjoy the light and warmth." The thing lifted its knotted hands—Edward's hands, as they had seemed such a short time ago—in a greedy gesture of seizure. "As you said, this is a war. We want what you have." It laughed, and for the first time the voice sounded nothing at all like his godfather's familiar tones. "And we are going take it from you. All of you."

"I don't think so. Because if you need bodies to survive here, then those bodies can be taken back from you..." And even as Nightingale spoke his gun flashed and roared and the thing in his godfather's shape staggered and fell back against the wheelchair cushions, chin on chest. A moment later the so-familiar face came up again. Smiling.

"Jenkins," it said. "If you would be so kind..."

Something knocked the gun from Nightingale's hand and then an arm like an iron bar slammed against his neck. He fought but it was like being held by a full-grown gorilla. His struggles only allowed him to slide around enough in his captor's grip to see Jenkins' blank eyes and the huge hole in the side of the caretaker's head crusted with bits of bone and dried tissue.

"I lied about giving him the night off," said the pseudo-Edward. "The living get impatient, but my colleague who inhabits him now was perfectly willing to stand in the dark until I needed him." Now Arvedson's body stood again, brushing at its clothes; the hole Nightingale's gunshot had made in its shirt was bloodless. "Bullets are a poor weapon against the risen dead, Nightingale," it pointed out with no little satisfaction. "You could burn the body, I suppose, or literally pulverize it, and there would be nothing left for us to inhabit. But of course, you will not get the chance to tell anyone about that."

"Bastards!" He struggled helplessly against the Jenkins-thing's grip. "Even if you kill me, there are hundreds more like me out there. They'll stop you!"

"We will meet them all, I'm sure," said his godfather's body. "You will introduce us—or at least the new resident of your corpse will. And one by one, we will remove them. The dead will live, with all the power of age and riches and secrecy, and the rest of your kind will be our uncomprehending cattle, left alive only to breed more bodies for us. Your driver was right, Mr. Nightingale—the storm door really is open now. And no power on this earth can shut it."

Nightingale tried to say something else then, shout some last words of defiance, but the pressure on his neck was crushingly strong and the lights of the world—the lamp, the headlights passing in the street below, even the storm-shrouded stars beyond the window—had begun leaching away into utter darkness.

His last sight was of the cold, hungry things that had been hiding behind that darkness, hiding and waiting and hating the living for so long, as they hurried toward him to feed.

THE STRANGER'S HANDS

PEOPLE IN THE VILLAGE HAD been whispering for days about the two vagabonds in Squire's Wood, but the boy Tobias was the first to speak to them.

Tobias was a somewhat wayward lad, and the fact that he should have been grazing his father's sheep on the hill above the forest at that hour more or less assured the sheep in question would be wandering along the shady edges of the wood instead, with Tobias wandering right behind them.

It was not until he saw a drift of smoke twining like a gray scarf through the trees that the boy remembered that strangers had been seen in the wood. He felt a moment of fear: why would anyone live out of doors in the cold nights and flurries of autumn rain if they were God-fearing folk? Only robbers and dangerous madmen dwelt under the unsheltered sky. Everyone knew that. If he had been a fraction less headstrong, Tobias would have turned around then and hurried back to the hillside, perhaps even remembering to take his father's sheep with him, but there was a part of him, a strong part, that hated *not knowing* things worse than anything. It was the part that had once caused him to pull the leg off a frog, just to find out what it would do. (It did very little, and died soon after with what Tobias felt guiltily certain was an accusatory look in its bulging eyes.) It was also the reason he had dented his father's best scythe when he had used it to try to cut down a tree, and why he had dumped the contents of his mother's precious sewing basket all over the ground—a search for knowledge that ended with Tobias spending all afternoon in the fading light on his hands and knees, locating every last needle and pin he had spilled. Once this rebel voice had even led him several miles out of the village, on a quest for the town of Eader's Church, which he had heard was so big that the streets actually had names. His father and two other men had caught up to him an hour after sunset as he sat exhausted and hungry by the side of the road. He had got a whipping for it, of course, but for young Tobias whippings were part of the cost of doing business.

So now, instead of turning and leaving the woods and its perilous inhabitants behind (for the sake of his father's livestock if nothing else) he followed the trail of smoke back to its source, a small cookfire in a clearing. A small man with a rat-like face was tending the flames, his wrinkles made so deep and dark by grime he looked like an apple-doll. His large companion, who sat on a stone beside the fire and did not look up even when Tobias stepped on a twig and made the little man jump, was so odd to look at that the boy could not help shivering. The large man's head was shaved, albeit poorly in some places, and the skull beneath the skin bulged in places that it should not. His bony jaw hung slack, the tongue visible in the space between top and bottom teeth, and although he did not seem blind, the eyes in the deep sockets were dull as dirty stones.

If the big man was paying no attention, the little man was. He stared at Tobias like a dog trying to decide whether to bark or run.

"Your wood's too wet," the boy told him.

"What?"

"You'll get mostly smoke and little fire from that. Do you want smoke?"

The small man frowned, but in dismay, not anger. "I want to cook this fish." He had the sound of a southerner, the words stretched and misshapen. Tobias wondered why they couldn't learn to speak properly.

He squinted at the man's supper with the eye of an experienced angler. "It's small."

"It's better than starving," the man pointed out.

"Well, then, I'll show you." Tobias quickly found enough dry wood to rebuild the fire and within a short time the little man was cooking the fish over it on a long stick. His large companion still had not moved or spoken, had not even seemed to notice the newcomer in their camp.

"Thanks for your kindness," the small man said. "I am Feliks. We are new to this."

"My name's Tobias," the boy said, basking in the glow of his own helpfulness. "What does that mean, new?"

"We have been living somewhere there was food." Feliks shrugged. "The food ran out."

Tobias stared at the other man, who still gazed at nothing, only the slow movement of his chest behind his dark, travel-worn robe showing that he was something other than a statue. "What's *his* name?"

Feliks hesitated for a moment. "Eli." He said it in the southern way, the last syllable rising like a shorebird's cry—Eh-*lee*. "He was my master, but he...something happened to him. He lost his wits."

Tobias now examined the big man with unhidden interest—if he had no wits, it couldn't be rude to stare, could it? "What happened?"

"The roof fell on him." Feliks took the fish from the stick, burning his fingers so that he almost dropped it—Tobias was amused by how many things the man didn't know how to do—

and then cut it into two pieces with a knife, handing the larger piece to the silent giant. Eli moved for the first time; he took fish without looking at it, put it in his mouth, and chewed with bovine patience. Feliks began to eat the other piece, then turned shamefacedly to Tobias. "I should offer some to you, for your kindness."

Tobias was old enough to understand this would not be a small sacrifice for Feliks. "No, I'll eat at home. And I'd better go now or Father will have the strap out." He looked through the trees to the angle of the sun, which was definitely lower than he would have liked. "He'll have the strap out, anyway." The boy stood. "I'll come back tomorrow, though. I can help you catch better fish than that one." He hesitated. "Have you been to other places? Other villages, even towns?"

Feliks nodded slowly. "Many places. Many cities all over the Middle Lands."

"Cities!" Tobias swayed a little, faint-headed at the thought. "Real cities? I'll be back!"

The tall man named Eli suddenly put out his hand, a gesture so startling after his hour of near-immobility that Tobias recoiled as though from a snake.

"He...I think he wants to thank you," Feliks said. "Go ahead, boy—take his hand. He was a great man once."

Tobias slowly extended his own small hand, wondering if this might be the beginning of some cruel or even murderous trick—if he had been too trusting after all. Eli's hand was big, knob-knuckled and smudged with dirt, and it closed on the boy's slim fingers like a church door swinging closed.

Then Tobias vanished.

When two days had passed with no sign of the boy, suspicion of course fell on the two strangers living in Squire's Wood. When the man named Feliks admitted that they had seen the child and spoken to him, the shireward and several local fellows dragged them out of the forest and chained them in wooden stocks beside the well in the center of the village, where everyone could see them and marvel at their infamy. Feliks tearfully continued to insist that they had done nothing to harm the boy, that they did not know where he had gone—both things true, as it turned out—but even if the two men had not been strangers and thus naturally suspect, the villagers could see that the big one was plainly touched, perhaps even demon-possessed, and almost no one felt anything for them but horror and disgust.

The lone exception was Father Bannity, the village priest, who felt that it was a troubling thing to imprison people simply because they were strangers, although he dared not say so aloud. He himself had been a stranger to the village when he had first arrived twenty years earlier (in fact, older villagers still referred to him as "the new priest") and so he had a certain empathy for those who might find themselves judged harshly simply because their grandfathers and great-grandfathers were not buried in the local churchyard. Also, since in his middle-life he had experienced a crisis of faith, leading him to doubt many of the most famous and popular tenets of his own religion, he was doubly unwilling to assume the guilt of someone else simply because they were not part of the familiar herd. So Father Bannity took it on himself to make sure the two prisoners had enough food and water to survive. It would be a long wait for the King's Prosecutor General to arrive—his circuit covered at least a dozen villages and lasted a full cycle of the moon—and even if the two were guilty of killing the poor child and hiding his body, Father Bannity did not want them to die before this could be discovered for certain.

As the small man, Feliks, grew to trust him, he at last told Bannity what he swore was the true story of what had happened that day, that the boy had touched big Eli's hand and then disappeared like a soap bubble popping. Father Bannity was not quite certain what to think, whether this was a true mystery or only the precursor to a confession, a man easing gradually into a guilty admission as into a scalding bath, but he stuck by his resolution to treat them as innocent until they told him otherwise, or events proved the worst to have happened.

One day, as he was holding a ladle of water to Eli's dry lips, the big man suddenly looked at him almost as if seeing him for the first time, a flash of life in the dull, bestial eyes that Bannity had not seen before. Startled, the priest dropped the ladle. The big man lifted his hand as far as he could with his wrist restrained by the stocks and spread his long fingers like some strange flower blooming.

"Don't," whispered Feliks. "That's what the boy did."

Father Bannity hesitated for only a moment. Something in the big man's strange gaze, something solemn and distant but not unkind, convinced him. He reached out and allowed Eli's hand to fold around his.

For a startling moment Bannity thought he had become a fish, jerked thrashing out of the river and up into the day-light, blinded by the sun and its prismatic colors, dazzled by the burning air. Then, a half-instant later, he realized it was as though he had been out of the water for years, and now had suddenly been plunged back *into* it: everything that had with-ered in him suddenly sprang back to life, all the small losses of the passing days and months—color, feeling, ecstasy. The feeling was so strong, so overwhelming, that he could not even answer Feliks' worried questions as he staggered away.

Bannity *knew* again. He had forgotten what it felt like, but now he remembered, and the thunderous force of belief returning betrayed how much he had lost. God had sent him a miracle in the person of the silent giant, and with that single touch, a world which had slowly turned gray around him over the years had been kindled back into flaming life.

God was in everything again, just as He had been when Bannity had been a child, when he had been able to imagine nothing better than to serve Him.

God was alive inside him. He had experienced a miracle.

It was only when the first surge of ecstatic happiness had become a little more ordinary, if no less pleasurable, that Father Bannity realized nothing tangible had actually changed. It wasn't so much that God had shown him a miracle, a sign, it was more as if touching the giant's hand had reawakened him to the love of God he had once had, but which had slipped away from him.

It was Eli, he realized, although undoubtedly acting as God's messenger, who had given him back his love of the Lord, his belief in a living Creation, and most of all, his certainty that what *was*, was meant to be.

The silent, damaged man had given Bannity his heart's desire, even though the priest himself had not known what it was.

Grateful, renewed, the priest resolved to speak on behalf of the two prisoners when the Prosecutor General returned to the village, to tell the truth even if it meant admitting that he had, for a time, lost his own faith. Father Bannity would undoubtedly have been their only defender, except that on the day before the traveling lawspeaker rode into town, the boy named Tobias came back.

He had been, the boy told the villagers (and very gleefully too) in the town of Eader's Church, and it was just as big and wonderful as he had imagined. "They have lots of dogs!" he said, his eyes still bright with the spectacle he had seen. "And houses that go up and up! And people!" He seemed to feel that the whipping his father had just given him—on general principles, since the actual mechanics of the boy's disappearance were still a mystery—was a small price to pay for all he'd seen.

Tobias knew nothing about how he had got from the village to the far-off town—it had happened in an instant, he said, from clasping Eli's hand to finding himself in the middle of the Eader's Church marketplace—but unfortunately there had been no equally magical way of returning. It had taken him all the days since he'd been gone to walk home.

When the Prosecutor General arrived the next day, there was no longer a case for murder to be tried, although several of the villagers were talking darkly of witchcraft. The Prosecutor General, a small, round, self-important fellow with a beard on his chin as small and sharp as an arrowhead, insisted on being taken to see the two former prisoners, who had been released to their campsite in Squire's Wood, if not to their previous state of anonymity.

Holding out his rod of office, the lawspeaker approached Eli and said, "In the name of the State and its gracious Sovereign, His Majesty the King, you must tell me how you sent the boy to Eader's Church."

The big man only looked at him, unbothered. Then he extended his hand. The Prosecutor General, after a moment's hesitation, extended his own small plump hand and allowed it to be grasped.

When Father Bannity and the other men watching had finished blinking their eyes, they saw that instead of his prosecutor's tunic, the Prosecutor General was now unquestionably wearing a judge's robes, cowl, and wreath, and that a judge's huge, round, golden emblem of office now hung on a chain around his neck. (Some also suggested that he had a stronger chin as well, and more penetrating eyes than he had heretofore possessed.) The ex-Prosecutor General, now a full-fledged Adjudicator, blinked, ran his fingers over the leafy wreath on his head, then fell down on his knees and uttered a happy prayer.

"Twelve years I've waited!" he said, over and over. "Thank you, Lord! Passed over and passed over—but no more!"

He then rose, and with fitting jurisprudential gravity, proclaimed, "These men have not practiced any unlicensed witchcraft. I rule that they are true messengers of God, and should be treated with respect."

Finding that his pockets were now richer by several gold coins—the difference between his old salary and new—the new-minted Adjudicator promptly sold his cart and donkey to Pender the village blacksmith and left town in a covered carriage, with a newly-hired driver and two new horses. Later rumors said that he arrived home to find he had been awarded the King's Fourteenth Judicial Circuit.

In the wake of the Prosecutor General's astonishing transformation, Squire's Wood began to fill with people from the village and even some of the surrounding villages—for news travels fast in these rural areas—turning the two men's camp into a site of pilgrimage. The size of the gathering grew so quickly that Father Bannity and some of the wood's nearer and soberer neighbors worried that the entire forest soon would be trampled flat, but the squireward could not turn the newcomers away any more than he could have held back the tide at Landsend.

Although none of this swarm of postulants was turned away, not all received their heart's desire, either—Eli's hand opened only to one in perhaps three or four and it was impossible to force the issue. One man, a jar maker named Keely, tried to pry the big man's fingers apart and shove his own hand in, and although he succeeded, nothing magical happened to him except that he developed a painful boil in the middle of his forehead the following day.

Some of the pilgrims' wishes turned out to be surprisingly small and domestic: a man whose sick cow suddenly recovered, a woman whose youngest son abruptly discovered he could hear as well as he had before the fever. Others were more predictable, like the man who after clasping Eli's hand discovered a pot of old coins buried under an ancient wall he was rebuilding.

To the astonishment of many, two blighted young folk who lived on neighboring farms, a young man with a shattered leg and a girl with a huge strawberry blotch on her face, both went to Eli, and both were gifted with a handclasp, but came out again looking just the same as they had before. But within the next few days the young man's drunkard father died of a fit, leaving him the farm, and the girl's cruel, miserly uncle who treated her like a servant fell under the wheels of a cart and died also, leaving her free to marry if anyone would have her. The two young people did indeed marry each other, and seemed quite happy, although they both still bore the disfigurements that had made them so pitiable to the rest of the village.

The only apparent failure of Eli's magical touch was Pender, the blacksmith, who went to the campsite a massive, strapping man with a beard that reached halfway down his chest, and went away again with the shape and voice and apparently all the working parts of a slender young woman. He left town the same night, trading the Prosecutor General's old cart for a pair of pretty dresses before setting off on the donkey toward the nearest city to start his life over (at least so he told his neighbors), so no one was ever able to find out exactly how such a strange thing had happened when others had been served so well.

Soon the lame youth and other grateful folk came and built a great tent in Squire's Wood for Eli and Feliks to shelter in, and began bringing them daily offerings of food and drink. People were coming to see the two strangers from all around, and even the villagers who had not obtained a supernatural gift from the silent giant came to realize how valuable his presence was: the village was full of pilgrims, including some quite well-to-do folk who were willing to pay exorbitant prices to be fed and housed near the miracle worker.

Father Bannity, still basking in the joyful light of his newly-recovered faith, did not doubt that Eli and Feliks were gifts from God, but he had not lost all caution or good sense, either, and he was worried by what was happening to his quiet village. He sent a messenger describing recent events to Dondolan, the nearest accredited wizard, who had an eyrie near the top of Reaching Peak. The wizard had not passed through the village for years—but he and the priest had met several times, and Bannity liked the mage and trusted his good sense, certainly beyond that of the village elders, who were growing as greedy of pilgrimage gold as children tumbled into a treacle vat, happily eating themselves to death.

Dondolan the Clear-Eyed, as he had been named back in his Academy days, took one look at the priest's letter, then leaped out of his chair and began packing (a task which takes a wizard a much shorter time than the average traveler). The messenger asked if there would be any reply, and Dondolan told him, "I will be there before you." Then, suiting deed to word, he promptly vanished.

He appeared again in the village at the base of the mountain, and took his horse from the livery stable there—even an accomplished wizard will not travel by magic for twenty leagues, not knowing what he will find at the other end, for it is a fierce drain on the resources—and set out. Other than an ill-considered attempt by some local bandits to waylay him just outside Drunken Princes' Pass, an interaction which increased the frog population of the highlands but did not notably slow Dondolan's progress, it was a swift journey, and he reached the nameless village within two days. Spurning more ordinary couriers, he had sent a raven ahead, and as a result Father Bannity waited at the crossroads outside of town to meet him.

When they had greeted each other—fondly, for the respect was mutual, despite their differences on the theological practicalities—Bannity led Dondolan through the fields around the outskirts of the village, so as not to cause more ruckus and rumor than was necessary: already the village practically breathed the stuff, and the pilgrims arriving daily from all over only made things more frantic.

"Do you wish to speak to the two of them?" Bannity asked. "It will be difficult, but I might persuade the village elders to let us close off the camp, although it will not be easy to remove all the addled folk who are living there now—they have practically made a new town in the middle of the forest."

"We should decide nothing until I see these miracle men," Dondolan said. "Although I must say that the description of them in your letter gave me an unpleasant feeling in the pit of my stomach."

"Why?" asked Bannity with some alarm. "Do you think they mean harm? I worried mainly that so many pilgrims would jeopardize the safety of our little town, drawing thieves and confidence tricksters and such. But surely God has sent those two to us—they have done so much good!"

"Perhaps. That is why I will restrain my conjectures until I have seen them."

They made their way through the woods, between groups of revelers singing and praying, gathered around so many camp-fires it seemed more like the eve of a great battle than twilight in the woods outside a quiet village too unassuming even to have its own name. As they grew close to the great pale tent and the crowd of people waiting there—some patiently, others loudly demanding that they be allowed to be next to see the wonder-workers because their need was so great—Bannity found it increasingly difficult to make headway through the throng. It was a mark of how many of these people were strangers to the area that the village's well-respected priest almost got into two fights, and only Dondolan's discreet use of a quelling-charm got them past those at the front of the line without real violence.

They slipped through the tent's flap-door. Dondolan looked across the big tent at the miraculous pair sitting like minor potentates on high-backed chairs the villagers had built them, the small man Feliks and the big man with the misshapen skull. Feliks was scratching himself and laughing at something. Eli was staring down at one of the kneeling postulants before him, his expression as emptily self-absorbed as a bullfrog waiting for a fly of sufficient size to happen past. Dondolan swallowed, then stepped back out of the tent again, and Bannity followed him. Even by torchlight, the priest could see the wizard had gone quite pale.

"It is indeed as I feared, Bannity. That is no poor traveler, innocently touched by God—or at least that is not how he began. The large man is the dark wizard Elizar the Devourer, scourge of the southern lands, and greatest enemy of the archmage Kettil of Thundering Crag."

"Elizar?" Bannity suddenly found swallowing difficult. Even a village priest knew the Devourer, who had burned whole towns because he liked the gloomy skies their smoking ruins provided, who had performed vile rites to turn men into beasts and beasts into men, and whose campaign of violent conquest had only been stopped by Kettil himself, the greatest wizard of the age, who had come down from his great ice caverns atop Thundering Crag and helped the young King defeat Elizar's vast army of slavering beast-men at the field of Herredsburn. Kettil himself had dueled Elizar before the gathered forces of both armies—the skies above Herredsburn, everyone remembered, had lit up as if with half a dozen simultaneous thunderstorms, and although neither had managed definitively to best the other, it had been Elizar who had fled the field, his plans in ruins, and who had retreated into a dark obscurity that had covered him for years—an absence that had lasted until this very moment. *That* Elizar?" murmured Father Bannity. "*Here?*"

"I would stake my life on it," said Dondolan, "and may be doing so. Even if his mindlessness is real, just seeing someone like me that he has known might shock him back to his prior self."

"But we cannot simply...leave it. We cannot leave things this way."

"No, but I dare not go near him. His miracles, you tell me, are real, so he still wields mighty powers. Even if he stays witless, I cannot afford the chance he might decide to give *me* my heart's desire." Dondolan shook his head, his white beard wagging. "The heart of a wizard, even a relatively decent one like myself, is full of dark crevices. It is the world we inhabit, the wisdoms we study, the powers we have learned to harness, if not always to understand." He smiled, but there was not much pleasure in it. "I truthfully do not know my heart's desire, and have no urge to discover it this way."

"I'm...I'm not certain what you mean."

"What if my heart's desire is to be the greatest wizard of my age? I felt that way once, when I was young and first entering the Academy. What if that desire has not gone, only hidden?" He shook his head again. "I dare not risk it."

"But what if an ordinary mortal—someone not a wizard—has the same thing as *his* heart's desire? Or something worse, asking for the end of the world or something."

Dondolan gave the priest a shrewd, sober look. "So far, that has not happened. In fact, the power Elizar wields seems not to have harmed much of anybody, except, by your account, a pair of nasty old folk who deliberately stood in the way of their children's happiness. And even there, we cannot prove that coincidence did not carry them away. Perhaps there is something to Elizar's magic that is self-limiting—something that prevents him from granting any but mostly benign wishes. I do not know." He looked up. "I *do* know that we must discover more before we can make up our minds. We cannot, as you said, simply leave things be, not with Elizar the Devourer here, surrounded by eager supplicants, busily creating miracles, however kind-hearted those miracles may seem." Dondolan ran his fingers through his long beard. "Not to mention the evil chance that this is all some cruel trick of Elizar's—that he only shams at having lost his mind, and plots to seize the Middle Lands again." He frowned, thinking. "When do they stop for the night?"

"Soon. When my sexton rings the church bell for evening prayer."

"Wait until that bell rings, Father, then bring me the man Feliks."

The small man seemed almost relieved to have been found out. "Yes, it is true. He was once Elizar, the greatest wizard of all."

"After Kettil the archmage, you mean," said Dondolan.

Feliks waved his hand. "My master poured his soul into five thousand beast-men at Herredsburn, animating them throughout the battle. Even so, he duelled Kettil Hawkface to a standstill."

"This is neither here nor there," said Father Bannity impatiently. "Why is he the way we see him? Is this some new plot of his, some evil device?"

"Tell the truth, minion, and do not think to trick me," Dondolan said harshly. "Even now, Kettil himself must be hearing news of this. He will not take longer than I did to deduce that your Eli is in fact his old arch-enemy."

Feliks sighed. "Then we must be moving on again. Sad, that is. I was enjoying it here."

"Damn it, man, one of the most dangerous men in the world sleeps twenty paces away! Talk to us!"

"Dangerous to you, perhaps." Feliks shook his head. "No, not even to you—not now. There is no trick, wizard. What you see is the truth. The old Elizar is gone, and dumb Eli is what remains.

"It was after Herredsburn, you see, when the king and your Wizard's Council turned us away. With all his beast-men dead or changed back to their former selves, my master left the field and retreated to his secret lair in the Darkslide Mountains."

"We suspected he had a bolthole there," murmured Dondolan, "but we could never find it."

"He was determined to have his revenge on Kettil and the others," continued Feliks. "I have never seen him thus. He was furious, but also weary, weary and distraught." The small man peered at the priest and the wizard for a moment. "Once, in middle-night when I was awakened from sleep by a strange noise, I found him weeping."

"I cannot believe that," said Dondolan. "Elizar? The Devourer?"

"Believe what you will. There was always more to him than you folk on the Council understood. Whatever the case, he became fixed on the idea of securing the Amulet of Desire, which can grant its possessor whatever gift he most wants. He spent many months—a year, almost—pursuing its legend down many forgotten roads, in old books and older scrolls. He spoke to creatures so fearsome I could not even be under the same roof while they were conversing." The memory still seemed to make Feliks fearful, and yet proud of his bold master. "At last the time came. Deep in our cavern home in the Darkslide Mountains, he prepared the spells. I helped him as best I could, but I am just a servant, not a necromancer. I stoked the fires, polished the alembics, brought the articles he needed from our reliquary. At last the hour came when the spheres were in alignment, and he began the Summoning of the Empty Gods.

"He had been nights on end without sleep, in the grip of a fever that I had never seen in him before, even on the night before Herredsburn, when dominion over all the world was still at his fingertips. Pale, wide-eyed, talking to himself as though I was not even present, he was like a prisoner desperate for release, whether that release came from the opening of the prison door or from the hangman's rope."

Feliks sighed and briefly wiped his eyes while Dondolan tapped impatient fingers.

"The spell went on for hours," the small man continued, "names shouted into the darkness that hurt my ears. At one point I fled, terrified by the shadows that filled the room and danced all around me. When I came back, it was because I heard my master's hoarse cry of triumph.

"He stood in the center of his mystical diagram, holding up something I could barely see, something that gleamed red and black..."

"Something cannot gleam black," Dondolan said—a trifle querulously, Bannity thought. "It makes no sense."

"Little of what had happened that night made sense, but I will not change my tale. It gleamed red and black. Elizar held it over his head, crying out with a ragged voice, 'My greatest wish made real...!'—and then the roof collapsed."

"Collapsed?" said Bannity. "How? I thought you were in some mountain cavern."

"We were," Feliks agreed. "I still am not certain how it happened—it was like being chewed in a giant's mouth, chewed and chewed and then spit out. When I woke up, we both lay on the slope beneath the entrance to the lair, which was choked with fallen rock. Elizar was as you see him now, crushed and silent, his head all bloody, poor fellow. The Amulet was gone. Everything was gone. I helped him up and we stumbled and crawled down the hill to a cotsman's deserted shack—the owner had fled when the mountain began to shake. I shaved my master's head and doctored his wounds. We ate what supplies the cotsman had laid in, but when we ran out, we had no choice but to become wandering beggars." The small, wrinkled man spread his hands. "*I can do no magic, you see.*"

"Was the boy in the village, the one Elizar sent to Eader's Church, the first to be...touched?"

Feliks shook his head. "My master took a few people's hands, mostly folk who gave generously to our begging bowl, and sometimes things happened. None were harmed, all profited," he added, a little defensively.

"And you," Dondolan demanded. "You must have touched his hands many times since this occurred. What of you?"

"What could happen? I already have my heart's desire. All I have ever wanted was to serve him. From the first moment I saw him outside the Academy, I knew that he was my destiny, for good or bad."

Dondolan sighed. "For bad, certainly, at least until now. You are not a true villain, Feliks, but you have served an evil man."

"All great men are thought evil by some."

"Not all great men graft the heads of wild boars onto the shoulders of peasant farmers," Dondolan pointed out. "Not all great men wear the skins of other wizards for a cloak."

"He killed only those who turned against him," said Feliks stubbornly. "Only those who would have killed him."

Dondolan stared at him for a moment. "It matters little now," he said at last. "As I said, Kettil will have heard by now, and guessed who is here. The archmage will come, and things will change."

"Then we must go," said Feliks, rising to his feet with a weary grunt. "We will move on. There are still places we can live in quiet peace, if I only help my poor master to keep his hands to himself."

"I dare not try to stop you," Dondolan said. "I fear to wake your master if he really sleeps inside that battered skull—I admit I was never his match. But even if you flee, you will not outrun Kettil's power."

It does not matter. What will be, will be, Bannity thought to himself, but a little of his newfound peace had gone with Eli's unmasking. *Whether Elizar is a man transformed or a villain disguised, surely what happens next will be as God wills,*

*too. For who can doubt His hand when He has shown us so
many miracles here?*

But Eli would not leave the wood, despite Feliks' urging. The
mute man was as resistant as a boulder set deep in mud: none
of his servant's pleas or arguments touched him—in fact, he
showed no sign of even hearing them.

Dondolan and Bannity, armed with the knowledge of the
miracle worker's true identity, convinced the suddenly terrified
village elders that for a while at least, the crowds should be
kept away. With a contingent of solders from the nearest
shirepost, hired with a fraction of the profits from the long
miracle-season, they cleared the forest of all the supplicants,
forcing them out into the town and surrounding fields, where
local sellers of charms and potions gleefully provided them
with substitute satisfaction, or at least the promise of it.

Even as the last of the camps were emptied, some of the latest arrivals from beyond the village brought news that Kettil
Hawkface himself was on the way. Some had seen nothing
more than a great storm swirling around Thunder Crag while
the sky elsewhere was blue and bright, but others claimed to
have seen the archmage himself speeding down the mountain on a huge white horse, shining as he came like a bolt of
lightning. In any case, those who had been turned away from
Squire's Wood now had something else to anticipate, and the
great road that passed by the nameless village was soon lined
with those waiting to see the most famous, most celebrated
wizard of all.

Father Bannity could not help wondering whether Elizar
sensed anything of his great rival's coming, and so he walked
into Squire's Wood and across the trampled site of the camp,
empty now but for a couple of hired soldiers standing guard.

Inside the tent wrinkled little Feliks looked up from eating a bowl of stew and waved to Bannity as if they were old friends, but Elizar was as empty-faced as ever, and seemed not to notice that the crowds of pilgrims were gone, that he and Feliks were alone. He sat staring at the ground, his big hands opening and closing so slowly that Father Bannity could have counted a score of his own suddenly intrusive heartbeats between fist and spread fingers. The man's naked face and shaved scalp made the head atop the black robe seem almost like an egg, out of which anything might hatch.

Why did I come here? he asked himself. *To taunt the blackest magician of the age?* But he felt he had to ask.

"Are you truly gone from in there, Elizar?" The priest's voice trembled, and he prayed to God for strength. He now realized, in a way he had not before, that here sat a man who was of such power that he had destroyed whole cities the way an ordinary man might kick down an ant-hill. But Bannity had to ask. "Are you truly and completely empty, or is there a spark of you left in that husk, listening?" He had a sudden thought. "Did you bring this on yourself, with your magical amulet? When the time came for your heart's desire to be granted, did God hear a small, hidden part of you that was weary of death and torment and dark hatreds, that wanted to perform the Lord's work for your fellow men instead of bringing them blood and fire and terror?"

Eli did not look up or change expression, and at last Father Bannity went out. Feliks watched him go with a puzzled expression, then returned to his meal.

He came down the main road with crowds cheering behind him as though he were a conquering hero—which, after all, he was. Bannity watched the people shouting and calling Kettil's name as the wizard rode toward the village on his huge white horse, the same people who only days before had been crouched in the dirt outside Eli's tent, begging to be let in, and the priest wondered at God's mysterious ways.

Kettil Hawkface was younger than Bannity would have guessed, or else had spelled himself to appear so. He seemed a man in the middle of life, his golden hair only touched with gray, his bony, handsome face still firm in every line. His eyes were the most impressive thing about him: even from a distance, they glittered an icy blue, and up close it was difficult to look at him directly, such was the chilly power of his gaze.

Bannity and Dondolan met the archmage at the edge of the wood. Kettil nodded at his fellow wizard, but hardly seemed to see the priest at all, even after Dondolan introduced him.

"He is in there..." Dondolan began, but Kettil raised his hand and the lesser mage fell silent.

"I know where he is." He had a voice to match his eyes, frosty and authoritative. "And I know what he is. I have battled his evil for half my long life. I do not need to be told where to find him—I smell him as a hound smells his quarry."

Strange, then, that you did not find him before, thought Bannity, then regretted his own small-minded carping. "But he is not the monster you knew, Archmage..."

Kettil looked at him then, but only a moment, then turned away. "Such creatures do not change," he said to Dondolan.

Bannity tried again. "He has done much good...!"

Kettil smirked. "Has he revived all those he killed? Rebuilt the cities he burned? Do not speak to me of things you do not understand, priest." He slid down off his massive white horse. "I will go, and we will see what devilry awaits."

Bannity had to admit the archmage was as impressive as legend had promised. He strode into the forest with no weapon but his staff of gnarled birch, his long hair blowing, his sky-blue robes billowing as though he still stood on the heights of Thundering Crag. Bannity looked at Dondolan, whose face bore a carefully composed expression that betrayed nothing of what he was thinking, then they both followed the Archmage Kettil into Squire's Wood.

To Bannity's astonishment, Eli himself stood in the doorway of the tent, looking out across the great clearing. "Ho, Devourer!" Kettil's voice echoed, loud as a hunting horn, but Eli only looked at him incuriously, his large hands dangling from his sleeves like roosting bats. "I have found you again at last!"

The hairless man blinked, turned, and went back into the tent. Kettil strode after him, crossing the clearing in a few long paces. Bannity started to follow, but Dondolan grabbed his arm and held him back.

"This is beyond me and beyond you, too."

"Nothing is beyond God!" Bannity cried, but Dondolan the Clear-Eyed looked doubtful. A few moments later little Feliks came stumbling out of the tent, flapping his hands as if surrounded by angry bees.

"They stand face to face!" he squawked, then tripped and fell, rolling until he stopped at Bannity's feet. The priest helped him up, but did not take his eyes off the tent. "They do not speak, but stare at each other. The air is so thick!"

"It seems..." Dondolan began, but never finished, for at that instant the entire clearing—in fact, all the woods and the sky above—seemed to suck in a great breath. A sudden, agonizing pain in Bannity's ears dropped him to his knees, then everything suddenly seemed to flow sideways—light, color, heat, air, everything rushing out across the face of the earth in all directions, pushing the priest flat against the ground and rolling him over several times.

When the monstrous wind died, Bannity lay for a long, stunned instant, marveling at the infinite skills of God, who could create the entire universe and now, just as clearly, was going to dismantle it again. Then a great belch of flame and a roar of rushing air made him roll over onto his knees and, against all good sense, struggle to sit up so he could see what was happening.

The tent was engulfed in flame, the trees all around singed a leafless black. As Father Bannity stared, two figures staggered out of the inferno as though solidifying out of smoke, one like a pillar of cold blue light, with flame dancing in his pale hair and beard, the other a growing, rising shadow of swirling black.

"I knew you but pretended, demon!" shouted Kettil Hawkface, waving his hands in the air, flashes of light crackling up from his fingertips. "Devourer! I know your treachery of old!"

The shadow, which had begun to fold down over the archmage like a burning blanket, instead billowed up and away, hovering in the air just above Kettil's head. A face could be seen in its roiling, cloudy midst, and Bannity could not help marveling even in his bewildered horror how it looked both like and unlike the silent Eli.

"I will make sure your dying lasts for centuries, Hawkface!" shrieked the dark shape in a voice that seemed to echo all the way to the distant hills, then it rose up into the air, flapping like an enormous bat made of smoke and sparks, and flew away into the south.

"Master!" screamed Feliks, and stumbled off through the woods, following the fast-diminishing blot of fiery blackness until he, too, disappeared from sight.

Kettil Hawkface, his pale robes smeared with ash, his whiskers and hair singed at the edges, strode away in the other direction, walking back toward the village with the purposeful stride of someone who has completed a dangerous and thankless job and does not bother to wait for the approbation he surely deserves.

As he emerged at the forest's edge, he stood before the hundreds of onlookers gathered there and raised his hands. "Elizar the Devourer's evil has been discovered and ended, and he has flown in defeat back to the benighted south," the archmage cried. "You people of the Middle Lands may rest safely again, knowing that the Devourer's foul plan has been thwarted."

The crowd cheered, but many were confused about what had happened and the reception of his news was not as whole-hearted as Kettil had perhaps expected. He did not wait to speak again to his colleague Dondolan, but climbed onto his white horse and galloped away north toward Thundering Crag, followed by a crowd of children crying out after him for pennies and miracles.

Bannity and Dondolan watched in silence as the ramrod-straight figure grew smaller, and then eventually disappeared. The crowds did not immediately disperse, but many seemed to realize there would be little reason to collect here anymore, and the cries of the food sellers, charm hawkers, and roving apothecaries became muted and mournful.

"So all is resolved for good," Father Bannity said, half to himself. "Elizar's evil was discovered and thwarted."

"Perhaps," said Dondolan. "But a part of me cannot help wondering whose heart's desire was granted here today."

"What do you mean? Do you think...they clasped hands?"

Dondolan sighed. "Do not misunderstand me. It is entirely possible that the world has been spared a great evil here today—Elizar was always full of plots, many of them astoundingly sub-tle. But if they *did* touch hands, I think it is safe to say that only one of them was granted his heart's desire."

"I don't understand."

"Elizar may not have seemed entirely happy as Eli the dumb miracle-worker," Dondolan said, "but he did seem peaceful. Now, though, he is the Devourer again, and Kettil once more has an enemy worthy of his own great pride and power."

Bannity was silent for a long time, watching the sky darken as the sun settled behind Squire's Wood. "But surely God would not let Elizar's evil back into the world simply because his enemy missed it—God must have a better plan for mankind than that!"

"Perhaps," said Dondolan the Clear-Eyed. "Perhaps. We will think on it together after we return to the church and you find the brandy you keep hidden for such occasions."

Father Bannity nodded and took a few steps, then turned. "How did you know about the brandy?"

The priest thought Dondolan's smile seemed a trifle sour. "I am a wizard, remember? We know almost everything."

Bad Guy Factory

Issue #1: "Heatseeker"

PAGE 1

PANEL ONE: SPLASH—*the* SEVEN ROOKIES
(HEATSEEKER, DOLLY, MINK, COLDBLOODED,
CELL, THROWBACK, SNAIL) *are standing by themselves
under a* SPOTLIGHT, *looking* UP *at* BYZANTINE, *a
nasty,* COLD-FACED *old man in an ornate bronze battlesuit
standing on a platform; next to him is his right-hand
man,* FARSIGHT.

*(WE DON'T HAVE TO SEE BYZANTINE'S FACE IN
THE FIRST PANEL.)*

A CROWD *of other* COSTUMED VILLAINS *fills the
huge, warehouse-sized room, the main meeting space of
the* FACTORY, *watching this* SPECTACLE—*most with
amusement or disdain. (We might see* PRETTY BOY, TIME
MASTER, WALRUS *and* CARPENTER, FLAK, SAILOR,

TAD WILLIAMS

OCHO, MADAME MIRAGE/MIMOSA, PROFESSOR NACHTIGAL among them.)

CAPTION 1:
There are some things you
never like to hear...

CAPTION 2:
"Your credit card has been
declined."

CAPTION 3:
"Your tests are back, but we
didn't get the results we'd hoped
for."

CAPTION 4:
"You're being deployed to the
Middle East."

CAPTION 5:
This is a new one...

BYZANTINE:
In less than two minutes, one of
you is going to be DEAD.

A) TITLE:

BAD GUY FACTORY

1: HEATSEEKER

B) CREDITS

PAGE 2

PANEL ONE: We see a GLOVED HAND, powerful-looking, raised to knock on a door.

CAPTION:
Hakim Anthony—now calling
himself Anthony Hack after
being reported AWOL from
the military—should have seen
it coming. After all, the day
pretty much started OUT like
shit...

PANEL TWO: Looking over ANTHONY's shoulder (he's in civilian clothes as he opens the door.) We see GUARD #1 (black) and GUARD #2 (white) just beyond him, looking through the door, which is still on its chain. They are wearing sunglasses and wool watch caps and wearing coveralls. The letters "BGF" are printed on their chest pockets. GUARD #2 has a HIDEOUS DWARF about TEN INCHES HIGH ("CARPENTER") RIDING on his SHOULDER.

GUARD #1:
You Anthony Hack?
Heatseeker?

ANTHONY:
Could be. Who are you?

PANEL THREE: GUARD #2 points to the pocket of his coveralls.

GUARD #2:
We're from Byzantium Gates
Fabrication.

PANEL FOUR: ANTHONY, *a lithely muscular black man in his mid-20s, opens the door and steps back.*

ANTHONY:
Yeah, that's me—but how
about you? Got some I.D.?

PANEL FIVE: GUARD #1 *reaches into his POCKET.*

GUARD #1:
Oh, yeah, no problem. You got
all your stuff ready?

ANTHONY
(pointing toward two duffel bags) :
Right there.

GUARD #1:
Good.

PAGE 3

PANEL ONE: *(Splash)—A HUGE ARC of electrical plasma ZAPS from the object in Guard #2's fist to ANTHONY, knocking him off his feet him with a huge and painful jolt.*

SFX:
GzzzZZZZAPPP!

GUARD #1:
And HERE'S my I.D., BITCH!

PANELS TWO, THREE, FOUR: (Small, at bottom, panels black except for the guards' words, unless we want to show the DISTORTION, THEN BLACK of a progression of ANTHONY passing out.)

GUARD #1
(Off Panel, as CAPTION):
Now the gas to make sure he
stays out.

GUARD #2 (OP, as CAPTION) :
Why didn't you just use the gas
in the first place?

GUARD #1 (OP, as CAPTION) :
Because burnin' his no-respect
ass was more fun.

GUARD #2 (OP, as CAPTION) :
Christ, where'd that freaky little
thing go? Damn, he's in the
wastebaskets looking for food.
Come help me catch the dwarf
or we'll never get back.

GUARD #1 (CONT.) :
Shee-it. You hear that punk?
Askin' ME for I.D...

TAD WILLIAMS

PAGE 4

PANEL ONE: CLOSE ON ANTHONY'S FACE—TINY DROPS OF SWEAT, BUT HE'S POKER-FACED.

> ANTHONY
> THOUGHT CAPTION 1:
> Man, I hate this place, and I
> truly hate being underground.
> Reminds me WAY too much of
> the Russian's place...and those
> motherfucking flies...
> the FLIES...

> BYZANTINE (OP):
> Two minutes to live—it's not a
> very long time, is it?

PANEL TWO: MEDIUM SHOT on BYZANTINE, FARSIGHT.

> BYZANTINE (Cont.):
> In any case, now that I have
> your attention...listen carefully
> and understand this: You are
> now part of Byzantine Gates
> Fabrication, sometimes known
> as The Factory, the most
> successful program ever devised
> for training metahumans and
> their associates to a life in the
> unregulated marketplace. You
> belong to me.

BYZANTINE (Cont.):
I am Byzantine...and while you
are here, I am your god. If you
offend me in any way, you will
suffer. After you leave, you will
still be mine until you have paid
off your debt. You know this.
You all accepted the bargain
before you came.

PANEL THREE: CLOSE on BYZANTINE'S FACE.

BYZANTINE:
But spies and traitors—that is a
different story. For them, there
is only one penalty.

ANTHONY
THOUGHT-CAPTION 2:
Do they know about me? Can't
be. They don't know about
me. He's just trying it to see if
anyone flinches.

ANTHONY
THOUGHT-CAPTION 3:
But I don't flinch.

*PANEL FOUR: SHOT ON ANTHONY in the midst of the
other ROOKIES.*

BYZANTINE:
Anthony Hack—Heatseeker.

ANTHONY
THOUGHT-CAPTION 4:
Shit. They MUST know.

ANTHONY
THOUGHT-CAPTION 5:
Damn! No side-arm, no way
to fight back—what kind of
dumb-ass gets himself into
something like this...?

ANTHONY:
Sir?

PANEL FIVE: BYZANTINE—EVIL-LOOKING old dude,
the COLD, ANGRY GRANDPA from HELL.

BYZANTINE:
What do you think we do with
traitors and spies here, Mr.
Hack?

ANTHONY
THOUGHT-CAPTION 6:
Shit!

PAGE 5

PANEL ONE: ANTHONY and MINK and THROWBACK
and SNAIL.

ANTHONY:
I don't know, sir.

BYZANTINE:
Letisha Angel—tagging, as you
young people say, as "Mink."
Tell me what you think happens
to people who spy on the
Factory, Miss Angel.

MINK:
Don't know. Trouble.

PANEL TWO: SAME as ONE.

BYZANTINE:
Mr. Carter?

THROWBACK:
Oh, f'sure. BIG trouble.

PANEL THREE: SAME as ONE.

PANEL FOUR: SAME as ONE.

SNAIL:
Trouble. Double.

PANEL FIVE: EVERYONE TURNS TO LOOK AT SNAIL.
HE'S STARING DOWN NERVOUSLY.

SNAIL (Cont.):
Mister Bubble.

PAGE 6

PANEL ONE: BYZANTINE walks down from the PODIUM, LOOKING THEM UP AND DOWN. We see/hear his SERVO MOTORS CLICKING.

SFX:
Ssss-klik. Ssss-klik. Ssss-klik.

BYZANTINE:
Which of you is the one called
Cell? Benny Santos?

CELL:
That would be me.

PANEL TWO: BYZANTINE STOPS, stares at him like a VULTURE at a DYING MAN. We can see FARSIGHT behind BYZANTINE, still up on the PODIUM.

BYZANTINE:
No, I'm afraid it wouldn't.
Mr. Farsight?

FARSIGHT:
Your real name is Anselmo.
You told our recruiter you're a
TP specialist for a Midwestern
crime syndicate who wants to
go solo. In fact, though, you're
an undercover police officer out
of New Columbia PD H Plus
Division.

PANEL THREE: CELL points ANGRILY at FARSIGHT.

CELL:
That's a lie, man! You got it
all wrong!

FARSIGHT:
I can feel him firing, sir, even
through the damper effect. He's
broadcasting at full strength.

BYZANTINE:
Thank you, Mr. Farsight. You
see, I have my own telepath.

PANEL FOUR: CELL TURNS on BYZANTINE.

CELL:
All right, you crooked bastard.
You can do anything to me you
want, but I just sent out a call
that's already been heard by
every TP-sensitive meta in the
area. You're going to have Force
Five or even U.P. all over your
ass in about two minutes.

BYZANTINE:
Please, give us a little credit—
we're professionals. Surely
you heard Mr. Farsight
mention the damper effect?
The Factory has special field

generators that prevent anyone
from broadcasting out on any
wavelength—INCLUDING
the theta-plosive frequencies of
most telepathy.

*PANEL FIVE: SOME GUARDS are MOVING FORWARD
(and ANTHONY and the others are BACKING AWAY) but
BYZANTINE holds up his HAND.*

CELL:
Yeah? Yeah? I can still do a few
tricks with microwaves—I'll
take some of your thugs down
with me!

BYZANTINE:
And now, Factory newcomers,
we answer the question that
was in all your minds: We are
giving out valuable knowledge
and equipment. How do we
make sure our students pay us
back after they graduate our
little program?

*PANEL SIX: CLOSE on BYZANTINE's COLD FACE,
COLD SMILE.*

BYZANTINE (Cont.):
The answer is—the same
way we keep order among
a collection of immature,

super-powered sociopaths,
of course. We knock them
unconscious before we bring
them here, then inject them
with nanobots. Pyroactive
nanobots that we can
activate...any time we want.

PAGE 7

PANEL ONE: (BIG) BYZANTINE GESTURES and CELL GOES UP IN an INFERNO of FLAME.

CELL:
AAAAHH!
AAAAAAAUUUUUUUGGH
GHHHHH!

PANEL TWO: Everybody SCRAMBLING AWAY while CELL burns.

PANEL THREE: NOTHING MUCH LEFT of CELL BUT A CHARRED SKELETON.

BYZANTINE:
I trust this little demonstration
has refined the thinking of our
new trainees. Until you have
learned all the rules, I suggest
you consider your every action
in the Factory very carefully.

BYZANTINE (Cont.):
Welcome to Byzantium Gates.

PAGE 8

PANEL ONE: *The SIX ROOKIES are walking back toward their SLEEPING ROOMS. Some other FACTORY "students" move in either direction in the background—it's a main corridor. NEED MORE CHARACTER DETAIL, FOR THE TEXT-READER, OF THE ROOKIES - ?*

THROWBACK:
Jesus! Did you SEE that?

ANTHONY:
We all saw it.

ANTHONY
THOUGHT-CAPTION 1:
And now we're all accessories,
too.

PANEL TWO: *THROWBACK, in his horrified enthusiasm, accidentally brushes COLDBLOODED's SHOULDER.*

ANTHONY
THOUGHT-CAPTION 2:
As far as I can tell, the ones
who came in with me—or who
got kidnapped and booby-
trapped with me, to be more
exact—are a cross-section of
street kids and psychopaths.

THROWBACK:
I mean, that was CRAZY!
They burned that guy UP! That
was…it was…

COLDBLOODED:
Take your hand OFFA me,
cracker.

THROWBACK:
Whoa, yeah, sorry…

ANTHONY
THOUGHT-CAPTION 3:
Like Coldblooded there. I know
him, even though I never met
him before today. He's half
the brothers I used to run with
before I went into the service
and out of the life. He'll fight
you for anything—or nothing.
There's no doubt I'm gonna
have to throw down with him
before this is over. The only
question is, should I get it out
of the way fast or wait 'til it
happens on its own?

PANEL THREE: THROWBACK *has stopped to watch
PROFESSOR NACHTIGAL walking by, a very tall, thin
middle-aged man with gelled-down hair and a face so thin and
bony you can see the SKULL underneath the skin. The other
ROOKIES pay no attention.*

PANEL FOUR: THROWBACK IS EXCITED. MINK notices, and watches the retreating NACHTIGAL.

> THROWBACK:
> DUDE! Did you see? That was
> Professor Nachtigal, I swear
> it was! What's he doing here?
> He's a major supervillain!

> MINK:
> Major or not, you can bet HE
> don't get it without payin'
> double for it.

> ANTHONY
> THOUGHT-CAPTION 4:
> And the women, oh God, I
> know them too—battered,
> abused, living off men because
> they can't see any other way,
> hating every minute of it.

> SNAIL:
> Nightingale. Fight in jail.

> ANTHONY
> THOUGHT-CAPTION 5:
> The white boys I can't figure
> out at all. Well, maybe little
> Darren there, what's he call
> himself, Snail? He's a bit crazy
> to start with, and he's from
> one of those backward country
> places like my daddy was.

ANTHONY
THOUGHT-CAPTION 6:
Even a life of crime is better
than that.

PANEL FIVE: THROWBACK approaches ANTHONY.

CODY:
You saw him, right? Professor
Nachtigal?

ANTHONY:
You a fan?

*PANEL SIX: ANTHONY is darkly AMUSED by
THROWBACK.*

CODY:
Not so much him, but he's
FAMOUS, man—I got one of
his skins! He fought Twilight
Man. He even broke out of
Las Sombras, so you know he's
earnin' the big cheddar! The
Godzilla scrilla!

ANTHONY:
Oh, yeah, sure. Nothing like
doing time in an institution for
the criminally insane to boost
your earning power.

ANTHONY
THOUGHT-CAPTION 7:
This Carter kid—what IS his
damage? He's stronger than any
of us, he can't shut up for ten
seconds, and he seems to think
this whole thing is a game. A
man was just burned to death
in front of him, and he...

ANTHONY
THOUGHT-CAPTION 8:
Screw it. Doesn't matter,
Hakim. He's picked his own
path—they all have. I'm not
here to save souls. I'm here to
get some PAYBACK...

PAGE 9

PANEL ONE: *An old man (his GRAMPA) opens the door to ANTHONY, in STREET CLOTHES. GRAMPA looks shocked, nervous.*

CAPTION:
EIGHTEEN MONTHS AGO.

GRAMPA:
Hakim? Jesus, what happened
to you? Those army fellows
keep coming to the door, asking
about whether we heard from
you yet!

BAD GUY FACTORY

PANEL TWO: GRAMPA *hurries* ANTHONY INSIDE—*a modest living room.* ANTHONY *is wearing his* SUNGLASSES *even in the* HOUSE.

GRAMPA:
We hear you in trouble, boy. Dorothy said they're gonna arrest you. I don't think she wants you around, see, and I'm sorry, but you know it IS her house...

ANTHONY:
Tell Dorothy not to worry— I'm not going to be around long enough to get anyone in trouble. It's not like there's anything to MY side of the story...

PANEL THREE: ANTHONY *looking toward a* PHOTO *on top of the TV.*

ANTHONY (Cont.):
No, forget it. I don't have time for this. Where's Jameel?

PANEL FOUR: *We see the* PHOTO—ANTHONY, *about 12 years old, and* JAMEEL, *a skinny 8 year old with a* LEG BRACE, *both trying to look* TOUGH *in their Sunday school clothes.*

— 133

GRAMPA (Off Panel):
That little brother of yours is
no good. Always in trouble.
He left my house and my rules
months ago.

PANEL FIVE: ANTHONY has let the picture FALL OVER
on the television and he's WALKING OUT.

ANTHONY:
It's not your house, Grampa,
remember? It's Dorothy's.

GRAMPA:
Now boy, come back. Don't be
that way! We're kin!

PANEL SIX: BANG—ANTHONY hits the front door and
he's down the steps to the STREET, a seedy but not dreadful
neighborhood. He looks MAD.

ANTHONY
THOUGHT-CAPTION:
When I heard he wasn't there,
I went cold. I knew then that
everything I'd heard on the
street was true. After I enlisted,
Janeel had started running with
gangbangers. He was small,
but he had powers, just like I
did. He could kind of SMELL
thoughts—get a feeling for what
someone was thinking, what they
were going to do. And sometimes

he could even make people do
what he wanted. Everybody
called him Headcase, and a lot of
folks in the neighborhood were
afraid of him, but he was still my
baby brother.

PANEL SEVEN: ANTHONY *with his* CAP PULLED
DOWN, *walking out of the* NEIGHBORHOOD.

CAPTION:
When we were little, he used
to crawl into my bed at night
when Mama was fighting
with one of her boyfriends.
Sometimes, if the screaming got
too bad, he'd be so scared he'd
pee in my bed. I beat him about
that a couple of times, but I
never hated him for it—after
all, I was all he had.

CAPTION:
I guess he was all I had, too.

PAGE 10

PANEL ONE: *In the* GENERAL DORM AREA, *between
the* MEN'S *and* WOMEN'S RESIDENCE. THROWBACK
is still trying to get some ATTENTION *from* DOLLY *and*
MINK—*right now, he's trying* MINK.

ANTHONY
THOUGHT-CAPTION 1:
The last anyone in the
neighborhood heard about
Jameel, he got accepted to
come here—the FACTORY.
Then nothing. Nobody's seen
him, nobody's heard from him.
I turned all of South Quartz
searching for him. I busted into
the City Pathology Department
files and looked at so many
autopsy photos of unnamed
DOAs that I see 'em every night
when I close my eyes—but
no Jameel. He went into the
Factory, but he never came out.

ANTHONY
THOUGHT-CAPTION 2:
I'm going to find him. And if
he's dead, I don't care if it was
Silas Winter himself who did it,
someone's got some shit to pay.
WHO'S SILAS WINTER?

THROWBACK:
So how come a girl as fine as
you is in here? Gonna join the
Fatal Femmes?

MINK:
Look, scrub, if you HAD any I'd
just cut 'em off, so move along.

PANEL TWO: THROWBACK—BLINK TAKE.

PANEL THREE: THROWBACK points PAST MINK at DOLLY.

> THROWBACK:
> Yo, actually, I was talking
> to HER.

> THROWBACK
> (Cont. Now to DOLLY):
> So how come a girl as fine as
> you is in here? I couldn't help
> noticing you got all that sexy
> Barbie thing goin' on.

> DOLLY:
> It's kinda more like Raggedy
> Anne, really—that's cause my
> tag is "Dolly".

> THROWBACK:
> Well, you're fine. I like the way
> you move. You ever model?

> DOLLY:
> Sort of. I used to be a dancer.
> Then I found out I could make
> more money in breaking and
> entering...

PANEL FOUR: MINK and DOLLY SQUARE OFF.

TAD WILLIAMS

> MINK:
> A DANCER? Bitch, please. You
> didn't make your money just
> SHOWING it to people.

> DOLLY:
> Are you calling me a whore? At
> least men like me. I heard about
> you—I heard how you had to
> kill your boyfriend...

PANEL FIVE: SPLAT! MINK KICKS—her BOOT lashes around and hits DOLLY so hard DOLLY's head BLOWS UP! (Except it DOESN'T—SEE DESCRIPTION OF DOLLY'S POWERS, REFERENCE #.) THROWBACK is ALARMED and IMPRESSED.

> SFX: SKELCH!

> THROWBACK:
> Holy SHIT!

PAGE 11

PANEL ONE: A river of DOLLY flies out of the COLLAR of her COSTUME from the force of MINK'S kick, leaving the costume on the floor.

PANEL TWO: The river of DOLLY-FLESH hits the ground and then two ARMS form and flip it over, back toward MINK.

PANEL THREE: The BATTERING-RAM-like FEET hit MINK in the head, knocking her backward.

DOLLY:
You're dead, bitch!

PANEL FOUR: *MINK's wrist blades come out as DOLLY reforms.*

SFX: CHING-CHING! CHING-CHING!

MINK:
Fine. Let's see who stops
breathing first.

PANEL FIVE: *PRETTY BOY is SUDDENLY standing between them—POP! He has CAUGHT MINK'S WRIST IN HIS HAND. We can see that DOLLY has just started to SAG away from the strike. (SEE REFERENCE #)*

PRETTY BOY:
Ah-ah-ah. You *chicas* going
to have to find a better way to
work this out.

PAGE 12

PANEL ONE: *PRETTY BOY in the midst of the ROOKIES, willing to be ADMIRED.*

THROWBACK:
Who are YOU?

PRETTY BOY:
They call me Pretty Boy—yes,
yes, I know you can see why.

> Now move along. You all
> supposed to be in your rooms.

PANEL TWO: PRETTY BOY is irritated with COLD-BLOODED, who's giving him the EYE.

> PRETTY BOY
> (Cont.—to COLDBLOODED):
> You, too. Go on. I know you
> worried, first night away from
> your mamas...

> COLDBLOODED:
> Shut up, bitch! Don't talk to me
> like you know me!

PANEL THREE: COLDBLOODED is now LEANING INTO PRETTY BOY's grill while the others watch with various degrees of interest/nervousness.

> PRETTY BOY:
> Oh, you going to throw some
> *catos* with me? You want to
> mix it?

> SNAIL (quietly):
> Fix it.

> COLDBLOODED:
> You disrespect me, you're
> disrespecting all the Los Reyes
> Screwtops.

PRETTY BOY:
Oh, man, you sniffin' the big
time and you're STILL reppin'
that gang shit? Are you gonna
take a shot or just stand there
like a pussy?

PANEL FOUR: COLDBLOODED *takes a swing. PRETTY BOY is gone.*

PANEL FIVE: PRETTY BOY *taps him on the shoulder from behind.*

PANEL SIX: COLDBLOODED *swings on him again. PRETTY BOY is gone.*

PAGE 13

PANEL ONE: PRETTY BOY *has reappeared, GRINNING. COLDBLOODED POINTS at him with his RIGHT HAND.*

COLDBLOODED:
Motherfucker...! I don't have to
hit you to mess you up!

PANEL TWO: COLDBLOODED's *HAND turns GLOWING ORANGE HOT, so fast there are little SPARKS of BURNING DUST.*

PANEL THREE: PRETTY BOY *hits him HARD, and so fast it seems simultaneous—we see him STRIKE THREE TIMES.*

TAD WILLIAMS

SFX: CHUD! CHUD! CHUD!

PANEL FOUR: COLDBLOODED is down on the ground with PRETTY BOY's foot on his throat and the other on the wrist of his HOT HAND.

PRETTY BOY:
Check it—there are only
thirteen people faster than me
in the WHOLE WORLD. You
ain't one of 'em. Now get the
hell back to your block before I
pull your eyeballs out and play
hacky-sack with 'em, *chavalo.*

PANEL FIVE: THROWBACK puppydogs PRETTY BOY.

THROWBACK:
Thirteen? Wow! You must be a
Level 8. Even Overdrive's only
a Level 9.

PRETTY BOY (to THROWBACK):
You into that stuff, huh?
Actually, I was only number
fifteen in the world until last
week, then this East Coast guy
named Courier got a rip in
his friction suit when he was
doing, like, Mach Mucho—
vato blew up like a Tijuana
bottle rocket...

PAGE 14

PANEL ONE: DOLLY and MINK are leaning in the MEN'S DORM doorway—well, DOLLY does, MINK hangs back, looking CONTEMPTUOUS. SNAIL and THROWBACK are looking at something on SNAIL'S FOLD-DOWN computer screen (SEE REFERENCE#)

> DOLLY:
> We're going upstairs to get new costumes.

> THROWBACK:
> Yo, Doll. Make sure they don't cover up TOO much.

> DOLLY:
> Ooh. Aren't YOU a bad boy...

> MINK:
> Shit. You think you're Big Mack, but you're only Vanilla Shake, white boy. And speakin' of dumb as shit, what is that you're looking at? Oh, jeesus, is that Plusdotcom? That shit is so OLD.

> ANTHONY:
> The superhero website? Explains a lot.

TAD WILLIAMS

THROWBACK:
I hope you ain't putting down
Plusdotcom, because they got
it ALL. Where else a beginner
gonna get some face? Look,
they got an article on one of
the guys who's in here with us!
Toxin, his name is. They made
him one a' their YVORs.

MINK:
Why vee oh WHAT?

THROWBACK:
Young Villains on the Rise.

ANTHONY
THOUGHT-CAPTION:
I swear to god, has this whole
country gone crazy while I was
overseas?

DOLLY:
Little boys and their toys.

THROWBACK:
Hey, I ain't playin'—I take this
stuff seriously. This is research.

ANTHONY:
That ain't research. That's
self-abuse.

PAGE 15

PANEL ONE (SMALL): *The MEN are getting out of an INDUSTRIAL ELEVATOR. THROWBACK (wearing a NEW SHIRT—See REFERENCE #) is looking REPROACH-FULLY at ANTHONY.*

> THROWBACK:
> ...But you didn't have to do me
> like that in front of the ladies.
> That was cold.

PANEL TWO (BIG): *They are in the midst of a HUGE INDUSTRIAL AREA with LOTS OF BRANCHES, CORRIDORS, WEIRD EQUIPMENT, ETC. This could be our chance to see a lot of OTHER "STUDENTS" like TOXIN, some TEACHERS, ETC. (SEE REFERENCE #)*

> THROWBACK (Cont.):
> Man, how are you supposed to
> find ANYTHING around here?

> ANTHONY:
> They said the weapon shop was
> on level 5. We're on level 5.
> Follow the blue line. I'm relying
> on you—I can't even SEE color
> with these things on.

PAGE 16

PANEL ONE: *THROWBACK is INTERESTED, in a fan-boy way.*

THROWBACK:
So, what's your trip? I mean,
like, your powers?

ANTHONY:
I see into the infra-red and
ultra-violet. And I can do some
other stuff.

THROWBACK:
Oh, kind of like Pipistrel, huh?
That bat-chick? You a mutant,
too?

PANEL TWO: THROWBACK sees TIME MASTER/
MASTER TIME (He's both, actually: See REFERENCE #),
who is pushing past COLDBLOODED—THROWBACK'S
EYES WIDEN. He's STOPPED LISTENING.

ANTHONY:
No. I got my powers the old-
fashioned way.

ANTHONY (Cont., quietly):
Shot in the back by my best
friend, then shoved into a vat of
active nanobuilders...

TIME MASTER:
No! Don't go! They're waiting
for you—they know!

COLDBLOODED:
Look out, you crazy mother...!

PANEL THREE: TIME MASTER STOPS right in front of ANTHONY, GRABS his LAPELS (or the equivalent.) ANTHONY is TAKEN ABACK.

TIME MASTER:
Don't you understand? They're way ahead of you—HE'S way ahead of you.

ANTHONY:
What the hell are you saying?

PANEL FOUR: TIME MASTER STUMBLES AWAY, leaving ANTHONY shaken.

TIME MASTER:
Well...then you better take sun block. And plenty of it.

ANTHONY:
What was THAT about?

THROWBACK:
I don't know, but, dude, that was Time Master! He fought everyone! He's the guy that dropped that dinosaur into the Tonight Show! Ate like a hundred people before Regent showed up and knocked it out! A T-Rex!

SNAIL:
S-s-special effects.

PANEL FIVE: THROWBACK pissed—SNAIL looking ASHAMED.

THROWBACK:
No way! It was real! From, like, TIME.

SNAIL:
Sorry. I can't help it. I just...say things. They rhyme, sometimes.

COLDBLOODED:
What, you trying to be a rapper?

PANEL SIX: ANTHONY has found a DOOR, MARKED "ARMORY"

SNAIL:
No, it's a s-syndrome. I've got a...a syndrome.

COLDBLOODED:
So do I. It's called "I'm sick of hearin' your retarded ass."

ANTHONY:
I think I found the place.

PAGE 17

PANEL ONE: IN THE WEAPONS SHOP with FLAK, a middle-aged black man in a functional BATTLE-SUIT. He looks like he might have been a top-sergeant in the military—very short gray-flecked military cut, no facial hair. He has an unlit cigar in his mouth at almost all times. He's addressing COLDBLOODED and THROWBACK.

FLAK:
You two I got no use for.

THROWBACK:
Why? What do you mean?

PANEL TWO: FLAK frowns at THROWBACK.

FLAK:
'Cause you ain't got no
weapons, stupid.

THROWBACK:
You could give us some.

PANEL THREE: FLAK STARES at THROWBACK.

PANEL FOUR: FLAK to THROWBACK.

FLAK:
Boy, you have no idea of the
countless ways in which I could
permanently fuck you up. It's
only because you haven't yet

earned back a single penny
for this facility that I'm gonna
refrain from ripping off your
nutsack right this moment. Go
on. You boys get the hell out
of here.

PANEL FIVE: FLAK TURNS to ANTHONY and SNAIL. Behind him, THROWBACK and COLDBLOODED are heading briskly for the exit.

FLAK:
As for you two, I'm not sure
what I'm supposed to do for
you...

FLAK (Cont.):
Special Forces Paladin-class
defensive suit. Doesn't need
much but routine maintenance.
Stolen?

ANTHONY:
Not exactly. Put it this way—I
was wearing it when I left.
You've seen one of these before?

PANEL SIX: FLAK turns to SNAIL.

FLAK:
Seen it? Pretty much designed
it. And how about YOU, son?
That's an interesting suit you

got there. Looks like it's made
of old car parts. Where'd you
steal it?

SNAIL:
I didn't. I...I made it.

FLAK:
Oh, really? All by your little old
self? Where?

SNAIL (Cont.):
In shop class.

PANEL SEVEN: FLAK raises an eyebrow.

FLAK:
Well, boy, if that's true, you
and I may have a few things to
talk about after all...

PAGE 18

PANEL ONE: IN THE COSTUME SHOP, with SAILOR
AND OCHO. (See REFERENCE # for description of
SHOP and SAILOR AND OCHO.) MINK and DOLLY
are just leaving as HEATSEEKER and SNAIL come in.
THROWBACK is having a fitting while COLDBLOODED
struggles with HOMOPHOBIC PANIC.

SAILOR:
Now, when you meet him,
ladies, you remember what

I told you! I know he's
DELICIOUS—but stay away.
He's got that name for a reason!

SAILOR (Cont.):
Oh, look, more BOYS! What
was it the Coast Goddess used
to say? "Ten men waiting for
me? Send one home—I'm
tired tonight."

PANEL TWO: TALKING and WORKING around the
COSTUMING TABLE while THROWBACK stands on a
LOW STOOL.

SAILOR:
Come on in. I'm Sailor. I used
to work her, you know—you've
heard of her, right, Coast
Goddess, she had the floating
palace, always threatening
to shoot Polaris missiles at
public buildings? Was SHE
Miss Stampy-Crampy most of
the time—oh my GOD. That
woman just had her bitch on
TWENTY-FOUR SEVEN. But
the food was pretty good.

SAILOR (Cont.):
My handsome Ocho was
muscle for Eightball 'til he got
taken down by Twilight Man
and all the Eights got laid off.

We met at one of the Sultan's
cattle calls. It was the Sultan,
wasn't it? Or was it one of the
Crimson Conjuror's?

OCHO:
Yeah, Sultan. What's this
coat thing?

SAILOR:
It's coming off, don't worry. I'll
say one thing for the Sultan, he
was one of the good old TVs.

THROWBACK:
A television?

PANEL THREE: SAILOR rolls his eyes.

SAILOR:
No, silly boy, Traditional
Villains. You might get hit
in the jaw a lot, and do some
jail time, but when you were
working for him you got your
check every Friday and you got
bailed out in 24 hours or less.
Not like Silas Winter. I don't
know why ANYONE works for
that mess.

OCHO:
Pays good. But he crazy.

SAILOR:
Tell me about it. He
electrocuted someone I knew
to death for bringing him the
wrong kind of breakfast! TO
DEATH!

PANEL FOUR: THROWBACK has his ARMS PULLED
BACK UNCOMFORTABLY because OCHO'S grabbed the
back of his HOODIE between SHOULDERS.

THROWBACK:
Hey!

OCHO:
Look what happen when I grab
you coat. Can't move you arms.

SAILOR:
He's right, we need something
less restrictive. And does it all
REALLY have to be black?

PANEL FIVE: THROWBACK protesting—he LOVES his
COSTUME.

THROWBACK:
I wear all these different shirts.
It's my gimmick. And black
goes with everything.

SAILOR:
Oh my GOD. Yes, it goes with
everything, but so do Levi's.

You don't see Black Dog
wearing 501s, do you? Colonel
Breakskull in relaxed-fit
Dockers? No, no—there's such
a thing as TOO casual.

*PANEL SIX: SAILOR is looking CRITICALLY at
THROWBACK. OCHO has THROWBACK's arms pulled
back even TIGHTER—THROWBACK looks like he's
STRANGLING.*

> SAILOR (Cont.):
> How about slate gray instead—
> that's nice, but not quite so
> Weekend Goth? Or, well, you'd
> be surprised at how many
> things go with teal…

PAGE 19

*PANEL ONE: THE DORM—LIGHTS OUT. ANTHONY
is strapping on his GEAR by the dim NIGHTLIGHT, getting
everything ready. His SUNGLASSES are STILL ON.*

> ANTHONY
> THOUGHT CAPTION #1:
> Locked and loaded. Going into
> some shit you don't know—
> the only certain thing is, you
> get unlucky, you're dead, like
> that poor cop. Like me in the
> Forces…at Benne Yhaar. Why
> am I DOING this again?

TAD WILLIAMS

PANEL TWO: *The NIGHTLIGHT, seen from BELOW.*

> ANTHONY
> THOUGHT-CAPTION 2:
> Benne Yhaar—even the name's
> still like poison. The place
> where everything changed.

PANEL THREE: *FLASHBACK—the NIGHTLIGHT is now
a MOON ABOVE HELICOPTER BLADES.*

> ANTHONY
> THOUGHT-CAPTION 3:
> We had just helped the
> Northern Alliance take Mazar-
> al-Sharif. About the time
> everybody else in Afghanistan
> was going south after Bin
> Laden, chasing him into Tora
> Bora, my squad was sent
> on a mission north, into the
> mountains where the borders
> get crazy—me and Jojo and
> the rest, accompanying three
> strangers with the hardest eyes
> I'd ever seen.

PANEL FOUR: *FLASHBACK—THREE WHITE GUYS
TALKING, being watched by ANTHONY and his friend
JOJO (See REFERENCE #)*

ANTHONY
THOUGHT-CAPTION 3:
I thought they were CIA, but
I still don't know for sure.
Could have been Red River or
one of the other private firms.
They didn't bother to tell us
anything, so I don't even know
the lie.

PANEL FIVE: FLASHBACK—*About a DOZEN MEN walking down a MOUNTAIN TRAIL at NIGHT, IN FULL GEAR.*

ANTHONY
THOUGHT-CAPTION 4:
All we knew was that we were
going in to secure some kind
of site named Benne Yhaar.
I dimly grasped that it had
something to do with weapons,
but like I said, those dudes were
close-mouthed. At the time I
didn't even know why us Forces
guys were going along, but I
found out.

ANTHONY
THOUGHT-CAPTION 5:
Because they needed RAW
MEAT...

PANEL SIX: *The SILHOUETTED MEN become the SILHOUETTE of THROWBACK tossing in his BUNK.*

THROWBACK:
Mmrrnh.

ANTHONY
THOUGHT-CAPTION 6:
Shit. Focus, Hakim—FOCUS.
You got a job here.

PAGE 20

PANEL ONE: *ANTHONY is out the OPEN DOOR of their cell/dorm room. He's still wearing his SUNGLASSES and he's holding up a little OBJECT like a LIMPET MINE.*

ANTHONY
THOUGHT-CAPTION 1:
Man, I bumped tougher
locks than that when I was a
freelance removal expert.

PANEL TWO: *He sticks the OBJECT on the wall by the CELL.*

ANTHONY
THOUGHT-CAPTION 2:
This is the dangerous part.
Either this transponder
preempts the digital security
cameras and feeds them a loop
of the last ninety seconds for
as long as I'm out of my dorm
room, or cell, or whatever you
call it...

ANTHONY
THOUGHT-CAPTION 3:
...Or I'm going to get cooked
like that poor cop this morning.

PANEL THREE: *He takes his SUNGLASSES OFF, LOOKS AROUND. For the first time, we see his WEIRD EYES. (See REFERENCE #)*

ANTHONY
THOUGHT-CAPTION 4:
I can't afford more than a quick
recon—too many ways to get
into trouble...

PANEL FOUR: *ANTHONY'S POV (See REFERENCE #) ??— sees HEAT-PATTERNS OF GUARDS coming around corner*

PANEL FIVE: *GUARD who hit ANTHONY JAWING with the other GUARD (from pages 2-4.) We don't see ANTHONY.*

GUARD #1:
Oh, I'm gonna notch me some
of these new punks, you damn
bet...

PANEL SIX: *NOW we see ANTHONY—WEDGED IN A CORNER of the CEILING, right above where the GUARDS just walked.*

ANTHONY
THOUGHT-CAPTION 5:
Damn! I HATE that guy.
Memo to self: if there's ever

a chance to push his face in
without blowing my cover, I'm
gonna take it.

PAGE 21

PANEL ONE: Still ANTHONY'S POV—his SPECIAL VISION. HE has CHANGED LEVELS. We see HEAT-TRACES on the floor (footprints) and the air (where bodies have passed) and from machinery, etc.

>ANTHONY
>THOUGHT-CAPTION 1:
>This must be their main office.
>Even if they've wiped out all
>Jameel's records, I might be
>able to find some evidence
>of what happened. The only
>question is, is someone on duty
>here 24/7?

PANEL TWO: An OFFICE WINDOW, in HEATSEEKER-VISION—it's FARSIGHT.

>ANTHONY
>THOUGHT-CAPTION 2:
>That Farsight guy. Well, that
>makes sense, I guess—I didn't
>figure Byzantine for the kind
>of dude who sleeps in his store
>at night.

PANEL THREE: FARSIGHT turns toward him, as if he senses ANTHONY'S PRESENCE.

>ANTHONY
>THOUGHT-CAPTION 3:
>Shit! Does he know I'm here?
>But this place damps TP, and
>I've got my suit shields on, too!

PANEL FOUR: ANTHONY going hurriedly down STAIRS.

>ANTHONY
>THOUGHT-CAPTION 4:
>I got a bad feeling about that
>guy. I don't want anything to
>do with him yet...

PANEL FIVE: A DARK SHAPE SWOOPS THROUGH THE AIR. ANTHONY IS KNOCKED SIDEWAYS by a FOOT IN THE BACK.

PANEL SIX: FOOT ON ANTHONY'S THROAT—He is GENUINELY CHOKING. We can't see WHO'S DOING IT.

>THROWBACK (OP):
>Oh, man, you are SO DEAD.

NEXT ISSUE: THE PLACE OF FLIES ??

PAGE 22

(This is going to be a page representing the PLUSDOTCOM website: It should LOOK like an ENTERTAINMENT

TAD WILLIAMS

SITE—LOTS OF PICTURES, POINTLESS GRAPHICS, Etc. I'm rewriting it because the original was written with DC references, characters, etc. It will have a tie-in to the story, and we'll probably have one page each issue. Here's the first article, just as an example.)

SPECIAL ALL-VILLAINS ISSUE!

THE SHADOW CIRCUIT— A GRAY MARKET FOR EVIL?

People think of supervillains stealing bullion from Fort Wayne or holding the world to ransom with giant laser weapons, but in an exclusive for PlusDotCom, investigative reporter K. Allen Lilly says that many professional bad guys and gals reap a sizeable income from the Shadow Circuit, lecturing and consulting with other criminal organizations, foreign governments, and a few "straight" businesses that don't mind having a reputation as "sharks" in mainstream corporate waters. Disgraced former governor and international arms dealer Hart Huon is of course the biggest act in this shadowy world, but such criminal masterminds as General Disorder, Maxim Nachtigal, Professor Tyrus Trinch, and the frankly frightening Silas Winter also command big appearance fees and are reported to be booked months or even years in advance.

"It's a wonder some of them even bother with regular crime anymore," says reporter Lilly. "Trinch or Huon could live the rest of their lives on under-the-table appearance fees from straight corporations and legitimate governments. If they're committing crimes or fighting superheroes, it's 'cause they WANT to."

(READ ARTICLE)

162 —

BAD GUY FACTORY

HEROES BELIEVE A HIGHER POWER HELPING THE HORROR

The powerful lawbreaker known as the Horror is responding well to a dose of religious education, according to a spokesman for Regent and his fellow born-again Christian hero, the Flag.

"He's not mindless," the source told PlusDotCom, "and he didn't want to be a villain. Ever since the original accident that made him what he is, he's had moments of sanity and remorse. Regent believes he has a responsibility to use his unique position to minister to lost souls, not just imprison them, and Flag has agreed to throw his own popular name behind a campaign to rehabilitate human-plus prisoners through faith."

Not all the members of United Powers agree with Regent and the Flag, however: other sources suggest that Twilight Man, who captured the Horror in a televised battle on top of the San Amaro Bay Bridge, has announced his disenchantment with the project, suggesting the superstrong criminal is only pretending to feel sorry about his numerous crimes to get more lenient treatment.

(READ ARTICLE)

BAD BOYS AND BAD GIRLS

Highlights of the Year in Villainy, including Butcher Baker's spectacular airport robbery, Knave of Hearts pre-empting the Super Bowl, and unforgettable video of the pitched battle between the Chain Gang and Force Five that leveled Jefferson City Hall—as well as a look at our Young Villains on the Rise at work and play, and new and fascinating killer faces like Hooligan, Fog, Toxin, and Murder One.

TAD WILLIAMS

(READ ARTICLE)

If they're mad, bad, and dangerous to know, PlusDotCom's got 'em—in the SPECIAL ALL-VILLAINS ISSUE!

THE THURSDAY MEN

YOU KNOW ANYONE FAMOUS NAMED 'Monday'?" Liz asked.

"You mean like Rick Monday? Used to play for the Dodgers back in the '70s?" That was from Ted the technician. I never cared much about baseball myself.

"Okay," said Liz. "So that's one for Monday. And there's Tuesday Weld, the actress."

"I thought of another one—Ruby Tuesday, that Rolling Stones song," said Ted, and began to hum it—or at least he hummed what he thought, in his tuneless way, it sounded like. He's a decent enough kid and a pretty good technician, but if the BPRD ever fires him he's not going to be making a living on the pro Karaoke circuit.

"I thought we were going to play cards," I said. My cigar had gone out and I couldn't find my lighter. "What is all this crap?"

Liz kindled her fingertip and re-lit my stogie. "I've just been thinking about the days of the week and people who have them as names," she said. "Wednesday from the Addams Family. Robinson Crusoe's Man Friday."

"No!" shouted Ted. "Has to be Joe Friday! From *Dragnet*."

"You weren't even alive when that was on," I growled.

Liz went on as if we weren't talking. "And there's Baron Saturday—he's one of the voodoo gods, I guess you'd call them. You know about them, right, HB?"

I have had more than a few strange adventures in the New Orleans area over the years. "Yeah. But that doesn't mean I want to talk about it. What's your point?"

"And Billy Sunday was a famous evangelist or something— my grandmother used to talk about him." She frowned. "But I still can't come up with a Thursday. I don't think there are any."

"Ooh, I thought of one," said Ted. "There's a pretty famous spy book called 'The Man Who Was Thursday'."

"Yeah, but it was just his code name," I pointed out.

Ted looked at me in surprise. "You read G. K. Chesterton?"

"Does that seem so unlikely?" I put my cigar in the corner of my mouth and did my best to look intellectual—not that easy to do when you're seven feet tall, literally ugly as sin, and red as a fire truck from head to foot. "But I'll give you a real one, if you promise to shut up and play some damn cards. Grayson Thursday. In fact, there were a whole bunch of Thursdays, when you get down to it."

"It doesn't count if nobody's ever heard of them," Liz said, pouting. She makes those grumpy-kid faces, you almost forget she could napalm a city block if the urge took her.

"But it does sound familiar," said Ted. "Why is that?"

"Maybe you read the file," I said, knowing he probably had. The kid studied up on me when he came here like a Yankees fan memorizing all the stats of his favorite player. When it came to me, he could tell you the BPRD equivalent of my on-base percentage or average with runners in scoring position for every year of my career.

Hey, I said I didn't care much about baseball, I didn't say I didn't know anything about it.

I looked at the two of them. They were waiting expectantly. "Crap," I said. "We're not going to play cards, are we?"

"Come on, tell about this Thursday guy," Liz said. "If I know who he is, then maybe it'll count for my list."

"Wait, was that back in the '80s? The guy with the magical grandfather clock?" Ted said. "I think I remember..."

"Just shut up," I suggested. "And keep it shut. I'm the one telling the story."

It was the first time I'd been on the California coast above San Francisco. It's interesting how quick you can go from a place packed with people and lights and car horns and things like that to the middle of nowhere. Once you get about an hour or so north of the Golden Gate Bridge, most of it's like that—the kind of place where you realize you've been listening to the seagulls and the ocean all day and not much else. Or at least that's how it was when I went to Monk's Point back in early March of 1984. Maybe it's different now.

Albie Bayless met me off the BPRD plane at Sonoma County Aiport. Bayless was a former reporter with the *San Francisco Examiner* who'd retired to his hometown a few years back and taken over the local shopper, the *Monk's Point Beacon*. He'd had some past contact with the BPRD and me— you remember that Zodiac guy, the murderer everyone says he was never caught? No, nobody knows the BPRD had anything to do with that—I didn't file an official report on that one. Probably never will. Anyway, when Bayless stumbled onto the weird death of Rufino Gentle and what happened after, he called my bosses at the bureau and suggested they send me out to have a look-see.

Bayless was wearing shorts and had grown a beard. He looked a good bit older and saggier than the last time

I'd seen him, but I was there to work with him, not marry him. "Still got that bad sunburn, I see," he said as I came down the ladder. Funny guy. I squeezed into the passenger seat of his car and he filled me in on details along the way. The town was called Monk's Point because there used to be a Russian monastery out on the rocky headland overlooking a dent in the coastline called Caldo Bay. The population of monks had dwindled until the last of them went back to Russia at the end of the 19th century. Later the monastery was turned into a lighthouse when the Caldo Bay fishing industry hit its stride. Those glory days passed too, and the lighthouse was decommissioned in the 1960s. The property on the point now belonged to some out-of-town rich guy who hardly anybody ever saw. But the place itself had a bad reputation going back even before the Russians arrived. The local Indians had been a tribe called "Zegrado", which, Bayless informed me cheerfully, was a corruption of the Spanish word for "cursed."

As I discovered, "cursed" and "dying" were the two words that seemed to come up often in almost any conversation about Monk's Point. The reasons became clear when we drove through the center of town, a handful of weathered plank buildings beside a tiny harbor at the mouth of a little dent in the coastline called Caldo Bay. There were half a dozen stores and a coffee shop and a bar, plus a few more places that looked like they'd been boarded up for a while. I doubt there were a thousand people in total living there. Things had gone downhill since the cannery closed. The town's young people were leaving as soon as they were old enough, and except for Albie Bayless, no one was moving back in.

"Everybody always says the place is dying," Bayless told me. "But they still get upset when someone actually dies—at least when there's no good explanation for it. That's what happened here last week. A kid named Gentle—Rufino Tamayo Gentle, how's *that* for a name?—was out here with some friends. I guess Gentle and his buddies were troublemakers by small town standards, but nothing too bad, a couple of busts for pot and loitering, some suspicion of breaking into tourists' cars. Anyway, on a bet, young Gentle climbed over the fence and went up to the famous haunted house. His friends waited for him. He never came back, never showed up for school. One of the kids mentioned it to a teacher. Result was, a local cop came by, cut off the bolt and walked up to the house. He found young Gentle standing on the front path, head slumped like he'd fallen asleep standing up. Body was stone cold—he'd been dead for hours."

"Standing up?"

"That's what the cop swears. He's not the type to make things up, either."

"You said one of the kid's friends told a teacher. What about the Gentle boy's parents? Didn't they notice he didn't come back?"

Bayless smirked. "You'll have to meet the kid's dad. *There's* a piece of work."

"Okay," I said, "'dead standing up' is definitely an interesting trick, but it isn't why you called us, is it?"

"Nope. That would be 'Rufino's Escape.' But first I'm gonna take you to my place, get you some dinner."

Just a half mile or so past the not-so-bustling downtown, Bayless pulled up to a gate across a private road. It was surrounded by weeds and sawgrass and looked like it didn't get opened much. Beyond it a long, curving driveway led away toward the top of the hill. The house itself, the ex-monastery, was mostly hidden from view behind the headland, but the lighthouse loomed in clear view, pale as a mushroom. The windows at the top went all the way around, but the impression was nevertheless of someone looking away from you, staring out over the sea—someone you didn't want to disturb, and not just out of courtesy.

"I don't like it," I said.

"You're not alone," said Bayless. "Nobody likes it. Nobody ever has. The local Indians hated the place. The monks only stayed about thirty years, then they all went back to Russia, saying the place was unholy. Even the guy who owns it now hardly ever shows up."

Albie Bayless lived in a mobile home on the outskirts of town—not a trailer, but one of those things that look pretty much like a house with tin sides. He kept it up nice, and he wasn't too bad a cook, either. As I listened to him I spooned up my bowl of chili. He made his with raisins and wild mushrooms, which actually worked out pretty good.

"The reason the dad didn't report his son missing is that he's a drunk," Albie said. "Bobby Gentle. Supposedly an artist, but hasn't sold anything that I know of. One of those ex-hippie types who moved here in the late sixties. Kid's mother left about five or six years back. Sad."

"But that's not why you called us."

"I'm coming to it. So they found the kid dead, like I told you. No question about it. No pulse, body cold. Took him to the local medical examiner over in Craneville and here's the good part. The body got up off the examination table, sort of accidentally slugged the examiner—it was thrashing around a lot, I think—and escaped."

"So he wasn't actually dead."

Albie fixed me with a significant look. "Think again, *kimo sabe*. This was *after* the autopsy."

That didn't sound good at all. "After?"

"Yeah. Chest cracked and sewn up again. Skull sawed open. Veins full of embalming fluid."

"Jesus. That's nasty."

"Imagine how the guy felt who'd just done the sewing."

"And you're sure the coroner's not in on some body-selling scam?"

"Kind of a stupidly vivid story to tell if you don't want to attract attention, don't you think?"

I had to concede that one. "Okay, so the kid goes to Monk's Point lighthouse on a dare, dies standing up, then walks off the autopsy table and runs away. Weird. Anything else?"

"Oh, yeah. You see, I was already doing research as soon as I heard about the boy being found dead. I didn't know him, but I thought it might make an interesting wire service piece—you know, 'Old ghost story haunts modern murder'..."

"Old ghost story?"

"Like I said, everybody's scared of this place, and it turns out there's good reason. A lot of weird stuff's happened there and in the area just around it, going back as far as I can research, everything from noise complaints to murders, old ghost stories and local kid's rhymes and other odd stuff, even some UFO sightings. It kind of goes in cycles, some years almost nothing, other years things happening a few times a month. It began to remind me of some of the places you told me about back in San Francisco, when we were working on, y'know..."

"I know," I growled. "Don't remind me." I took out a cigar. "You mind?"

"Go ahead." Albie got up and opened the window.

I could hear the frogs outside kicking up their evening fuss, and, dimly, the sound of seabirds. "I think I want to have a look at the place close up."

I stood in front of the gate. The lighthouse was nothing much more than a big dark line blocking the stars like paint. "I think I'm going to have a look around. You were going to tell me something about the guy who owns the place."

Bayless pulled his jacket a bit tighter. It was cold for the time of year. "Grayson Thursday. It's been in his family for a long time. He's hard to get hold of, but he's supposed to see us the day after tomorrow."

"Good enough," I said. "See you in the morning."

"Are you sure you want to do that?" He looked upset, but I didn't know whether it was because he was scared for me or he'd been looking forward to the company. "What if you're not back in the morning?"

"Tell the children that Daddy died a hero." I ground out my cigar on the gravel driveway, then vaulted over the gate. "See ya, Albie."

The local real estate market wasn't losing anything by having the Monk's Point property in the hands of one family. It was kind of butt-ugly, to tell the truth. As I came around the headland so I could see the buildings properly, my first thought was, *So what?* There really wasn't much to it—the lighthouse, plain and white as vanilla, and a big, three-story barnlike structure with a few other outbuildings pushed up against it like they were all huddled together against the hilltop wind. Still, my feelings from earlier hadn't changed: something about the place, as subtle as a trick of light or angle of land, made it easy not to like. In the dark it had a thin, rotten sheen like fungus.

I stopped on the pathway in front of the barnlike building's front door, figuring this must be where the kid had ended up. I looked around carefully, but couldn't see anything that was going to stop someone's heart. The front door was locked, but the pockets of my coat were full of remedies for a problem like that, and a few moments later I was inside, swinging a flashlight around.

If this Thursday guy and his family had hung on to the house for a while, it looked like it was mainly to keep their old junk. It was like some weird flea market, with the stuffed heads of deer and other wild animals on the wall, with dozens of other examples of the taxidermist's art in glass cases or stands all over the huge front room, even a stuffed Kodiak bear looming almost ten feet high on its hind legs. The shelves were piled with books and curios, an old pipe organ stood against one wall, and a grandfather clock the size of a phone booth stood against another. Some of the junk actually looked kind of interesting and I strolled around picking things up at random—a model sailing ship, a conch shell the size of a tuba, some giant South American beetles that had been preserved and posed and dressed like a mariachi band. Three quarters of an hour or so passed as I wandered in and out of the various rooms, some of which seemed to have been dormitory rooms for the monastery, all of which seemed to have the same kitschy decorator as downstairs, as though the place had been planned as a museum but never opened. I even walked up the winding stairs of the lighthouse itself, which was as bare as the rest of the place was cluttered. It didn't look like the beacon had been lit in recorded memory—the wires had been torn out, the big lamp removed. I took the long walk back down.

I looked at my watch. A little after eleven. I sat on an overstuffed chair that didn't cramp my tail too badly, switched off my flashlight, and settled in to wait.

I may have dozed off. The first thing I noticed was a glow in the high windows, a sickly, pale gleam, pulsing slowly. It took me a moment to realize what it was—above my head the lighthouse had smoldered into a sort of weird half-life. I started across the room, but before I got to the foot of the stairs I heard a strange, rustling sound, as though a flock of birds was nesting in the high rafters. I stopped. The noises were getting louder, not just rustles but creaks, crackles, pops and snaps, as if the room was a bowl full of cereal and someone had just poured the milk.

I swung my flashlight around. A stuffed seagull on a stand meant to look like a dock piling was stretching its wings, glaring at me. The deer-head on the wall behind it was straining to get loose, rattling and bumping its wooden plaque against the wall. Something moved beside me and I snatched my hand back. It was a replica of a Spanish galleon, its sails inflating and deflating like an agitated blowfish.

"Oh, this is just CRAP!" I said.

Outside the windows the green light was still dim but the pulses were becoming more rapid and the whole room was growing more *wrong* by the moment—the air had gone icy cold and smelled harsh and strange, scents I had no name for. I took a few steps back and something broke on the other side of the room with a splintering crash, then a huge shape came thumping and stumbling out of the shadows. It was the stuffed bear, walking like a stiff-legged drunk, swinging its clawed arms as it went.

"You must be kidding me," I said, but the thing wasn't answering. It wasn't even alive, just moving. One of its glass eyes had popped out, leaving behind a hole full of dangling straw. I stared at this for a half a second too long and the thing caught me on the side of the head with one of those swinging paws. It might have been stuffed, but it felt like it was poured full of wet cement. It knocked me halfway across the room and I'm no feather. Something other than the latest improvements in taxidermy were definitely going on, but I didn't really have time to think about it too much, since the giant bear was on top of me and trying to rip my head off my neck. It felt like it weighed about twice as much as a real bear, and trying to throw it off was already making me tired. I dragged out my pistol and shoved it up against the furry belly.

I emptied the gun into it. "No picnic basket for YOU, Yogi!" I shouted. BAM! BAM! BAM! BAM! No soap. The thing just kept bashing me. Trying to shoot a stuffed bear—stupid, stupid, stupid.

Eventually I rammed the thing through the wall and got its head stuck deep enough that I could finally pull myself loose.

No sooner had I got rid of the bear than a tiger rug wrapped itself around my ankles and started trying to gnaw off my feet. The whole place was nuts—the paintings on the wall with their eyeballs bulging, trying to talk, the stuffed animals jerking around like they'd been electrified. I'd had enough of this crap. I kicked the rug up into the rafters where it hung, gnashing its teeth and swiping at me with its claws, then I made a run for the front door. I couldn't help but notice as I ran past that the grandfather clock was lit up from within like a jukebox, glowing and, well, sort of *pulsing*. And the air around it was murky with strange, colored shadows which were streaming into the clock like salmon swimming upstream to spawn. Every one that went past me burned icy cold and made my skin tingle. It didn't take much to know that this was the center of the haunting or whatever it was. It was pulling on me, too, a strong, steady suction like a whirlpool in dark, cold water. I had to struggle against it to reach the door.

I was happy enough to get outside at first.

The sickly glow from the top of the lighthouse was barely strong enough to light the long grass waving on the hilltop, but it was enough to illuminate the thin shape standing at the bottom of the path, swaying a little, head hanging down as though in some kind of hypnotic trance. Whoever it was, they didn't have a prayer against that stuff behind me.

"Hey!" I shouted. "Get out of here!" I hurried down the path. If I had to, I'd just throw whoever it was over my shoulder and carry him...

The first thing weird I noticed was that the Y-shaped pattern on the guy's chest wasn't a design on a shirt. I realized that because of the second weird thing—he was naked. The third thing was that the shape on his chest was made of stitches. Big ones. In fact, it wasn't a guy in any normal sense at all—it was Rufino Gentle's body, fresh off the autopsy table, standing just about where it must have been found in the first place.

— 175

I've seen a lot of creepy stuff in my time, but that doesn't mean you get *used* to it, you know.

I grabbed at his hair as I got close and lifted his head so I could look into his eyes. No resistance at all. Nothing in his eyes, either. Dead—I'm telling you, dead. Not like you say it about someone who doesn't care any more, I mean dead as in "not alive." There was nothing like a soul or a sensibility in that corpse, but it was still standing there, swaying a little in the wind, long dark hair flipping around, a livid new autopsy scar stretching up past his navel and forking to both collarbones. When the wind caught his hair again I couldn't help noticing that the top of his skull was gone, too, his brain sitting right there like a soft-boiled egg in a cup. He was holding the rest of his skull in his dead hand, clutching it like it was an ashtray he'd made at summer camp.

I'd had a rough night. I don't think anyone will blame me for not bringing Rufino Gentle's body back with me. He looked pretty comfortable standing there, anyway, so I left him there and hurried down to the fence and Albie Bayless waiting in his car.

"Did you see the lights?" Albie asked me, wide-eyed.

"We'll talk about it," I told him. "But first I need to drink about nine beers. Do you have nine beers at your place? Because if not, I really, really hope there's somewhere open in this godforsaken little town where we can get some."

"The Gentle kid's body, just...standing there?" Albie asked again as we got into the car the next morning. This was about the twentieth time. "You really saw it?"

I don't think Albie had slept very well. I wondered if maybe I'd told him too much.

"Trust me—I've seen worse things in my day. I have to admit, though, you've developed a few new wrinkles here."

Grayson Thursday was waiting for us in his office, a little storefront place that looked like it might have been the site of one of those telemarketing boiler rooms. There was a computer—the 1980s kind, so it looked like the mating of a Hammond organ and a typewriter—a television, a telephone, and that was about it. He had a desk with a single notepad on it. Not a file cabinet in sight. Thursday himself was a kindly looking gentleman of about sixty, although his face was a little odd in a way I couldn't entirely put my finger on at first. Like he'd been in an accident and had gone through some cosmetic surgery afterward that didn't quite iron out all the bumps. His voice was a little odd, too, as though he'd been born deaf but had learned to talk anyway. But what really worried me was that he didn't seem to think there was anything unusual about me at all—didn't even look twice when we were introduced. *That* I'm not used to, and it gave me a bad feeling.

"I'm sorry to have kept you waiting for this meeting, Mr. Bayless, Mr. Boy," he said. "I don't get into town very often."

"Oh, yeah? Where do you live?" I asked him.

"Quite a long way away." He smiled as if he was thinking of something else entirely and adjusted the sleeves of his expensive sweater. "Now, what can I do for you gentlemen?"

"My associate and I want to ask you a few things about the Monk's Point property," Albie told him.

"Is this about the Gentle boy?" He shook his head. "Terrible thing—tragic."

Oddly enough, he really sounded like he felt bad about it. It didn't make me any more comfortable with him, though.

Thursday proceeded to answer a bunch of questions about the house—how long his family had owned it (seventy years or so), what they used it for (it had been a local museum, but never earned enough money, so for now it was just sitting there), and why they didn't sell it to a hotel company (family sentiment and the historical value of the property.) All very expected, but

I was watching Thursday more than listening to the answers. Something about him just didn't quite seem right. He seemed... distant. Not like he was on drugs, or senile, just weirdly slow and detached.

"I hope that's been some help to you," he said and stood up, indicating that our time was over. "What happened to the boy was very sad, but as I told the police already, it's nothing to do with me. Now I'm afraid I have some important errands to run. Please leave a message with my answering service if there's anything else I can do for you. I won't be back in town until next week."

As we went out into the parking lot, I asked Albie, "Did he say he wasn't going to be back until next week?"

"Yeah, why?"

"And didn't you tell me he made you wait a week for this meeting?"

"I guess."

"And it just happens today's Thursday. And his last name's Thursday."

"I'm not following you."

"Never mind. Can you look some stuff up for me this afternoon? I'll give you a list. And before you start, drop me off at Bobby Gentle's house."

"The dead kid's father? Why?"

"His name was on a notepad on Thursday's desk."

Albie shrugged. "You're the boss. Try not to scare anyone to death."

"There's been enough of that already," I said.

After the Baylessmobile rolled away, I walked up the long, overgrown driveway but stopped and stepped into the trees before I reached the house. I waited for no more than a quarter hour before Grayson Thursday rolled up the driveway past me in his spanking new Mercedes. I waited a couple of minutes then followed, but the yard around the ramshackle house was covered with dry grass that hadn't been mowed in months, not to mention all kinds of other trash, and it was hard to get close without making a noise. Thursday didn't stay very long, anyway. I had to duck back into the trees again as he came out, got into his beautiful car and bumped off down the driveway.

When he was gone, I knocked on the peeling paint of the front door.

"Jesus Christ!" said Bobby Gentle when he saw me, and jumped back into his shabby living room, then darted out of sight. That was the kind of reaction I was used to. I felt better already.

"Don't bother getting out a gun," I called after him. "I don't mean you any harm, but I am armed and I'm probably a better shot than you are. I just want to talk." I looked around the living room. The place was a mess, cigarette butts and beer bottles everywhere, along with greasy fast-food wrappers, a month's worth. A couple of not-very-good seascapes hung on the nicotine-stained walls. If they were Gentle's, I knew why he wasn't selling much.

He came out of the back room slowly, his hands open wide. He hadn't been able to find the gun, anyway.

"Swear you ain't gonna hurt me?"

"I promise. Sit down."

He squinted. "What the hell are you? Some kinda lobsterman? You ain't gonna pinch me with that claw, are you?"

Gentle Senior was a piece of work, no doubt about it. He stank of booze and it wasn't even noon yet, so I figured he must be sweating it out of every pore. He was as pale as his son, but without the excuse of having had all the blood pumped out of him. I kind of doubted he'd been outside more than a couple of times in the last six months. His hair was long in the back, thin on the top, and stringy and greasy all over and he hadn't killed himself keeping up with his shaving, either. Still, the last week couldn't have been easy on anyone. "Sorry about your son," I said. "Rufino, that was his name, right?"

"Yeah. His mama named him after some famous spick painter. Before she took off and left me. But I got the boy back off her. Went to court for it." For a moment his angry little red eyes lost what focus they'd had. "Bitch wasn't taking my boy to live in some commune full of tofu-eating losers."

Tempting as it was, I didn't really want to spend the whole day with this charmer. "I'll cut to the chase, Mr. Gentle. You've just had a visit from Grayson Thursday. I suspect it has something to do with your son's death. Would you mind telling me what he saw you about?"

He looked at me in surprise and confusion, then his pale skin turned almost as red as mine. Before I could react, he bolted out of the living room and down the hall. He pulled a door shut behind him and locked it. I was patting my pockets for a lockpick when I looked again at the state of the rest of the place, then I just broke off the knob.

The bathroom was empty except for a stack of Hustler magazines beside the toilet and an ancient no-pest strip dangling from the lightbulb. The window was open, the screen kicked out.

I caught him in the woods a hundred yards away. He was pretty fast for a rummy, but for some reason he was carrying a suitcase, and I can get this bulk of mine moving pretty quick when I want to.

"No!" he screamed when he saw me, and threw the suitcase end over end into the deep undergrowth. "You can't have it! I never got anything else for him! All that boy ever did was cost me! You can't take it away!"

I picked him up by one arm and let him sway in the wind a little bit until he stopped yelling and started whimpering.

"What are you talking about? Why did you run away? What did you throw?"

He stared at me, or did his best to focus in my direction, anyway. "You don't want to take it away from me? You're not going to steal it?" He grimaced. "Damn! I shoulda kept my big mouth shut!"

"I'm sure that's not the first time you've said those words—and I'll bet it won't be the last." I put my face really close to his, doing my best not to breathe in. "Now, if you don't want me to swing you around in a circle until this arm of yours comes off, you'd better tell me what you're babbling about."

"The money Mr. Thursday gave me. It was 'cause my boy died! He said so! There's no crime in me having it!"

I shook my head. "He gave you money? How much?"

Now his eyes got shifty. "I don't know. A couple of thousand…"

I lifted him higher. I heard something pop in his shoulder and he shrieked. "Don't lie to me, Gentle."

"A hundred thousand! He said it was a hundred thousand!"

I set him down. A hundred thousand? That was crazy. "Go get it."

He came back with the suitcase cradled in his arms. I swear he was tearing up at the thought I was going to take it off him. I couldn't help wondering if he'd ever expressed that much care and concern for his own son. "Open it," I told him. He did. If it wasn't a hundred thousand dollars, you could have fooled me. Stacks of new bills, side by side. I made a face and turned around, heading back toward the road. This whole thing was pissing me off.

"So…I can keep it?" he called.

"Far as I'm concerned. But you'd better keep your mouth shut about it or someone less genteel than me will come out here and take it away from you."

Last I saw of him he was scurrying back toward his falling-down house, suitcase once more gripped tight against his chest.

It was well into the afternoon by the time I had hiked back to Albie's mobile home. He met me at the front door.

"Guess what I found out," he said. "Oh, and do you want some chili? I was just going to heat some up."

"Later," I said. "And you can tell me what you found out while you're driving me back into town. We're going to talk with that lying son of a gun Thursday before he takes off again."

"Why's he a liar?" Albie asked as he maneuvered his car out onto the main road.

"You remember him saying the murder was nothing to do with him, right? Well, he was just over at Bobby Gentle's place and gave the guy a hundred thousand dollars. Does that sound like nothing-to-do-with-me money? Or like some kind of pay-off instead?"

Albie whistled. "I never knew my little town was so exciting."

I scowled. "In my business, there's a thin line between 'exciting' and 'multiple fatalities,' and I hope we stay on one side of it."

Nobody was in at the office, so I sent Albie into the coffee shop to buy me a couple of burgers and we sat in the car and ate while we kept a watch on the place. "So what did you find?" I asked him.

He handed me a stack of green print-out pages about the width of my thumb. My bigger thumb. "I pulled every story I could on weird stuff happening near that house, going back to the monastery days. There are lots of Indian legends, but they didn't have what we're looking for, of course..."

"And?"

"And guess what I found. Almost every single murder, UFO sighting, public panic, you name it, for the last hundred and forty years, happened on..."

"Thursday," I said.

"Well, no. But you were half-right."

I was stunned—my theory had just been shot to hell. I squinted at the print-out. "What do you mean?"

"Look. A few did happen on Thursday, or at least that's when they were reported. And a few seemed to have happened on Tuesdays. But almost every other freaky thing—dozens of them—happened on a *Wednesday*, between midnight and midnight. Which, if you remember, was also when the Gentle kid must have died."

So it wasn't back to square one, after all. I felt mighty relieved. But it probably meant I was going to be spending at least another week on this one, so I was a bit disappointed, too. "Wednesday, huh?"

"Thursday."

Now I was losing my temper. "But you just said...!"

"No, I mean that's Thursday—over there." He pointed to where a silky black Mercedes was just pulling into the reserved parking space in front of the office. "He's back."

We waited until he'd gone in before following. I didn't want to spook him. I'd chased enough weirdos for one day.

The inner office door was locked, but I leaned on it and it popped open. Grayson Thursday looked up at us. He didn't look as surprised as he should have, but I don't think it's because he was expecting us. He just wasn't very good at showing human emotions.

"Okay," I growled. "Sit down. You aren't going anywhere until we have some answers."

He did manage "puzzled" pretty well. "Didn't we finish our conversation earlier?"

"Can that crap. Tell us the truth about Monk's Point." I flopped the stack of print-outs down on his desk. "Tell us why stuff's been happening there for a hundred years, and probably more. And why it always seems to happen on the same damn day of the week."

His mouth worked for a moment. He really didn't look right and it was starting to bug me. If you're going to wear a disguise, at least *try* and be convincing. I yanked out my gun and stuck it in his face. "I'm losing my temper here. You're a lousy fake, you know? Your watch is upside down, your shoes are on the wrong feet, and your pupils don't contract when the light changes. Now talk to us or I'll blow your head into little bits. That may not bother you personally very much, but I'm betting it will be at least an inconvenience." I was also betting on the fact that he wouldn't know and couldn't guess that I'm not the kind of guy to shoot except in self-defense. Sometimes when you're huge and red and scary-looking like me, a bluff is your best move.

He waved his hands frantically. "No! Don't! We have no right!"

Now he'd confused me again. "No right to what?"

"We have no right to damage this body." He patted himself gingerly, as if it was a rented tux and he was afraid he might wrinkle it. "It is only borrowed. Its owner is in a comatose state, but he may recover someday. Please do not ignite your weapon."

I turned to Albie Bayless, who looked pretty confused. I felt sorry for him. Even I'm not completely used to this stuff, even though I do it for a living. "Sit down, Albie," I said. "I think we're finally going to get some answers."

"As you've guessed," Grayson Thursday said, "my people are not natives of your earth. Or, to be more exact, we are native only to a small part of your world—the portion that happens on the day you call Thursday."

"I'm lost already," said Albie cheerfully. "Or I've finally gone crazy."

"Our dimension intersects with yours, but at an angle, so to speak—our lives only touch yours once every seven of your days. We have explored your dimension, but we have no physical existence here and normally cannot interact with the inhabitants, so our visits had only ever been for the furtherance of science...until things went wrong. You are so far from us, so different, that other than these few scientific expeditions we might as well be in different universes."

"Thursday's child has far to go," I said.

"What's that?" Thursday asked.

"A nursery rhyme. Bayless, you must know it. 'Monday's child is fair of face, Tuesday's child is full of grace, Wednesday's child is full of woe, Thursday's child has far to go...' And Grayson's people are Thursday's children, I guess."

Grayson Thursday nodded. "Very appropriate—disturbingly so. Because it is not us but Wednesday's children who are the problem. The are indeed 'full of woe', and it is our fault. We bred them too well. We gave them enough life to be aware of their own condition, their own...shortcomings."

"Okay, now you lost me," I said. "Try again."

"We are an old race." He shook his head. "We were tired of striving, of struggling. We wanted rest. So we created a race of servants for ourselves. Not like us—we made them primitive, without emotions...or so we thought. Creatures that would not object to servitude."

"To slavery, you mean." I scowled. "Let me guess. They didn't feel the same way about it as you expected them to."

"After many thousands of years, yes, they did become restless." It was hard to tell, but the stiff face looked a little ashamed. "There was an...uprising. We realized that we had created a permanent problem. Our servants were more numerous than us. We could not destroy them—we are not that kind of race."

"In other words, you could make and keep slaves but you couldn't kill them."

"You mock the complexity of our problem," Thursday said sadly. "But it is more or less true. So our greatest thinkers devised a way to solve the problem. We found a parallel dimension, one that had no outlet back into our world. We transported our unruly servants there and left them to make their own lives. We even apologized, but they were too savage, too discontented to feel anything but hatred toward us."

"Imagine that." I sat up and tucked my gun back in its holster. "Let me guess. The place you dumped your slaves leaks into our dimension. Right here at Monk's Point."

He sighed. It was the closest to human he'd seemed so far. "Yes. We did not know that at the time, of course, or we would have sent them somewhere else. Apparently all our parallel dimension intersect your timeline here in this dimensions. Thus, the Wednesday Men, as you might term them, imprisoned one dimension over from us. Full of woe—and anger. And once a week, if conditions are right, their prison touches on this world."

"So why are *you* here? And what are you doing about Monk's Point?"

Thursday grimaced. "We have done the best we could to keep them there. We have filled the place with attractive host-bodies—you see, like my people and I, they have no physical forms here, and must find things to occupy. Thus, we have provided once-living shells that attract them. And the house is warded with various defenses. It does not always work, I'm sad to say. Sometimes the flow from what you would call the Wednesday dimension is very strong and they spill out past the barriers we have made. That is when...unfortunate things happen."

"Yeah. And your job is to show up here once a week, when the Thursday dimension opens into ours, and pay off the victims or their families. To keep them quiet, or just to ease your own consciences?"

"Please." He actually looked pained. "We encourage silence, of course, but I am here to repair, in a small measure, the harm we have done." He shook his head. "We did not mean this to happen, but we no longer have the power to move our former servants to another place. They have grown too strong, too canny—we could never trick them again as we did the first time."

"Well, isn't this just sweet," I said, and looked at Albie, who was busy scribbling notes. "Why are you bothering, Bayless? You'll never be able to print this story."

He looked shocked, his face suddenly old and helpless. "What do you mean?"

"Well, leaving out the fact that you'd get put in a nuthouse, let's not forget that you called in the BPRD, and this is now government jurisdiction. But we've got bigger problem, anyway." I turned back to Grayson Thursday. "Do you want to make up for what you've done? End this problem once and for all?"

"Of course, but it cannot be done..."

"Hey, buddy, in our dimension, we never say 'cannot'. For one thing, we use contractions." I stood up. "I'll tell you what you need to do." I grabbed Albie's pen and handed it to him. "You'd better write it down, because I'm guessing your dimension goes back out of phase with us at midnight, so we won't be seeing each other for a week. If you get this wrong, we're all in trouble. *Big* trouble."

"Like what?" Albie Bayless asked.

I would have liked to reassure him, but I wasn't in a reassuring mood. "Like end-of-the-world trouble."

It was Tuesday morning when I landed again at the Sonoma County airport. Albie was waiting for me. He was definitely looking old and tired, like maybe he was wishing he'd taken this being-retired thing more seriously. Getting a glimpse of what squirms under the rock of everyday reality can do that for you. I definitely wasn't going to let him get any closer to the lighthouse than I had to.

"How was your trip?" he asked.

"Connecticut, what's there to say?" I told him. "The guys at the bureau say hi. A bunch of them still remember you from '69."

"That's nice," he said. "How was New Orleans?"

"Even freakier than usual. I did get to spend a nice night on the town." I have more than a few friends in New Orleans, and there are a few places I can go and eat red beans and listen to music where nobody bats an eye at me. I like that.

"And your...shopping?"

"Good, I think—I hope. We'll see. There's no recipe book for this stuff—we kind of make it up as we go along."

It was a pleasant enough trip west toward the coast and Caldo Bay—you could smell and see spring on the way—but I wasn't really looking forward to visiting Monk's Point. As he drove, Albie filled me in on what had been happening, not that there was much news. The only excitement in town was that Bobby Gentle was spending what he called "his insurance money" like it was water, and there was a permanent 24-hour party going on out at his house, with all the local rummies and freeloaders prominently represented.

"I can't help thinking about that poor kid—or at least his body," I said. "You never saw anything so empty and so lost."

Albie shuddered. "Come on, don't."

When we arrived *chez* Bayless I opened my two suitcases and started spreading stuff out on the table. Albie watched me with wide eyes as I counted and sorted. "What *is* all that?"

"Fighting gear," I said as I shoved things into a knapsack. "And some other tricks. It's how we're going to take it to the Wednesday boys, basically."

"How's that going to work?"

"You mean, how do I *hope* it's going to work? I'd rather tell you after I live through it, if I manage. It'll be less embarrassing that way." I wasn't feeling all that confident, to be honest. "You got a beer?"

The afternoon ticked away in small talk and me packing and repacking my knapsack and coat pockets about a hundred times. At one point I was making Albie so nervous I got up and took a walk along the headlands above the ocean. The lighthouse at Monk's Point stuck up like a warning finger. I turned my back on it and concentrated on the dark-green water, the white chop kicked up by the rising wind. Seagulls banked and keened. It was like standing at the edge of the universe. Which, if I thought about what was going to open up in a few hours just half a mile away, was pretty much the case.

So much for putting my mind at ease.

After dark had come down good and solid, I let Albie drive me up to the bottom of the hill at the edge of the Monk's Point property. "You go home now," I said. "Don't get any stupid ideas about coming to help me, no matter what happens— you'll wind up doing the 'Thriller' dance alongside the Gentle kid. Come back at dawn Thursday."

"That's more than twenty-four hours from now!"

"I'm aware. If I'm not waiting for you then, go home and call the bureau."

Albie shook my hand and tried to smile. "Second time, damn it," he said.

"Second time what?"

"First Zodiac, then this," he said. "Second time I've been sitting on the story of the century and both times you wouldn't let me write it."

"Oh, you can write it," I told him as I got out and headed for the fence. "Feel free. You just can't show it to anyone."

Inside the house I picked a spot just a few yards away from the grandfather clock, which was almost ten feet tall and as ornate as a baroque chapel. Once I'd got my equipment set up, I hunkered down to wait. I might even have drowsed a little. About ten minutes to midnight, with the wind blowing hard outside and the breakers crashing below, I turned on the special lights. They didn't make the place any brighter, of course—they weren't that kind of lights. But when I put on the blue quartz goggles the boys at the bureau had whipped up for me, all of a sudden I could see all kinds of things I couldn't before, including how the air seethed and glowed around the big clock, and how the thing itself didn't look much like a clock anymore, but like something a lot less ordinary and a lot more complex.

"We put it there to keep the fabric of the wound in space/time from getting any larger," Thursday had told me. "We can't close the hole back up, but the clock-construct will keep it from getting any worse."

Based on what he could tell me, I'd had the bureau's tech boys and girls get to work, and so, with my special lights and special goggles, I was actually able to see what was happening as midnight came and the Wednesday dimension opened into our own.

It wasn't pretty.

The clock began to strike midnight. On the twelfth toll, the space around the clock—there's no other way to put it—split open. What came pouring out was light like a bad bruise and wisps of something smoky yet as liquid as dripping glue that nevertheless had the shape of living creatures, with limbs and a depressing bump where a head should be. Their eyes were empty black holes, but they were holes that melted and ran like the yolks of soft-boiled eggs. Flapping, ragged mouths gaped beneath them, and I was grateful I couldn't hear the noise they made, because I could feel it vibrating in my bones and even that was sickening.

I turned on the "brass knuckles", as the technicians had named them, which looked like a couple of glass and wire watchbands, one of them big enough to stretch over the Hand of Doom. For a moment I felt the vibration they made, then my hands just...weren't anymore. I couldn't feel them at all. I hoped that meant that the Wednesday Men would. I stepped toward the clock.

"You're not going anywhere, Sloppy Face," I told the nearest of them and swung at him. There wasn't much in the way of a satisfying impact, but a kind of snap and sizzle like an electrical shock, and the thing flailed backward, its nasty mouth all hooty and shocked. I grinned. "Didn't like that, huh? Well, come and see what we're serving on Wednesdays around here from now on!"

It was the donnybrook of all donnybrooks and it went on for hours. It was like flying all the way to Asia with in-flight entertainment by the Spanish Inquisition. I could only touch them with my hands, but they hit, scratched and bit. Sometimes they grabbed me and it burned, burned bad. Then for a little while they'd retreat and huddle in the glowing depths of the clock, just inside the gap into their dimension, and look out at me like eels hiding in the rocks, whispering to each other in a deep, soundless rumble I could feel in my teeth. That would give me a few minutes to rest before they broke out and tried me again. Like I said, hours went by, and I had only one thought: Keep 'em here. Don't let 'em past.

I had a few other weapons from the tech boys, but I knew ultimately I wouldn't be able to push them all back by myself. I just had to hang in and keep them in the vicinity of the clock until the rest of the plan kicked in. When I absolutely couldn't make it another moment without rest, I chucked one of my precious supply of vibration-augmented grenades at them, which disrupted them and probably hurt them like hell, too—in any case, each grenade sent them flapping and slurping back into the breach for a bit. Then they'd get back their courage and come at me again.

It was pretty much like the Spartans at Thermopylae. I had to stop them and keep them here. As long as they were busy trying to kill me, or occupying the various stuffed animal corpses, we had a chance. If they got beyond the perimeter, we were in trouble.

And, yeah, they used everything—stag and boar heads jumping off the walls, gouging and biting, stuffed ferrets breaking loose from their pedestals to run snapping up my trouser legs. Even the giant Kodiak bear made a re-appearance about six in the morning, at a moment when I was feeling particularly exhausted. I was ready for it this time, though, and after about half an hour rolling around with it I broke off its arms, then let out all its stuffing with a Gurkha knife.

Things got a little quieter as the sun rose—the Wednesday Men didn't seem to like the light very much—but I couldn't afford to turn my back on them and I certainly didn't dare sleep. I popped a few amphetamine tablets I'd brought with me and did my best to pay attention. I walked around the place beating the random crap out of anything alive that shouldn't have been, trying to keep all activity confined to the area around the clock. I did have time to eat a sandwich in the middle of the day, which was nice. I'd brought a sack lunch, including two packages of Twinkies. It's the little things that make fighting for the survival of our dimension worthwhile.

Damn, I was tired, though. Things began to ramp up again as the sun set on Wednesday night—the things might not have understood who I was or what I was doing, but they were clearly getting frustrated as hell. As soon as the dark came they were all over me again in earnest, and I can't really tell you what happened for the next several hours. I just fought to stay alive, using my vibration-enhanced hands and weapons on the things themselves, using the clubs and knives I'd brought with me to beat the unholy bejabbers out any of the stuffed corpses they hid themselves in the way hermit crabs used seashells.

The last hour before midnight was the worst. I think they'd begun to get an inkling that I meant to do more than deprive them of their fun for a single week, and if I thought they'd fought hard before, I hadn't seen anything. I wished for about the hundredth time I'd brought more help from the bureau, but I hadn't wanted to risk anyone else. I still had no idea what was going to happen at the end—for all I knew, we'd wind up with a scorched hole a mile wide where the town had been, or something even worse, like a blackened rip in the space/time continuum itself.

At the end, they finally got me. I was boneless as a flatworm, exhausted, battered, sucking air but not catching my breath, and to be honest, I couldn't even remember why I was fighting. A bunch of them charged and pulled me down, then they swarmed over me like giant moaning jellyfish. That was it, I knew. All over. I was too tired to care.

Then, from what seemed like a hundred miles away I heard the grandfather clock begin to chime, a surprisingly deep, slow sound, and suddenly the light around me changed color, from purple-blue to a bright reddish-orange. The things on top of me rolled off, buzzing in surprise, as a host of new shapes burst from the clock. They didn't look a thing like human beings, but they didn't look like the Wednesday Men either, and I knew that Grayson Thursday had kept his word and brought his friends. The cavalry had come.

"Pull them back in!" I shouted, although the Thursday folk probably couldn't understand me or perhaps even hear me. Nevertheless, they knew what to do. The orange, glowing shapes grabbed my attackers and the other Wednesday Men and began to drag them back toward the shimmering lights of the big clock. Not that the moaning jellyfish-things went without a fight—people were dying, that was clear, even if they didn't look like people.

It seemed to go on for an hour, but it must have happened during the twelve times the clock struck. At the end, the last of the glowering Wednesday shapes had been pulled back into the breach, and one of the Thursday Men looked back at me with his face that wasn't a face.

"Thanks, buddy!" I shouted. "Now I suggest you all duck!" I pulled out the egg grenade. I'd saved it for last, saved it carefully. Not only was it set to the same vibrational field as the Wednesday Men—and that of their entire dimension—but I'd had one of my friends down in New Orleans prepare it for me, so the grenade itself was taped to a black hen's egg full of serious hoodoo powder. See, hoodoo magic is crossroads magic, and if a place where one world runs into another isn't a crossroad, I don't know what is. I'd gone to see some folks who knew how to deal with such things.

One of the Wednesday Men had got away and was oozing back toward the breach, mouth wide in an unheard roar of frustration. "Hey, Soupy," I shouted. "Regards from Baron Saturday!" I pulled the pin and threw the hoodoo egg grenade.

I've never seen half the colors that explosion made, and I hope I never see them again—they hurt my eyes something fierce and made my brain all itchy. Not only did the blast seem to close the breach, it blew the clock itself to fragments and started big pieces of roof beam falling down as well. It was all I could do to crawl out into the post-midnight darkness before the walls themselves started to collapse. The last thing I saw before I passed out was the lighthouse tower shiver and then crumble, falling down into the ocean in big white chunks.

Albie Bayless found me in the morning. He stared at the ruins like a kid who's not only seen Santa Claus but been given a supersonic ride to the North Pole strapped onto the runners of the fat man's sleigh.

"What happened?"

"I held the pass," I told him. "It's closed now."

"For good?"

I groaned as I sat up. "I'm not sure. That's why I've got one more thing to do." I limped over to the spot at the edge of the property where I'd left my last little surprise. I ached all over, and judging by the worried expression on Albie Bayless' face, I must have looked pretty bad, too. It hurt even to lift the lead box, which was about the size of a tool chest. Normally I could have picked it up with a finger and thumb.

"What's that?"

"Something we're going to leave behind." I led him back to the wreckage of the Monk's Point house and picked a patch of open ground. I dug a hole and put the lead box in it. I tried not to read the stuff scratched on it. My friend in New Orleans had said it would work and that's all I needed to know. She's a smart lady.

"But what *is* it?" Albie asked as I kicked dirt over it.

"That box contains the mortal remains of a man named Albert Dupage," I said. "Killed half a dozen men because he claimed they were cheating him at cards. Killed his family too, wife and kids, but that was another time. Killed a sheriff and a deputy, and the local circuit preacher as well. Meanest, craziest man in all of St. Bernard Parish, everyone says. When a posse finally tracked him down in the swamp and shot him down like a mad dog, he was buried at the crossroads just to keep his evil spirit from finding its way back home." I smiled. Even that hurt. "I figure we'll leave him here to guard *this* crossroad, just in case those Wednesday boys get an idea about coming back. They'll have to get through Albert, and I don't think it'll be easy."

There was one more part of the Monk's Point story. As I was recuperating the next afternoon in the sunshine of the front yard at Albie Bayless' place—Albie himself was in the house, putting raisins in his chili—I heard a rustling in the bushes and looked up. The figure standing there wasn't naked any more.

It was wearing somebody's pink bathrobe, but the new garment was a little too small to conceal the Y-shaped autopsy scar. This time, though, he was looking right at me, and there was an intelligence to his face that hadn't been there last time.

"Rufino?" I asked. "That you?" I asked calmly, but I was a little worried in case it was one of the Wednesday Men who'd got out before the breach was shut.

"Roof," he said. "That's what everyone calls me." The boy shook his head slowly. "Used to call me. 'Cause I'm dead now."

"So I heard." I beckoned him over. "Sit down. How are you feeling?"

"Not too bad. I don't like the sun much, though, so I think I'll stay here. It makes my skin feel bad—makes it smell, too. Kinda like bad bologna. You know what that smells like?"

"Yeah, 'fraid so. What brings you here?"

He shrugged. He was still a teenager, just a dead one. "I don't know. You saved me, kind of. I mean, I got out of that place when you blew up the door. Found my way back into my body, I guess."

"Ah. So they were sort of—holding you prisoner?"

"I guess. It's all kind of confusing. One minute I was looking at the old haunted lighthouse, the next minute I'm in some kind of dark, windy place listening to these weird noises. It was like going to a really, really slow Day on the Green concert. On bad acid. Then a bunch of *really* weird stuff happened, and there was you, and an explosion, and...and I was back in here again." He frowned and shook his lank hair out of his face. "But look what those doctors did to my body! I don't even have blood any more."

"Yeah, that can't be fun."

"Thing is, you're leaving, right? You're not from around here. I want to go with you. I already hated this place when I was alive. Can you imagine how messed up it's going to be for me now I'm dead?"

I thought about it for a moment. "You know, I think the folks at the bureau would be willing give you a place to stay, Rufi...Roof." I nodded. "Just hang around for a little while, then Bayless can drive both of us. I've got a private bureau plane waiting in Sonoma." I smiled. "It's not like you've got a lot of stuff to pack."

"No," he said seriously. "But there is one thing I gotta do first. Can you come along?"

"Where?"

"I need to say goodbye to my dad."

You haven't heard a houseful of drunken rummies scream until you've heard how these guys sounded when Roof showed up at his dad's house in mid-party—bloodless, scalpless, and very obviously dead. The few who could keep their legs (and bladders, and sphincters) under control long enough to run outside all ran into me, which probably didn't help their state of mind, either. Albie told me later that about half of of Bobby Gentle's friends ran straight into to town after this life-changing experience and threw themselves on the mercy of Jesus, care of the nearby Monk's Point Presbyterian Church.

"I told him he ought to get his act together," Roof said as he rejoined me. I could see his dad lying slumped in the doorway of the house where he'd fainted, a beer still clutched in his fist. "I don't think he'll listen, though."

"Don't underestimate your powers of persuasion," I said as I led him up the driveway. I could hear some of the guests still shrieking inside. "You may have a future on the religious circuit, kid."

I took him back to Albie's place, and found him some duct tape so he could stick the top of his head back on until we could fix him properly back at the bureau.

⌒ℳ

"Wow," said Ted. He looked a little pale himself. "I mean…
Jeez. That's pretty… So what happened to the kid?"

"He stayed with us for a couple of years. Worked a few mis-
sions for BPRD, but his heart wasn't in it." I smiled as I thought
of Roof. He had been a slacker before the word existed—he
had just happened to be a dead one. The last thing he wanted to
do was spend his afterlife working an office job. "Last I heard,
he was in Yakutata, Alaska, surfing year-round. He likes it
'cause it's real cold there, and nobody ever asks why he always
wears a wetsuit."

"And the Thursday Men?" asked Liz.

"Haven't heard from them—*or* their woeful buddies. But I
can't help but worrying about it sometimes."

"Why's that?" Liz smiled at me. She thinks I think too
much. She's probably right.

"Well, if those two dimensions just happened to run smack
into ours, what about the others? What about the rest of the
days of the week? Why haven't we heard anything yet from the
Monday Men or the Tuesday Men?" I re-lit my cigar. "They're
probably here already, and we don't even know yet. In fact, you
could be one of them, Ted. It would explain your singing voice."
I slapped my hand on the table. "Now, who's playing cards?"

THE TENTH MUSE

WHEN I FIRST GOT TO know Balcescu, I didn't like him much. A snob, that's what I thought he was, and way too stuck on himself. I was right, too. One of the things that drove me crazy is that he talked like George Sanders, all upper-crust, but I didn't believe for a moment he actually knew who George Sanders *was*. Old Earth movies wouldn't have been highbrow enough for him.

He also loved the sound of his own voice, whether the person he was talking to had time to listen or not.

"There you are, Mr. Jatt," he said one day, stopping me as I was crossing the observation deck. "I've been looking for you. I have a question."

I sighed, but not so he could tell. "What can I do for you, Mr. Balcescu?" Like I didn't have anything better to do coming up on twelve hours 'til Rainwater Hub than answer questions from seat-meat. Sorry, that's what we call passengers sometimes. Bad habit. But I hate it when people think they're on some kind of a pleasure cruise, and that just because I'm four feet tall and my voice hasn't broken yet I'm the best choice to find them a comfy pillow or have a long chat about the business they're going to be doing planetside. What a lot of civilians don't get is that this is the Confederation Starship *Lakshmi*, and when you're on my ship, it's serious business. A cabin boy is part of the crew like anyone else and I've got real work to do. Ask Captain Watanabe if you think I'm lying.

Anyway, this Balcescu was a strange sort of fellow—young and old at the same time, if you know what I mean. He had all his hair and he wasn't too wrinkled but his face was thin and the rest of him wasn't much huskier. He couldn't have been much older than my cabin-mate Ping, which would make him late thirties, maybe forty at the most, but he dressed like an old man, or like someone out of an old movie—you know, those ancient films from Earth where they wear coats with patches on the elbows and loose pants and those things around their necks. Ties, right. That's how he dressed—but no tie, of course. He wasn't crazy, he just thought he was better than everyone else. Wanted you to know that even though he was some kind of language scientist, he was *artistic*. It wasn't just his clothes— you could also tell by the things he said, the kind of the music he listened to. I'd heard it coming out of his cabin a couple of times—screeches like cats falling in love, crashes like someone banging on a ukulele with a crescent wrench. Intellectual stuff, in other words.

"I can't help but noticing that much ado is being made of this particular stop, Mr. Jatt," he said when he stopped me on deck. "But I went through four Visser rings on the way out to Brightman's Star and nobody made much of that. Why such a fuss over this one, this...what do they call it?"

"People call Rainwater Hub 'the Waterhole'," I told him. "You can call it a fuss, but it's dead serious business, Mr. Balcescu."

"Why don't you call me Stefan, my young friend—that would be easier. And I could call you Rolly—I've heard some of the others call you that."

"Couldn't do it, sir. Regs don't allow it."

"All right. How about something else, then? You could call me something amusing, like 'Mr. B'..."

I almost made a horrified face, but Chief Purser always says letting someone know you're upset is just as rude as telling them out loud. "If you don't mind, I'll just keep calling you Mr. Balcescu, sir. It's easier for me."

"All right, then, Mr. Jatt. So why is Rainwater Hub such a serious business?"

I did my best to explain. To be honest, I don't understand all the politics and history myself—that's not our job. Like we rocket-jocks always say, we just fly 'em. But here's what I know.

When Balcescu said he went all the way out to Brightman's Star and there was no fuss about wormhole transfers, he was right, but that's because he'd left from the Libra system and his whole trip had been through Confederation space. All those Visser rings he went through were "CO&O" as we say— Confederation Owned and Operated. But when he hopped on the *Lak'* to join us on our run from the Brightman system to Col Hydrae, well, that trip requires one jump through non-Confederation space—the one we were about to make.

Not only that, but for some reason not even Doc Swainsea can explain so I can understand, the Visser ring here at Rainwater is hinky, or rather the wormhole itself is. Sometimes it takes a little while until the conditions are right, so the ships sort of line up and wait—all kinds of ships, the most you'll ever see in one place, Confederation, X-Malkin, Blessed Union, ordinary Rim traders, terraform scouts out of Covenant, you name it. They call it the Waterhole because most of the time everybody just...shares. Even enemies. Nobody wants to shut down the hub when it means you could wind up with an entire fleet stranded on this side of the galaxy. So there's a truce. It's a shaky one, sometimes. Captain Watanabe told us once in the early days the Confederation tried to arrest a Covenant jumbo at another hub, Persakis out near Zeta Ophiuchus—the Convenant had been breaking an embargo on the Malkinates. Persakis was shut down for most of a year and it took twenty more for everyone to recover from that, so now everybody agrees there's no hostilities inside a hub safety zone—like predators and prey sharing a waterhole on the savannah. Once you get there, it's sanctuary. It's...*Casablanca*.

I mentioned I like old Earth movies, didn't I?

After I'd explained, Balcescu asked me a bunch more questions about how long we'd have to wait at Rainwater Hub and who else was waiting with us. For a guy who'd traveled to about fifteen or twenty different worlds, I have to say he didn't know much about politics or Confederation ships, but I did my best to bring him up to speed. When he ran out of things to ask, he thanked me, patted me on the head, then walked back to the view-deck. Yeah, patted me on the head. I guess nobody told him that any member of a Confederation crew can break a man's arm using only one finger and thumb. He was lucky I had things to do.

The weird stuff started happening as we entered the zone. Captain Watanabe and Ship's Navigator Chinh-Herrera were on the com with Rainwater Hub Command when things started to get scratchy. At first they thought it was just magnetar activity, because there's a big one pretty close by—it's one of the things that makes Rainwater kind of unstable. The bridge lost Hub Command but they managed to latch onto another signal—com from one of Rainwater's own lighters—and so they saw the whole thing on visual, through a storm of interference. Chinh-Herrera showed it to me afterward so I've seen it myself. I wouldn't have believed it if I hadn't.

First there was the huge alien ship, although even after several views it takes a while to realize it *is* a ship. Shaped more like a jellyfish or an amoeba, all curves and transparencies, and not particularly symmetrical. In another circumstance you might even call it beautiful—but not when it's appearing out of a wormhole where it's not supposed to be. The Visser ring wasn't supposed to open for another several hours, and it certainly wasn't supposed to open to let something *out*.

Then that…*thing* appeared. The angry thing.

It was some kind of volumetric display—but what kind, even Doc Swainsea couldn't guess—a three-dimensional projected image, but what it looked like was some kind of furious god, a creature the size of small planet, rippling and burning in the silence of space. It just barely looked like a living creature—it had arms, that's all you could tell for certain, and some kind of glow around the face that might have been eyes. Its voice, or the voice of the alien ship projecting it, thundered into every com of every ship within half a unit of Rainwater Hub. Nobody could understand it, of course—not then—it was just a deafening, scraping roar with bits along the edges that barked and twittered. "Like a circus dumped into a meat grinder, audience and all," Chinh-Herrera said. I had to cover my ears when he played it for me.

If it had stopped there it would have been weird and frightening enough, but right after the monstrous thing went quiet some kind of weapon fired from inside it—from the ship itself, cloaked behind the volumetric display. It wasn't a beam so much as a ripple—at the time you couldn't even see it, but when we played it back you could see the moment of distortion across the star field where it passed—and the nearest ship to the Visser ring, a Malkinate heavy freighter, flew apart. It happened just as fast as that—a flare of white light and then the freighter was gone, leaving nothing but debris too small to see on the lighter's com feed. Thirteen hundred men dead. Maybe they were X-Malkins and they didn't believe what we believe, but they were still shipmen like us. How did it feel to have their ship, their home, just disappear into fragments around them? To be suddenly thrown into the freezing black empty?

A few seconds later, as if to show that it wasn't an accident, the god-thing roared again and convulsed and another ship was destroyed, one of Rainwater's lighters. This one must have had some kind of inflammable cargo because it went up like a giant magnesium flare, a ball of white fire burning away until nothing was left but floating embers.

This was too much, of course—proof of hostile intent— and a flight of wasps was scrambled from Rainwater Station and sent after the jellyfish ship. Maybe the aliens were surprised by how quickly we fought back, or maybe they were just done with their giant hologram: in either case, it disappeared as the wasp flight swept in. A moment later the wasps were in range and began to fire on the intruder, but their pulses only sputtered and flashed against the outside skin of the jellyfish ship. A moment later every one of the wasps abruptly turned into a handful of sparks flung out in all directions like spinning Catherine wheels—an entire flight gone.

After that, everybody fell back, as you can imagine. "Ran like hell" might be a better way to put it. The Confederation ships met up in orbit around the nearest planet, several units away from Rainwater, and the officers began burning up the com lines, as you can imagine. Nobody'd seen anything like the jellyfish before, or recognized whatever it was on that volumetric or how it was done. We accessed some of the Hub drones so we could keep a watch on Rainwater. The alien ship was still sitting there, although the Visser ring behind it had closed again. There were moments when the angry-god display flickered back into life, as if it was waking up to have a look around, and other moments when crackling lines of force like blue and orange lightning arced back and forth between the jellyfish and the ring, but none of this told anyone a thing about what was really going on.

Our first major clue came when one of the Hub's own lighters got close enough to pick up some of the wreckage of the Malkin jumbo. The ship had not been blown apart in any normal sense—no shear and no heat, or at least no more than would be expected with sudden decompression. The carbon ceramic bones and skin of the ship had just suddenly fallen apart—"delatticed" was Doc Swainsea's term. She didn't sound happy when she said it, either.

"It's not a technology I know," she told Captain Watanabe the day after the attacks. "It's not a technology I can even envision."

The captain looked at her and they stood there for a moment, face to face—two very serious women, Doc tall and blonde, Captain W. a bit shorter and so dark haired and pale skinned that she looked like an ink drawing. "But is it a technology we can beat?" the captain finally asked.

I never heard the answer because they sent me out to get more coffee.

About two hours later, while I was bringing more whiskey glasses to the captain's cabin—which meant, I assumed, that the doctor's answer had been negative—I found Balcescu standing waiting for the lift to the bridge.

"I think I have it, Mr. Jatt," he told me as I went by.

I was in a hurry—everyone on the ship was in a hurry, which was strange considering we obviously weren't going anywhere soon—but something in his voice made me stop. He sounded exhausted, for one thing, and when I looked at him more closely I could see he didn't look good, either: he was pale and trembling, like he hadn't had anything but coffee or focusmeds for a while. Maybe he was sick.

"Have what, Mr. Balcescu? What are you talking about?"

"The language—the language of the things that attacked us. I think I've cracked it."

Two minutes later we were standing in front of the captain, Chief Navigator Chinh-Herrera, Doc Swainsea, and an open com line going out to the other Confederation ships.

"I couldn't have done this if it had been pure cryptography," Balcescu explained, standing up after all the introductions had been handled. His hands were still shaking; he spilled a little of his coffee. He obviously needed some food, but I was damned if I was going to leave the room right then.

Sorry. We spacemen swear a lot. But I wasn't going to rush out to the galley just when he was about to explain.

"What I mean to say is," Balcescu went on, "if it is anything like the languages we already know—and I think it is—then they haven't given us enough of a sample to do the standard reductions. For one thing, we couldn't know that we were even hearing all of it..."

"What are you talking about?" asked Chinh-Herrera. "Not heard it all? It nearly blew our coms to bits!"

"We heard the part that was in our audio register. And there were other parts above and below human hearing range as well that we recorded. But who could say for certain that there weren't parts of the language outside the range of our instruments? This is a first encounter. Never make assumptions, Chief Navigator."

Chinh-Herrera turned away, hiding a scowl. He didn't like our Mr. Balcescu much, it was easy to see. The chief navigator was a good man, and always nice to me, but he could be a bit old-fashioned sometimes. I actually understood what Balcescu was saying, because I've spent my life living with other people's assumptions, too. That's what happens when you're my size.

"So you're saying the sample wasn't enough to form a basis for translation, Dr. Balcescu?" This was Doc Swainsea. "Then why are we here?"

"Because it *is* a language and I know what they're saying," said Balcescu wearily. By his expression, you'd have thought he was being forced to explain the alphabet to a room full of four-year-olds. "You see, we've enlarged the boundaries of human-contact space quite a bit in the last couple of hundred years—the Hub system has seen to that. Just a few weeks ago I was out in the Brightman system doing something that would have been unthinkable only generations ago—xenolinguistic fieldwork with untainted living cultures." He gave Chinh-Herrera a bit of a sideways look. "In other words, speaking alien with aliens. Our linguistic database has also expanded hugely. So I figured it was worth a try to see if there were any similarities between what we heard at Rainwater Hub and any of the other cultures we've recorded on the outskirts of contact space. I spent hours and hours going through different samples, comparing points of apparent overlap..."

"And, Doctor Balcescu?" That was Captain Watanabe. She wasn't big on being lectured, either.

"And there are similarities—distant and tenuous, but similarities nevertheless—between what we heard yesterday and some of the older speech systems we've found out toward the galactic rim. I can't say exactly what the relationships are—that will take years of study and, to be honest, a great deal more information about this latest language—but there are enough common elements that I think I can safely translate what we heard, at least roughly." He looked around expectantly, almost as if he was waiting for polite applause from the captain and the others. He didn't get it. "I used what we already know about these particular rim dialects as a ratchet, combined with some guesswork..."

"Get to the point, Doctor," said the captain. "Tell us what it said. A lot of good men and women are dead already, and the rest of us are stranded 46 parsecs from the nearest Confederation hub."

"Sorry, of course." He pointed to the com screen and the picture of the monstrous apparition jumped back onto it. I'd seen it before, of course—everyone had been watching it over and over, trying to understand what had happened—but it still scared the brass marbles off me. It was like something out of an old ghost story, the kind they tell down in the engine bay on a slow shift, with the lights down. The thing was like some wailing spirit, a banshee heralding death—and not just the death of a few, but of the whole human race. How could we beat something like that?

As the image billowed and stretched in achingly slow motion, like living flame, Balcescu spoke.

"What it seems to be saying, as far as I can tell, is unfortunately just as bellicose as its actions suggest. It boils down to this." He said it like a man reciting a memorized speech, all emotion squeezed out of his voice. " '*Your death is upon you. Only black ash will show that you ever lived. The Outward-reaching Murder Army*'—that's the best I can do, that's pretty much what they're saying—'*will spit upon the stars that give you life, extinguishing them all. The cold will suck the life from you. All memory of you will be obliterated.*' " Balcescu shook his head. "Not exactly Shakespeare. In fact, a rather crude translation, but it makes the main points."

The monstrous shape still rippled slowly on the com screen, its face glowing like a dying sun.

"Well," said Captain Watanabe after a long silence. "Now that we know what it said, I'm sure we all feel a lot better."

Everybody on board the *Lakshmi* continued to hurry around as the days went past, but with what seemed like an increasing hopelessness. Rainwater was one of the longest and most important holes—without it, it would take us years, maybe decades, to make our way back. There was no other shortcut from this part of the rim.

Under emergency regs most of the passengers had been put into cryo, except for those like Balcescu who had a job to do.

I didn't have much to keep me occupied so I spent a lot of time with the people who had time to spend with me. Chinh-Herrera the navigator didn't have much to do either, once he'd plotted the various ways back home that bypassed Rainwater, but when he was done he didn't really want to talk. I'd bring him wine and stay a while, but it wasn't much fun.

One evening I got called up to Balcescu's room, an unused officer's cabin he'd been given. To my surprise, as I got there Doc Swainsea was just leaving, dressed in civilian clothes—a dress, of all things—and carrying her shoes. She smiled at me as she went past but it was a sad one and she didn't really seem to see me. Balcescu was sitting in the main room listening to music—kind of pretty, old-fashioned music for a change—and when he saw my face he smiled a little bit too.

"We all deal with fear in different ways," he said, as if that explained something. "Did you bring my coffee, Mr. Jatt?"

I put the tray down. "There's plenty of coffee down in the commons room," I told him, a touch grumpily I guess. "Cups, spoons, you name it. Even stuff that tastes like sugar. It's practically a five-star restaurant down there." I wasn't sure what that meant, but I'd heard it in old movies.

He raised an eyebrow. "Ah. Is it the revolt of the proletariat, then, Mr. Jatt?" he asked. "*The Admirable Crichton*? If we are all going to die, let it be as equals?"

I'd seen *The Admirable Crichton*, as a matter of fact, but I didn't remember anyone using a word like "proletariat". Still, I got the gist. "Some would say we were already equals, Mr. Balcescu," I said. "The Confederation Constitution, for one. I've read it. Have you?"

He laughed. "Touché, my good Jatt. As it happens, I have. It has its moments, but I think it would make a dull libretto. Unlike this." He gestured loosely to the air and I realized he was drunk, so I started pouring the coffee. We might die as equals but it probably wouldn't be soon, and in the meantime

I'd be the one who'd have to clean up any messes. "I said, *unlike this*," he told me again, more loudly. The music was getting loud too, some men singing in deep voices, all very dramatic.

"I heard you!" I practically shouted back. "Here's whitener if you want some. And sweetener."

"I haven't been able to get this out of my head for days!" He waved his hand over the chair arm and the music got quieter, although I could still hear it. "*Don Giovanni*. That...thing... that alien projection we saw reminds me of the Commendatore's statue. Come to drag us all to hell." He laughed and reached clumsily for the coffee. I held the cup until he had a grip on it.

"I have no idea what you're talking about, Mr. Balcescu," I said. "Unless you want something else, I'd better be going."

"That's what...Diana said."

"Pardon?"

"Dr. Swainsea. Never mind." He laughed again, another in a line of some of the saddest laughs I had ever heard. "Don't you know *Don Giovanni*? My God, what do they teach cabin boys these days?"

"How to deal with drunken idiots, mostly, Mr. Balcescu. No, I don't know *Don Giovanni*. One of those old Mafia films?"

He shook his head. He seemed to like doing it enough that he kept it up for a bit. "No, no. *Don Giovanni* the *opera*. Mozart. About a terrible man who seduces women—preys on them, really." He began to shake his head again, then seemed to remember that he'd done that already, and for a good long while, too. "At the end, the murdered spirit of one of the women's fathers, the Commendatore, comes after him in the form of a terrible statue. In his foolishness and his pride, Don Giovanni invites the ghost to supper. So the statue, the ghost, whatever you want to call it—it *comes*. It's going to take him to his judgment. Listen!" He cocked an ear toward the music. "The Commendatore's statue is saying '*Tu m'invitasti a cena, Il tuo dover or sai. Rispondimi: verrai tu a cenar meco?*' That means, 'You invited me to dinner—now will you come dine with *me*?' In other words, he's going to take him off to hell. And Don Giovanni says, 'I'm no coward—my heart is steady in my breast.' He'd rather go to the devil than show himself afraid—that's panache!" Balcescu was lost in it now, his eyes closed as the music swelled and the voices boomed. "The ghost takes his hand, and Don Giovanni cries out, 'It's so freezing cold!' The ghost tells him it's his last moment on earth—repent! '*No, no, ch'io non me pento!*' Don Giovanni tells him—he won't repent!" Balcescu sat back in his chair, eyes still closed, and sighed. "That is Art. That's what Art can do!"

He said it—slurred it a bit, actually—as though it were the end of a beautiful dream, but I could hear the music in the background and nobody sounded very happy—not even the stony-voiced thing that I guessed was the Commendatore's statue. Made sense. What did the poor old Commendatore have to look forward to after his revenge, anyway? He was already dead.

"I don't get you, Mr. Balcescu."

He frowned. "You really should call me 'Doctor', Mr. Jatt. I am a doctor, you know. *Art*, I said. Art teaches us the things that reality can't. Teaches us to live with the things that seem beyond endurance. Missed chances. Failed love affairs. Suffering and death— the stuff of actual life."

He was lecturing again and I didn't like it. "But what's so good about that?" I asked. "I don't *like* your kind of art—that high-falutin' stuff that's just like real life. Why can't it be the other way around—why can't life imitate the stuff *I* like? Like *Casablanca,* y'know? Some scary bits, some laughs, then the good guys win—a decent ending, y'know? Why can't life be like *that*?" I was getting kind of angry.

"Ah, well. You know what Oscar Wilde once said? 'God and other artists are always a little obscure.' " Balcescu looked just as struck by dark thoughts as I was, his thin face sagging into lines of weariness. All of us on the *Lak'* were feeling that way, trying to follow our routines in the long shadow of doom—or at least permanent exile. "You know, I shouldn't even be here," he said after a while. "I was going to go back to my home in the Gliese Ring, but a colleague asked me to come to the opening of an exhibit at the Xenobiology Gardens on Col Hydrae 7. Just a big party, basically, but he used some of my material from the Xenolinguistic Encyclopedia and thought I'd like..." He shook his head. "And here I am. Never going home, now. 'Cause I said yes to a goddamn cocktail party..." He fell silent again for a long moment. "Never mind, Mr. Jatt. I've kept you long enough. I'm sure you have more important people to help."

As I've told you, I didn't really like Balcescu much, and I usually don't give a crap for other people's self-pity, but I suddenly felt sorry for him. Don't ask me why—he wasn't any worse off than the rest of us—but I did. A little.

"Mr. Balcescu, how old do you think I am?"

The reaction was slowed by alcohol, but when it came he looked mildly startled. "How *old* are you? My dear Mr. Jatt, how the hell should I know? Ten? Eleven but small for your age?"

"Has it ever occurred to you to wonder why a Confederation cruiser would have an able-bodied shipman ten or eleven years old?"

"But you're...you're a cabin boy, aren't you?"

"That's the name of my job, yes. But I'm a legit grade CS6 shipman, bucking for grade seven. I'm forty-three years old, Mr. Balcescu. I've been shipping out on Confederation ships for twenty-five years."

His eyes went wide. "But...look at you! You're a kid!"

"I look like a kid, but I'm just about your age...right? Although right now you look about ten years older. You look like crap, in fact."

He straightened up a little, which was what I'd intended. "What happened to you? Is it some kind of genetic thing?"

"Yeah, but not in the way you mean. My parents were Highfielders—they were subscribers to Reverend Highfield's generation ship. You may have heard of that—the Highfielder movement started up about the same time the X-Malkins were splitting off. My parents' church said that the Confederation system was full of sinners and was doomed to be destroyed by the Lord, so they planned to send their children away to find another home outside the system, somewhere far away across the galaxy. And to make sure we'd be able to survive on ship as long as possible, they worked with geneticists to retard our aging processes—see, they started this project before we were even born. That was supposed to give us an advantage for a long haul trip—keep us small, easy to feed, revved-up immune systems. So don't worry about me, Mr. Balcescu—I'll hit puberty eventually, but it won't be for another twenty or thirty years. I'm looking forward to sex, though. I hear it's a lot of fun."

"What...what happened?" Balcescu was listening now, all right. "Why didn't you go?"

"Do you remember Katel's World?"

For a moment he couldn't place it. Then he went a little pale. I see that a lot when I tell people. "Oh my God," he said. "Those were your parents?"

"My folks and about a thousand other Highfielders. And of course a few thousand of their children. That's why the Confederation went in, to protect the children. But as you probably remember, things didn't work out so well with that. I was one of about eight hundred that were rescued alive. I grew up in an orphanage, but I always wanted to see the big black— I figure it's sort of what I was born for. So here I am."

He stared at me. "Why are you telling me this?"

"Don't know, exactly, Mr. Balcescu. I hate to see people lose track of what's important, I guess. And I hate to see people make assumptions. And I definitely don't like to see people being underestimated."

"Are you saying I underestimated you?" He sat up and wiped his hand across his face. "Well, I suppose I did, Mr. Jatt, and I apologize for..."

"With respect, Mr. Balcescu, I'm not talking about that. I'm talking about you underestimating *yourself*. Instead of sitting around listening to weepy music and feeling sorry for yourself, there must still be useful work you can do. You figured out what those aliens were saying—what else can you figure out about them?"

When I left with the empty wine glasses he was drinking his coffee and staring up at the ceiling as if he was thinking about something real. The music had started again, Don Giovanni and his doomed pursuit of pleasure. Oh, well, better than the caterwauling modern stuff, I guess.

Honest, I've got nothing against art. I hope I've made that clear. I just don't like moping. Waste of everyone's time. "Life's a banquet," as good old Rosalind Russell said in one of those ancient films I like, "and most poor suckers are starving to death."

The thing that finally made it all happen was Doc Swainsea's report. I don't know what happened between her and Balcescu, but after the night I saw her she pretty much disappeared from social life on the ship, spending something like twenty hours a day in her lab. I know, because who do you think brought her meals to her, cleared away the old trays, and tried to get her to sleep and take a sonic occasionally?

Anyway, it happened during one of the meetings where I was off duty and my roomie Ping was serving at the bridge conference table—he gave me the lowdown the next morning. Doc Swainsea was just finishing up her final report. The energies she'd been able to analyze in the destruction of the Malkinate ship and the Hub lighter were like nothing else she'd seen, she told the captain and the others. The wreckage was like nothing else she'd seen, either. The projection mechanism had to be like nothing she'd seen. And she'd been in touch with a xenobiologist on one of the other trapped ships and he agreed that the projected apparition looked like nothing he'd seen, either. If it was an image of a real life form, it was one we hadn't come into contact with yet.

"Extragalactic, most likely," was Balcescu's one contribution, Ping said. Nobody argued, but nobody seemed very happy about it, either. Then the odd part happened.

Doc Swainsea closed with one last point. She said that in analyzing the projection she'd discovered a regular pulse of complex sound buried deep in the roaring, blaring audio, at a level too low for humans to hear without speeding it up. It didn't sound anything like the speech Balcescu had translated—in fact, she wasn't sure at all that it *was* speech, although it seemed too regular and orderly to be an accident. She said she didn't know what that signified, either—she just thought she should mention it. Ping said she looked exhausted and sad.

And just at this point Balcescu got up and walked out.

When Ping told me I couldn't help wondering what was going on. Was it something to do with that evening the two doctors had spent together, the one I'd walked in on? It had just looked like a less-than-satisfactory date to me, but maybe my lagging biochemistry had betrayed me—maybe there had been something more complicated going on. Ping said Doc Swainsea had looked surprised too when Balcescu left so abruptly, surprised and maybe a little hurt, but she didn't make a big deal of it. That upset me. I really liked Doc Swainsea, although the difference in our ranks meant I didn't get to talk to her much.

I didn't have much time to think about Stefan Balcescu, though. That morning as I came on duty, right after I talked to Ping, we heard that five Malkinate cruisers had attacked the jellyfish ship. The black starfield around Rainwater Hub looked like a Landing Night celebration back home—fireworks everywhere. But silent, of course. Completely silent. The X-Malkins were obliterated in a matter of minutes.

Things got a little crazy after that. Some of the passengers who were supposed to be in deep sleep staged a sort of mini-mutiny. We didn't do much to 'em once we put an end to their uprising—just put 'em back in cryo where they were supposed to be in the first place. One of the passenger cabin CS4s turned out to be the sympathizer who'd let them out, and he wound up in cryo himself, except in the brig. Captain Watanabe knew she had a lot of unhappy, worried shipmen on her hands but she also wanted to make sure she did the right thing. The problem was, at that moment nobody believed anything good could happen from staying near Rainwater Hub: everybody figured if we were going to take years getting home, we might as well get started. But the captain and some of the other Confederation officers hadn't given up yet—and strangely enough, the one who had convinced them to hang on was Stefan Balcescu.

I only found out what was happening when I got called to the bridge one evening almost a week later. It was about day twenty of the crisis. Captain Watanabe was in the conference room with Lt. Chinh-Herrera, Dr. Swainsea, First Lieutenant Davits who headed up the ship's marines, and several men and women from Engineering whose names I didn't know—they've kind of got their own world down there.

I asked the captain what I could bring her.

"Just sit down, Jatt," she told me. "Shipman Ping's handling your duties. You're here as an observer."

"Observer?" I had no idea what she was talking about. "Begging your pardon, Captain, but Observing what?" It was a mark of how sure she was of her command that I could ask my commanding officer a question that easily. A lot of 'em want you to treat anything they say like it's written on a stone tablet.

"This," she said, and one of the engineers turned on the com screens.

The first thing I saw was a group of perhaps a half-dozen red circles moving across a star field, heading toward the immensity of the alien jellyfish ship. It took me a few more seconds until I figured out that the red circles were only on our screen, that they were markers outlining the position of several small Confederation ships which would otherwise have been almost too dark to see. The weird thing, though, was that I could see as I focused on their silhouettes when they crossed in front of the alien vessel that they weren't Confederation cruisers or jumbos or even attack ships, but...

"Lifeboats," said the captain as if she'd heard my thought. "One from each of the Confederation ships."

"I'm sorry, Captain Watanabe, I'm still not getting any of this..." I looked around to see if anyone else was as puzzled as I was, but they were all watching the screens intently. I noticed that Balcescu, who lately had been at all these sort of meetings, was conspicuously absent. Had he given up? Or just pissed everyone off so much that they hadn't invited him for this... whatever it was?

"Bear with us, Shipman Jatt," the captain said. "You're here by special request, but we're in the middle of an actual mission here and we don't have time to..." Her attention was distracted by a murmur from the first lieutenant.

"They're not going for it," he said.

"Maybe they're just not in a hurry," said Doc Swainsea. "Their approach is slow. Give it time..."

Even as she said it, one of the lifeboats suddenly flew apart. The others scattered away from their stricken comrade in all directions, but slowly—too slowly. The small ships dodged and dived, but within only a few minutes every one of them had been reduced to shattered flotsam. I blinked hard as my eyes filled with tears.

"There he is!" said Captain Watanabe. "See, Jatt?" When she turned to me she saw my face. "No, look, he got through!"

"He? What are you talking about? They're all dead!" It was all I could do to keep from sobbing out loud at the waste, the murderous stupidity of it all.

"No! No, Jatt, the lifeboats were unmanned. They were cover, that's all." She pointed to the screen again, at what I had taken for another small, rounded chunk of debris. "See, that's him! He's almost reached them!"

"He doesn't know, Captain," said Chinh-Herrera suddenly. "Balcescu didn't tell him."

"For Christ's sake, who is this *he* you keep talking about...?" Then suddenly it hit me. "Wait a minute...Balcescu? Are you telling me that's *Balcescu* out there? What's he doing? What's going on?" I was almost crying again, and if you don't think that's embarrassing for a guy my age no matter *how* tall he is, you're a damn idiot.

"He's in one of our exterior repair pods," said Chinh-Herrera, pointing to the tiny, avocado-shaped object floating across the starfield toward the jellyfish, which loomed above it now like a frozen tidal wave. "The engineers modified it. Wait'll you see what it can do."

"If the ship lets it get close enough," said Doc Swainsea. I noticed for the first time that her eyes were red, too.

I still didn't really understand, but I sat in silence now with everyone else, holding my breath as I watched the tiny object float closer to the monstrous ship. At last it touched and stuck. Everyone cheered, even me, although I still wasn't quite sure why. Slowly, the rounded shape of the repair pod flattened against the side of the jellyfish ship until had turned itself into a wide, shallow dome like a black blister.

"It's slicing its way through," said Chinh-Herrera. "Monofilament cutter."

"Put on the helmet feed," said the captain.

A moment later another picture jumped onto the screen—a close-up view of something falling away—a section of the alien ship's skin that had been cut away now falling into the ship, I realized. The hole it left pulsed with blueish light.

"How's the pod holding up?" the captain called to the engineers.

"The blister beams have gone rigid—no loss of pressure. We're solid, ma'am!"

A moment later we could see feet in an excursion suit fill the screen as Balcescu looked down while he stepped through the hole cut in the alien hull. It seemed crazy—the aliens must know he was there. How many seconds could he have until they were on him? And what the hell was he supposed to do in that little time—plant a bomb? Why would they send Balcescu to do that instead of one of the marines?

But all I asked was, "Why isn't he talking to us?"

"Radio silence," Chinh-Herrera whispered. "To make sure we give him as long as possible before he's detected."

"He likes it better that way, anyway," said Doc Swainsea.

As Balcescu moved inside it was as though he had been swallowed into some giant living thing—the blue-lit corridor was mostly smooth except for low bumps in strange formations, and as shiny-wet as internal organs. I half expected him to be swept up like a corpuscle in a blood stream, but instead he turned into the main passage, which seemed to be about half a hundred feet tall and nearly that wide, and began to move down it. He was walking, I realized, which meant that the ship had to have some kind of artificial gravity.

"What's he looking for?" I whispered, but nobody answered me.

Suddenly a trio of inhuman shapes emerged from a side-corridor into the main passageway. I heard several of the observers swear bitterly—I must confess Captain Watanabe was one of them—as the horrors turned toward Balcescu. I couldn't make a sound, I was so frightened. They were at least twice human height, rippling like ash in a fire, but undeniably real, even seen only on com screen. Whatever complicated arrangement was at the bottom of their bodies didn't touch the floor, but they did not give the impression of being light or airy or ghostly. And their faces—if those were their faces…! Well, I'll just say I think I know now what was under the Commendatore's mask.

Balcescu stopped and stood waiting for them. We could tell he'd stopped because the walls around him stopped moving. I guess he thought there was no point in running away, although if it had been me I sure as hell would have given it a try. The entire bridge was silent. You know that expression about hearing a pin drop? If someone had dropped one just then we all would have jumped right out of our skins.

The terrible things approached Balcescu until they were right in front of him—and then they glided right past him.

"What the hell…?" I said, louder than I meant to, but nobody seemed to care. They were too busy cheering. For a second I thought they'd lost their minds. "Has he got some kind of cloaking device…?" I asked.

Balcescu had turned around for some reason and was following the floating aliens. To my horror, he actually hurried after them until he caught them, then reached out and shoved the nearest one in the back. The creature stumbled slightly, or at least bobbed off balance, but then righted itself and went on as if it hadn't noticed anything unusual. Neither of them even looked back.

I felt like crying again, even as everyone else was celebrating. I just didn't get it. I almost thought I'd lost my mind.

"I hope you all saw that," Balcescu said. I realized it was the first time I'd heard his voice in days. Who would have guessed I'd be hearing it over a comlink from the alien ship? "I humbly submit that I have won the argument."

"You sure did, you arrogant sonuvabitch!" shouted Chinh-Herrera, but I think the comlink was only working one way.

"What happened?" I asked Doc Swainsea. She seemed more restrained than the others, as if she didn't quite believe this was the victory everyone else seemed to think it was.

"They're not real," she said. "He was right, Rahul." The doctor is the only person who calls me by my true name.

"Not real? But they blew up our ships! And just now...he pushed one of them!"

"Oh, they're real enough—they have weight and mass. But they're constructs. They're not real people, any more than a child's toy soldiers are real." She frowned. She looked very tired, like it was taking all her energy just to keep talking to me. "No, that's a bad analogy. They're not that kind of toys, they're puppets. This was all a show."

"A show? They killed people! Hundreds of shipmen! What kind of show is that?"

But before she could answer me I heard Balcescu's voice and turned back.

"This looks like it, don't you think?" he asked, as if having a conversation with an old friend. "Time to make a little trouble for the local repertory company, I think." George Sanders, maybe even Cary Grant—I have to admit, the superior bastard did have style. He seemed to be standing in a large chamber, one that was even more intestinal than the passageway, if such a thing was possible. At the center of it floated a huge, shifting transparency, a moving gob of glass-clear gelatin as big as a jumbo jet. Balcescu walked toward it, then stopped and held up his com wand, thumbed it. A deep rasp of sound echoed through the room and the jelly rippled. Then a vast pseudopod abruptly reached out toward Balcescu and engulfed him. I must have cried out, because Chinh-Herrera turned to me and said, "Nah, don't worry. He was right again, damn him. Look, it understood!"

The pseudopod was lifting him as gently as a mother with her child. Balcescu's point of view rose up, up, up until he was at the top of the gently swirling jelly, up near the roof of the intestinal, cathedral-sized room. He stepped onto a platform that emerged from the bumps and swirls of the wall, then held up his com wand again. A single sound, loud and rough as a tree pulling up its roots as it fell, then Balcescu and the rest of us waited.

Nothing happened.

"Maybe I'm being too polite," he said. Balcescu still sounded like he was on a day-hike in the hills. Even I had to admire him—me, who'd seen him drunk and feeling sorry for himself. I can't tell you how annoying that was.

He lifted the com wand and thumbed it again and another wash of sound rolled out, this one harsher and more abrupt. We waited.

The jelly thing abruptly shrank away beneath him like water down a drain. Then the lights faded all though the vast room. Everything was black. A moment later, Balcescu's helmet light flicked on, but the view now was almost all shadows, the chamber's far walls a distant, ghostly backdrop.

"Mission accomplished, Captain Watanabe," he said. "It's turned off."

The bridge erupted in cheers, some of them almost hysterical. I still didn't really understand what I'd just seen, or why I was even there, but when Ping appeared a few moments later with something that looked as near as damnit to champagne, I took a glass. God knows everyone else was having some, even the captain.

I was taking my second sip when I noticed someone standing over me.

"I've got something for you, Rahul," said Doc Swainsea. She showed me her ring with its glowing spot. I let her touch mine so the data could transfer. "He asked me to make sure you got it."

"He?" I asked, but I knew who she meant. It was just something to say as I watched her walk away and out of the conference room. She was the only one beside me who didn't seem happy, and I wasn't sure I understood my own reasons.

I stayed on the bridge a little while, but I wanted to see what he'd left for me. Anyway, I never liked champagne much. Any alcohol, in fact. Too many people over the years have thought it was funny to try to get the little guy drunk, and I used to be stubborn and stupid enough to try to prove them wrong.

"Hello, Mr. Jatt. I'm sorry I didn't get to say goodbye properly, but the last few days have been a bit of a whirlwind, getting ready for this thing we're trying. But I did want to say goodbye. I'm glad I got a chance to know you, even a little bit. I intend no joke, by the way."

Balcescu was wearing an exosuit. The message looked like it had been recorded just before he left, which explained why he was talking like he wasn't coming back.

"But I owed you of all people an explanation, because you were the one that gave me the idea. I guess you must know by now whether I was right or not."

Like you ever really doubted it, you arrogant s.o.b., I thought. But then I wondered, hang on, if he was so sure of himself, why did he leave me this message?

"I should have suspected something right away—or at least as soon as I translated the message," he went on. The Balcescu of half a day ago was putting on his exosuit gloves. "I mean, really—'The Outward-Reaching Murder Army will spit upon the stars that give you life'? 'Only black ash will *show that you ever lived.' A bit over the top, isn't it? But I didn't see it. I took it at face value.*

"Then you asked what else I could figure out about the aliens. I began to wonder. As you said, we knew what they'd said—but not why. Were they just roving the universe like Mongol horsemen, conquering and slaughtering? But why? What was the plan? Why leave a ship with immensely superior firepower to defend a Visser ring when they could have wiped out every ship in the vicinity in minutes? But it was the way they talked that really puzzled me. Bloody melodrama, that's what it was. It was like something out of one of those ancient movies you told me you like so much..."

"Those aren't the kind of movies I like," I told the recording. "Not that John Wayne crap—well, except for 'Stagecoach'... and maybe 'The Quiet Man'. I like *characters*."

"...but I still couldn't figure out what was making me itch. Then Diane...Dr. Swainsea...came in with her wide-spectrum audio analysis of the sounds that we hadn't noticed at first, the ones that were largely out of our hearing range. Think about it. Behind those overly dramatic words they were pumping out a huge range of sounds—higher, lower, faster, slower— not exactly synchronized to the words, but emphasizing them, heightening the effect. What does that sound like?"

It hit me like a blow. "A soundtrack," I whispered. "Like a movie."

"Right," the recording said. *"A score—as in an opera. As in Don Giovanni."* The recorded Balcescu had closed all his seals and sat calmly, as if we were in the same room at the same time, having an ordinary conversation. *"So I kept thinking, Mr. Jatt—why would someone go to such lengths, write an entire space opera, so to speak, just to kill innocent people? I couldn't wrap my head around it. But then I started thinking that maybe they didn't know they were killing anyone? But how could that be?"* He smiled that infuriating smile of

his. *"Because maybe they didn't think there was anyone left to kill. Remember, this thing came to us through the Rainwater Hub, the most compromised wormhole in known space. Who's to say they even came from our galaxy? Remember, I only found traces of their languages in some of the very oldest civilizations we know out near the galactic rim. Maybe the originals that spoke those languages are long gone—at least in physical form."*

I had no idea what he was talking about, and I was about to run the recording back when he picked his helmet up off the clean pad where it had been sitting. The mirrored visor made a brief infinity loop with the recording wall screen—a million helmets strobed. *"Look, if you saw this by itself, up close, you would assume someone was in it, right?"* He slid the visor up to show the empty interior. *"My guess is, these people— let's call them the Company, like an opera company—have left their physical forms behind long ago. They might even be dead and gone, but that's another libretto."* Again, that irritating grin. *"But what they haven't done is given up art. Just as our operas often imitate the past in which they were written, the Company's art mimics the time when they had bodies. Entire constructs that perform acts of aggression and destruction and who knows what else? Programmed, operating in empty space at the edge of a distant galaxy, for the nostalgic pleasure of bodiless alien intelligences. Of course they would violently destroy what they come into contact with—because they're pretending to be the kind of ancient savages that would do that. But that's why I'm guessing that the Company are no longer wearing bodies— they assumed that anything they came in contact with would be more of their own lifeless constructs, part of this art form of theirs that we can't hope to understand...yet.*

"So that's my idea, and in an hour or so we'll find out if it's true. I've convinced the captain it's worth a try, and she's

brought in the other Confederation ships, so at the very least I will be the center of a fairly expensive little drama of my own." Balcescu stood then, his helmet under his arm as though he were some kind of antique cavalier. *"Sorry I couldn't explain this to you in person, but as I said, it's been a busy last 48 hours or so, putting together my hypothesis and then getting ready to test it."* He turned toward the door. *"But I did want to thank you, Mr. Jatt. You opened my eyes in a couple of ways, and that doesn't happen very often."*

I'll bet it doesn't, I thought, but suddenly I wished I'd told him my first name.

"And now one of two things are going to happen," the recorded Balcescu said. *"Either I'm wrong somehow—about the purpose of that ship, or about how realistic and thorough its defenses are, in which case by the time you see this I'll have been delatticed, as Diane puts it. Or, I'll be right, and I'll be able to use the little bit of Company language I've put together, along with some useful algorithms from Dr. Swainsea, to override the programming and cancel the show, as it were."* He moved to the door of his cabin, so that he stood just at edge of the recorded picture. *"And if I succeed with that, then I'm going to start looking for some kind of emergency return pod. You see, the Confederation are welcome to the ship itself. I don't give a damn about how it works or how far it came to get here or anything of the things they want to know. I just want to go where the show is happening—where the opera, or religious passion play, or children's game, or whatever this thing represents, is really going on. I'm hoping that the Company has some kind of recoverable module—like a ship's black box—and that it will return to their space, wherever that might be. I intend to be on it.*

"How could I miss that chance? A whole new culture, language, and even more importantly, a whole new art form! Nine muses aren't going to be enough anymore, Mr. Jatt. So that's why I made this recording, my friend. Either way, I wanted

to say thank you—and goodbye." And with that the recorded Balcescu held out his com wand and the recording went black.

Maybe he hadn't guessed how soon I'd watch the recording—maybe he was still on the alien ship. I commed the captain's cabin but she was on the observation deck with everyone else, celebrating. I rushed up, but before I could say a thing to Captain Watanabe or any of the other officers I spotted Dr. Swainsea leaning against the biggest view-portal looking out at the jellyfish ship, so strange, so large, so distant.

"Doc...Doc...!" I called as I ran up.

"I know, Rahul," she said without turning. "Look—there it goes." She pointed. I thought I could see a dim streak of light moving away from the alien ship—but not toward the Visser ring, I was surprised to see. "God only knows what kind of path those things travel," she said. "Well, Stefan will find out soon enough."

"You knew what he was going to do?"

"Of course. I helped him." She looked at me. "Oh, Rahul, what else was I going to do? Beg him to stay? We had...maybe the beginning of something. How could that compete against a Big Idea, especially for a man who lived for big ideas? No, I couldn't have asked him and he couldn't have agreed—we both would have hated ourselves. You'll understand someday."

I understand now, I wanted to say, but everyone needs to tell their own story their own way. You don't have to be six feet tall to know that. "It was just..." I shook my head. "At first I didn't like him. But then, I kind of thought he and I might be... we might..."

"It might have been the beginning of a beautiful friendship?" she asked. Something in my expression must have amused her, because she laughed. "You don't think you're the only one who watches old pictures, do you?"

"I guess not." I frowned. "I think Balcescu's crazy, anyway. We've already got music and art and Fred Astaire and

Katharine Hepburn and Howard Hawks—do we even need a tenth muse?"

"I need a drink," she said. "Then maybe I'll feel a little bit less like Ingrid Bergman."

We walked across the observation deck, threading our way through the happy crew members, many of whom were already well into the champagne. She still looked sad, so I reached up and took Doc Swainsea's hand...Diana's hand. Lose a friend, make a friend. Sometimes life does imitate art, I guess.

"Well," I told her—my best Bogart—"whatever else happens, we'll always have Rainwater Hub."

THE LAMENTABLY COMICAL TRAGEDY (OR THE LAUGHABLY TRAGIC COMEDY) OF LIXAL LAQAVEE

I AM NOT A MAGICIAN," Lixal Laqavee announced to the shopkeeper who had come forward at the ringing of the bell upon the counter, "but I play one in a traveling show."

"Then you have come to precisely the right place, sir," the man said, smiling and nodding. "Twitterel's Emporium is known throughout the length of Almery for its unrivaled selection of effects, marvels, and confidence enhancers."

"And are you Twitterel?" Lixal inquired. "The one whose name is above the door of this establishment?"

"I have that honor," said the small, bewhiskered man and brushed a fleck of dust from his velvet robe. "But let us not waste time on such trivia as my name. How may I serve you, sir? Flash-dust, perhaps? It gives the impression of a great outrush of thaumaturgical energies while posing no great danger to its employer." Twitterel reached into a ceramic jar on the scarred counterop and produced a handful of silvery dust, which he threw to the floor with a flick of his wrist. It burst with a percussive crack and produced a voluminous puff of white smoke. The shopkeeper then fanned vigorously with his hand until he and Lixal were face to face again. "As you see, it also provides ample distraction for a well-conceived disappearance or sleight-of-hand effect."

Lixal nodded thoughtfully. "Yes, I think a portion or two of flash-dust might serve admirably, although by no means will it fulfill all my needs."

"Ah!" Twitterel smiled, showing fewer teeth than one might expect even in a man his age. "A gentleman who wishes his impostures to be both believable and exciting. May I say, sir, that your audience will thank you for your care. Perhaps this length of rope, which when properly exhibited seems to have the living qualities of a serpent? Or this Benaraxian Cabinet, whose interior can comfortably contain a shapely female assistant—the type whose curvaceous form, and your menacing of same with these cleverly constructed sabers, will particularly stimulate your audience..."

"No, no," said Lixal, waving his hand. "You have incorrectly conceived my needs. I do not wish to employ mere trickery, especially of the expensive variety embodied in this monstrous, mirrored sarcophagus." He flicked a finger at the lacquered surface of the Benaraxian Cabinet. "The performing troop with which I ply my trade is a small one, accustomed to the back roads of Almery, and we have but one wagon to carry all our goods. Also, and far more importantly, in the vicinities we frequent the distinction between performing the *role* of magician and *being* a magician is often a blurry one."

The shopkeeper Twitterel paused. He reached up and plucked out a bit of his breakfast that had lodged in his beard (or at least Lixal hoped it was from a meal no less recent.) The old man seemed oddly disturbed by his customer's words. "I am not sure I grasp the sum of your meaning, sir," Twitterel said. "Elucidate, please, so that I may better serve your needs?"

Lixal frowned. "You force me to greater crudity than I would prefer. However, I will do my best to make plain my desire." He cleared his throat.

"I travel with a troop of performers, providing entertainment and instruction, and sometimes even hope to those who previously found that quality in short supply. Not all perceive us in this wise—in fact, some ungenerous souls have suggested that I and my associates are little better than venal tricksters, a claim I reject vigorously.

"In the course of our educational performances we offer to our auditors certain medicines and tonics of a curative nature. Despite the slurs of the uncomprehending, our record of cure is bettered by no other similar organization, and even compares favorably with the more common medicinal advice offered by the sort of physic to which our rustic audiences generally have access. Do you grasp my meaning?"

"You sell dubious cures to the peasantry."

"In a nutshell, good shopkeeper, in a nutshell, although I might take exception to the word 'dubious'. By certain measures life itself is dubious. However, generally speaking, your perception is admirable. Now, because my part in this organization is a portrayal of magicianship, at times I am approached by members of the buying public separately from the rest of the cast, customers who believe the illusions they have seen are real. Many of them wish only to know whether the silver coin I produced had truly been lodged in their ear in the first place, and if so should it not then belong to them." Lixal shook his head ruefully. "Others, though, have requests for magical assistance of a more precise nature, usually concering some petty problem in their lives—a failure of certain human apparatus of a privy nature being the most common. Then there are those who would like to see a family member hastened to peace so that the division of his or her possessions might be practiced sooner rather than later." Lixal held up his finger. "These commissions I would not take, I hasten to assure you, even had I the means, and not only because of my naturally ethical composition. Our rural folk tend to carry both grudges and sharp hand tools, so I have no urge to excite malice." He cleared his throat. "Other supplicants have desired lost objects found, unpleasant creatures or relatives confined, and so on—in short, a galaxy of requests, most of which I am unable to fulfill, and so a healthy sum remains dispersed in the pockets of the rustic population instead of concentrated in my own where it might form the foundation of a burgeoning fortune." Lixal shook his head sadly. "I have come to tire of this woefully imbalanced state of affairs. So I come to you, good shopkeeper."

Twitterel looked back at Lixal with more consternation than the casual observer might have expected. "I still do not grasp with certainty your desires, sir," the old man said nervously. "Perhaps you would be better off visiting the shop of my good friend and colleague Dekionas Kroon a scant four leagues away in the pleasant hamlet of Blixingby Crown Gate—he also specializes in fine acoutrements for the performing of magic to discerning audiences..."

"You tease me, sir," said Lixal sternly. "You must have grasped by now that I am not interested in the *accoutrements* of the magical arts, not in elaborate stage artifices or even the potware and piping of alchemy or other scholarly but unsatisfying pursuits. I wish to buy actual *spells*. There—I can make it no clearer. Just a few, selected for one like myself who has no magical training—although, it must be said, I do have a wonderful, firm voice that any magician might envy, and a certain physical presence concomitant with a true thaumaturge, as you must have noticed yourself." Lixal Laqavee stroked his full brown beard slowly, as if comparing its lushness to the sparse clump of yellowed whiskers which decorated the shopkeeper's receding chin.

"Why would I, a mere merchant, have such things?" Twitterel questioned in what was almost a squeak. "And why, even if I did possess such objects of powerful wisdom, would I share them with someone whose only claim to wizardly dessert is a velvet robe and an admittedly handsome beard? Sooner would I put a flaming brand into the hands of a child residing in a house made of twigs and dry leaves!"

"You misunderstand me again, good Twitterel," Lixal replied. "You protest that you are a mere merchant, and yet unless I much mistake things, the name etched above your door does not conform to your true identity. In other words, I believe you are in fact not 'Twitterel' at all, but rather Eliastre of Octorus, who was once reknowned in the most powerful circles as 'The Scarlet Sorceror'—a pleasantly dramatic name, by the way, that I would quickly adopt for my own performances were it not that I make a better appearance in dark colors such as blacks and moody, late-evening blues." Lixal smiled. "You see, it happens that by mere chance I studied your career while honing my impersonation of someone in your line of endeavor. That is also how I recognized you when I saw you drinking in the tavern up the road yesterday and began to conceive of my current plan. What a piece of luck!"

"I...I do not understand." Twitterel, or Eliastre, if that was indeed his name, retreated a little farther from the countertop behind which he stood. "Why would such an unlikely set of affairs mean luck for you?"

"Step back in this direction, please. Do not think to escape me," Lixal said. "And neither should you attempt to bluff me with the powers you once so famously owned. I know full well that after you failed in an attempt to seize leadership among your fellow magicians and wizards, the Council of Thaumaturgic Practitioners removed said powers and placed you under a ban of trying to regain them or *in any other way dabbling in the profession of wizardry*, under pain of humiliating, excruciating and lingering death. Please understand that I will happily inform the Council of your whereabouts and your current occupation if you resist me. I am inclined to believe your current profession, peddling alembics and flash-dust, might well fall within the scope of their ban."

Twitterel seemed to have aged twenty years—decades he could ill-afford to add to his tally—in a matter of moments. "I could find no other way to make a living," he admitted sadly. "It is the only craft I know. The Council did not take that into account. Better they should have executed me outright than condemn me to starve. In any case, I wished only to reform certain insufficiencies of the transubstantive oversight process—what was once a mere prophylactic has become a hideous, grinding bureaucracy..."

Lixal held up his hand. "Spare me. I care not for the details of your rebellion but only for what you will do next—namely, provide me with several easily-learned spells that will allow me to supplement my performing income by rendering assistance to those pastorals who seek my aid. I am not a greedy man—I do not wish to raise the dead or render gold from dry leaves and river mud. Rather I ask only a few simple nostrums that will put me in good odor with the country-folk—perhaps a charm for the locating of lost livestock..." He considered. "And surely there is some minor malediction which would allow the sending of a plague of boils to unpleasant neighbors. Such a thing has been requested of me many times but heretofore I had no means of answering the call."

Eliastre, or Twitterel as was, rubbed his hands together in what looked like genuine unease. "But even such minor spells can be dangerous when improperly used—not to mention expensive!"

"Never fear," said Lixal, with a certain air of *noblesse oblige*. "When I have begun to earn the money I so richly deserve by employing these spells, I will most certainly return and pay you their full worth."

"So," the shopkeeper said bitterly. "You would extort me *and* rob me."

"Not at all." Lixal shook his head. "But lest such an ill-considered notion set you scheming to punish me somehow for merely trying to better my situation in this uncertain life, let me show you the warding bracelet on my wrist, an object of true power." He flourished the twist of copper he wore around his arm, which indeed seemed to have a glow greater than the ordinary reflection of metal. It had been given to Lixal by a young lady of the troop during a time of pleasurable intimacy— a charm that she swore would protect him from premature death, inherited by her from her aunt at the time of that elderly lady's quite timely demise. "Oh, by the by," Lixal continued, made uneasy by the speculative way Eliastre was examining his wrist jewelry, "if in your misdirected bitterness you decide that some knowledge or stratagem of yours could overcome the efficacy of this ornament, I would like you to be aware that the bracelet is not my only protection. Should anything untoward happen to me an associate of mine unknown to you will immediately dispatch to the Council of Thaumaturgic Practitioners a letter I have prepared, detailing both your recent crimes and your exact location. Remember that as I choose my spells and you guide me in their recommended usages."

The old man stared at him for a long time with an expression on his face that it would have been difficult to call either friendly or forgiving. "Ah, well," Eliastre said at last. "My hands appear tied, as it were, and the longer I resist the more the binding rope shall chafe me. Let us proceed."

When he had completed the transaction with the ex-wizard to his satisfaction, Lixal took the manuscript pages of the new spells and bade Eliastre goodbye.

"By the by, I frown on the word 'extortion'," Lixal called back to the old man, who was still glaring at him from the doorway of the shop. "Especially when I have given you my word of honor that I will come back at a time when my pockets are full and repay you at market rate. The expression on your face suggests that you doubt this promise, or else that you are otherwise unsatisfied with our exchange, which to me seems to have been more than fair. In either case, I am displeased. Until that cheerful day when we meet again, I suggest you cultivate an attitude of greater humility."

Lixal made his way back out of the city of Catechumia toward the forested outskirts where his traveling theatrical company had made its camp. He wished he had been able to force the old man to recite the spells himself, as proof that none of them had been primed like a springe trap to rebound painfully or even fatally on its user, but since Eliastre had been forcibly curtailed from using magic by the Council of Thaumaturgic Practitioners Lixal knew there would have been little point: no flaws would have been exposed because the spells themselves would not have worked. He would have to trust to the curbing effect of his threat to have a colleague notify the Council if anything hurtful should happen to Lixal. The fact that this colleague was an invention, created on the spur of the moment—Lixal had long practice in improvisation—would be unknown to Eliastre, and therefore no less effective an intimidation than an actual confederate would have been.

Most of the rest of his fellow players were still in town, but Ferlash, a squat, ill-favored man wearing the cassock of a priest of the Church of the Approaching Horizon was toasting a heel of bread at the campfire. He looked up at Lixal's approach.

"Ho!" he called sourly. "You look cheerful. Did you bring something to eat? Something which, by sharing it with a deserving priest, you could store up goodwill in the afterlife? I do not doubt your soul's post-horizontal standing has need of a little improvement."

Lixal shook his head in irritation. "As everyone in our company knows, Ferlash, you have not been a celebrant in good standing of your order since they expelled you years ago for egregious impregnation of congregants. Thus, I suggest you leave off discussion of my own particular afterlife. I would no more listen to your speculations about the health of my soul than I would accept similar advice from the piece of bread you are toasting."

"You are a testy young man," Ferlash said, "and too pleased with yourself by half. In fact, I must say that you seem even more self-satisfied than usual today."

"If I am, it is a condition well-earned. I have made no small contribution today to my own well-being and, indirectly, yours as well, since the spread of my fame as a thaumaturge will bolster the reputation of our entire troop."

Ferlash scowled. Along with Lixal and another man who called himself Kwerion the Apothecary, the once-priest acted the part of authority figure for the troop, explaining matters of religion and its accommodations with commerce to the rural audiences. "Your thaumaturgic credentials are even more tenuous than mine as a priest," he now told Lixal, "since I at least once legitimately wore the sacred mantle. What claim to genuine wizardship have you?"

"All the claim in the world, as of today." And, because he was indeed pleased with himself, he went on to tell Ferlash what he had done. "So here you see the fruits of my intellect and ambition," he finished, waving the sheaf of spells. "Once I have conned these, I shall be a form of magician in truth and thereafter I will rapidly better myself."

Ferlash nodded his head slowly. "I see that you have indeed done well today, Lixal Laqavee, and I apologize for lumping you in with the rest of us poor posers and counterfeits. Since you are soon to become such an accomplished wonder-worker, I suppose you will no longer have any use for that bracelet you wear, the one that is such a fine talisman against premature death? There are times during our travels when the agnosticism of our audiences slips from doubt of my sincerity into actual bad temper—especially among those for whom the prayers and holy artifacts I sold to them did not work as effectively as they had hoped. I would value such a protection around my own wrist against those more strenuous gainsayers of my methods."

Lixal drew back in irritation. "Nothing like that shall happen, Ferlash. The bracelet is mine and mine alone, given to me by a woman who loved me dearly, even though she chose security over romance and married that toadlike proprietor of a livery stable last year. The idea that you would be rewarded for nothing but beggary with such a puissant token is laughable." He sniffed. "I go now to learn my spells. When next you see me, I shall be even less a person with whom you might wish to trifle."

The thaumaturge-to-be left Ferlash sitting by the fire, staring after him with envy and dissatisfaction.

Lixal Laqavee had chosen the incantations carefully, because without the decades of conscientious practice which most wizards devoted to their craft—a routine far too much like hard work to attract Lixal, who knew there were many more amusing uses for his spare time—it was entirely possible to misspeak an incantation or muddle a gesture and find oneself in an extremely perilous situation, taslismanic bracelet or no. Also, due to his lack of experience, it was doubtful that Lixal

Laqavee would be able to employ more than one spell at a time, and of course after each employment he would need to learn the spell anew before its next usage. Thus, Lixal had demanded only four spells of Twitterel-who-was-in-truth-Eliastre, a selection that he believed would prove both versatile and easy to manage.

The first was the Rhinocratic Oath, which allowed its perpetrator to create amusing or horrifying changes to the nose of anyone he designated, and then to undo those changes again if he so desired. The second, the Cantrip of Notional Belittlement, allowed its wielder to make any idea or sight seem smaller or less important to one or more people, the length of the effect varying with the amount of people ensorceled. The third was a charm of romance named Dormousion's Pseudo-Philtre, which tended to create lust even when lust would normally not have existed or exacerbate it in even its most tenuous manifestations until the designated recipient of the pseudo-philtre would take ridiculous risks to scratch the amatory itch.

Last, most difficult to memorize, but also undoubtedly the most powerful of all the spells he had chosen, was the Thunderous Exhalation of Banishment, a weapon which would instantly move an unwanted personage or creature to the farthest end of the earth from the point at which the spell was employed, and then keep that individual there perpetually. An enraged husband or hungry leucomorph so banished anywhere in Almery would instantaneously be flung to the farthest ends of the unknown regions of ice on the far side of the world, and be held in that vicinity in perpetuity as long as he lived.

This spell drew such great reserves of strength from its user that it was practical only for select occasions, but since those occasions would likely be of the life-or-death variety, Lixal did not doubt it had been a wise and valuable choice. In fact, his selection of the Thunderous Exhalation had particularly seemed to nettle old Eliastre, so that the shopkeeper muttered the entire time he transcribed it, which only convinced Lixal he had done well in his selection.

And indeed, over the following months Lixal and his newfound thaumaturgical skills did indeed prosper. He enlivened countless local feuds with the sudden provision and subsequent recusal of nasal grotesqueries, and created a giant efflorescence so like a starfish on the end of one old woman's nose that she completely rewrote her will in favor of a nephew she had not previously favored, who happily passed on a percentage to Lixal, who then rewarded the old woman's good sense by returning her proboscis to its natural (if only slightly less unlovely) state. On separate occasions he used the Exhalation to banish three mad dogs, one dauntingly large and aggressive tree-weasel, and two husbands and a father who had all taken violent issue with Lixal's use of the pseudo-philtre on their wives and daughters, respectively. (Two wives and two daughters, because one of the cuckolded husbands also had a comely daughter slightly past the age of consent. Lixal had made sure of this last—he was scrupulous that his amatory coercions should be used only on adults, another of his many traits that he felt was deserving of greater admiration than it received.) And the belittling cantrip had also been employed in several cases where his other methods could not prevail, enabling Lixal to find escape and even reward when he might otherwise fail in one or both areas. He began to develop no small reputation in the environs through which his troop traveled.

Thus, one evening, in a town called Saepia, a committee of local grandees led by Saepia's aldermayor approached Lixal at the conclusion of the troop's nightly show with a request for his assistance. He invited them to drink a glass of stock wine with him and discuss their needs. After a string of successes in surrounding towns Lixal felt secure in what he had to offer, and thus in what he was empowered to charge.

"We could not help admiring your demonstrations tonight," the aldermayor opened, clutching his many-pointed ceremonial wool hat in his hands in the submissive manner of a tardy schoolboy. "Nor could we help to be impressed by the arguments of your colleagues, Kwerion and Reverend Ferlash, as to the value to a town like ours of being forward-thinking in regard to the benefits of your advanced knowledge."

"By the way, speaking of such aids to fortune, is it true that those apothecarical potions will allow me to satisfy my wife?" asked one of the grandees shyly. "If so, I would like to buy some from your colleague Kwerion. My lady has a powerful appetite, if you know what I mean, and I often despair of being able to keep her from looking elsewhere for sustenance."

"Oh, Kwerion's potions could no doubt help," Lixal assured him. "But if you will send your wife to me to be examined, as a personal favor I will give her something to curb those hungers— and I will not charge you a single terce! Is that all you good folk wished, then?" he asked as the local grandee stammered his thanks.

"In fact, there is another matter," said the aldermayor. "Small and insignificant to the great and powerful Lixal Laqavee, but large and ruinous to such as ourselves, and to the resources of our small backwater. A deodand has taken up residence in the local cuttlestone quarry, and we can no longer work the crystal beds there, which had long been source of the greatest part of our revenue. To add to the indignity, not only does his presence inhibit the quarry's workings but also he sallies forth at intervals to steal our town's babies from their cribs or seize unwary citizens walking home by night. He then takes these unfortunates back to his cavern and devours them. We have sent several doughty hunters after him and he has defeated and digested them all. It has cast a pall over even the smallest activities in Saepia's usually vibrant civic life."

"And you would like me to rid you of this vile creature?" said Lixal, thinking cheerfully of the Thunderous Exhalation of Banishment. "Easily done, but owing to the danger of the work, even to a trained and experienced practitioner of the mystical arts such as myself, the price will not be insignificant." And he quoted them an amount in gold that made the grandees blanch and the aldermayor fretfully detach one of the wool horns from his ceremonial hat.

After a great deal of bargaining they settled on a slightly lower amount, although it was still as much as Lixal would have expected to make over the next half-year in the ordinary course of things. He pleaded weariness that evening, wanting a chance to study and memorize the banishing spell, then bade them goodnight with a promise to meet them in the morning and solve their problem.

The next day, after a leisurely breakfast with the grandee's wife, whose curative visit had run long, Lixal made his way from his wagon in the troop's camp—he now had one all to himself— to the aldermayor's house, a humble but well-constructed building in the domelike local style. That gentleman stood waiting in the road with an even larger swarm of townsfolk than had accompanied him the previous night. Lixal greeted them with casual nonchalance and allowed himself to be led up the hill toward the cuttlestone quarry behind the town.

He was left at the edge of it, without guides, but with directions toward the deodand's cave. Lixal made his way across the floor of the silent quarry, noting with interest the tools dropped as though their users had simply run away and never returned, which had likely been the case. Dispersed among these discarded tools were the bones of both animals and people, most of which had been snapped in half so that their marrow could be accessed. The quarry itself was hung with early morning mist that mostly blocked the sun and made it hard for Lixal to see what was around him, which might have made a less confident man nervous, but he knew it took only a heartbeat to shout the single, percussive syllable which enacted the Thunderous Oath. After all, had he not been surprised by that cuckold back in

Taudis, so that he had only begun to speak the word as the ax was already swinging at his head? And yet was not he, Lixal, still here, while the ax-wielder was doubtless shivering miserably in the snows of uttermost Ultramondia, wishing he had thought twice before assaulting the Dire Mage Laqavee?

"Hello!" he called now, tiring of the walk. "Is anyone here? For I am a lost traveler, plump and out of shape, wandering helplessly in your abandoned quarry."

As he expected, a dark form came toward him out of the mists, in no great hurry, lured by the promise of such an easy meal. The deodand, in the manner of its kind, looked much like a man except for the flat, sooty black of its skin and the bright gleam of its claws and fangs. It stopped now to inspect him through slitted, bile-yellow eyes.

"You exaggerate your own plumpness, traveler," it said disapprovingly. "Except for that moderate roll of fat around your middle I would not call you plump at all."

"Your eyes are as faulty as they are inhumanly strange," cried Lixal, nettled. "There is no such roll of fat. I described myself thusly merely to lure you out so that I might dispose of you without wasting my entire morning in search."

The deodand looked at him curiously. "Are you a warrior, then? I confess you do not resemble it. In fact, you have the slack, well-fed look of a merchant. Do you plan to end my reign of terror here in Saepia by offering me better employment elsewhere? I confess that I feel an urge to explore other places and to eat newer, more exotic people."

Lixal laughed in scorn. "Do not be impertinent. I am no simple merchant, but Lixal Laqavee, the Dire Mage in Late-Evening Blue. If you do not know my name already you will have ample time to reflect on it with rue in the cold place to which I will send you."

The deodand moved closer, stopping only when Lixal raised a hand in warning. "Strange. I have never heard of such a magician as yourself, and other than that small talisman on your wrist I see no evidence of power about you. If I wrong you please forgive me, but you do not strike me as much of a wizard at all. Could you be mistaken?"

"Mistaken? Can you mistake *this*?" His irritation now become something closer to blind rage, Lixal waved his hand and uttered the Thunderous Exhalation of Banishment in his loudest and most impressive voice. The sky rumbled as if in terror at the great forces employed and a flash of light surrounded the deodand as though lightning had sprung out of the creature's carbon-colored pores. But the next instant, instead of shrinking into utter vanishment like a man falling down an endless well, as all the previous men and beasts struck with the Exhalation had done, the deodand suddenly came sliding toward Lixal as rapidly as if the foul creature were a canal boat dragged by a magically superanimated donkey. Lixal had time only to throw his hands in front of his face and give out a brief squeak of terror, then the deodand smacked to a sudden halt a scant two paces away from him as though the creature had run into a soft but inflexible and unseen wall.

Lixal looked between his fingers at the deodand, whose hideous aspect was not improved a whit by close proximity. The deodand looked back at him, an expression of bemusement on its cruel, inhuman features.

"A strange kind of banishment," it said, taking a step back. A moment later it leaped at Lixal, fangs bared. Whatever had prevented it from reaching him before stopped it this time as well: the deodand bounced harmlessly back from him. "Hmmm," the creature said. "Your spell seems to have worked in reverse of the way you intended it, drawing me toward you instead of exiling me." The deodand turned and tried to walk away but could not get more than a step before it was again brought up short. "I am held like a leashed moon circling a planet, unable to move away from you," it said in frustration.

"But that talisman on your wrist seems to prevent me reaching you and completing my earlier intention, namely, to destroy you and eat you." It frowned, hiding its terrifying pointed teeth behind a pouting lower lip. "I am not happy with this state of affairs, magician. Release me and I will go my way without molesting you further. You have my word."

Lixal stared at the creature, who was so close he could smell its sour, feral scent, the odor of bones and rotting flesh that hovered in its proximity like the morning fogs that hung over the quarry. "I...I cannot," he said at last. "I have not the capability to undo the spell."

The deodand made a noise of disgust. "As a both a wizard and deodand-slayer, then, you are close to an utter failure. What are we to do now?" A look of calculation entered its yellow eyes. "If you cannot release me in the conventional way, you must consider removing your bracelet and letting me kill you. That way at least one of us will live his life out the way the spirits of the void intended."

"On the contrary!" said Lixal, piqued. "Why would I permit you to kill me? You may just as easily kill yourself—I imagine those sharp claws will work as efficaciously on your own jugular as mine. Then I can go on with my own life, which has much more to recommend it than your skulking, marrow-guzzling, baby-stealing existence."

"Clearly we will not easily find agreement on this," said the deodand. "A thought occurs to me. Have you offended another wizard lately?"

Lixal thought immediately of Eliastre and the impression of dissatisfaction he had displayed at their parting, but was unwilling to broach the subject to the deodand after such a short acquaintance. "Anything is possible in the rarefied yet contentious circles in which I travel. Why do you ask?"

"Because if so, it is likely that even death will not release us. If this misfiring of your incantation is the result of thaumaturgical malice, it may well be designed so that even if one of us dies, the other's fortunes will not improve. For instance, I am compelled to be in your vicinity. If you die and become motionless bones, it is quite logical that I will be compelled to remain in the spot where you fell. Similarly, should you achieve the unlikely result of killing *me*, the corpse would probably still adhere to your person no matter where you traveled. The material shells of my tribe decay loathsomely but extremely slowly. In short, you would spend the rest of your life dragging my rotting corpse behind you."

Lixal closed his eyes in disgust and dismay. "Eliastre!" he said, and it was a bitter curse upon his tongue. "I know this is his hand at work. He has treated me shamefully with this trick and I will have revenge on him, somehow!"

The deodand stared at him. "What name is this?"

"It is the name of one we apparently must visit," Lixal said. "That is our only hope to escape our unpleasantly twinned fate. Come with me." He grimaced sadly. "I think we must steer clear of Saepia as we leave these environs. The townspeople now will have several reasons not to love me, and I will tell you honestly that they never cared much for you."

Like two climbers bound by a rope, Lixal and the deodand made their way through the forest and back to the camp outside town where the traveling troop was still ensconced. The players would have been at worst indifferent to the arrival of Lixal in other circumstances, but his companion filled the whole camp with unhappiness.

"Do not move," shouted the apothecary Kwerion. "A terrible beast pursues you! Throw yourself down on the ground and we will do our best to slay it!"

"Please offer the creature no harm," said Lixal. "Otherwise, and in the doubtful circumstance that you destroy it, I will be condemned to drag its stinking, putrefying corpse around with me for the rest of my natural days beneath our dying sun."

When Lixal had explained what had befallen, the rest of the troop was much amazed. "You must find a sorceror of great power to help you," said Kwerion.

"Or a sympathetic god," suggested Ferlash, who was having trouble keeping amusement off his face.

"Surely someone as clever as yourself will find a solution," said a young woman named Minka, who had replaced the young woman who had given Lixal the bracelet in the role of the troop's primary educational dancer. Minka had of late expressed a certain warmness toward Lixal, and though she was clearly disappointed by this latest turn of events, she seemed determined to at least keep her options open. "Then you will find your way back to us."

"In any case," Kwerion said authoritatively, "you must embark on your quest for salvation immediately!"

"But I think I should prefer to remain with you—the troop is headed back toward Catechumia soon," Lixal said. "I would appreciate the security of company. I will find some way to incorporate the deodand into our presentation. It will be a sensation! What other troop has ever boasted such a thing?"

"No other troop has ever performed while infected with the Yellow Death, either," said Ferlash. "Novelty alone is not enough to promote attendance, especially when it is the novelty of horrid mortal danger, and is accompanied by such a dreadfully noisome and pervasive odor of decomposing flesh."

The rest, even Minka, seemed to agree with the false priest's objections, and despite Lixal's arguments and pleading he and the deodand were at last forced to set off on their own toward distant Catechumia with nothing more in the way of possessions than what they could carry, since the troop also saw fit to withdraw their gift to Lixal of a private wagon, as being inappropriate for one no longer appearing in their nightly dissemination of knowledge to the deserving public.

Lixal Laqavee's first night in the wilderness was an uncomfortable one, and the idea that he was sleeping next to an inhuman creature who would happily murder him if it could did not make Lixal's slumbers any easier. At last, in the cold hours before dawn, he sat up.

The deodand, which did not seem to have even tried to sleep, was visible only as a pair of gleaming eyes in the darkness. "You awaken early. Have you reconsidered letting me take your life and now find yourself eager to begin your adventurous journey into That Which Lies Beyond?"

"Unequivocally, no." Lixal built the fire back up, blowing until it filled the forest dell with reddish light, although the deodand itself was still scarcely more than a shadow. He had no particular urge to converse with the ghastly thing, but neither did he want to sit beside it in silence until sunrise. At last, Lixal reached into the rucksack that contained most of his remaining possessions and pulled out a box which unfolded into a gaming board of polished wood covered with small holes. He then shook a handful of nail-shaped ivory spikes from a bag that had been inside the box and began to place them in holes along the outer edge of the board.

"What is that?" asked the deodand. "An altar to your god? Some kind of religious ritual?"

"No, far more important than that," Lixal said. "Have you ever played King's Compass?"

The glowing eyes blinked slowly—once, twice, three times. "Played King's Compass? What do these words mean?"

"It is a contest—a game. In my childhood home in the Misty Isles we play it for amusement, or sometimes as a test of skill. At the latter times money is wagered. Would you like to learn the game?"

"I have no money. I have no need of money."

"Then we will play for the sheer pleasure of the thing." Lixal extended his arms and set the game down an equal distance between the two of them. "As for the distance that perforce must always separate us, when you wish to reach out and move your pieces I shall lean back a compensatory amount, allowing you to manipulate the *spinari*."

The deodand stared at him, eyes narrowed in suspicion. "What is a spinari?"

"Not 'a spinari'—it is plural. One is called a *'spinar'*. The collective refers to these pale spikes. For every one you move to your right, you must move another to your left. Or you may choose to move two in the same direction. Do you see?"

The deodand was silent for long moments. "Move one to my right…? What is the point of it?"

Lixal smiled. "I will show you. You will learn it in no time—in the Isles even the youngest children play!"

By the time they reached Catechumia they had traveled together nearly a month and played several hundred games of King's Compass, each of which Lixal had won handily. The deodand was somewhat literal in its employment of strategy and had trouble understanding Lixal's more spontaneous decisions. Also, the concept of bluffing and feinting had not yet impinged on the creature's consciousness in the least. Still, the deodand had improved to the point where the games were now genuine, if one-sided, and for that at least Lixal was grateful. The life of a man tethered to a living deodand was bound to be a lonely one, and so his had proved in these last weeks. Solitary travelers fled them without even stopping to converse on the novelty of Lixal's situation. Larger groups often tried to kill the deodand, the reputation of whose kind was deservedly dark, and such groups bore scarcely more good will toward Lixal, who they deemed a traitor to his species: more than once he was forced to flee with the creature beneath a hail of fist-sized stones. Twice the barns in which they had taken refuge for the night were set on fire with them inside, and both times escape had been no certain thing.

"I confess I had not fully understood the unhappiness of your existence," Lixal told the deodand. "You are hunted by one and all, with no succor to be found anywhere."

The creature gave him a look that mingled amusement with scorn. "On the contrary, in the general run of things one and all are hunted by *me*. In any average meeting, even with three or four of your fellows, the advantage is mine owing to my superior speed and strength. Our current plight is unusual—no sensible deodand would go into the midst of so many of his enemies in broad daylight when his inherent duskiness provides no shield against discovery. It is only being tethered to you by this confluence of spells that puts me in such a vulnerable position. Not to mention how it hampers my diet."

This last remark, the most recent of several, pertained to Lixal's insistence that the creature with whom he was bound up not consume the flesh of human beings while they were in each other's company—which meant, perforce, all the time. This the deodand had acceded to with bad grace, and only after Lixal pointed out that he could easily warn away all but the most deaf and blind of potential victims. When he accompanied this injunction by employing the Rhinocratic Oath, showing the deodand how Lixal could cause the creature's nose to grow so large as to block its creature's sight entirely, the deodand at last submitted.

They both needed to eat, however, so Lixal had a first-hand view of the sharpness and utility of the deodand's claws and teeth when they were employed catching birds or animals. Because the distance between them had to remain more or less identical at all times, it meant that Lixal himself also needed to learn something of the deodand's arts of silent hunting and swift attack. However, this level of cooperation between the two distinct species, although interesting and unusual, only made Lixal Laqavee more aware of how desperately he wanted to be out of the creature's presence.

Since the Exhalation of Thunderous Banishment had proved worse than useless when employed on deodands—and that, Lixal suspected, had been the exact nature of Eliastre's deadly ruse—it was only the talismanic bracelet around his wrist which kept the deodand at a distance. He no longer had any illusions that he could resist the creature's fatal strike in any other way: the Rhinocratic Oath would not deter it for more than a moment, the Pseudo-Philtre was laughably inappropriate, and even the Cantrip of Notional Belittlement, which Lixal had employed early on in their forced companionship, had only slightly reduced the creature's obsession with the day when it would be free of him (and, the implication was clear, equally free to destroy him.) He might have used the cantrip on himself to reduce his own level of unease but feared becoming oblivious to looming danger.

One interesting concomitant of the situation was that the cantrip-calmed deodand became more conversational as the weeks rolled on. There were evenings, as they leaned back and forth like rowers to access the King's Compass gaming board that the creature became almost chatty, telling of his upbringing as an anonymous youngster in a teeming nest, surviving against his fellows only by employing those impressive fangs and talons until he was old enough to escape the nest and begin killing things other than his own siblings.

"We do not build towns as your kind does," the deodand explained. "We share territories, but only at a distance except for those times when we are drawn together to mate and settle grievances, the latter of which we effect by contests of strength which inevitably end in exoneration for one party, death for the other. I myself have survived a dozen such disputes. Here, see the deep scar of one such honorably concluded disagreement." The creature raised its arm to show Lixal, but in the firelight he could make out nothing against the flat darkness of its skin. "It has never been in our nature to cluster together as your kind does or to build as your kind builds. We have always been content to take shelter where it is found. However, as I play this game of yours I begin to see advantages in the way your kind thinks. We deodands seldom plan ahead beyond the successful conclusion of a given hunt, but I see now that one of the advantages your people has over mine is this very quality of forward thinking. Also, I begin to comprehend how misdirection and even outright untruth can be useful for more than simply catching a wary traveler off-guard." The deodand abruptly moved two spinari in the same direction, revealing a sortie he had prepared, but which had been previously hidden behind them. "As you see," he pointed out with a baring of fangs which was the deodand equivalent of a self-satisfied smile.

Despite the creature's unusual strategem, Lixal won again that night. He had been put on notice, however: the deodand was learning and he would have to increase the effort he put into the games if he wished to maintain his supremacy and his unbroken record. He found himself regretting, as he had many times before, that hundreds of consecutive victories in a game of skill should net him exactly nothing in the way of monetary reward. It was a suffering more poignant than anything Eliastre could have devised for him.

At last they reached the small metropolis of Catechumia, home of Twitterel's Emporium. Lixal and the deodand paused and waited for nightfall in a glade on the outskirts of town, not far from the place where Lixal's troop had once camped.

"Do not trouble yourself with speech when we meet Eliastre," he warned the deodand. "It will be a tense negotiation and best served by devices I alone can bring to bear. In fact," he said after a moment's thought, "it may be best if you remain outside the door while I step just inside it, so that the treacherous one-time mage knows nothing of your presence and can prepare no defense against you, should I find it necessary to call upon you."

"You have tried once already to trap me on the other side of a door, Laqavee," the deodand said sourly. "Not only that, but it was a church door, which you thought might increase the efficacy of the strategem. And what happened?"

"You wrong me! That was weeks ago and I intend no such trickery here...!"

"You discovered you could not go forward while I remained on the other side of the door," the creature reminded him. "Like the golden links of a magister's cuff, we are bound together, willy-nilly—one cannot proceed without the other."

"As far as our current plan, I desired only to keep your presence a secret at the outset," Lixal said in a sulky voice. "But you will do as you feel you must."

"Yes, I shall," said the deodand. "And you would be wise to remember that."

When midnight came they crossed town swiftly and mostly silently, although Lixal was forced to remonstrate severely with the deodand who would have eaten a drunkard he found sleeping in an alcove outside a shuttered tavern.

"He is of no interest to anyone except me," the creature argued. "How can you prevent me when you have starved me of proper man-flesh for so long?"

"Because if we are discovered things will go badly for both of us. If the gnawed bones of even the lowliest of townsfolk come to public attention, will not the presence of such as yourself in Catechumia instantly be inferred?"

"They might suppose a wolf had snuck into town," suggested the deodand. "Why do you continually thwart me? You will not even let me eat the flesh of the dead of your species, which your people scorn so much they bury it in the ground, far from their habitations!"

"I do not let you eat the flesh of corpses because it sickens me," replied Lixal coldly. "It is proof that, no matter how you aspire to be otherwise, you and your ilk are no better than beasts."

"Like those you call beasts, we do not waste perfectly edible tissues. Our own kind, at the end of their days, are perfectly happy to be returned to the communal stomach."

Lixal shuddered. "Enough. This is the street."

But to his great unhappiness, when Lixal approached the doorway of what had once been Twitterel's Emporium it gave every sign of being long deserted. "Here," Lixal cried, "this is wretched in the extreme! The coward has decamped. Let us enter and see if there is any clue to his present whereabouts."

The deodand easily, if somewhat noisily, broke the bolt on the door and they went into the large, dark room that had once been densely packed with Twitterel-who-was-Eliastre's stock in trade. Now nothing lined the shelves but cobwebs, and even these looked long-abandoned. A rat, perhaps disturbed by the deodand's unusual scent, scurried into a corner hole and disappeared. "He seems to have left you a note, Laqavee," said the deodand, pointing. "It has your name on it."

Lixal, who did not have the creature's sharp vision, had to locate the folded parchment nailed to the wall by touch, then take it outside into the flickering glow of the street-lantern to read it.

> To Lixal Laqavee, extortionist and counterfeit thaumaturge,
>> the missive began,

If you are reading this, one of two things has occurred. If you have come to pay what you owe me, I stand surprised and pleased. In this case you may give thirteen thousand terces to the landlord of this establishment (he lives next door) and I will receive it from him at a time in the future and in a manner known only to myself. In a spirit of forgiveness, I will also warn you that at no time should you attempt the Exhalation of Thunderous Banishment on a deodand.

If you have not returned to erase your debt, as I think more likely, it is because you have used the Exhalation on one of the dusky creatures, but for some reason my intention of teaching you a lesson has been thwarted and you mean to remonstrate with me. (It is possible that my transposition of two key words, because hurried, was not as damaging to the effect as I hoped. It is even remotely possible that the protective charm you wore on your wrist was more useful than it appeared, in which case I must blame my own overconfidence.) If any combination of these is the case for your return, my various curses upon you remain in force and I inform you also that I have moved my business to another town and chosen another name, so that any attempt by you to stir up trouble for me with the Council of Thaumaturgic Practitioners will be doomed to failure.

You, sir, may rot in hell with my congenial approval.

signed, He Who Was Twitterel

Lixal crumpled the parchment in his fist. "Repay him?" he growled. "His purse will groan indeed with the weight of my repayment. His account shall be paid to bursting!"

"Your metaphors are inexact," the deodand said. "I take it we shall not be parting company as quickly as we both had hoped."

TAD WILLIAMS

Like two prisoners condemned to share a cell, Lixal and the deodand grew weary of each other's company in the weeks and months after they left Catechumia. Lixal searched half-heartedly for news of the ex-wizard Eliastre, but he was inhibited by the constant presence of the deodand, who proved a dampening influence on conversation with most of humankind, and so he all but gave up hope of ever locating the author of his predicament, who could have set up shop anew in any one of hundreds of towns and cities across Almery or even farther countries still.

While they were everywhere shunned by men, they came occasionally into contact with other deodands, who looked on Lixal not with fear or curiosity, but rather as a potential source of nutrients. When his bracelet proved more than these new deodands could overcome, they settled instead for desultory gossip with their trapped comrade. Lixal was forced to listen to long discussions criticizing what all parties but himself saw as his ridiculous opposition to the eating of human flesh, living or dead. The deodand bound to him by the Exhalation was inevitably buoyed after these discussions with like-minded peers, and would often bring an even greater energy to bear on their nightly games of King's Compass: at times Lixal was hard-pressed to keep up his unbroken record of victories, but keep it he did, and, stinging from the deodandic imputation of his prudishness, did not hesitate to remind his opponent as often as possible of that creature's campaign of futility.

"Yes, it is easy to criticize," Lixal often said as the board was packed away. "But one has only to review our sporting history to see who has the superior approach to life." He was even beginning to grow used to this mode of existence, despite the inadequate nature of the deodand as both a conversationalist and competitor.

Then, almost a year after their initial joining, came the day when the talismanic bracelet, the admirer's gift that had so long protected Lixal Laqavee's life, suddenly ceased to function.

Lixal discovered that the spell was no longer efficacious in a sudden and extremely unpleasant manner: one moment he slept, dreaming of a charmed scenario in which he was causing Eliastre's bony nose to sprout carbuncles that were actually bigger than the ex-wizard himself, and laughing as the old man screeched and pleaded for mercy. Then he awoke to discover the deodand's stinking breath on his face and the demonic yellow eyes only an inch or two from his own.

Lixal had time only for a choked squeal, then the taloned hand closed on his neck.

"Oh, but you are soft, you humans," the thing whispered, not from stealth it seemed but from pure pleasure in the moment, as if to speak loudly would be to induce a jarring note into an otherwise sublime melody. "My claws would pass through your throat like butter. I will certainly have to choose a slower and more satisfying method of dispatching you."

"M-my b-b-bracelet," stuttered Lixal. "What have you done to it?"

"I?" The deodand chortled. "I have done nothing. But as I recall, it was meant to protect you from untimely death. Apparently in whatever way these things are calculated your time of dying has arrived. Perhaps in a different state of affairs, a paralleled existence of some sort, this is the moment when you would have been struck lifeless by a falling slate from a roof or mowed down by an overladen horse cart whose driver had lost his grip on the reins. But fear not! In this plane of reality you shall not have to go searching for your death, Laqavee, since by convenience I am here to make certain that things proceed for you as just the Fates desire they should!"

"But why? Have I mistreated you so badly? We have traveled together for a full round of seasons." Lixal raised a trembling hand with the intention of giving the deodand an encouraging, brotherly pat, but at the sight of the creature's bared fangs he swiftly withdrew it again. "We are as close as any of our two kinds have ever been—we understand each other as well as our two species have ever managed. Surely it would be a shame to throw all that away!"

The deodand made a noise of sarcastic amusement. "What does that mean? Had you spent a year chained against your will to a standing rib roast, do you suggest that when the fetters were removed you would suddenly wish to preserve your friendship with it? You are my prey, Laqavee. Circumstances have pressed us together. Now circumstances have released me to destroy you."

The grip on his neck was tightening now. "Hold, hold!" Lixal cried. "Do you not remember what you yourself suggested? That if I were to die you would be held to the spot where my bones fell?"

"I have considered just that during this long night, since I first realized your magical bracelet no longer dissuaded me. My solution is elegant: I shall devour you bones and all. Thus I will be confined only to the vicinity of my own stomach, something that is already the case." The deodand laughed in pleasure. "After all, you spoke glowingly yourself of the closeness of our acquaintanceship, Laqavee—surely you could wish no greater proximity than within my gut!"

The foul stench of the thing's breath was almost enough to snatch away what little remained of Lixal's dizzied consciousness. He closed his eyes so that he would not have to see the deodand's terrible gaze when it murdered him. "Very well, then," he said with as much aplomb as he could muster, although every limb in his body trembled as though he had an ague. "At least I die with the satisfaction of knowing that a deodand has never beaten a human at King's Compass and now never shall."

He waited.

He continued to wait.

Lixal could not help remembering that the deodand had earlier spoken of a death both slower and more satisfying than simply having his throat torn out—satisfying to the murderous creature, Lixal had no doubt, rather than to himself. Was that why the thing hesitated?

At last he opened his eyes again. The fiery yellow orbs were asquint in anger and some other emotion, harder to discern.

"You have put your finger on a problem," the deodand admitted. "By my account, you have beaten me thrice-three-hundred and forty-four times out of an equal number of contests. And yet I have felt for some time now that I was on the verge of mastering the game and defeating you. You yourself must admit that our matches have become more competitive."

"In all fairness, I must agree with your assertion," said Lixal. "You have improved both your hoarding and your double sentry maneuver."

The deodand stood, keeping its claw wrapped around Lixal Laqavee's neck and thus forcing him to stand as well. "Here is my solution," the creature told him. "We will continue to play. As long as you can defeat me I will let you live, because I must know that when I win, as ultimately I feel sure I must, it will be by the sole fact of my own improving skill."

Lixal felt a little relieved—his death was to be at least momentarily postponed—but the knowledge did not bring the quickening of hope that might have accompanied such a reprieve in other circumstances. The deodand did not sleep, while Lixal felt the need to do so for many hours of every day. The deodand was swift and powerful while he, Lixal, was a great deal less so. And no human with any wit at all would try to help him.

Still, perhaps something unforeseen might happen that would allow him to conquer the beast or escape. The events of Lixal's life had taught him that circumstances were bound to change, and occasionally even for the better.

"You must also keep me well-fed and healthy," he told the deodand. "If I am weakened by hunger or illness any victory of yours would be hollow."

"Fair enough." The creature transferred its iron grip to his arm, then without further conversation began to walk. It made a good speed through the patchy forest, forcing Lixal to hurry to keep up or risk having his limb pulled from its socket.

"Where are we going?" Lixal called breathlessly. "What was wrong with that particular camping spot? We had a fire, and could have started a game at our leisure once you had provided us with some dinner."

"I am doing just that, but dinner of the kind I seek is not so easily obtained near our previous camping site."

Sometime after this unsettling declaration, just as the morning sun began to bring light to the forest, the deodand dragged Lixel out of the thickest part of the trees and into an open grassy space dotted with lumps of worked stone, some standing upright but many others tumbled and broken, all of them much patched with moss.

"Why have we come here?" Lixal asked. "This is some ancient graveyard."

"Just so," said the deodand. "But not truly ancient—burials have taken place here within relatively recent years. You have long forbidden me the chance to dine as I please, on the meat that I most like. Now I shall no longer be bound by your absurd and cruel strictures. And yet I do not want the vigilante impulses of your kind to interfere with our contest, so instead of sallying forth for live human flesh we will encamp ourselves here, where suitably aged and cured specimens wait beneath only a shallow span of topsoil." The creature grinned hugely. "I confess I have dreamed of such toothsome delicacies for the entire span of our annoying and undesired companionship."

"But what about me?" said Lixal. "What shall I eat? Will you hunt game for me?"

"You seem to think you still hold the upper hand, Laqavee." The deodand spoke as sternly as a disappointed father. "You are far away from the assistance of any of your fellows and in the passing of a single heartbeat I can tear your throat with my talons. Hunt game for you? Nonsense." The deodand shook its head and shoved him down onto his knees. "You will eat what I do. You will learn thrift as the deodands practice it! Now set up the gaming board and prepare to defend the honor of your species, Lixal Laqavee! In the meantime, I will begin digging for breakfast."

THE TERRIBLE CONFLAGRATION AT THE QUILLER'S MINT

(From the diaries of Finn Teodoros, discovered and edited by Tad Williams)

W HEN I WAS BUT A young man newly come to this great city from my mother's house near the ocean cliffs of Helmingsea, I had no friend or family here who could give me houseroom, so I paid a few copper pieces each week for a bed at the ancient inn known as The Quiller's Mint. The place was owned in that time by a man named Arvald, although in this our present day it has a different owner. He was a dour and secretive fellow, as are many of the Vuttish who live in the March Kingdoms—he had been born in the islands but had traveled all over the world on merchant ships in his youth, much as had my own father, born in Krace but buried on the foggy hills of Helmingsea. It was a strange thing to see, a Vuttish taverner—odd as an extravagant Settlander or a chaste Syannese—and he was as thrifty with words as you might guess. I think not many people who occasioned the inn favored Arvald much or would have chosen his establishment above any other, but that his prices were low.

I slept near the top of the building, three floors above Squeakstep Alley, in a room with a tiny window that looked out at a dark warehouse so close I could almost touch its timbered walls. Several others shared the poorly-furnished room with me, most of them merchants staying only a few nights, and even the louse-ridden bed could not be called my own, for Arvald was not prey to the sort of foolish generosity that would let a bed go unused half the day. I slept my fitful sleep in it when the world was dark, and in the daylight hours a riverman who worked at the night-docks outside the walls would make it his. Many were the evenings I came home to find the sheets still dank with river water. Once I found a small fish in the blankets that I suspicion had come from out of his boot, for others who shared the room told me the riverman wore his sodden old pair even in bed.

Before I found my position in the royal tax office, I earned a bit of my lodging-fee back by helping Arvald serve his guests, and a strange, sad lot they were. Even today, when it has a slightly better name for hospitality, the folk lining the tavern benches of The Quiller's Mint are a motley collection at best, rhymers and other less lawful blather-men, snitches, sharpers, and shave-pennies.

For those who have not visited the place, it stands inside the outer wall of the keep like a man who has been backing away from a brawl and run out of room, between Fitters Row and Tin Street, with Squeakstep Alley running past its front door like a narrow, muddy river. Its painted sign is a faceless woman veiled and dressed in black, for no reason anyone knows. The tavern sits just a short distance from Skimmer's Lagoon on the Fitters Row side, and while the skimmers themselves do not visit the place—they have their own establishments into which the rest of us are not welcomed—the smell of the lagoon is always in the place, especially when the sun is high or the tide is low, and the cries of seabirds are its usual music, when they can be heard above the bellowing of drunkards and slatterns. It is an old building, and in fact at the rear it is built straightly into the city's outwall, as though the wall were built around it rather than the other way round. No one claims to know when it was first put up, or even how far it extends. I could not tell you myself, despite having worked there for a year. There are several rooms down beneath the main tavern, pantries and other places I never explored. It troubled my heart to go down there by myself because it was quiet and dark and the corridors twisted most confusingly, and thus kept my visits short. When Nevin Hewney—perhaps Southmarch's most famous playwright, and certainly its most frequently drunken playwright—is in his cups and claims another entire tavern lies deep beneath the one in current use, deserted but preserved, it will not be me who calls him a liar.

In any case, the Mint (as many called it then and still do) was not so much different in my youth than it is now. Most of the patrons, as is generally the case with poets and criminals, swung between extremes of morbid silence and loud bragging, often prodding each other to some dangerous bet or inflicting childish pranks. One that I remember is when a young poet with a demanding mistress was told that the pie-plant growing in the Mint's kitchen yard was a sovereign prompter of the gallant reflex. This foolish versifier ate several uncooked stalks and grew so ill he nearly died, prompting amusement in all but the most charitable customers.

On the night of the conflagration, I recall little happening that was not of the ordinary. It was a chillsome late autumn, especially down by the lagoon where the winds blew unchecked, and a fire had been set in the fireplace. The air was thick with smoke and my eyes stung. Nevin Hewney, who was then still such a young man that he had no beard upon his face at all, but only a yellow fluff like dandelion, was bragging about having finished his first play, a piece of what we suspected must be dubious skill and even more doubtful virtue, which told the story of a famous Trigonarch's mistress. To our surprise, a year later this play, *The Eidolon of Devonis,* was performed at the Firmament Theater and became quite popular, and Hewney received his first post with Earl Rorick's players.

In another corner a trio of strangers, who despite the warmth of the room had not taken off their hooded cloaks, drank moderately and spoke quietly among themselves for most of the evening. I have heard it said in after days that these were the Lord Constable's guardsmen, but what their purpose in the tavern should have been I do not know, and I doubt the story. There are places closer to the inner keep than the Quiller's Mint where guardsmen can drink, and in fairer circumstances as well. I have even heard it claimed that one of these hooded men was young Prince in disguise—he is said to have liked to sit with ordinary men and women to learn something of their lives—but I suspicion this is a false claim. People will see the hands of princes and hierarchs in any fateful event, but there are fateful events enough in this world that princes and hierarchs would have to forego sleep entirely to have a hand in them all.

A few other of the tavern's regular patrons were in the main room on that night, including a poet and occasional swindler named Thom Regin (although most who knew him would have said that it was the poetry that was occasional and the swindling his fulltime vocation) and a Jellonian woman named Doras, of whose virtues the most charitable thing that can be said is that she did not haggle much about prices. Doras, who from time to time kept a sort of company with big-bellied, booming-voiced Regin when he was sober, had on this night brought in a stranger, a dark-haired, pale man who she introduced as John Sommerle or Summerlea (I have seen the name spelled in diverse ways) who she said was a sailor. Sommerle himself did not speak much.

As I said, I remember little about the night that was odd or untoward. At one point Thom Regin—who I thought was not happy about Doras keeping company with another man, but had not said so straightly—recited a bit of poetry about a man who beds a fairy-princess and wakes up in the morning to find that the Twilight People have ensorceled him and that his companion is a sow. Sommerle for some reason took exception to this foolish rhyme and threatened Regin with a dagger, although the knife was never actually produced. Arvald the tavern-owner intervened, and only Doras' tearful pleading kept him from ejecting John Sommerle from the Mint on the instant.

The three hooded men took little interest in this brawl, as far as I could see.

Later in the evening, while I was busy playing potboy and thus did not see what happened, Sommerle and the woman Doras fell into a disagreement for some reason and Sommerle left the Quiller's Mint. He did not come back, at least while the tavern was open.

When the bell rang in the temple of the Trigon and closing hour came round, the Jellonian woman and Thom Regin seemed to have been reconciled. She was fondling his face and lovingly tweaking his beard while he recited her some bit of doggerel, this one a tale of women who give their hearts to fairy-princes. Since he seemed to be likening himself to such an immortal and magical lover, I thought he was overbuilding himself a bit—Regin was not the most presupposing of men. In any case, that was the last time I saw him. Arvald called for those who were present to empty their scoops. He had not locked the doors yet, and a few of the patrons were still in the tavern when he sent me to my bed. That was the first thing in the evening that felt odd to me, since Arvald generally kept me at my labors until every tankard was rinsed and every bench and table wiped.

I was awakened in the middle of the night by a woman's voice raised in a scream. My nostrils were instantly full of the harsh scent of smoke. Tripping over the other inhabitants of my shared room, who were slower to wake than I, I made my way to the stairs and started downward. Between the ground floor and the first story I almost ran into a dark figure. It was the woman Doras, her hair and clothes in disarray, looking as though she had just been pulled from bed, although whether also from sleep would have been another question.

"Where is my Riggin?" she said, her Jellonian accent making it hard for me to understand what she was saying. "My Rig, where has he gone?"

I shoved past her and made my way down to the tavern. A fire was burning, not in the fireplace, but in the straw floor on the opposite side of the main room. Lying beside this new blaze but not in the flames was a dark shape. I leaned over to see the poet Regin with his forehead caved in like a broken eggshell and blood running from his nose and mouth. He was lying near one of the room's wooden ceiling-pillars. I suppose that if he had been running across the room, not looking where he was going, he might have hit the pillar hard enough to crack his poll that way. I am not certain I believe that, but I cannot say it is impossible.

In any case, I had no time to think about it then. The fire was already spreading across the straw and in a moment more I would be surrounded and hemmed in by the blaze. I tried to drag the poet's corpse with me, although I knew he was already dead, but he was too heavy. It must be remembered that at the time I was only a stripling, and Regin must have carried almost twice my weight.

The Terrible Conflagration at The Quiller's Mint

I ran out of the tavern then and through the inn, shouting for Arvald, calling out that there was fire in the house, fire! Soon the halls and stairwell were full of confused guests and tavern patrons—apparently Arvald had allowed a card game in his own chambers after the main room was closed. I saw Arvald trying to enlist the help of some of the scurrying cardplayers to go to the lagoon to fill buckets of water, but no one paid him any attention in the smoke and shouting and darkness lit only by flickering flames. One man was killed in the crush at the front door, trampled until his ribs cracked and pierced his heart, and several more had broken limbs and other injuries trying to get out. As the fire swiftly spread, some had to leap out of the upper stories into the ordure of Squeakstep Alley. It was only due to the mercy of Zoria, I believe, and of Honnos who watches over travelers, that more were not killed inside the tavern.

But many others did die as the fire spread to some of the nearby roofs, and to the tenement houses on Tin Street where hundreds of people lived in each single three- or four-story house. All told, something more than two dozen folk were killed in the terrible Quiller's Mint fire and hundreds more lost their homes. The conflagration would have burned far more of the city had not two sides been blocked from spreading by Skimmer's Lagoon, and one side by the city wall itself.

There was not much strange in the events of that evening, as I said, but there was much that was strange that happened afterward.

Arvald, the owner of the tavern, disappeared within a few days after the fire. Some said that was because there was nothing except an expensive and pointless salvage to detain him in Southmarch any longer and so he had gone back to the Vuttish islands, others suggested it was because his conscience was something less than clean. Why he should have set a fire in his own tavern, though, has not yet been convincingly explained even by those who suggest his guilt.

TAD WILLIAMS

When Thom Regin's body was brought out of the ashes, it was naught but black bones and charred meat, and thus nothing I said would have made any difference, so I told no one of how I had found him. I was young and not keen for the eye of authority to fall on me in such an unflattering situation. I might have spoken up if John Sommerle had remained, but he too had vanished, never seen again after Arvald shoved him out of the Quiller's Mint front door. The Jellonian woman Doras was little help in answering questions. She could never speak of the evening without bursting into tears, and the pox took her within a year or two in any case.

Was it simply by chance that the Mint burned down? It matters little, I suppose, because a new tavern was soon built on the ashes of the old, and because the oldest parts of the place are in any case below ground or in the city walls and thus went unscathed.

It still seems odd that the fire should have started on the opposite side of the room from the fireplace, on a damp night, and that I should find Thom Regin's corpse on the ground near the place where it had caught. But if John Sommerle came back to murder Regin and set the fire to cover his deed, why did he not simply drag the poet's corpse out through one of the side doors and leave it in an alley instead? Regin would have been thought only the most recent in a long line of Quiller's Mint patrons who never made it back to their homes through the Lagoon District's sometimes inhospitable streets.

There are even wilder speculations, most based around the reputed presence of the man who would someday be our King Olin, but I have never heard one of these tales yet that did not sound to me like the ravings of a madman. The idea that a king who has always shown kindness even to his lowest and poorest subjects would instruct his guards to set a deadly fire simply to hide the fact that he was visiting a tavern...well, there is just no sense to it.

270 —

The Terrible Conflagration at The Quiller's Mint

So there it is, the tale of the conflagration that destroyed the old Quiller's Mint. In fact, I am told that even this terrible deed or accident was merely a reenactment of a larger historical tradition—that the Mint which burned was at least the fourth or fifth building of that name on that spot in Squeakstep Alley between Fitters and Tin. It is that most unsatisfying of tales, a true one. What it means, if it means anything at all, must be up to you, kind reader, to decide.

—Finn Teodoros, by his hand, on the ninth day of the eleventh month of the year 1314

Black Sunshine

FADE IN:

EXT.—PIERSON HOUSE, 1976—NIGHT

From blackness to shadowy trees—a tangled orchard in moonlight. We move through them toward a three-story turn-of-the-century house with lights in the windows. As we track in, we hear Black Sabbath's "Iron Man" playing distantly on a stereo.

CUT TO: ERIC'S DREAM POV—*Micro close-up on a carpet—it's ALIVE, squirming with intricate patterns. "Iron Man" is ear-splitting now.*

YOUNG JANICE
Eric! Eric, talk to me!

YOUNG ERIC'S POV swivels up from the carpet—things are dreamlike, compressed, distorted—it's an acid trip. YOUNG

TAD WILLIAMS

JANICE is so close that her face is distorted. We dimly see she is fifteen, maybe sixteen, wearing 70s clothes.

> YOUNG JANICE
> Eric, I want to get out of here...!

YOUNG BRENT lurches into view, looming above JANICE. He's chunky, teenage, clutching his hands against his stomach, panicky but trying to stay calm.

> YOUNG BRENT
> Shit, it's bad—Topher's freaking
> out for real up there.

> YOUNG JANICE
> What's going on, Brent?
> Where's Kimmy?

> YOUNG BRENT
> I don't know! I can't find her.
> I think...I think something
> bad happened! I tried to help
> Topher, and I...

Just now realizing, BRENT lifts his hands away from his body and stares at them. They are smeared with blood. His eyes bug out.

> YOUNG JANICE
> Oh my God!

Something is THUMPING on the ceiling above—something heavy thrashing around upstairs. As the POV looks upward, the ceiling suddenly becomes TRANSPARENT, a spreading puddle of translucency as though the ceiling were turning to smeared glass. A dark human shape (YOUNG TOPHER) is lying on the floor of the room above, face pressed against the transparent ceiling as though it were a picture window, looking down on them. All we can make out of him is a huddled shape, distorted face, and a single staring eye.

YOUNG TOPHER
Hey, Pierson—I seeeeee you...!

YOUNG JANICE
(screaming)
Eric!

FADE *with JANICE's cry still echoing as we* CUT TO:

INT.—ERIC'S MOTEL—NIGHT

ADULT ERIC as he sits bolt upright in a motel bed, sweating.

YOUNG JANICE
(very faint now)
Eric!

ERIC PIERSON is sweaty, trembling. He's in his early 40s, nice-looking, slender, but at this moment he could be twenty years older. He fumbles for a cigarette and sits smoking in the dark as we:

ROLL CREDITS

TAD WILLIAMS

EXT.—THE PIERSON HOUSE, NOW—MORNING

ADULT ERIC drives down a long, dirt driveway. From atop a rise we see the house—the same house, but now sitting in a wide, empty DIRT FIELD several acres across: the orchard has been cut down. The house looks grim—peeling paint, screen door hanging halfway off. Hesitantly, he moves up the front steps and through the front door.

INT.—HOUSE

There's nothing Gothic or creepy about the place, it's just stripped and empty—carpets removed, no furniture, wallpaper peeling. ERIC hesitates again, then moves toward the dark stairwell. He flicks the switch—no light. He looks up the stairs, but a noise outside distracts him. A car with "Red Letter Realty" has pulled up beside his and someone is getting out.

EXT.—HOUSE

ERIC has returned to the dry front lawn, and stands with his back to the drive, looking up at the house. As an attractive, dark-haired woman in her late thirties approaches, he talks over his shoulder to her.

> ERIC
> Things seem smaller when you
> see them after a long time. I
> remembered this place as being
> so huge...

JANICE

That's funny, because I
remembered you as being much
shorter.

ERIC turns, startled.

ERIC

Janice? Janice? Oh, my God,
what are you doing...

(looks at car)
Jesus. Are you the...

JANICE

The real estate agent? Well,
someone else in the office is
actually handling it, but when
I heard you were coming back
to town to sign the sale papers,
I said...

(shrugs)
Well, it seemed to make sense.

ERIC is still staring at her.

ERIC

You look...you look great.

JANICE

I look old. But thanks. You look
okay yourself. I was sorry to
hear about your grandmother.

                    ERIC
          Well, ninety-two. We should all
          last so long. I thought she'd sold
          this years ago.

                    JANICE
          She wasn't stupid, Eric. She was
          making the developers bid up
          the price—you can see this was
          the last property here. She did
          you a good turn.

                    ERIC
                    (turns back to the house)
          It's hard to believe, huh? Those
          days seem like...like a dream.

                    JANICE
          Not to me. I live around here,
          remember?

ERIC turns at the harshness in her voice.

                    ERIC
          Is that bad?

                    JANICE
          You didn't want to stay much.
          No, I guess it's all right. Not as
          exciting as Los Angeles, I'm sure.
                    (she frowns, then tries to smile)
          But it's nice to send the kids
          off to school without firearms
          training.

> ERIC
> You...have kids?

> JANICE
> Callie and Jack—eight and six.
> But no, not at the moment.
> They're with their dad for the
> summer. We're divorced.

ERIC *is staring at the house again.*

> ERIC
> I was just going to visit Topher,
> then drive back, but...hey,
> would you like to have dinner?
> It'd be nice to catch up.

> JANICE
> You're...going to visit Topher?

> ERIC
> Thought I should. You want to
> come along?

> JANICE
> *(shakes her head; then:)*
> You haven't seen him lately.
> It's bad.

> ERIC
> *(shrugs)*
> Yeah, that's what they told me.
> So, dinner. What do you say?

> JANICE
> I don't think it's a good idea,
> Eric.

> ERIC
> Just talk. Catch up. I...really
> feel like I need to.

> JANICE
> You don't want to catch up, Eric.
> It's better to leave things alone.

> ERIC
> C'mon...Jan-Jan.

JANICE looks at him for a long moment, both touched and irritated by the use of the name. She rolls her eyes like a schoolgirl.

> JANICE
> Asshole.

FADE TO: EXT.—LAS LOMAS CONVALESCENT HOSPITAL—DAY

It's a quiet, decent place. ERIC pulls into the parking lot.

INT.—HOSPITAL

ERIC walks down the hallway, past various geriatrics in wheelchairs and one young man twisted with palsy. As ERIC's gaze sweeps across the young man's face, a voice speaks behind him.

OLD WOMAN
Stop! Stop!

He turns. A scowling OLD WOMAN in a wheelchair is following him.

OLD WOMAN
It's all a mistake! Call my
mother!

ERIC walks on a little faster than before.

CUT TO: INT.—HOSPITAL LOUNGE

The room is filled with old people on benches, in chairs, mostly staring into space. ERIC is talking with a NURSE in the lounge doorway. She points toward the corner. As ERIC approaches, looking around, he doesn't see TOPHER until the last moment—then a look of SHOCK runs across his face.

FLASH CUT TO: *TOPHER as a teenager in 1976, handsome, blonde, surfer-ish, a shit-eating grin on his face as he lounges on a couch.*

YOUNG TOPHER
Eric, my man! Have I got
something for you...

CUT TO: TOPHER NOW, *in his wheelchair. He is startlingly grotesque, hairless and hunched, but his SKIN is the worst part—a crusty brown SHELL over his whole body, as though he's covered with dried mud. He sits as stiff as if paralyzed. Two pale blue eyes peer out of the masklike face.*

>   ERIC
>   *(trying to cover his shock)*
> Topher, man. Long time. Long
> time... I'm sorry I haven't been
> to see you in a while. Life, man,
> it's just...you know.

A horrible silence. TOPHER peers outward, not even looking at ERIC.

>   ERIC (cont.)
> I never...I never stop being
> sorry, man. It was just so
> screwed up. You...we never
> thought...

>   NURSE
>   *(appearing over his shoulder)*
> Is everything all right?

ERIC suddenly gets up and lurches toward the door.

CLOSE-UP: TOPHER'S FACE, staring at nothing.

In the doorway, the NURSE nods understandingly.

>   NURSE
> It's very disturbing if you
> haven't seen it before.

>   ERIC
>   *(still in shock)*
> It's been years...

NURSE
It's come on very badly lately.
Nobody knows what it is. It's
flexible at the joints, though,
when he moves. When we
move him, that is—he doesn't
do anything himself, doesn't
talk... The skin tissue is
unusual—hard and brittle,
like...what is it insects make?
A chrysalis?
(she looks at ERIC)
I'm sorry, am I upsetting you?
Is he a relative?

ERIC
(shaking his head)
High school friend...

FADE TO: EXT.—RURAL ROAD—DAY,
MINUTES LATER

ERIC is driving, face troubled. He fumbles for a tape and pushes it into the player. Something contemporary begins to fill the car as we CUT TO:

INT.—HOSPITAL—SAME TIME

CLOSE-UP on TOPHER's strange face. The eyes blink for the first time, slow-motion, as we CUT TO:

TAD WILLIAMS

INT.—REAL ESTATE OFFICE—SAME TIME

JANICE, phone against her ear, is looking for something on top of her desk, holding a styrofoam cup of coffee in her hand.

> JANICE
> ...I think they're looking for
> something a bit less pricey...

She looks at the coffee, which is suddenly black as ink. There is black on her hand, too, and smeared up her arm. She drops the black liquid to the floor, but her desk is covered in black smears too, and it's all over her legs and skirt and chair. She screams and leaps up, rubbing frantically at herself as we CUT TO:

TOPHER'S EYES: Another SLOW BLINK

INT.—ERIC'S CAR

The contemporary music abruptly twists sideways into the drum-and-screams intro of the Stones' "Sympathy for the Devil". Eric stares at the tape player, starts to pop the tape, then hears:

> YOUNG TOPHER
> Hook a right, man—time we
> got back to your place.

The high-school TOPHER is sitting in the passenger seat, grinning, thumb pointing down a side road. ERIC gasps and hits the brakes. The car fishtails to a stop on the side of the road. ERIC stares. The passenger seat is EMPTY. The music is back to normal.

CUT TO: INT.—REAL ESTATE OFFICE

JANICE is standing up, perfectly clean, her desk clean too, everything fine but for the coffee she spilled on the floor. All her co-workers are STARING at her as we CUT TO:

EXT.—GAS STATION—MINUTES LATER

ERIC has pulled his car into a small service station. The CASHIER, a fifty-something skinny guy with a beard and ponytail, wanders out. ERIC gets out and leans against the car, stunned.

> CASHIER
> It's self-serve. Hey, you feel all
> right?

> ERIC
> Yeah, I guess so.

> CASHIER
> We got a bathroom if you need
> to puke or something.

> ERIC
> No, I...I think I just...had a
> flashback.

> CASHIER
> *(chortles)*
> I know about that shit, man.
> Between acid and that Post
> Traumatic Stress shit, I've had

so many of them things I prolly
spend more time in the old days
than I do in the right-now...

ERIC *is looking back over the fields and through the trees as
we DISSOLVE TO:*

INT.—RESTAURANT—NIGHT

ERIC *and* JANICE *eating dinner in an upscale Mexican
restaurant. She has dolled up a bit, but has a sweater over her
shoulders as though unwilling to relax too much. Neither is
eating very heartily.*

> ERIC
> ...Had no idea. Oh my God, he
> looks like...like...

> JANICE
> Like a monster. I know.

> ERIC
> It really got to me. I kind of
> freaked out on the ride back.

JANICE *looks troubled, but also angry.*

> JANICE
> Yeah. Tension and guilt will do
> that to you.

ERIC
Are you saying I should feel
guilty, Janice? I do. Of course I
do. But it's not all my fault.

JANICE
You sure left town like you
thought it was.
(*She has been fidgeting with her
silverware. She waves a waiter over.*)
Could you please give me a
clean fork, if it's not too much
to ask? This fork is dirty. It's
disgusting.

The waiter leaves. ERIC looks at her. She stares defiantly back.

JANICE (cont.)
Well, you did, didn't you?

ERIC
What did you want me to do?
I had a scholarship that fall,
remember? Did you want me
not to go to UCLA?

JANICE
To become a journalist and save
the world.

ERIC
To become a journalist, yeah,
even if I didn't know it then.
Should I have just stayed?

JANICE

Of course not. Then you would
have had to break up with me
face to face.

ERIC

C'mon—it was as much your
idea as mine, wasn't it?

JANICE

Maybe. But I didn't get to leave.
I had to go to that high school
for two years. How do you
think that felt? To have people
pointing at me, whispering
about me...?

ERIC

If you want me to say I'm sorry,
Janice, I will. I'm sorry.
(He toys with his food.)
Didn't you have anyone else to
talk to? What about Brent?

JANICE

Oh, sure, Brent. I hardly saw
him. He got all weird—started
reading like Tibetan Buddhism
and stuff.

ERIC

Brent? Reading books?

                    JANICE
He's a lot different, Eric.
You'd hardly know him. He's
done really well, actually. He
lost a lot of weight, married
some ex-model, owned his
own advertising agency in Los
Angeles for a while, then sold
out and moved back here...

                    ERIC
Advertising agency? Oh,
shit, he wasn't the Zenger in
Zenger-Kimball, was he?
That's too weird.

                    JANICE
Like I said, you wouldn't
recognize him...

DISSOLVE TO:

INT.—BRENT'S HOUSE—SAME TIME

*The ADULT BRENT ZENGER looks fit and successful—nice
haircut, buff body, expensive casual clothes. His wife TRACY
and daughter JOANIE look up from the couch where they're
watching television. BRENT heads for the closet to hang up
his coat.*

                    BRENT
The man is home.

                    TRACY
          Hi.

                    JOANIE
          Hi, daddy. The class hamster
          had babies.

                    BRENT
          I'd love to hear about it after
          I get myself one little, much-
          deserved drink.

                    TRACY
          You're home late.

                    BRENT
          Dinner with a client...

*He reaches the closet and throws open the door, starts to hang
up his coat, then sees there's a light of some kind at the back
of the closet. BRENT is surprised. He pushes through the
coathangers and discovers a door on the back of the closet,
where clearly none has ever been before. He steps through it
and into an EXACT DUPLICATE of the living room he's
just left.*

                    BRENT
          What the hell...?

                    TRACY
          (looking up in alarm)
          Who are you? What are you
          doing in here?

JOANIE
Mommy? Mommy!

BRENT
What are you talking about...?

TRACY
(pulling JOANIE backward toward the phone)
I don't know what you think you're doing, but I'm calling the police. Don't move!

JOANIE
(crying)
Who is that man, Mommy?

Terrified, stunned, BRENT takes a stumbling step backward and falls into the closet. After a confused moment, he fights his way out of darkness again.

TRACY
Brent? What on earth are you doing? Do you need some help?

JOANIE
Daddy's tangled up in the coats!

CLOSE UP—BRENT, pale and shaken, as we dissolve to:

TAD WILLIAMS

EXT.—RESTAURANT PARKING LOT—NIGHT

JANICE and ERIC are walking through the lot. She has her sweater pulled tight around her shoulders.

> ERIC
> ...And she put all my stuff in
> boxes and put them out on
> the sidewalk with—you know
> those label guns? With a label
> on each one reading "property
> of shit head". Which is how I
> became single again.
> (a beat)
> Hey, I thought you would have
> enjoyed hearing about my
> hopeless love life.

> JANICE
> Oh, Eric, I never wished you
> bad luck. Not really.
> *(a beat)*
> I'm sorry if...if I wasn't very
> good company tonight. I told
> you this was a poor idea.

> ERIC
> I said I'm sorry about everything,
> Janice. I really am, I...I was just
> scared of the whole thing. You,
> life, what happened...

They have stopped beside his car.

JANICE

I accept the apology. I did
stupid things too. Let's just say
goodnight and maybe we can
be friends again. That would be
something, wouldn't it? After
all this time?

ERIC

It sure would.

He reaches out and takes her hand, holding it awkwardly for a moment—he's trying to find a way to pull her closer but she's quietly resisting. Abruptly he drops her hand and walks to his car.

JANICE

Eric?

ERIC

Hang on a second.

He fumbles around, then pops a tape into the player and leaves the door open as he walks back. The quiet intro to Traffic's "Low Spark of High Heeled Boys" begins to play.

JANICE

I know that.

ERIC

Of course you do. This is now
officially middle-aged-people's-
music.

He suddenly takes her hand again, then pulls her toward him.

> ERIC (cont.)
> Remember slow dancing?

> JANICE
> The only kind you could do.
> A casualty of the Disco
> Invasion is what you were.
> C'mon, Eric, stop.

> ERIC
> Just a dance. Better than
> arguing. Come on.

JANICE allows herself to be drawn slowly into a dance.

> JANICE
> You do know you're going back
> to your motel alone, don't you?

> ERIC
> All the more reason to be quiet
> and let me enjoy this...

They circle across the parking lot, under the lights. A foursome walks past them and makes joking comments, but sweetly— it's a nice moment. We dissolve slowly to:

EXT.—PIERSON HOUSE, 1976—NIGHT

Another quiet song rises up, supplanting the Traffic—it's Roxy Music's "In Every Dream Home A Heartache". Five people are sitting on the roof of the house. It's a summer evening, last rays of sunset just vanishing, and the lights of other houses are far on the other side of the orchard.

Five teenagers are sitting along the edge of the roof, passing a joint. YOUNG ERIC and YOUNG JANICE are pressed close. Chunky YOUNG BRENT, wearing cutoffs and deck shoes, is dangling his feet over the edge and taking his turn with the joint. KIMMY, a small girl with glasses, a hooded sweatshirt, and overalls sits a yard or so from him but close to YOUNG JANICE. YOUNG TOPHER sits against the chimney, swigging from a bottle of Bacardi.

> YOUNG ERIC
> Last night of summer.

> YOUNG JANICE
> Shut up. You'll ruin it.

> YOUNG BRENT
> *(inhaling deeply)*
> Nothing could ruin it but
> running out of dope. I love this
> song. Manzanera rocks so bad
> on this solo that it isn't funny.

> YOUNG ERIC
> The last night of the last
> summer we're all in high school
> together. The night summer
> vacation dies forever.

> TOPHER
> *(reaching down to take the joint)*
> Oh, shit. Poetry alert!

Everbody laughs.

> YOUNG ERIC
> Okay, I'll just shut up.

> YOUNG JANICE
> No, baby, you're so sweet when
> you talk. But just be quiet for a
> little while, okay?

She presses in against his side. TOPHER passes the joint to KIMMY. After a hit, she starts to cough. JANICE leans over to slap her back.

> YOUNG JANICE (cont.)
> Kimmy, just take little hits! You
> always do that.

> KIMMY
> *(raspy, almost unable to talk)*
> At least I didn't throw up.
> This time.

> TOPHER
> Erky. Throw me a cigarette,
> man.

ERIC tosses up his pack. TOPHER takes one and lights it.

                    KIMMY
How long are your
grandparents gone, Eric?

                    YOUNG ERIC
Weeks. Months. Years.

                    YOUNG BRENT
                    (laughing)
Erky is high.

                    YOUNG JANICE
They missed their plane. They
were supposed to be back
today.

*The Roxy Music song has been playing under all this, and it's
building to a climax now. YOUNG TOPHER stands up and
begins playing air-guitar, using the rum bottle as the guitar neck.*

                    YOUNG BRENT
                    (repeating after song)
"In every dream home a
heartache..."

                    YOUNG ERIC
Yeah, and if you get too fucked
up and put a foot through my
grandparents' roof, it'll be my
fucking heartache, all right.
Topher, what are you doing?

                    YOUNG BRENT
Topher's higher than Erky.

YOUNG JANICE
Topher, be careful...

The climax of the song comes. TOPHER strides down to the edge of the roof and braces himself, serenading the orchard and surrounding town. He begins to sing, quiet but getting louder, then bellowing the final line:

TOPHER
"Inflatable dolly—dee-luxe and
dee-lightful. I blew up your
body...but you blew my mind!"

As the guitar solo comes wailing in, TOPHER staggers for a moment on the edge of the roof, air-strumming the bottle. Abruptly, he pitches over the edge and vanishes. After a stunned second:

YOUNG ERIC
Shit!

KIMMY
(almost crying)
Is he hurt? Is he hurt?

YOUNG ERIC
Topher, man? You all right?

YOUNG TOPHER
(weakly; offscreen)
It was all great, except the last
little bit. But I think I spilled
some of my Bacardi.

YOUNG BRENT
(relieved)
You are such an asshole, man!

YOUNG ERIC
Are you sure you're okay?

*As ERIC begins climbing down from the roof, TOPHER
suddenly sits up.*

YOUNG TOPHER
Shit!
(fumbles in pockets)
If those fuckers get lost...
(finds what he's looking for)
Ah. Far out.

YOUNG ERIC
Don't do shit like that, man.

YOUNG TOPHER
I fucking thought I smashed
these or something.

YOUNG ERIC
Smashed what?

YOUNG TOPHER
Let's go in, man, put on some
more tunes—I'll show you. It's
a surprise...

As Roxy Music plays out, we DISSOLVE TO:

TAD WILLIAMS

EXT.—ERIC'S MOTEL—NIGHT

Just to establish the transition, we see the outside of a mid-grade side-of-the-road motel. We move in on ERIC'S room.

INT.—ERIC'S MOTEL—NIGHT

ADULT ERIC is sleeping. We move in on his face, lips moving a little, hear his voice in a dreaming whisper:

> ERIC
> Topher, don't...

CUT TO: Quick FLASH of TOPHER's distorted current face coming out of shadow, as though it were in ERIC's room.

ERIC wakes up, gasping, but there's nothing in the room but a little light from the streetlights leaking through the curtain. ERIC lets his head fall back, then we hear a faint noise. ERIC sits up: he hears it. It's someone CRYING.

Looking really disturbed, ERIC glances at the digital clock, which reads 3:17. We hear the crying a little louder—a woman's voice, a hopeless, quiet weeping. ERIC stands up by the bed, turning his head slowly, locating the source of the sound. It's more upsetting to him than us, because he RECOGNIZES it.

ERIC moves slowly across the dark room toward the bathroom door, which is closed. He slowly leans his head against the door and we hear the crying louder. He looks terrified. The crying gets louder.

ERIC
K-K-Ki...Kimmy?

The crying continues, a little more frightened and miserable now.

ERIC
Kimmy, is...is that you?

KIMMY
(tiny, whispery voice)
I'm so scared.

ERIC, hands shaking violently, tries the door. It's locked.

ERIC
Kimmy, let me in.

KIMMY
I'm...scared. Eric, where is
everyone? What's happening?

Something THUMPS, as though someone has just climbed into the bathtub. The thumping gets louder—something very strange is happening in the bathroom.

ERIC
Kimmy? Kimmy!

Her weeping has changed to sounds of panicked grunts, like someone fighting for their life or being raped.

KIMMY
Why...why can't...I...see? You

told me...you told me I could
see...everything!

*On "everything", the door finally pops open in ERIC's hand.
He throws on the light. The bathroom is EMPTY. He staggers
back, looks wildly at the clock. It reads 3:18, as we CUT TO:*

INT.—HOSPITAL—NIGHT, SAME TIME

*We see TOPHER's strange head on a pillow, eyes open, staring
straight up into the darkness. A light from outside is making tree-
branch shadows flail on the walls and across his expressionless
face, but he is utterly, utterly still as we CUT TO:*

INT.—JANICE'S KITCHEN—NIGHT

*ADULT JANICE is in her dressing gown, hugging herself
against a chill, stumbling a little as though just awakened.
There's street-light coming through the blinds and a bathroom
light in the hall. She takes a glass and fills it from a dispenser
bottle of water by the refrigerator, then drinks it as we
CUT TO:*

CLOSE UP: RIM OF GLASS

There's an ANT on the glass, feelers waving.

*JANICE makes an "urp" of shock and jerks the glass away
from her mouth, then slams it down in the sink. A moment later
she snatches it up again, plunges it under the faucet and washes
the ant down the drain. She looks, and there are a few ants on
the dispenser bottle as well. A little less surprised now, but*

just as unhappy, she starts to lift the bottle into the sink, then snatches her hand back. There are more than a couple of ants— at least a dozen are running along the counter and in a line to the refrigerator door. She takes a napkin and flicks them off the handle, then pulls open the refrigerator, spilling out the light.

CUT TO: INTERIOR OF REFRIGERATOR

There are MILLIONS of ants in the refrigerator—a boiling black mass that tumbles out the door and all over the linoleum. JANICE leaps back, shrieking and shrieking and shrieking as we go to BLACK and then, when the screams have faded, DISSOLVE TO:

INT.—MOTEL COFFEE SHOP—MORNING

ADULT JANICE and ADULT ERIC are having coffee. They both look like hell—they clearly haven't slept.

> ERIC
> I...I've been having bad dreams
> for a few weeks now. About...
> that night. That's one of the
> reasons I decided to come back.
> I thought, y'know, seeing the
> place again...

> JANICE
> But not me. Just the place.

> ERIC
> I didn't think you'd WANT to
> see me. Stop playing games.

You've been having them too,
haven't you?

JANICE
Yeah. But it wasn't bad at first.
Just a couple of nightmares,
and I used to have those all the
time. But...things have started
happening. In the daytime.

ERIC
Me too. Bad. Bad stuff.

JANICE
But why? It's too weird, Eric. It
doesn't make sense. I'm scared
I'm going crazy.

ERIC
I don't think so—not both of us
at the same time.
(he stands up)
Well, as long as I'm back in
town, I guess it's time to go see
another old friend...

We DISSOLVE TO:

EXT.—BRENT'S HOUSE—HALF AN HOUR LATER

*The house is big, nice, with two SUVs in the driveway. ERIC
and JANICE are on the front porch.*

JANICE
We could have called first...

ERIC
If he's really Zenger-Kimball,
I don't trust ad guys on the
phone.

JANICE
He's still Brent!

ERIC
Yeah. Whatever that means
after twenty-five years.

The door opens. BRENT ZENGER doesn't look good. In fact, he looks worse than ERIC and JANICE: it's early in the morning and he has a drink in his hand and a sour, sick expression on his face.

BRENT
Hey, Janice. Pierson. Long time.

ERIC
You don't seem surprised to see
us.

BRENT shrugs and turns, waving for them to follow him. He leads them across the entry into the large living room. The television is playing and there's a Bacardi bottle on top of it, half-full.

BRENT
Drink?

ERIC
A bit early.

BRENT
Tracy and Joanie are out at the
park.
(looks at Eric)
My wife and kid. Sit down.

ERIC
Like I said, Brent, you don't
look surprised to see us.

BRENT
Not feeling very surprised today,
I guess. Watching Jenny Jones'll
do that to you—kind of burns
the surprise glands right out.

ERIC
Me and Janice—we've been
having some weird dreams.
Ring any bells?

BRENT
Yeah, and it's nice to see you,
too, Pierson. It HAS been a
long time. I'm doing well,
thanks for asking.

JANICE
Neither of us has had much
sleep, Brent. Eric doesn't mean
to be rude.

BRENT

That's pretty good, Pierson.
Back after twenty years and
already she's sticking up for
you again.
(he looks around)
Do you think there's too
much white in this room?
Tracy kind of bugged out on
the all-white thing.

ERIC

Have you been to see Topher?

BRENT

I saw him. Once. That was
enough.

JANICE

He's gotten a lot worse.

BRENT

No shit.

ERIC

(angry)
Look—enough! Brent, man, I'm
sorry I haven't been around.
You could have called me too,
for that matter. But the fact is
that we went different ways.

BRENT

Yeah. It happens.

ERIC

So let's cut the bullshit, okay?
I knew you in the fucking
third grade, man. Being a
grown-up sucks, cool, we'll all
agree. Now let's get down to
business. There's something
really strange going on.
Janice and I have been having
hallucinations, all about that
night. THAT night. Nothing
else. How about you?

BRENT

I don't really want to spend
a lot of time thinking about
that shit.

ERIC

It doesn't feel like we have
much choice.
        (a beat)
It's happening to you, too, isn't
it? How long?

BRENT

I don't know what you're
talking about.

ERIC

Don't give me that, man, I
know you. How long? Weeks?

BRENT
(after a pause)
Yeah. For a while. But it goes
away sometimes.

ERIC
Maybe it did, but now it's
getting worse. We have to do
something.

BRENT
(laughs)
Oh, yeah? What's that?
Write a little Sunday magazine
section piece? "High School
Nightmare Reunions"? Or
maybe call the cops? The
dream police? What the fuck
do you think we can do about
it, Erky?

ERIC
It's something to do with
Topher. I could feel it when I
saw him. There's something...
alive in there. Angry.

JANICE
That doesn't make any sense.

ERIC
None of this does—but it's
happening. We have to go
see him. All of us. If this is

something to do with...that
stuff...that stuff he took...

> BRENT
> Talk to him? You really have
> turned into a liberal dickhead,
> Pierson, just like I always
> thought you would. What are
> we going to say? "If that's
> you fucking with our minds,
> Topher, could you please stop?"
> You must be joking.

> ERIC
> He was our friend...

> BRENT
> And look at him now! You think
> talking to that...thing is going
> to change anything? Is it going
> to change the past? Is it going to
> make up for what happened to
> him, to... to Kimmy?

Shockingly, BRENT suddenly bursts into tears—he's had quite a lot to drink.

> BRENT (cont.)
> Kimmy. Oh, man, poor
> Kimmy... Shit!

> JANICE
> It's okay, Brent. It wasn't your
> fault, either...

BRENT
Okay? It fucking well is not.
And if you want to go talk to
that...that thing...go ahead. But
don't expect me to come with
you. I wouldn't go within a mile
of that freak.

ERIC
That doesn't make...

BRENT
Just get out. Get out of here
before my wife comes home.
I used to tell her about what
great friends I had. Don't fuck
it up for me.

JANICE
Brent, come on...

BRENT
(shouting)
Get out of my damned house!

We CUT TO:

INT.—ERIC'S CAR—MINUTES LATER

They are driving out of BRENT's nice neighborhood.

ERIC
That went well, didn't it?

                    JANICE
          He's terrified. What's going on?

                    ERIC
          Guess what. I'm terrified too...

DISSOLVE TO:

INT.—HOSPITAL—AN HOUR LATER

JANICE and ERIC are talking to an ADMINISTRATOR at the main desk, a lady in her fifties or early sixties.

                    ADMINISTRATOR
          I don't quite understand
          what you're asking, sir.
          Mr. Holland's records are
          private, but I can assure you
          he's been getting the best
          possible care.

                    ERIC
          Who DOES have access to his
          records? His father's dead—he
          must have a legal guardian.

                    ADMINISTRATOR
          He has an aunt in Northern
          California. But I'm not sure
          I should be discussing any
          of this with you. He's been
          a patient with us for almost
          thirteen years now. I recognize

Mrs. Moorehead, but I don't
think I've even seen you before.

> ERIC
> *(to JANICE)*
> Mrs. Moorehead?

> JANICE
> *(to ADMINISTRATOR)*
> That's fine, thanks. We were
> mainly wondering about
> whether there had been any...
> changes. To his condition.

> ADMINISTRATOR
> Only the skin problem, which
> seems to be getting worse.

> ERIC
> But what did they say when
> they sent him here...?

JANICE pulls him away.

> ERIC (cont.)
> He was in a government
> psychiatric hospital—under
> security. I still have the
> clippings. Would they really just
> let him go?

> JANICE
> *(a little angry)*
> This isn't some big investigative

report, Eric. Topher hasn't
spoken or moved in years. His
dad went to court and asked to
have him sent here, so he'd be
closer to home.

                    ERIC
                  (disgusted)
His old man must have been
happy Topher couldn't get into
trouble any more.

*The OLD WOMAN ERIC has seen earlier rolls out in
front of them, then paces them until they stop in front of
TOPHER's door.*

                  OLD WOMAN
                  (eyes wide)
You going in there?

                    JANICE
We're going to see a friend.

                  OLD WOMAN
              (grabbing ERIC's arm)
You tell my mother I been
good. Tell her I never went in
there.

As they open the door, she rolls herself backward down the hall.

                OLD WOMAN (cont.)
That's where the devil lives...

The door swings open. It's a small room, but with TOPHER at the far end it seems very large. He is sitting in his wheelchair by the bed, staring at nothing. ERIC and JANICE hesitate, then JANICE at last moves forward and sits on the bed. ERIC picks up a chair and puts himself on the other side of TOPHER.

> JANICE
>
> Eric and I are here to see you,
> Topher. We've been thinking
> about you a lot.

> ERIC
>
> Yeah. A lot.

> JANICE
>
> We've been having...bad
> dreams. About that night. We
> thought...you might be having
> bad dreams too.

ERIC looks at her, a little surprised; this is an unexpected approach. He struggles to find the wavelength.

> ERIC
>
> We...want to help you. God,
> man, we're so sorry that this
> happened to you. To all of us.

TOPHER is rigid as a statue, staring past them.

> ERIC (cont.)
>
> But it isn't anybody's fault. It
> just...happened.

JANICE hesitates, then reaches out and takes TOPHER's hand. It's a brave act—we can sense how weird it must feel.

                    JANICE
          I haven't slept well in months,
          Topher. You know I've tried to
          help you, come visit you. How
          can I do that if I'm scared all
          the time? If I can't get
          any sleep?

                    ERIC
          We were all friends, remember?
          Before that...that bad night.
          We're still your friends. We...
          we miss you.
                    (after a long moment, he touches
                    TOPHER's other hand.)
          Please, man. Please.

The strange tableau falls silent, two people holding hands with a rigid monstrosity, as we DISSOLVE TO:

EXT.—BRENT'S HOUSE—SAME TIME

ADULT BRENT is loading things into his SUV. It looks like he's getting the family ready for a camping vacation, but not a happy one: he's very blank and silent, even though his wife TRACY is standing at the front door, talking to him.

                    TRACY
          Brent? What are you doing?
          Are we going somewhere?

He continues to load the SUV, not answering.

> TRACY (cont.)
> Whatever it is you're doing,
> we're not going anywhere until
> you talk to me. What's going
> on? It's like I don't even know
> who you are anymore...!

BRENT slows and then stops in the middle of the driveway like a toy winding down. He puts his hands over his face, shoulders shaking.

> TRACY
> Brent? Brent, you're scaring
> me...

INT.—ERIC'S CAR—LATE AFTERNOON

They are driving along a tree-lined road. Both look troubled.

> ERIC
> ...I mean, what was that all
> about? Are we saying that it's
> Topher who's making us see these
> things? There are a lot of better
> explanations, Janice. Janice?

JANICE shakes her head, too tired to talk about it. We close on JANICE's face, her eyes closed, thinking, hand on head like she's got a migraine coming on. The sound of The Doors' "Riders On The Storm" comes up slowly, filling the car.

> JANICE
> I don't want to hear any music,
> Eric. Could you turn the tape
> off?

> ERIC
> *(sounding strange)*
> It's not the tape player.

> JANICE
> *(opens eyes)*
> Then turn off the fucking
> radio! My head hurts.

> ERIC
> I didn't turn it on. It's not on.

As they both stare at the dark radio dial and the music grows louder, something suddenly appears for an instant in front of the car—a dark shape. JANICE and ERIC both shout in terror and ERIC jams on the brakes, sending the car squealing and sliding. Something THUMPS against the car as they screech to a halt, halfway across the road.

> JANICE
> We hit somebody! We hit
> somebody!

ERIC is sitting stunned in his seat, trying to get his breath, when something large and dark lands on the windshield. For a moment there's a dim glimpse of YOUNG TOPHER'S face, distorted against the glass, then he bursts into roaring FLAMES which surround the car.

TOPHER
(*screaming with laughter in the flames*)
I see you! I see you!

An instant later the flames vanish. Everything is NORMAL, the car still skewed across the empty road, but no sign of anything else. ERIC turns to JANICE, bloodless, shocked. She's just as devastated.

JANICE
Oh, my God, Eric, what's
happening to us...?

We pull back slowly from the pair of them, back until we see the car in the middle of the country road, back and back as we DISSOLVE TO:

EXT.—HOSPITAL—NIGHT

The wind is blowing the trees, hard. Except for a light in the front lobby, the hospital windows are all dark. The wind gets stronger, the tree-shadows flailing along the walls.

INT.—BRENT'S HOUSE—SAME TIME

BRENT is sitting cross-legged on the floor in front of the television. The sound is off. As we pan around we see that he has a bottle and glass on the rug in front of him. The glass is upside-down. BRENT has arranged five BULLETS in a little circle on the bottom of the glass, and is holding the sixth in his hand, looking at it. A gun is lying on the carpet next to his leg.

INT.—JANICE'S HOUSE—SAME TIME

JANICE and ERIC have finished a meal of take-out food. JANICE is washing the few dishes while ERIC wanders around in the kitchen/dining room. We can hear the wind getting LOUD outside. He picks up a picture of JANICE'S CHILDREN and looks at it.

> JANICE
> I'm glad you're here. I don't think I could have faced spending the night here by myself.

> ERIC
> I felt the same about the motel. So...tell me about your marriage. Was he a good guy?

> JANICE
> Terry? I don't know. He's an engineer. Not the most talkative guy in the world. I thought I could make it work. It seemed like a good idea at the time...

> ERIC
> What went wrong?

> JANICE
> Nothing, really. But nothing went right after a while, either. Another guy I cared more about than he cared about me.

(turns, drying her hands)
But it's different when a
marriage goes off the tracks
and you have kids. It's...there's
still something that worked. I
love my children. I miss them
so much.

ERIC
I can't seem to get a handle on
it. You married. Children.

JANICE
It's been a quarter of a century,
Pierson. You haven't exactly
stayed in touch.

ERIC
All I've been doing since I
came back here is saying I'm
sorry, and it doesn't seem to be
working on anyone. But I am
sorry, Janice, especially about
the way I treated you. Shit, I
didn't know what was going
on—I was numb, crazy. I was
a kid! We were all kids. I just
wanted it all to go away.

JANICE sits down on the couch. ERIC joins her.

JANICE
I used to call you. You never
called back. It was horrible,

having to keep leaving messages
with those guys in your
dorm—I could just hear them
thinking, "Oh, no, it's that
pathetic hometown chick that
Pierson dropped..."

ERIC
It wasn't like that...

JANICE
But you know what the worst
thing was? Do you remember
that stupid song about the
telephone? It was playing every
time I turned the radio on
that fall.
(she sings, a little hoarse)
"Okay, so no one's answering...
so I'll just wait a little longer,
longer..." I couldn't get away
from that fucking song.

JANICE blinks angrily, fighting tears.

ERIC
I never liked Electric Light
Orchestra, anyway. Brent really
hated 'em. Said they'd gone
downhill after Roy Wood left
the group.

JANICE
Boys. You can talk about guitar

solos, but anything else just
paralyzes you, doesn't it?

ERIC
Look, for years there wasn't a
fucking day that went by when
I didn't think about how things
went so wrong—with you and
me, that night...everything.
Over and over. Thinking
about how if I'd only done this
thing different or that thing
different...

JANICE
(after a pause)
What are we going to do, Eric?
I'm frightened.

ERIC shakes his head, then moves closer to her and puts his arm around her. She relaxes into his chest.

ERIC
I have no idea at all. I'm scared
shitless myself. But this feels
good. It's the first thing that's
felt that way for a while.
(a beat)
I haven't really been able to
make it work with anyone.
Scared I never will. Sometimes
it feels like I'm getting paid
back for being a shit to you,
back then.

JANICE lifts her face to look at him. She has a tear on her cheek. ERIC gently wipes it away with his finger. After a moment, he touches her cheek again, letting his hand stay. She leans forward and they kiss. What starts out careful and tenative begins to turn passionate—JANICE is crying as they kiss, almost climbing onto his lap. Then she pulls away.

> JANICE
> No. No, it's not right.

> ERIC
> If you want...

> JANICE
> After all these years, I don't know what I want. But you don't know me any more, Eric. I'm not the same person, and neither are you. We can't just fall into bed. We'd be...I don't know, fucking our past, not each other.

> ERIC
> Seems like its our past that's fucking us. In more ways than one.

JANICE slowly moves back against his chest.

> JANICE
> You're still pretty funny, you know? Too bad it's true.
> *(after a moment)*
> I was so scared.

ERIC
It's been a weird day all around.

JANICE
No! Back then. That night. I
was acting cool because I hated
you guys treating me like a
wimpy girl, but I didn't really
want to take that stuff...

DISSOLVE TO:

INT.—PIERSON HOUSE, 1976—NIGHT

CLOSE ON: BRENT'S PALM

YOUNG BRENT is shaking a little bit of something out of a pill bottle onto the cotton wadding in his hand. As we pull back, we see that everyone is sitting in a circle on the living room floor, except TOPHER who is lying on the couch with his feet up.

YOUNG BRENT
Four-way windowpane. Decks
are cleared. Ready to beam up,
Mr. Spock.

KIMMY
(nervously)
I thought acid came in, like, a
sugar cube.

TAD WILLIAMS

YOUNG BRENT
That was in the old days. This
is the latest and greatest. Come
on, you don't know who your
friends really are until you trip
with them—right, Erky?

YOUNG ERIC
(singing)
"Oh I wish I was an Oscar
Mayer Wiener, that is what
I'd truly like to be-ee-ee,
'cause if I was an Oscar
Mayer Wiener..."

YOUNG BRENT
Five hits. Kimmy, put a record
on so we don't have to listen to
fucking Pierson.

YOUNG ERIC
(finishing)
"Everyone would be in love
with me!"

YOUNG JANICE
You wish.

KIMMY
What should I put on?

YOUNG BRENT
I don't know. You got anything
decent, Pierson? You got Yes?

"Fragile" would be pretty
bitchin'.

KIMMY
Here's a Yes album, I think. It's
hard to read the writing.

*As she's putting it on, YOUNG TOPHER swings his legs
down from the couch back and sits looking over the others as
the acoustic intro of "And You And I" begins. JANICE and
KIMMY are both clearly nervous.*

YOUNG JANICE
They're so tiny! How long is
this going to last?

YOUNG BRENT
A while. I wish I could have
got Stringer to get me this
stuff earlier—it's amazing to
go, like, to the park. The grass
looks alive.

YOUNG ERIC
The grass is alive.

YOUNG BRENT
You know what I mean.
(to Kimmy)
But wait 'til you see the stars.
They look just...far out.

TAD WILLIAMS

> YOUNG ERIC
> They are far out.

Everyone laughs, even BRENT.

> YOUNG BRENT
> *(in a bad Brooklyn accent)*
> Quit bustin' my balls, Pierson.
> *(holds out the acid; normal voice:)*
> Okay, boys and girls. Come and
> get it!

> YOUNG TOPHER
> Slow down, Zenger. I wanna
> show you guys something.

> YOUNG BRENT
> Fuck, Holland, this shit doesn't
> even come on for an hour. Let's
> just take it and then you can
> show us.

> YOUNG TOPHER
> *(enjoying his mystery)*
> No, you're definitely gonna
> wanta see this first.

There's a pause: TOPHER's clearly waiting to be asked.

> YOUNG ERIC
> Okay, what is it?

TOPHER extends his hand, in a fist, palmside down, then turns it over and uncurls his fingers to reveal five shiny BLACK PILLS.

> YOUNG BRENT
> What the fuck are those?

> YOUNG TOPHER
> The. Fucking. Best. High. Ever.

> YOUNG BRENT
> Looks like speed, man. Black
> beauties.

> YOUNG TOPHER
> Oh, no, my little Bent
> Zengerdenger. This is shit
> you've never seen. Ain't nobody
> ever seen this. This...is Black
> Sunshine.

> YOUNG ERIC
> Topher, what exactly the hell
> are you talking about?

TOPHER slides from the couch onto the floor, takes a theatrical swig from the rum bottle, enjoying everyone's attention. Just to piss them off, he takes an elaborate time lighting a cigarette, too.

> YOUNG BRENT
> Come on. Jesus!

YOUNG JANICE
Ooh, the mystery man.

YOUNG TOPHER
Okay, you know the lab? The
place my old man works?

YOUNG BRENT
Where you have a job pushing a
broom on Saturday mornings?

YOUNG TOPHER
(unfazed)
Yeah. That lab. Well, Castillo
the fuckin' head janitor had to
go home because he got sick—
he was, like, green—and he left
me the keys to lock up. Man,
normally he'd rather leave me
alone with his fuckin' daughter
than even let me touch 'em, but
he was in bad shape, pukin' his
lungs out all over
the restroom...

YOUNG ERIC
You have a gift for storytelling,
amigo.

YOUNG TOPHER
I do, don't I? So anyway, I
thought it might be a good
time to check out the drug
refrigerator, the one that's

always locked with this big old
fuckin' lock? Just in case they
had some like pharmaceutical
quality coke lying around, or
some shit like that.

KIMMY
Topher! You could go to jail.

YOUNG TOPHER
Not unless I was stupid enough
to get caught. So I'm checking
it out, and they've got a little
glass jar of these babies in the
back, in some kind of a plastic
envelope, with all these yellow
warning stickers. The name
was fucked up—Dee-oh-noxy-
somefucking or other—but
right there on the label it says,
"hallucinogen". You know what
that means, right, Pierson?
'Cause you're so smart and shit
in English?

YOUNG ERIC
You stole some drugs you don't
know anything about, except
they said "hallucinogen"?
You're crazy, Topher.

YOUNG TOPHER
(suddenly angry)
Don't fucking talk to me like

you're my dad or something,
Pierson. I'm not stupid. I
had the keys, remember, like
to the files and stuff? I
went and looked in the
folders, checked it out.
It's an experimental drug
they're working on for some
government project, and it's
basically just like acid, except
cleaner, 'cause there's a couple
of different electrons or some
chemistry shit like that.

YOUNG BRENT
Fuckin A. Experimental acid?
For the government? What kind
of shit is that?

YOUNG ERIC
And you just walked off with
'em? Like they're not going to
notice.

YOUNG TOPHER
Cool out, man. I found some
other pills that looked just
like 'em—some kinda water-
retention shit. So if they give
'em out to somebody for an
experiment they won't get
high, they'll just get...whatever.
Bloated.
(cackles)

And the scientist guys'll just
say it's like "a non-standard
reaction to the medication".
I hear my dad talk about this
stuff.
        (brightly)
So, whaddaya say? Let's get
high!

        YOUNG JANICE
        (incredulous)
Huh? You don't think we're
going to take those, do you?

        KIMMY
I think maybe I should go
home.

        YOUNG BRENT
No! No, don't, Kimmy. It's
cool. We're just going to take
acid—Topher's only playing
around.

        YOUNG TOPHER
I ain't fuckin' playin' around,
Zenger. This is fuckin' straight
up. What, are you all pussies?
No offense, ladies.

        YOUNG ERIC
Just cool out, Topher. It was
pretty amazing you did that,
but we're not going to take

something no one's ever heard
about. What is this "Black
Sunshine" shit, anyway? They
give their drugs names like that?

YOUNG TOPHER
I made it up. Pretty bitchin',
huh? I made a copy of Castillo's
key too. If this shit is half as
good as I think it is, I'm gonna
creep half the next batch and sell
it for ten bucks a hit. Send some
to Ozzy and the boys and get a
backstage pass forever. Come on,
Pierson—it'll be far fucking out!

ERIC *shakes his head grimly.* BRENT *has already begun
giving out his* WINDOWPANE ACID *to the girls.*

YOUNG BRENT
Just forget it, Holland. Come
on, you'll blow the mood. We're
just getting to the good part of
this song.

BRENT *puts his own portion on his tongue, then hands the
rest to* ERIC; *as* ERIC *takes his, the girls look at each other.*

YOUNG JANICE
We're just going to take half.

They break one hit of acid in half and each take part, KIMMY
having trouble swallowing. ERIC *turns and offers the last
squares of windowpane on his fingertip to* TOPHER.

> YOUNG TOPHER
> I can't fuckin' believe you guys.
> The last night of summer.
> Fuckin' lightweights! What
> have you got to lose, Erky? You
> ain't even staying around this
> asshole town.

He holds the five black pills in his hands and stares at them, then stares at ERIC's proferred acid. BRENT has his eyes closed, swaying to the music—one hand is against KIMMY's leg, which she's trying to ignore. TOPHER looks them all over, then abruptly THROWS the five pills up in the air.

CLOSE ON: BLACK PILLS, TUMBLING

As they come down, TOPHER lets them fall into his mouth like candy. It's hard to tell whether they all make it in—at least one bounces away—but from the way TOPHER holds his mouth closed, he's clearly got some.

> ERIC
> *(genuinely startled)*
> Fuck, man, what are you
> doing...?

> JANICE
> Topher? You're joking, right?
> Spit them out!

TOPHER swallows elaborately, then grins.

> YOUNG TOPHER
> Party time...!

TAD WILLIAMS

We DISSOLVE TO:

INT.—JANICE'S HOUSE—MIDNIGHT

ADULT ERIC and ADULT JANICE have fallen asleep on the couch, curled together. Shadows are moving across their faces—it's windy outside. JANICE is twitching. ERIC is murmuring in his sleep, small, unintelligible sounds of fear.

INT.—BRENT'S HOUSE—SAME TIME

ADULT BRENT is lying face down on the rug with the bottle of rum tipped over beside him, wind moaning in the chimney. At first we think he might be dead, but as we move closer we see the sixth BULLET is still gripped in his fingertips.

INT.—CONVALESCENT HOSPITAL—SAME TIME

We are looking down a long hospital corridor, from TOPHER's POV—it's his odd SHADOW we see on the wall beside us. The wind is loud now, wailing. As the shadow passes across the open doors of the patients' rooms, we hear some of them cry out loudly in nightmares. We see others flail in their beds. The shadow passes the nursing station where the DUTY NURSE is sleeping as though she's been poleaxed; as the shadow crosses her she flinches and whimpers. A few more steps and our POV reaches the hospital's front doors, which FLY OPEN so hard the glass shatters. The sound of the wind is a ROAR now. POV pauses for a moment, looking out on the dark and the trees.

We are now behind the dark humanoid SHAPE, which moves out the doors, out of our view. The doors swing back, as if the force that held them open has released them. A few more shards of glass tinkle. The winds are still fierce.

Our viewpoint turns, moving back down the hall much faster than we came the other way, past the sleeping nurse, past a few patients wandering in the hall, lost and weeping, to TOPHER's room.

On the bed is the hardened shell of TOPHER'S DISCARDED SKIN, a horrible relic, clearly empty now, lying cracked open, broken into several pieces on the white sheets.

SLOW DISSOLVE TO:

INT.—JANICE'S HOUSE—MORNING

CLOSE ON ADULT ERIC'S FACE: He's sleeping, still fully dressed on the couch. JANICE comes into the room in a bathrobe, toweling her hair. She stands over him, a look of troubled fondness on her face, then lays her hand on his cheek for a long moment before sliding it down to his shoulder and gently shaking him.

> JANICE
> Wake up, Rip Van Winkle.
> The power's off. I used most
> of the not-very-hot water on
> a quick shower, so you have
> a choice—a cup of lukewarm
> water to wash with, or a cup
> of lukewarm water to make
> instant coffee with.

ERIC
(groaning)
An embarrassment of riches.
Jesus, give me the coffee, please.
(a beat)
It was nice. Holding you
last night.

JANICE
Oh, shit! It's Saturday, isn't it?
I have to call the kids about
when they're coming in so I
can pick them up. Where's my
watch? (she examines it)
After ten. Damn.

ERIC
When are they due back?

JANICE
Tomorrow. School starts on
Monday.
(she picks up the phone)
Oh, damn, damn, damn, the
phone's out too. I knew I should
have gotten a cell phone.

ERIC
Use mine. Shit, dead battery.
Okay, we'll drive into town.
Maybe stop somewhere and
get some actually hot coffee,
hmmm?

                    JANICE
                (a sudden thought)
Eric, how can I let them come
back to...to this stuff? To their
mother having some kind of
breakdown, complete with
screaming daytime nightmares?

                    ERIC
I think the parenting magazines
always say, "Tell them the
truth."
                (a beat)
But speaking as a journalist,
I doubt the writers have ever
had this particular problem to
deal with.

                    JANICE
Speaking as non-journalist and
parent...thanks a lot.

CUT TO:

INT./EXT.—DRIVING THROUGH TOWN—MORNING

The storm damage is pretty extensive—trees down in the road, some power poles and phone poles tipped over. Many stores have plywood or plastic sheeting in place of windows and people are sweeping up the sidewalks. There's no power anywhere, including the traffic lights. ERIC stops at an intersection where a COP is directing traffic.

TAD WILLIAMS

> ERIC
> Hey, officer, do you know
> if any of the pay phones are
> working?

> COP
> Not right around here. Besides
> the wind, we must have had
> a little electrical storm or
> something—there's a lot of stuff
> on the fritz besides just phone
> lines. Screwing up our radios,
> too. And some of the power
> poles actually caught fire.

JANICE and ERIC for the first time look at each other, a dawning idea that something is not completely ordinary here. ERIC pulls out of the line of cars so he can continue talking to the officer.

> ERIC
> So...so where would the nearest
> working phones be?

> COP
> You'd practically have to get to
> the county line, I think, other
> side of the hills. PacBell's got
> crews out though. They should
> have the service on in a couple
> of hours. Power might take a
> little longer...

CUT TO:

INT./EXT.—DRIVING—MINUTES LATER

There are repair crews out along the road. ERIC and JANICE are behind an ambulance and firetruck, which turn down a side road.

> ERIC
> *(slowing car)*
> That's...

> JANICE
> They're going to the
> convalescent hospital. Have
> to be. It's the only thing down
> there.

ERIC pulls the car around and follows the ambulance as we CUT TO:

EXT.—HOSPITAL—MINUTES LATER

The front grounds of Las Lomas Convalescent Hospital are a surreal sight. Many of the windows are broken out, and a tree has crashed down on the front of the building, smashing the roof and damaging one of the walls. Several of the patients are wandering around the grounds, many still in nightgowns. Police and fire people are trying to clear some of them out of the driveway so the firetruck and ambulance can get in.

ERIC and JANICE park the car and walk across the front lawn. Some of the patients are just wandering. Others seem frightened or dreamy, but all turn to STARE fixedly at ERIC and JANICE as they walk past.

The ADMINISTRATOR is standing next to the fallen tree, talking to one of the police officers while the ambulance guys roll a stretcher in through the ruined doors. The ADMINISTRATOR looks up in surprise as ERIC and JANICE approach.

> ADMINISTRATOR
> Mrs. Moorehead? Did
> someone...? I mean, how could
> anyone have called you when
> the phones are out...?

> JANICE
> Called me? Why would anyone
> call me?

> ADMINISTRATOR
> *(flustered)*
> Oh. I just thought...because of
> your friend, Mr. Holland.
> *(her look grows sharper)*
> If no one called you, how did
> you know?

CUT TO:

INT.—HOSPITAL—MINUTES LATER

ERIC and JANICE are walking fast down the hallway, across leaves and other debris which have blown in through the broken doors and windows. The NURSE is walking with them, talking fast and nervously.

NURSE

He's the only one...it's a miracle
more didn't wander away—it
was terrible! Some of them were
so frightened they hid under the
beds and we missed them when
we did the count this morning.

JANICE

But you said he couldn't
move—that he couldn't even get
into a wheelchair by himself!

NURSE

It's so strange—I've never
heard of anything like it. In a
way, it's a kind of miracle...oh,
but I hope he's all right! Poor
Mr. Holland. Poor, poor Mr.
Holland...

*The OLD WOMAN that ERIC had met previously is standing
in the hall, wearing a jacket over her nightgown. As they push
through the door of TOPHER'S ROOM she calls after them:*

OLD WOMAN

He's gone home! I heard him
when I was sleeping! Tell
Mama I'm all right, 'cause he's
gone home!

*TOPHER's empty "shell" is still lying on the bed. JANICE
muffles a noise of fear and disgust behind her hand. After a*

*moment, ERIC steps forward and hesitantly touches it. He lifts
the masklike skin of the face, staring at the hollow eyeholes. It
breaks apart in his hand as we DISSOLVE TO:*

EXT.—BRENT'S HOUSE—LATER IN THE MORNING

*ERIC and JANICE are walking up BRENT'S walkway.
There's only one SUV in the driveway now.*

> JANICE
> He can't be more than a few
> hundred yards from there, Eric.
> He's crippled! He's been mostly
> bedridden for years!

> ERIC
> A chrysalis—that's what the
> nurse said the first time I saw
> him. Like a cocoon. And now
> he's hatched.

ERIC knocks at BRENT's door.

> ERIC (cont.)
> You don't think all that's a
> coincidence, do you? The power
> failures, all that shit, and Topher
> just sheds his skin and walks
> away? After all these years?

> JANICE
> What are you saying? That
> he did it, somehow? I thought

you were supposed to be the
rationalist.

> ERIC
> When the facts themselves
> are irrational, you still have
> to work with them. Just think
> about it for a second. Think!
> What night is it tonight?

JANICE *stares at him in incomprehension as the door opens.*
BRENT is standing there clutching his hand, with blood on
his arms and shirt. He looks numb and half-dead. JANICE
and ERIC gasp.

> BRENT
> I was wondering when you'd
> show up.
> > *(their expression finally penetrates; he*
> > *looks down at the blood)*
> Oh. I broke a glass. Guess you
> might as well come in.

He turns as if he couldn't care less and walks inside. After a
moment, ERIC and JANICE follow him.

INT.—BRENT'S HOUSE—HALF AN HOUR LATER

BRENT *is pretty drunk. He's sitting on the couch with his*
head in his hands while ERIC and JANICE make coffee on a
camping stove they've set up on the counter.

          BRENT
I sent Tracy and Joanie away.
Tracy didn't want to go, but
I think she thought I was going
to get violent or something...
Joanie wanted to take all
her dolls.
        (fighting tears)
Oh, God, I sent them away...!

ERIC *pours a cup of coffee for himself, sips it and burns his tongue. He blows and sips it again gratefully while JANICE takes a cup to BRENT.*

          BRENT (cont.)
I should have gone with them.
I don't want to be here. It's all
going to hell.

          ERIC
Shut up and get some coffee
into you. Jesus, Brent, do you
always drink like this?

          BRENT
        (indignantly)
What? Are you going to tell
me everything's normal? That
it's fucking inappropriate to be
drinking in the morning? You
think I should just sit here sober
waiting for that...thing to come
kill me?

JANICE
(sharply)
You knew he got out of the
hospital?

BRENT looks up with such SHOCK in his eyes that he clearly
did not. His hands begin trembling so badly that coffee spatters
the rug.

BRENT
(looking down at the mess)
Jesus. Jesus, look at that.

ERIC
Give it to me.

*He sets it on the table in front of BRENT. As he stares at
haggard, shivering BRENT, his face softens.*

ERIC (cont.)
You didn't know he'd gotten
out of the hospital?

BRENT
Christ, no. But I had dreams...

JANICE
We all had dreams. But he's a
sick man, catatonic—a cripple!

BRENT
He's coming for us. He wants...
he's angry. Because of...of what
we did.

> JANICE
>
> But that doesn't make any
> sense! We were his friends! And
> why now, after all these years?

> ERIC
>
> Maybe because he had to get
> ready. Like a caterpillar who
> had to wait until he could
> become a butterfly. He was just
> waiting all that time, changing
> inside, growing into...
> something else.
> *(turns to JANICE)*
> You know what tonight is,
> don't you? Don't you? Why
> are your kids coming back
> tomorrow?

> JANICE
>
> Oh, shit, I never called them.
> What do you mean, why are
> they coming back? Because they
> have to be back for school...
> *(it finally hits her)*
> Oh. Oh, God, tonight is...

> ERIC
>
> Yeah. The last Saturday night
> of the summer.

They look at each other across the sunlit living room of a nice, ordinary house as we DISSOLVE TO:

INT.—BRENT'S HOUSE—HOURS LATER

The living room is beginning to look a bit like a cage. A house of cards has fallen over on the coffee table. BRENT and ERIC are smoking. BRENT has sobered a bit—he just looks hellishly depressed. JANICE is clearing up in a sort of obsessive way, straightening things on shelves, etc.

ERIC
Leave it alone. It's okay.

JANICE
It's driving me crazy. All this
mess... It's something to do,
for God's sake. What are we
waiting for?

ERIC
The power to come back on.
The phone to start working.
A monster who used to be our
friend to knock on the front
door. Who knows?

JANICE
If you really think this is going to
happen, why don't we just leave?
Let's just get in the car and go!

BRENT
Won't do any good...

ERIC
For once I agree with Zenger.

What if the engine just happens
to die while we're driving down
some back road somewhere?
There we'll be, out in the
woods somewhere, stuck, no
walls, no locked doors...

JANICE

It just seems...it just seems so
stupid. All of it. This is stuff
that happened years ago!
What's it doing screwing things
up now? I just want it all to go
away so I can have my kids and
my life back.

ERIC

There has to be some kind of
sense to this. He was in that
psychiatric hospital for years.
What did they find? What the
hell was in those pills?

BRENT
(shaking his head)
Doesn't matter now.

ERIC

But it does! Was it some kind
of psychic warfare experiment?
Some kind of biological
modification thing? The CIA,
a bunch of other government

groups were working on all
kinds of crazy shit in the
Seventies. What did Topher get
his hands on?

JANICE has finished nervously clearing the living room. She
wanders into the hall and through the open bathroom door.
We can still hear ERIC's voice.

> ERIC (cont.)
> For a while, about ten years
> ago, I thought I might write an
> article about it—I even started
> researching. Nobody wanted
> to say a fucking word—total
> blackout. It was definitely
> something big. But I just
> couldn't go through with it, you
> know, dragging all that stuff
> back out again...?

JANICE is staring at herself in the mirror, hands on the
sink. ERIC's voice has become a faint murmur. As she
stares, the radio beside the bath begins to play Cat Stevens'
"Moonshadow". She stares at it in shock. When she looks
back at the mirror, it's her own YOUNGER FACE looking
back. At first she is terrified, but the impulse to look at this
lost version is irresistible. As she lifts her hand to touch her
own adult face, the YOUNG JANICE image mirrors her, and
we CUT TO:

EXT.—PIERSON HOUSE, 1976—NIGHT

It's dark now, and YOUNG ERIC *and* YOUNG JANICE *are sitting on the front porch overlooking the orchard. "Moonshadow" is wafting out the front door. There are stars in the sky and crickets chirping.* JANICE *is looking into the mirror of her compact, her hand in the same position we last saw it.*

YOUNG ERIC
(amused)
What are you doing?

YOUNG JANICE
You know Carly Heener?
She said that when she did
acid, she knew when she was
tripping because she looked
in the mirror and her face
was melting.

YOUNG ERIC
Carly Heener's brain was
already melted. Cool out, it
won't even hit for half an hour
or so. You're just high from all
that weed.
(a beat)
Man, Zenger must have a
serious crush on Kimmy. He's
actually in there listening to Cat
Stevens with her. Like the Pope
sitting down to have breakfast
with Satan.

YOUNG JANICE
(laughing, high)
You're so funny, Eric. But if you
guys all think Cat Stevens is so
bad, how come you have one of
his records? Busted!

YOUNG ERIC
I think my cousin must have
left it or something.

YOUNG JANICE
Yeah, sure.
(looks at him fondly, then frowns)
You know, you're kind of
sweating a lot.

YOUNG ERIC
I think it might be coming on
a little.

YOUNG JANICE
Do you think Topher will be all
right? Where is he, anyway?

YOUNG ERIC
Out running through the trees,
probably. Yeah, he'll be fine.
I saw him drink gasoline out
of a jug once. He thought it
was white wine. Crazy fucker's
invincible. Besides, I bet he's
bullshitting anyway. His dad
would beat the shit out of

him if he got caught ripping
that place off. I bet it's just
speed, or some psilocybin he
bought off Ricky Caffaro or
something...

*JANICE nestles against ERIC, looking out at the orchard.
"Moonshadow" ends and is replaced by Peter Frampton's
"Baby I Love Your Way". ERIC laughs.*

> YOUNG ERIC
> Man, Zenger's really got it bad.
> *(shouts toward the door)*
> Put on some decent music,
> will you?

> YOUNG JANICE
> I never noticed how close the
> trees are to the house. They
> look...I don't know. Like they're
> surrounding the place.

> YOUNG ERIC
> They are surrounding the place.

> YOUNG JANICE
> You already did that joke. But
> don't you think they're weird?
> Like they're reaching...

> YOUNG ERIC
> Ssshhh. You're just starting to
> come on. It's fine. It's all fine.

He puts his arm around her. After a moment, he starts to kiss her neck, then her mouth. She tries to respond, but when his hand moves up to her breast she pulls away.

> YOUNG JANICE
>
> Don't...

> YOUNG ERIC
>
> It's okay.

> YOUNG JANICE
>
> It's not okay. I feel weird. Like...
> like I've got a battery on my
> tongue. I don't think I like this.

> YOUNG ERIC
>
> Shit. You only took half a hit.
> *(he sits up)*
> I'm leaving in like a week, you
> know.

> YOUNG JANICE
> *(quietly)*
>
> I know.

> YOUNG ERIC
>
> And, I don't know, since I'm
> going to be in LA, and we'll
> only be able to see each other
> on weekends...I don't know,
> maybe we should start thinking
> about...about...

There is a loud CLATTER from just overhead, then something large and dark DROPS down from the roof above them and lands with a SLAM on the porch, making ERIC and JANICE shout and jump in shock. It's TOPHER, very wired and grinning. He's got his shirt off and tied around his waist. He looks like a wild man.

> TOPHER
>
> Take me to your leader!
> *(cocks an ear to music)*
> What is that queer shit?
> *(shouts)*
> Zengerdenger! Put on some Zep
> or some Sabbath or I'll kick
> your ass into next year!
> *(he leans over ERIC and JANICE)*
> Man, I'm so fucking thirsty—
> let's make a run for brews.
> C'mon, Erky, you drive.

> YOUNG ERIC
>
> I'm not driving, man. The acid's
> just starting to come on.

> TOPHER
>
> Then we'll walk. C'mon. Janice,
> make your fuckin' boyfriend get
> off his ass. Come on, come on!

> YOUNG JANICE
>
> Why do we need beer?

> TOPHER
>
> Why do we need beer? Why do

we need anything? Why do we
need fucking music? Why do
we need dope? Because life is
shit and I'm so fucking high I
can't believe it!
> *(he laughs and shadow-punches the air,*
> *circling ERIC and JANICE like a dog*
> *excited about going for a walk)*

Party time!

TOPHER *throws back his head and howls like a wolf, a rising,*
hoarse note that turns into ERIC yelling:

ADULT ERIC
Janice! Janice!

As we DISSOLVE TO:

INT.—BRENT'S HOUSE—EVENING

ADULT JANICE *is staring at the mirror, at her own grown-*
up face. She looks at her hand on the counter. There's an ANT
crawling on it. JANICE gasps and flails until she brushes it off.
ADULT ERIC appears in the bathroom doorway, obviously
upset. The house is dark, but there's light behind him from (as
we'll find out) a camping lantern in the living room.

ERIC
Where have you been?

JANICE
(near tears)
You were going to break up

with me, you bastard! Before
anything of that other stuff
even happened!

ERIC
What are you talking about?

JANICE
We were sitting on the porch,
and you were just about to tell
me we should break up...

ERIC
I have no idea what you're
talking about, Janice. Where
the hell have you been? I've
been looking for you for half
an hour all over the house. I've
been screaming your name! I
was worried to death!

JANICE
I've been right here...
            (a beat)
Half an hour?

ERIC
Brent's not doing too well.
Where were you?

JANICE suddenly grabs him.

JANICE
Oh my God. I am going crazy.

(looks around)
It's dark!

ERIC
Yes, it damn well is. That's
why I've been looking all over
for you—I didn't know what
happened. Where were you?

JANICE
Back there. Back there, Eric.

BRENT *stumbles into the hallway, haggard, haunted.*

BRENT
*(even more overwhelmed than
E. and J.)*
Can't get away. He's in our
heads! We're fucked.

ERIC
Come on, pull yourself
together.

BRENT
You think I'm useless, don't
you? But I know how to end
this.
(he produces his GUN)
It's easy. One bullet in
Topher Holland's brain and
everything's over...

> ERIC
> Jesus, Brent, put that thing
> away! That's all we need,
> you pulling some cowboy shit
> like that.

> JANICE
> Why is this happening to us?
> He was our friend!

> BRENT
> You have no idea how hard
> I worked to make a life for
> myself. Worked damn hard.
> It was a nice life, too. I just
> wanted to forget...

BRENT *pauses; then, as if he has really noticed ERIC and JANICE for the first time, he looks at them sorrowfully.*

> BRENT (cont.)
> I'm sorry. I'm so sorry. It's all
> my fault. I...

He turns and staggers out of the hallway. A moment later a CRASH startles ERIC and JANICE. They run to the living room. BRENT has knocked over the coffee table.

> ERIC
> Jesus, you almost busted the
> lantern...!
> (*realizes BRENT is staring in horror at
> the front door*)
> Brent, what's...

As JANICE comes up beside him, the three of them standing close together in the middle of the living room, the DOORKNOB of the front door turns a little, clicks, turns again. They stare at it, frozen. After a moment, the door clicks and slowly swings open... BRENT makes little panting noises of terror. JANICE and ERIC grab for each other's hands.

The door is all the way open. The street outside is dark. The doorway is EMPTY.

> ERIC
> *(hoarsely)*
> Who...?

He picks up a broken table-leg and the lantern and slowly moves toward the open door. JANICE grabs a heavy vase and moves up beside him. BRENT is on his knees on the floor behind them. They reach the doorway and peer out. Empty, dark street. ERIC cautiously extends the lantern, taking a step outside, looking, looking...

> ERIC
> There's no one here...

ERIC glances down. A symbol written in FLAMES on the porch—a crude drawing of an EYE, surrounded by rays like the sun—is flickering out. As it disappears, the PHONE rings, making them all JUMP in shock. It takes a second for the import to reach them.

> JANICE
> *(excited, relieved)*
> The phones! The phones are
> working!

The cordless phone is in the table-wreckage near BRENT, but he doesn't move. JANICE picks it up and listens for a second. Her eyes widen, her jaw drops. She turns like an accident victim in shock and hands the phone to ERIC.

> JANICE
> It's for you. It's...it's Kimmy.

> KIMMY
> *(on phone; as if from a great distance)*
> Help me...! I'm lost, and it's so
> dark! Come home, Eric! Come
> home...!

ERIC is pale and half-dead-looking as the phone drops from his hand. He looks at JANICE, then at weeping BRENT. He and JANICE turn to stare at the open door.

DISSOLVE TO:

EXT.—STREETS—MINUTES LATER

The ADULT versions of ERIC, JANICE, and BRENT walk down the dark, deserted suburban streets like they're going to their own execution. All the houses are lightless and look deserted.

> ERIC
> I told you the car wasn't going
> to start. It's not going to work
> that way—none of it.

JANICE
We could wait until tomorrow
and call the police! He's an
escaped patient! This isn't just
us having some hallucination—
he's real!

ERIC
You think that's going to
happen?

JANICE
It makes more sense
than walking into your
grandmother's deserted house,
looking for him. The lights
have to come back on some
time...the phones...

ERIC
Let's find out.

ERIC suddenly steps out of the road and walks across a lawn
toward one of the houses. He stops in front of the door and
pounds on it.

ERIC
Hello? Can you help us, please?
It's an emergency.
            (no answer; he knocks louder)
You don't have to open the
door, just talk to us.

            JANICE
    Eric, you're acting crazy...

            ERIC
    Am I?

He vaults over the hedge to the next yard and begins pounding on that door, too. No answer.

            ERIC
    Help! Nuclear war! Invasion of
    wild pigs! Call the police! Call
    the National Guard!

He picks up a porch chair, heaves it over his head, then SMASHES it through the picture window.

            JANICE
    Stop it! Why are you doing this!

            ERIC
    Because there's nobody
    there, Janice! No-fucking-
    body! Look at the windows—
    no candles, nothing. People
    in the real world have
    batteries, Janice. They have
    radios and flashlights. They
    still go out and walk their
    dogs, even when there's
    a blackout.

ERIC reaches for a chunk of the windowsill and pulls it away. It comes off like it's rotten and CRUMBLES into dust in his hands. He pushes his hand through the wall and another section breaks away and dissolves into powder.

> ERIC (cont.)
> He's playing with us. Don't you
> remember that night, when we
> were walking on this same road?

> JANICE
> Stop it. You're making it worse.

> ERIC
> Do you remember what I said?
> He remembers. He's pulled us
> back into it—it's all happening
> again, but twisted up...

As ERIC speaks, we do a slow DISSOLVE into 1976. The street is still dark, but only because it's a quiet neighborhood, late at night. There are a few lights in the windows, streetlights, the glow of a television through curtains. YOUNG JANICE and YOUNG TOPHER are walking with YOUNG ERIC, who has stopped in the middle of the street, clearly beginning to feel the acid. JANICE turns and starts back toward him.

> YOUNG JANICE
> Eric? What you doing?
> (quietly, now she's close)
> Would you come on? Topher's
> making me nervous.

ERIC lets himself be led. As they catch up to TOPHER, ERIC is clearly disoriented.

TAD WILLIAMS

                    YOUNG ERIC
          Is it...this year? In all the
          houses?

                    YOUNG JANICE
          What are you talking about?

                    YOUNG ERIC
          I thought...for a minute I
          thought... I mean, how do we
          know it's still now?

                    TOPHER
          Oh, he's coming on real good.

                    YOUNG ERIC
          No, really. I mean, we don't
          know. Time could have just...
          stopped. For us, I mean. And
          like everyone else just went on.
          So in all those houses, it could
          be twenty years later, but we're
          still stuck in this one night,
          forever. Like we were ghosts.

                    YOUNG JANICE
          Don't say things like that.
          You're giving me the creeps.

TOPHER is swigging from a beer, even more full of manic energy. He's carrying the rest of the two six packs in a bag.

                    TOPHER
          Twenty years there ain't gonna

be no town here—'cause one of
these days I'm gonna burn the
fucking place down. Maybe I'll
do it tonight.
(turns to ERIC)
You want another beer? It'll cut
the harsh on that buzz.

YOUNG ERIC
No. I don't think so. Not now.

YOUNG JANICE
I feel really strange, Eric. I wish
you hadn't said that. I feel...
empty.

TOPHER
(oblivious)
I told you we could pimp some
brews up at the One Stop, no
problem, man. It's cause we
had a chick along, just like I
told you. Those older guys, they
always want to look cool when
there's a chick around.

YOUNG JANICE
I can see my hand moving—
look. It's all blurry.

TOPHER
You got tracers, baby! It's
coming on!

> YOUNG ERIC
> *(forcing himself back to reality)*
> How 'bout you, Topher—you
> okay, man?

> TOPHER
> *(a flash of suspicion)*
> Why? You think I'm acting
> weird? You're just paranoid—
> you always get paranoid,
> Pierson. I'm fucking great.
> Black Sunshine, bay-bee! I'm
> so big I'm gonna blow up like
> a balloon!

> YOUNG JANICE
> I hope Kimmy's all right. We
> should have made her come
> with us. She's really nervous
> about all this...

> YOUNG TOPHER
> Zenger's sniffin' after her. Boy
> is workin' hard, workin' hard.

> YOUNG JANICE
> *(suddenly)*
> I probably will still be here in
> twenty years. This fucking dead
> town.
> *(she is suddenly very emotional)*
> You'll go off to college and
> you'll be some famous guy,
> and I'll see you on television,

and I'll still be working in that
coffee shop, refilling the catsup
bottles.

ERIC is lost in thought, silent, plodding along.

YOUNG TOPHER
Yeah, you'll be sixty years old,
wearin' that fucking little skirt.
"Hi, my name is Janice, happy
to serve you!"

YOUNG JANICE
Like you'll be doing anything
different, Topher. At least
I'll have a job, which is more
than you'll have when they
find out you were ripping off
the lab.

TOPHER
Man, I'll be so far out of
here. Once I bag fuckin' high
school, I'm gone, and my dad
can fuck himself. I'll join the
fuckin' Air Force, be a pilot.
I'll be all over the world,
checkin' out the señoritas, all
that shit.

*TOPHER's voice is getting strangely loud and off-key. He's
even twitching a bit. ERIC is staring at him.*

TOPHER (cont.)
I'll be so fuckin' high you
won't even be able to see me.
You and Pierson and all the
others, you'll be pretending
you're my friends, but you'll
be on the ground, living in
this dick town, on the ground,
round and round on the
ground...

YOUNG JANICE
(angry)
Shut up, Topher. You aren't
going to do shit. Your old man's
going to throw you out and
you'll wind up hangin around
on the benches at Tyner Park
like all the other losers...

TOPHER
(suddenly screams)
Fuck you, bitch!

TOPHER *is suddenly shaking with rage, eyes rolling. ERIC,
startled out of his reverie, takes a step forward.*

YOUNG ERIC
Hey, man, cool out...

TOPHER
Keep your woman in line, man!
She can't talk to me like that...!

YOUNG JANICE
You can't talk to me like that...

TOPHER
(screaming again)
I ain't stupid! I ain't fucking
stupid! I'll fucking show you!

TOPHER *turns and runs away down the street. ERIC looks at JANICE in worried irritation, as if to say it's her fault, then starts after him. They have reached the end of the wooded street that leads to the orchard and the Pierson House. TOPHER stops under the last streetlight before the orchard, huddled. ERIC approaches him slowly.*

YOUNG ERIC
Topher? Topher, man, just take
it easy...

As ERIC is reaching to put a hand on his shoulder, TOPHER looks up, grimacing in MISERY. His features appear for a moment to RIPPLE, like something powerful is shifting below the skin. As he shrieks at ERIC, the streetlight above them EXPLODES in a shower of glass.

TOPHER
Leave me alone!

ERIC reels back, shielding himself from falling glass, as TOPHER flees into the orchard and we CUT TO:

EXT.—STREET—SAME TIME, BUT THE PRESENT

ADULT ERIC is clutching the same streetlight, unbroken now but also unlit. ADULT JANICE is beside him, crying, staring out across the empty lot where the orchard was, while ADULT BRENT simply stares.

> JANICE
> I don't want to go there. I don't
> care if this is all real or not. I
> don't want to go there.

LONG SHOT: PIERSON HOUSE, NOW

Over her shoulder, we see the dark house in the empty field.

> BRENT
> *(almost like talking in his sleep)*
> He wants it back. He wants it
> back...

> ERIC
> I don't think we can run away
> from this, Jan-Jan.

> JANICE
> My kids. I'll never get back to
> them—never see my kids again.
> Callie...Jack...

> ERIC
> I don't want to go either. But I
> think the only way out is...there.

He takes an awkward step down toward the field. He reaches back for JANICE's hand. She looks at him, miserable but sobered. She reaches out as if to touch his hand, but lets her hand drop again as we DISSOLVE TO:

EXT.—ORCHARD—1974

YOUNG ERIC and YOUNG JANICE are holding hands, deep in the trees of the orchard. The branches are so close that they block everything except thin moonlight.

> YOUNG JANICE
> He...he was acting like he was
> crazy. Really crazy. I'm scared
> and I want to go home, Eric.
> Can you just take me home? I
> want this all to stop.

> YOUNG ERIC
> We can't leave Topher like that.
> We have to find him—he's
> freaking.

> YOUNG JANICE
> What about me, Eric?

ERIC shakes his head—a choice he does not want to be forced to make. Suddenly, something RATTLES the trees nearby. ERIC and JANICE freeze, startled. Whatever it is, it's making a strange MOANING sound and it's coming closer. JANET presses into ERIC as they wait, helplessly. The sound gets louder, then an instant later YOUNG BRENT blunders through the trees and almost runs into them.

> YOUNG ERIC
>
> Brent! Damn, man, you scared
> me to death. Have you seen...?

He suddenly realizes BRENT has tears on his cheeks.

> YOUNG ERIC (cont.)
>
> Oh, shit, what's up? Are you all
> right...?

BRENT *pushes him aside.*

> YOUNG BRENT
>
> Fuck off, Pierson. Leave me
> alone.

> YOUNG JANICE
>
> Where's Kimmy? Brent, where's
> Kimmy?

> YOUNG BRENT
> *(stopping for a moment)*
> Your friend is bitch, Janice. A
> total bitch.

His face screws up with anger and hurt and he blunders away.

> YOUNG ERIC
>
> Jesus, what's going on around
> here...?

He stops as JANICE pulls away from him and heads toward the house.

YOUNG ERIC (cont.)
Janice! Where are you going...?

YOUNG JANICE
I have to find Kimmy!

He tries to follow her, but stumbles on something and falls. He gets up, calling JANICE's name, and we have DISSOLVED TO:

EXT.—THE DIRT FIELD, NOW—NIGHT

ADULT ERIC is in the middle of the empty field. There is nothing in front of him but the dark, empty house several hundred yards away. He is ALONE.

ERIC
Janice? Brent?

CUT TO: ADULT JANICE, SAME SITUATION

She's alone, nothing but her and the house.

JANICE
Eric? Where are you?

CUT TO: ADULT BRENT, SAME SITUATION

BRENT is standing in the same field, also alone. As he stares at the house, light begins to GLOW in the windows—not sudden, like a light switch, but like something smoldering into life. The first spooky piano notes of David Bowie's "Time" begin to waft across the field of dirt. BRENT slumps to his

knees facing the house like a man awaiting execution as we
SLOW DISSOLVE TO:

EXT.—ORCHARD, THEN—NIGHT

The David Bowie song is playing, but a little more muffled, as
YOUNG ERIC makes his way through the trees, which seem
very tangled and dense. He stumbles into an open clearing and
sees TOPHER sitting cross-legged, eyes closed, at the base of
a tree.

> YOUNG ERIC
> Topher! Man, you okay?

TOPHER's eyes open very slowly. He looks at ERIC with an
expression almost of amusement.

> TOPHER
> Erky. Give me a smoke, man.

ERIC fumbles out a cigarette and hands it to him.

> YOUNG ERIC
> This is all crazy, man. I think
> I'm starting to peak...

As he's talking, TOPHER lights it simply by touching the tip of
his finger to the end of the cigarette. ERIC stares, open-mouthed.

> TOPHER
> Zenger tried to get himself
> some. He touched little Kimmy's
> tit and she smacked him.

YOUNG ERIC
Did he tell you that?

TOPHER
I saw it.

YOUNG ERIC
You were with us.

TOPHER
(*imperturbable*)
I saw it. I can see your old lady
right now. She and Kimmy're
having an argument because
she wants to go home and
Kimmy doesn't. Kimmy's kind
of digging the high.

YOUNG ERIC
What are you talking about?
You can't see them from here.

TOPHER
I can see everything, man. I can
see my fucking dad watching
television in the living room at
our house, drinking a fucking
beer and squeezing his dick.
Everything. I can see the,
like, radio waves between the
stars—they look like black
rainbows.
(*he stands and lets his head fall back*)
You don't know what I can

do. I can see the worms in
the ground under your feet,
these little silver strings
crisscrossing...
> *(lets his head loll forward until he's*
> *looking at ERIC; grins)*
I can even see inside your head,
Pierson. You've been thinking
all night about some little
blonde chick you met at Bader's
party who said she was going
to UCLA in the fall—thinking
about how she slipped you some
tongue when you went out with
her to get smokes...

TOPHER's *laugh is a cackle. ERIC takes a stumbling step backward. TOPHER opens his eyes wider—the pupils are so dilated that there is no iris, only* BLACK HOLES *in the middle of the white.*

TOPHER
Don't run away, Erky. It's all
starting to happen now—I
can feel it. I'm getting so big
that I'm not going to need my
body soon. I'll be flying, man,
flying...

TOPHER *actually begins to* FLOAT *up from the ground until he is hovering at least a foot in the air, head thrown back, laughing. ERIC turns and runs as we CUT TO:*

EXT.—PIERSON HOUSE, 1976—MINUTES LATER

*YOUNG ERIC stands on the front porch, gasping for breath:
he's run all the way. He braces his hands on his knees. David
Bowie is still playing inside.*

> YOUNG ERIC
> *(to himself; a terrified mantra)*
> Too high. Just peaking, that's
> all. Cool out, man. Cool out.

*Shakily, he stands and opens the door—the music comes rolling
out. YOUNG BRENT is crouched beside the stereo system,
records all over the floor, feverishly looking for something.*

> YOUNG ERIC
> Where's Janice?

BRENT shakes his head; he's too busy.

> YOUNG BRENT
> Gotta change the music—
> too many edges. You got some
> Floyd, don't you? Reverse the
> flow, you know what I mean?
> "Dark Side of the Moon"?
> No, no, too much electricity.
> The new one, the new one,
> the new one. "Wish You Were
> Here", yeah, that'd close up
> the holes.
> > *(he looks up at ERIC, eyes wild, face
> > flushed)*
> Where's your Floyd, Pierson?

You have "Wish You Were
Here", don't you? Don't you?

YOUNG ERIC
Take it easy, dude.

YOUNG BRENT
There's fucking electricity, man!
It's leaking all over the place! I
gotta put something on...!

YOUNG ERIC
Uh...I think I've got some
Crosby, Stills, and Nash...

YOUNG BRENT
Perfect!
    (he returns to pawing frantically
    through the records, not really looking
    at any of them)
Crosby, Nash, Stills, still crazy,
Crazy Horse, Young, young
gifted and black, Black Mariah,
Blackmore, Richie Blackmore, Black
Oak, blackout, Black Sabbath...
    (he pauses for a moment, startled)
No. No!
    (returns to his pawing and gibberish)
Nash, Stills, steel, steal your
face, Steely Dan, Steeleye Span,
Stealer's Wheel, wheels, wild,
child, chill, still, Stills, Nash,
Crosby, Nash...

ERIC is looking for JANICE. The living room is a mess. So is the kitchen, even worse. Someone has started to make a pot of Spaghetti-Os on the stove, but stopped partway through, leaving tomato sauce splashed on the counter. Someone has finger-painted a crude EYE on the counter with the tomato sauce—the eye with sun's rays we've seen on BRENT's doorstep—and a few ants are crawling around it.

As ERIC reaches the stairs leading upstairs, BRENT has put on a "mellower" record—King Crimson's "Court of the Crimson King". ERIC hesitates, then moves up into the shadowed staircase. As he reaches the landing, he pauses.

> YOUNG ERIC
> Janice?

He looks up and down the hall, then moves toward the only closed door—for a moment the hallway STRETCHES, so that it seems a VERY LONG WAY. He takes another step and his hand closes on the doorknob and the door swings open.

It's his grandparents' BEDROOM—fussy, tidy. The only light is from a small bedside lamp with a heavy shade, so the room is shadowy. A FIGURE is seated on the bed, back to him, very still. ERIC, clearly nervous, begins to walk around. It's KIMMY, head down as though she's asleep sitting up, her hair covering her face. As ERIC nervously reaches his hand toward her, she lifts her face, eyes wide.

> KIMMY
> Eric! I thought you were Janice.
> *(she smiles)*
> Not Janice-Janice, of course,
> but this Janice.

> YOUNG ERIC
> Where is she?

> KIMMY
> I don't know. She's mad at me
> because I want to stay. Maybe
> she went home. If she has a
> home here, I mean—do you
> think everyone has one here,
> just like in real life?

ERIC shakes his head in confusion and sits beside her.

> YOUNG ERIC
> This is such a weird night...

> KIMMY
> I think it's nice you're in my
> dream.

> YOUNG ERIC
> Huh?

> KIMMY
> Because I thought about it
> happening like this, and then it
> happened, so that's how I know
> I'm dreaming.

> YOUNG ERIC
> You're not dreaming, Kimmy.
> You're just tripping.

KIMMY

Maybe you dreamed it, too.
Maybe you just went to sleep,
and now you're dreaming the
same dream as me. That's okay.
It means no one can get in
except us.

YOUNG ERIC

Like ghosts...

KIMMY

Yes. Like we're ghosts, maybe.
I never knew that there were
so many places outside the
world, Eric. I never thought
there was any place I could
really talk to you.

She turns to him, very intent.

KIMMY (cont.)

I could never say this to you
in real life, but since this is a
dream it doesn't matter—I'm
just talking to myself. I've
been in love with you since
9th grade, Eric. Since we were
in that Social Studies class
together and did that project.
When Janice started to go out
with you, it hurt so much...
        (smiling but teary-eyed)
And I just thought, I can never

say it, she's my best friend. But
now you and I are dreaming the
same dream.

ERIC, *overwhelmed, just stares.*

> KIMMY (cont.)
> You'll never know how much
> I wished this could happen
> for real. I used to imagine that
> we met at a party, and that
> you didn't know Janice, and
> that we...
> > *(she turns her head away; when she*
> > *turns back, her expression is almost*
> > *feverish)*
> Sometimes I think about that at
> night, when I'm in bed, and I...I
> touch myself.

> YOUNG ERIC
> Jesus, Kimmy, I...

She leans over and puts her finger against his lips.

> KIMMY
> Ssshhh. I know—it doesn't
> matter. I never understood that
> before, but I do now. Because
> there are places like this where
> we can be together—where we
> were always together.
> > *(she giggles)*
> I wonder if I'm asleep now?

Lying on the floor, and you
guys are trying to wake me up...

KIMMY *takes off her glasses.*

> KIMMY (cont.)
> I want to learn everything, do
> everything. I probably won't
> even remember this when I stop
> dreaming, but...

She suddenly leans forward and kisses him. ERIC, still stunned, almost pulls back, but the intensity of her kiss is compelling and he is drawn into it. After a moment they roll over onto the bed. A couple of times ERIC starts to draw away, more from overload than moral resistance, but KIMMY is uninhibitedly PASSIONATE—kissing and even licking his face and neck, climbing onto him, slithering her body over his with abandon. The kissing grows more intense; both of them have their hands in each others' shirts and pants—ERIC has begun pulling KIMMY's pants down over her hips when he suddenly hears JANICE's voice loud in the hall just outside the door.

> YOUNG JANICE
> No, I don't know where the Led
> Zeppelin is, Brent. You've got
> the records all over the place,
> how am I supposed to know?

Startled, ERIC slides away from KIMMY and onto the floor with a painful thump, almost tipping over the lamp table. He begins zipping himself up. KIMMY shows no such guilt, still deep in her "dream".

KIMMY
Eric...? What are you doing?

ERIC *hurriedly finishes, then gets his hand on the door just as JANICE starts to open it. For a moment they stand face-to-face.*

YOUNG JANICE
What...?

YOUNG ERIC
(blustering)
Where have you been?

YOUNG JANICE
What do you mean, where have
I been? You're really sweating
again.

YOUNG ERIC
I'm high, Janice. I'm tripping. But
I was...I was worried about you.
*(he begins to move toward the stairs,
leading her away from the bedroom.)*
Topher's acting crazy.
Completely crazy. It's fucking
with my mind. Do you think he
really took all those pills?

YOUNG JANICE
I don't want to think about
him. Maybe I should just go
home—I don't feel very good.
Besides, my mom didn't answer

the phone, so I couldn't tell her
I was staying at Kimmy's. She'll
be pissed if she comes back and
I'm not there.

YOUNG ERIC
What are you talking about?
You already called her. Jesus,
Janice, you call her again and
she'll know you're high.

YOUNG JANICE
I called her already? Really?
(looks distraught)
Is that cause I'm tripping? I
don't like this stuff, Eric. I want
to come down.

ERIC *puts an arm around her, leads her back downstairs.*

YOUNG ERIC
I think there's some of that
sinsemilla left. We should have
a couple of hits, mellow
us out...

As they reach the bottom of the stairs, BRENT suddenly
lurches into view, holding a monstrous pile of records; some
are slipping out of their jackets onto the floor, but he doesn't
even notice.

YOUNG BRENT
I figured it out. It's okay. It's
all handled.

TAD WILLIAMS

YOUNG JANICE
What are you talking about?

YOUNG BRENT
See, I was thinking, "Stairway
to Heaven", but that's so
obvious, but Jimmy Page used
to play in the Yardbirds, just
like Clapton, and Clapton was
in Blind Faith. And "Yardbird"
means "prisoner", see?

YOUNG ERIC
You need to calm down, man.

YOUNG BRENT
No, no, you're not thinking.
You remember that Blind Faith
song, "Sea of Joy"? Get how
it connects? Because "Sea" is
not only "Sea" like "ocean",
but it's "C" like "Clapton"
and also "Crimson", right?
"Court of the Crimson King",
and that's the devil, right, the
devil's court—that's hell. So
how do you get out of hell,
that's the Stairway to Heaven.
Blind Faith. So it's also "C" like
"see"—seeing. With your eyes.
You have to just...close your
eyes, and you'll get out. We'll
all get out, someday, even...even
if it takes a thousand years.

(a long pause; BRENT looks haunted)
Don't you get it?

Before ERIC or JANICE can answer, the FRONT DOOR swings open. TOPHER stands framed in it, feet wide apart, head down, face obscured by dangling hair. When he lifts it, we see that his face is streaked with dirt and scratches and his eyes are wild and lost.

TOPHER
It's...getting too big...

He staggers forward, raising his hand to his friends. He looks so deranged that ERIC, JANICE and BRENT all step back from him.

TOPHER (cont.)
(a moment of focus; a cracked smile)
Hey, Erky, check it out.
(sings)
"'Cause if I were an Oscar
Mayer wiener, everyone would
be in love with me..."

He suddenly stumbles and falls to his knees in front of them, head back, this time the eyes rolled up until only the whites show.

TOPHER (cont.)
(almost whispering)
Help me...

DISSOLVE TO:

TAD WILLIAMS

EXT.—PIERSON HOUSE, NOW—NIGHT

ADULT ERIC stands by himself on the front porch of the house. He looks around. There's no one in sight, no lights but the strong glow of a full moon. The house itself is dark, too, and everything is dead silent. ERIC takes a breath, opens the front door and steps through. He is tensed, but moonlight streaming through the windows shows the house is stripped, EMPTY.

Coming up from silence, slowly, is T. Rex's "Bang a Gong". As ERIC hears it, he shudders and turns to locate the sound of the noise, and as he turns the MUSIC and LIGHT and MOVEMENT all EXPLODE simultaneously. "Bang a Gong" is playing earsplittingly loud, and the room is suddenly the LIVING ROOM, CIRCA 1976. But this time, the ADULT ERIC is right in the middle, a witness to everything, including the younger version of himself.

ADULT ERIC stands in the middle of the floor, blinking, astonished, as YOUNG TOPHER collapses to the floor and YOUNG ERIC, YOUNG BRENT, and YOUNG JANICE stand staring.

> YOUNG ERIC
> Oh, man, why did you take that
> shit?

As he bends over TOPHER, who is shaking violently, JANICE grabs at YOUNG ERIC's arm.

> YOUNG JANICE
> We have to call an ambulance.

YOUNG BRENT
No fucking way. The cops will
be all over this place!

YOUNG JANICE
He might be dying!

YOUNG ERIC
Topher? Can you hear me,
man? You're just tripping.

YOUNG JANICE
We have to get him to a doctor!

YOUNG ERIC
Topher?

TOPHER *looks up, ragged and pale, but suddenly smiling.*

TOPHER
Tripping? You wish, man.
I'm...I'm becoming.

YOUNG ERIC
Let me help you...

He reaches down to pull TOPHER to his feet, but TOPHER simply shrugs and is three feet to one side. He has MOVED INSTANTANOUSLY, like a jump-cut. YOUNG ERIC is holding empty air. He is stunned, and looks up at the others. YOUNG JANICE is blankly terrified. YOUNG BRENT suddenly turns away, scuttling toward the stereo.

>   YOUNG BRENT
> I definitely gotta put something
> else on...

He takes off T.Rex with a jagged scratch and begins scrambling among the albums scattered all over the floor.

ADULT ERIC has been watching this. Now he takes a step forward toward his younger self, reaching out as if to take himself in his own arms, but ADULT ERIC's hand passes right through YOUNG ERIC, who is still staring after TOPHER.

>   YOUNG ERIC
> What...what's going on?

>   YOUNG TOPHER
> Don't touch me, Erky. You can't
> stop it.

>   YOUNG JANICE
> Topher, you're scaring me...

She cautiously reaches toward him, as though he might be hot to the touch, but TOPHER is suddenly GONE again, having moved instantaneously to the base of the stairway leading upstairs.

>   ADULT ERIC
>   *(shouts)*
> Just get out of the house!
>   *(no one can hear him; his face*
>   *crumples in misery)*
> Get Kimmy...

> YOUNG BRENT
> Topher, man, I couldn't find
> the Sabbath, but check this out!
> You love this! You love this,
> man!

The choppy opening licks of Jimi Hendrix's "Voodoo Chile"
come out of the speakers.

> YOUNG BRENT (cont.)
> Just sit down and listen to Jimi,
> man.

> YOUNG TOPHER
> *(a big grin)*
> Listen to him? I'm talking to
> him, bro! I'm talking to all the
> dead people...

TOPHER turns and makes his way up the stairs into the darkness.

> YOUNG ERIC
> It's the acid. I didn't see it. It's
> the acid. It's the acid...

> YOUNG JANICE
> What are we going to do? We
> have to call an ambulance, the
> police, something...
> *(sudden realization)*
> Where's Kimmy?

*ADULT ERIC turns to YOUNG JANICE, who cannot see or
hear him. Tears are in his eyes.*

> ADULT ERIC
> I'm sorry, Jan-Jan. Oh, God,
> I'm so sorry. It was all my fault.

YOUNG ERIC *looks up at the mention of* KIMMY. *A look of guilt flashes across his face.*

> YOUNG ERIC
> Kimmy's fine. She's fine. I
> think...she went out walking.
> Yeah, she's out in front.

> YOUNG JANICE
> I can't stand this! I feel like
> things are crawling all over me.
> Eric, what are we going to do
> about Topher?

> ADULT ERIC
> I'm so, so sorry...

> YOUNG ERIC
> It's okay. We're all tripping—
> we're just high, having a bit of
> a freak-out. Stay with me. Stay
> with me. It'll be okay.

> YOUNG JANICE
> *(wanting to believe)*
> You think so? Will you put
> your arms around me? I'm
> really scared.

YOUNG ERIC wraps his arms around her and they stand swaying in the middle of the living room. ADULT ERIC slowly reaches his hand out to the two of them, then lets it drop as we SLOW DISSOLVE TO:

INT.—PIERSON HOUSE, NOW—NIGHT, SAME TIME

ADULT JANICE stands in a darkened, deserted hallway of the present-day house, moonlight coming in through the windows. A few objects left when the house was emptied and some windblown leaves lie on the floors. After a moment, she hears a sniffling sound—someone CRYING. Frightened, she makes her way slowly down the hallway, listening, until she stops in front of one of the doors. She opens that door, but instead of a room, there's ANOTHER HALLWAY—incredibly long, equally dark, with a huddled shape sitting at the far end. The crying is louder.

> JANICE
> K-Kimmy?

> KIMMY
> You never came back for me.

JANICE is suddenly near tears. Music rises quietly—ELO's "Telephone".

> JANICE
> I...I didn't know...

> KIMMY
> You followed Eric like you were
> his dog. He was so much more

important to you than me—
your best friend...!

JANICE moves toward her but the hallway does not seem to get any shorter. KIMMY is still far away, her back to JANICE, face hidden.

JANICE
I didn't know any better.
He was my boyfriend... Oh,
Kimmy, that was twenty-five
years ago!

KIMMY
(a cracked laugh)
Not for me. For me it's still
happening. For me, it's always
happening...

JANICE
I'm so sorry!

The distance suddenly telescopes—JANICE is right on top of KIMMY. She reaches out to touch her.

JANICE
Kimmy? Can I do anything...
anything to make it better?

KIMMY turns, except it isn't KIMMY, it's YOUNG JANICE, but still with KIMMY's voice. YOUNG JANICE lifts BLOODY HANDS.

YOUNG JANICE/KIMMY
You betrayed me...!

ADULT JANICE screams; it echoes down the long corridor, twisting, growing fainter as we follow it around many twists and turns, until it fades back into the music of Hendrix, still playing somewhere. ADULT BRENT is standing in a corridor of his own, an Escher-like impossibilty of stairs and weird angles. He turns, bewildered. A little SMOKE drifts along the passageway.

BRENT is frightened and clearly lost. He takes a step, then another. A shadow falls on the wall across from him, and he turns with eyes wide. A dark figure steps from an open door— it's the ADULT ERIC.

ERIC
Brent? That you?

BRENT
Oh my God. Oh my God. I've
been in here for hours—where
did you go? Where's Janice?

ERIC
I don't know. Everything's...
strange.

BRENT
We have to get out of here. We
should never have come. He's
going to...

                    ERIC
          There must be some kind of
          sense to it, like Janice said. A
          reason. We were his friends...!

                   BRENT
          No! He's crazy. It wasn't
          anybody's fault—things just
          went wrong.

                    ERIC
          Really? I thought you said it
          was all your fault.

                   BRENT
          Let's just get out of here.

                    ERIC
          No, you distinctly said it was
          your fault. In fact, you were
          going to say that you betrayed
          him, weren't you?

                   BRENT
          What...what are you talking
          about?

                    ERIC
          Come on...Brent. You know
          what betrayal is, don't you?

ERIC steps closer, resting his hands on BRENT's shoulders.
BRENT is struggling, but he can't get away.

ERIC
"You don't know who your
friends really are until you trip
with them..." Remember that?
Remember?

BRENT
(struggling)
Let go of me!

*ERIC's face is beginning to change—to harden and grow
brittle. BRENT struggles harder, but it's like being held by a
statue. ERIC's face grows completely rigid, like TOPHER's
SHELL. Then it cracks, and falls away, to reveal the YOUNG
TOPHER beneath.*

YOUNG TOPHER
(big grin)
It's all about the Court of the
Crimson King, Brent. And hell
has a special place saved for
traitors...

*BRENT's clothes start to smolder where TOPHER is holding
them. BRENT shrieks and flails and at last breaks away,
falling backward.*

YOUNG TOPHER
Wait! There's still the big
finale...

*TOPHER reaches up and PEELS AWAY his face, revealing
YOUNG BRENT's FACE underneath. ADULT BRENT
doesn't stay to watch—he drags himself to his feet, running*

down the distorted corridor, shrieking and crying, as we CUT TO:

INT.—LIVING ROOM—THEN AND NOW

ADULT ERIC is miserably watching his YOUNG ERIC self combing through the carpet of the living room floor while YOUNG JANICE watches him, worried. No music is playing.

> YOUNG JANICE
> Eric? Eric, what are you doing?

> YOUNG ERIC
> He's faking. He has to be
> faking. He couldn't have taken
> all of those pills...

YOUNG BRENT looks up from his records.

> YOUNG BRENT
> Hey, where's Kimmy?

> ADULT ERIC
> *(a hopeless whisper)*
> Just tell them...

> YOUNG ERIC
> *(hurriedly)*
> Outside! She went for a walk!

BRENT rises and heads for the front door. He pauses in the open doorway.

YOUNG BRENT
The moon! It's fucking huge—
like a big eye!

As he goes out, YOUNG ERIC is still on his hands and knees, running his fingers through the carpet, searching.

YOUNG ERIC
It's all bullshit. It has to be!
We're just too high.

YOUNG JANICE
What are you talking about?

YOUNG ERIC
(looks up, desperate-eyed)
It's not real. We're all just
tripping. Topher's trying to
freak us out. He just pretended
to catch those pills, but they're
here somewhere. I'll find them.
That'll prove it.

He goes back to his relentless combing of the carpet, crawling with his face practically down against the fibers. YOUNG BRENT comes back in and walks past them, then heads up the stairs. ADULT ERIC looks after him, then closes his eyes.

YOUNG JANICE doesn't know what to do. She looks up at the stairway, then toward the front door. She watches YOUNG ERIC for a moment then sits back, hugging herself and looking very frightened. ADULT ERIC moves toward her, and although she can't see him, he kneels in front of her.

> ERIC
> You were right. Oh, God, I
> was a fucking idiot, a terrified
> kid, trying to talk myself into
> thinking everything made
> sense.
> *(a beat)*
> And now I'm a just a ghost and
> you can't hear me...

For a moment YOUNG JANICE almost does seems to hear him: she tilts her head, as though searching for a tiny sound. Abruptly, the stereo comes on full-blast—"Iron Man", by Black Sabbath—and she jerks her head back around to stare at it. There's no one nearby: it has turned on by itself.

We begin to experience the first scene over again, but this time from ADULT ERIC's viewpoint.

> YOUNG JANICE
> Eric! Eric, talk to me!

YOUNG ERIC looks up blearily from the carpet.

> YOUNG JANICE
> Eric, I want to get out of here
> right now...!

YOUNG BRENT, staggers down the stairs, clutching his hands against his stomach, panicky but trying to stay calm.

> YOUNG BRENT
> Shit, it's bad—Topher's freaking
> out for real up there.

YOUNG JANICE
Where's Kimmy, Brent? What's
going on?

YOUNG BRENT
I don't know! I can't find her. I
think...I think something bad
happened! I...

As if finally realizing something, BRENT lifts his hands away from his body and stares at them. They are covered in blood, smeared to the elbows. His eyes bug out.

YOUNG JANICE
Oh my God!

ADULT ERIC stares at BRENT, then looks up at the ceiling. He SEES something no one else can see, and cowers back in horror, gasping in panic, covering his face.

YOUNG JANICE
Eric! Eric, what's going on?
Stop that!

YOUNG BRENT has just noticed the music playing.

YOUNG BRENT
Why is this on? Who put on
Sabbath? I hid the Sabbath!

YOUNG JANICE
(panicked, overwhelmed)
It just...came on. Why do you
have blood on you?

YOUNG BRENT
No, no, no! It's all wrong! It'll
fuck everything up!

BRENT runs to the stereo and starts trying to turn it off, but can't make the buttons work. Blood is smearing on the stereo knobs. He takes out the record and throws it on the floor, but "Iron Man" keeps on playing. He picks the record up and breaks it. He's crying. The music keeps on playing. Something begins thumping on the ceiling—weird sounds, like there's a large animal thrashing around up there.

YOUNG JANICE
(suddenly certain)
Oh, no. Kimmy's up there.
With him.
(to YOUNG ERIC)
She's up there.

YOUNG ERIC shakes his head, but it's not a denial.

YOUNG ERIC
(gesturing frantically at carpet)
He didn't take all the
pills. They're around here
somewhere. It's okay!
Everything's going to be okay...!

An even stranger NOISE comes through the roof, a long muffled shriek. The three teenagers look up. For a moment none of them move or speak, although the music continues loud.

YOUNG JANICE
I'm going to get her.

She reaches the stairs, then turns to the two boys. She's clearly terrified, but trying to be brave.

> YOUNG JANICE
> Well? Are you coming with me?

> YOUNG ERIC
> Everything will be all right.

> YOUNG BRENT
> *(dropping the bits of shattered record)*
> No. It won't.

JANICE waits until YOUNG ERIC drags himself off the carpet and stands. ADULT ERIC leaps to the stairs and tries to block the way with his body.

> ADULT ERIC
> Don't go up there! Don't...!

But he's insubstantial—they walk THROUGH HIM as we DISSOLVE TO:

INT.—STAIRS, THEN—MOMENTS LATER

We've dropped back into the shaky, distorted perspective from the beginning of the film, more or less YOUNG ERIC's POV. YOUNG JANICE leads, YOUNG ERIC and YOUNG BRENT right behind. We can still hear the music, but it seems odd, underwater.

Everything upstairs is very trippy—angles seem strange. The hall lights are FLICKERING between bright and dim. It makes for an eerie, almost "strobelight" effect.

>   YOUNG JANICE
> Kimmy! Kimmy, where are
> you?
>
>   YOUNG ERIC
> Where's...where's Topher?
>
>   YOUNG BRENT
> I don't know. He was here
> a minute ago—man, he was
> acting so strange... I think he
> cut himself or something...

The corridor is distorted, the walls so narrow that it seems they might crush the viewer. YOUNG ERIC looks down to the far end, sees the door to his GRANDMOTHER'S ROOM—the place he left KIMMY. He turns like a sleepwalker and moves toward it. We follow right up to the door, feel him hesitate, then push it open.

Inside, there's only the one light of the bedside lamp, flickering, making a little humming noise as though you can HEAR the ELECTRICTY. The bed is empty now, the sheets disarranged, smeared. On the wall over the head of the bed is the EYE WITH SUN RAYS, drawn crudely in smeared dark liquid, still wet.

There's a brighter light coming from under the bathroom door.

ERIC moves toward it slowly. He stands in front of it and we hear a strange muffled THUMPING noise, and also heavy breathing and moans, like someone quietly reaching orgasm. ERIC pushes the door and it swings open. There's something in the tub, moving clumsily, hidden from us by the shower curtain.

YOUNG ERIC
Kimmy...?

YOUNG JANICE is stuck behind YOUNG BRENT, and cannot see properly. She makes a face as something CRAWLS over her foot. She looks down blankly and sees that she's standing in a couple of dozen ANTS. She shudders and takes a step back, trying to brush them off.

YOUNG ERIC (cont.)
Is that you, Kimmy?

He pulls the shower curtain aside and we see that KIMMY is huddled on her hands and knees, face pressed against the wall, partially hidden by the curtain. She's breathing in a very jerky way, and her voice is very thin.

KIMMY
Eric? I'm...scared. It's dark,
Eric. But Topher's...going to
help me to see...like he does.
Could you turn off the water?
I'm getting all...wet.

YOUNG JANICE
(still behind BRENT, trying to get over the ants and past him)
Kimmy? Are you okay?

YOUNG ERIC reaches out to KIMMY and she turns. Her eyes are GONE—only RAGGED BLACK SOCKETS—and her face and shirt are soaked in blood. The wall where she's been leaning is smeared with blood and the bathtub is full of it—she's kneeling in it.

ERIC and BRENT both scream and reel back, knocking JANICE over, tumbling in a panic on top of her, which prevents her from seeing.

> YOUNG JANICE
> Kimmy! Kimmy? Eric, what's wrong?

> YOUNG ERIC
> Don't look! Don't look!

Scrambling away from the bathroom, he tries to pull JANICE with him, but she's fighting him, crying, trying to get to KIMMY. She manages to grab the doorframe of the bathroom and pull herself crawling onto the tiles. As she turns away from fighting with ERIC, she sees (with her face at floor-level) a black knot of ANTS, boiling, swarming over some small object lying on the tiles just a few inches from her nose. It's a bloody EYE—one of KIMMY's eyes.

The POV SWINGS CRAZILY as she flails backward, retching and shrieking, tangling with ERIC and BRENT as they try to rise. They tumble back into the bedroom, sprawling on the floor. The lights are still flickering slowly on and off, and in a moment of shadow we see that there's a LARGE DARK SHADOW on the ceiling—like a stain, but more complicated.

As the lights flicker up again, the shadow opens its EYES—it's TOPHER, stretched on the ceiling as though it were the floor. A trail of BLOODY HANDPRINTS leads up the wall and across the ceiling to where he is.

> TOPHER
> Seen enough?

The three terror-stricken teenagers crush themselves into the corner of the bedroom, staring as TOPHER crawls back across the ceiling and down the wall like a spider, until he reaches the floor and stands at the center of the room, blood-smeared arms held wide.

> TOPHER (cont.)
> It's almost done now. I can fucking feel it happening—I don't need this body anymore, don't need any of this...

> YOUNG JANICE
> *(a ragged screech)*
> What did you do to Kimmy...?

> TOPHER
> I helped her. Helped her to see... all the way...to the end...

TOPHER suddenly convulses—not just a twitch, but something that physically distorts his ENTIRE BODY. He SCREAMS—a whistling shriek of agony.

> TOPHER (cont.)
> Oh God! Oh God! Oh God!

He is thrashing now, his body BULGING and TWISTING. STEAM begins to rise from his skin, leaking from his mouth and nostrils, and his gasps and screams become even more tortured. The three teenagers are all weeping in terror, fighting to force themselves even farther back into the corner. TOPHER is between them and the door.

>   TOPHER (cont.)
> Oh, fuck, it hurts! Help me! It
> hurts it hurts it hurts! I don't
> want to be...inside this...any
> more... Ah! Ah!

TOPHER *suddenly staggers forward, his face seeming to* MELT *from within, little ripples of flame lifting from the skin. He grabs* YOUNG BRENT, *who shrieks and struggles.* ERIC *and* JANICE *do not try to help him, but only fight to get further away, clawing at each other.* TOPHER *pulls* BRENT *close so that their faces are only inches apart, wreathed in steam, and shrieks at him.*

>   TOPHER (cont.)
> Get me out of here! Fuuuuuck!
> Make it stop!

The biggest convulsion of all, a moment in which TOPHER *seems almost to turn* INSIDE-OUT, *and* BRENT *is flung away, slamming against the bedroom wall.* TOPHER *falls onto the floor, writhing like a smashed snake, making awful gargling noises.* YOUNG BRENT *slowly climbs to his feet, stumbling and gasping, then staggers out the bedroom door.*

>   TOPHER (cont.)
>   *(his voice is different now, weak and ragged)*
> Stop! Come back! It's...this is
> all wrong...

YOUNG ERIC *and* YOUNG JANICE *struggle onto their feet and sprint for the bedroom door.* TOPHER's *twitching has slowed—he raises a quivering hand after them.*

TOPHER (cont.)
Come...back! Eric! J-Janice!
Don't...leave me... Don't leave
me...

We are on ERIC and JANICE as they hurtle down the stairs in a distortion of sound and vision. YOUNG BRENT is already gone, the front door swinging, and they CRASH through it after him, still screaming into the darkness, screaming, SCREAMING...

As the door swings back and clicks shut (we see it from the inside) the screaming abruptly STOPS.

We are in the empty, current LIVING ROOM with ADULT ERIC, ADULT JANICE, and ADULT BRENT. They turn in unison from the front door and look at the entrance to the stairway. There is a long, grim silence.

JANICE
(a ragged whisper)
We should have taken Kimmy...

ERIC
We were afraid...

JANICE
We left her there to bleed to
death.

BRENT
(staring at them)
Who are you?

                    ERIC
What?

                    BRENT
Who are you? Is it you again,
another trick? Do we have to
do this all over again?
          (he begins to cry)
I've been here for years. There's
nothing left you can do to me...

                    JANICE
Brent, it's us. We're here. It's
really us.

                    ERIC
          (to nobody in particular)
You know what we need to do,
don't you?

                    BRENT
But how do I know that?

                    ERIC
We need to go upstairs.

JANICE closes her eyes, not arguing, knowing it's true.

                    BRENT
Upstairs? We can't!
          (whispers)
He's up there.

ERIC
(to JANICE)
I tried to make it all go away. I
was wrong. I lied to you about
Kimmy, because...she and I
were making out, getting it
on, and...and I was feeling like
everything would fall apart if
you found out.

JANICE
(startled)
Oh, God, Eric, really?

ERIC
But I lied and it killed her.

JANICE hesitates, trying to decide what she feels. At last:

JANICE
You can't change the past.
You can't let it haunt you. We
all wish we'd done things...
differently.

Without quite realizing it, they both look at BRENT, but he will not meet their eyes.

ERIC
We should have have called
someone—the police, an
ambulance. Instead of just
leaving Topher there all night,
turning into...whatever it was.

TAD WILLIAMS

> (a sudden, nasty thought)

Whatever it is.

> BRENT

He hates us. We betrayed him.

> JANICE

We didn't know any better.

She looks at ERIC, then holds out her hand, which he takes. As if they've had a silent conversation, they both move toward the STAIRS, then, with only the smallest hesitation, they mount up into the shadows. BRENT stares after them for a moment.

> BRENT
> (quietly)

Don't leave me here.

He stands for a moment, then—with an expression of great hopelessness—he pulls the GUN out of his pocket and starts up the steps after them.

BACK WITH ERIC AND JANET:

The stairway is impossibly long, as distorted as some of the earlier hallucinations. They climb silently, clutching each other's hands. A little MIST or STEAM drifts down from the doorway at the top and eddies past them down the stairs.

They finally reach the door at the top and look into the upper hallway. It's DISTORTED like 1976, with mist along the wood floor, but empty like "now". A few leaves rustle beneath their feet, blown in through the broken window at the end of the hall. Silently, ERIC and JANICE step up and begin to walk down the hall. A small cracked voice begins to sing close by.

> TOPHER
> "Oh I'm glad I'm not an Oscar
> Mayer wiener. That is what I'd
> never like to be-ee-ee..."

As ERIC and JANICE reach the bedroom door, it swings open. The empty bedroom has EXPANDED—it seems dozens of yards across. At the far end, a pale shape—TOPHER REBORN—sits in front of the wall in low mist, head sunken on his chest. The EYE WITH SUN RAYS is scrawled on the wall above his head in dried blood.

> TOPHER (cont.)
> "...'Cause if I was an Oscar
> Mayer wiener, there would
> soon be nothing...left... of...
> me..."

TOPHER lifts his head. He is VERY PALE all over, without any hair, his skin raw and clammy, like some sea creature that has been pulled from a shell. His eyes are all BLACK.

> TOPHER (cont.)
> Hi, Erky. Hi, Jan-Jan.

JANICE tries to say something, but TOPHER lifts his hand and her mouth works without sound. ERIC takes a step toward him, but TOPHER lifts his other hand and ERIC and JANET are both frozen in place.

TAD WILLIAMS

>   TOPHER
> Ssshhhhh. It's time for you to
> be quiet.

A strange SHIFT in perspective and TOPHER is suddenly right in front of them, still sitting cross-legged.

>   TOPHER (cont.)
> I spent a long time being quiet,
> while I changed. It was like
> being buried alive. Helpless in
> the dark—screaming but no
> one could hear me. Twenty-
> five years. Twenty-five years,
> screaming! Think about that.
> *(he reaches out and touches
> JANICE's face, then ERIC's.)*
> I thought of lots of ways to
> make you suffer for leaving
> me. Oh, I lay there a long time
> in the dark, trapped in that
> body, thinking about it. What
> I would do to you. When I had
> finished...changing.

TOPHER stands. He has no genitals, no nipples, no fingernails or toenails. Music begins to play—Roxy Music again, "In Every Dream Home A Heartache", slow and building.

>   TOPHER (cont.)
> I thought I might...melt you. Or
> turn you inside out. Or maybe
> just let you experience what
> happened to me—a quarter

of a century locked inside
yourselves—but that all seemed
so...obvious. And after a while,
I began to really think...

BRENT suddenly appears in the doorway—staggering, panting for breath.

BRENT
Leave them alone!

TOPHER
Hey, I was wondering when
you'd show up!

BRENT
Fuck you! You know it's not
them you want. You know it!

TOPHER
Do I? It's funny how you think
you know things about your
friends, isn't it?

BRENT suddenly levels the gun and shoots, five times in rapid succession, screaming as he does so.

BRENT
Fuck you! Fuck you!

When the smoke clears, the REBORN TOPHER is still standing there, unharmed but for five little puckered holes across his pale body. He smiles and looks down at the bloodless wounds. They close up.

TAD WILLIAMS

> TOPHER
> Did you really think you were
> in a place where that would
> work? This all belongs to me—
> don't you know that? This is
> all my dream, and this time I'm
> taking you along.

BRENT sobs and lifts the gun.

> BRENT
> There's one bullet left...

> TOPHER
> Go ahead. What was it you
> said? "One bullet in the brain
> of Topher Holland will end all
> this?"

BRENT slams the gun against his own head and pulls the trigger. Nothing. A moment later the gun crumbles into dust in his hand.

> TOPHER
> You didn't think it would be
> that easy, did you?

He turns to ERIC and JANICE; they tumble to the floor, moving again.

> TOPHER (cont.)
> I never finished my story. See,
> I spent a long time—years—
> thinking about what to do to

you. But then, slowly—oh, I
had a lot of time—I came to
understand that there are levels
of betrayal. Many levels. And
you were scared and young, just
like I was.
> *(a beat)*

But there are some betrayals
that can't be forgiven.
> *(he turns to BRENT)*

Right, Topher? Come here.

BRENT *(as we've been thinking of him) sways and crumples to
the floor. TOPHER (as we've been thinking of him) points, and
BRENT begins to crawl toward him, despite himself. TOPHER's
skin is giving off faint curls of smoke now. The music is growing
more insistent as it builds toward its slow climax.*

TOPHER
You ran, and ran, and ran,
didn't you? But you never really
got away.

BRENT
> *(weeping, fighting, crawling)*

No, please! I didn't mean to...!

TOPHER
But you did it, and that's all
that matters. Abandoned this
body like rats off a burning
ship. Pushed me out of my own,
so I had nowhere to go.
> *(a beat)*

Black Sunshine. We'll never
know quite what that shit was,
will we? The answer is probably
buried in some government
file forever. But it was sure
something strange, something...
bad. But no one asked you to
take those pills, Topher. It was
your own stupid idea. So why
didn't you live with it, you
selfish bastard?

> *(he leans down toward crawling
> BRENT/TOPHER)*

You wanted to get out of this
body bad, didn't you? What
you did to Kimmy, all the
other crazy shit—none of that
bothered you. But when the
pain came, then you wanted
out. And you got out. Jumped
right into my body, didn't you,
Topher? And I had nowhere to
go but this ruined, mutating
shell. You took my body, didn't
you? You took my whole life!

*BRENT/TOPHER has now arrived weeping at TOPHER's/
BRENT's feet.*

BRENT
I'm sorry! I'm so sorry!

TOPHER

Sometimes it's too late for
"sorry". Twenty-five years...
Yeah, I'd say it was too late.

ERIC struggles to his feet.

ERIC
(to TOPHER)
Brent...? It's you?

TOPHER

He took my body just like a
thief. Tried to make it his own,
like repainting a stolen car. But
it's over now, Holland, isn't
it...?

*TOPHER/BRENT pulls BRENT/TOPHER up off the
ground and into his arms. The smoke is rising in earnest now,
the first flames beginning to flicker from TOPHER/BRENT's
skin. BRENT/TOPHER is screeching and fighting, in pain,
but can't escape.*

JANICE
Don't! Oh, God, don't...!

ERIC
Brent, we'll help you...!

*TOPHER/BRENT shakes his pale head. As the Roxy Music
song comes up louder, he leans close to BRENT/TOPHER,
close as a lover, and stares into his eyes. BRENT/TOPHER
struggles even harder, like an animal in a trap, but it's no use.*

TOPHER/BRENT
(to ERIC)
No, there's no help now—only
loose ends. Only circles being
closed. Sometimes the future can't
begin...until you kill your past...

*Fire and smoke are leaking out of TOPHER/BRENT's mouth
as he turns back to BRENT/TOPHER.*

TOPHER
And now I want back all the
things you took. The things
that would have been mine...

*The smoke and light is leaking from BRENT's mouth, nose
and eyes now, being INHALED by TOPHER.*

TOPHER (cont.)
A life...you got to live a life...but
it should have been mine...

BRENT
(shrieking in terror)
No...no...!

TOPHER
We got married, didn't we...and
we even had a child! Ah, she's
beautiful...

BRENT
No! Not them! Tracy, Joanie!
Give it back!

TOPHER
(gently)
No, it's you who have to give it
back now, Topher. Everything
you stole. But don't worry—it's
only for a moment...

BRENT *is fighting, struggling, but his life and memories are
leaking out of him, being devoured by TOPHER—the real
BRENT. The music comes up—Roxy Music, swelling...*

TOPHER
So many things, that should
have been mine. My memories,
my future. Stolen. All you left
me was the past. All you left me
was that night.
(a beat)
Remember this song, Topher?
It used to be one of your
favorites...
(sings, almost a whisper)
"Inflatable dolly—dee-luxe and
dee-lightful. I blew up your
body...but you blew my mind!"

As the guitar solo wails in, the flames suddenly become an
INFERNO—a wall of fire. We see the two figures writhing
within it, hear BRENT/TOPHER's shrieks grow more and
more SHRILL, then descend into bubbling GASPS as the
figures in the flames slowly MELT TOGETHER...

A moment later, there is NOTHING: TOPHER and BRENT
and the painted EYE on the wall are gone. The music is gone.

ERIC and JANICE are huddled together in the deserted empty bedroom, with dawn light filtering through the cracked windowpane.

Silently, and as carefully as if they've both been badly bruised, they walk down the stairs, which look quite normal now. They make their way across the bare living room and out onto the front porch, where they stand for a moment, looking out across the empty dirt lot in the early morning lot, to the trees and town beyond.

JANICE
What happens now?

ERIC
The future.

JANICE
Brent...Topher...whoever he
was. He has a wife, a daughter.
What are we going to tell them?

ERIC
(shrugs)
The truth? Or some part of it?
(a beat)
Maybe not.

Without looking, they reach out and find each other's hands, then walk down the porch steps and out into the field that once was an orchard. We pull back, watching two small figures walk slowly, holding hands, across the empty field. Pink Floyd's "Wish You Were Here" comes up, sweet and sad:

"So, so you think you can tell
Heaven from Hell,
Blue skies from pain.
Can you tell a green field
From a cold steel rail?
A smile from a veil?
Do you think you can tell...?"

ROLL CREDITS.

THE END.

ANTS

I T FEELS GOOD TO SWING hard, to feel his muscles flex and the blade of the ax bite deep into the wood. It feels even better that it's the old apple tree, the one whose apples have never been any damn good, puny and sour. *But the blossoms,* she always says, *it blossoms so nice—it makes the whole yard look pretty!* Yeah, and who gives a crap about that?

Well, today he's made his mind up. If there's one upside of having lost his job down at the salvage yard, it's that he doesn't have to pretend to care about anything around here that isn't pulling its weight. The apple tree is a perfect example: a few useless blossoms versus the need to bring down the heating bills next winter equals the tree is history.

As he finishes setting the cut wood onto the pile, which is getting impressively high, he sees her watching from the window. Oh, God, that face. Like he was killing a family dog instead of just taking down an old eyesore of an apple tree. He gives her a mocking smile and wave, a little twiddle of the fingers. She turns away.

He married her. He must have—everybody tells him so. But he doesn't really remember it happening and certainly doesn't remember why. Sometimes, listening to her complain about all the things that (according to her) he should have done and hasn't, or shouldn't have done but did anyway, he has a sudden fantasy of just taking a big old swing at her with his fist, like something out of a Popeye cartoon, hitting her so hard she just flies away and he never has to hear that voice again.

He even sees it with a caption, like one of those rumpled, Xeroxed cartoons they used to pass around at the yard in the days before the internet: *Bitch In Space.*

"That's just great, Karl," she tells him as he comes in and sets the ax in the corner of the kitchen. It needs to go out to the garage to be oiled and re-sharpened and put away properly, but he's going to have a beer first because he goddamn well deserves it. He wipes sweat from his face and the back of his neck. Maybe two beers. He's only had a couple today so far and it *is* Saturday. Is there some law that says you have to have a job to enjoy a few beers on Saturday?

"What the hell are you talking about?"

"Just great. Spend an hour chopping down a harmless tree for firewood in the middle of July instead of doing something useful. It's ninety goddamn degrees outside—what do we need firewood for?"

He ignores her, feels the beer sliding down his throat, icy and perfect. If only there was a way to pour cold beer over his whole life. Yeah, drown the bitch with it...or at least drown her out.

"Have you done any of the other things I asked you to do? Did you call the exterminator?"

"We don't need any goddamn exterminator. Do you know what those cheating bastards charge? It's just a few ants."

"Just a *few*?" She stares at him like he's crazy. "If you were ever in here for any longer than than it takes to open another beer, you might have noticed that we're being overrun by the creepy little things. Look. Look!" She's waving her arm like her turn indicator's broken. He rolls his eyes, which just makes her more pissed off. "Look in that sink, damn you!"

He takes a long swallow of his beer, hitches his pants up, rubs some sweat from the small of his back and ambles over to the sink. It really would be nice just to plant her one, a shot in the nose to straighten her right up. Yeah, he'd probably go to jail, that's the way things are nowadays, but oh my God it would be like a dream come true... "So what?"

"Do you happen to notice about a thousand ants in there?" She points at them like he's stupid—like he really doesn't see them. "And in the cabinets, and on the table, and all over the floor. It's *gross*, Karl, it's goddamned gross and disgusting! I can't walk across the kitchen without stepping on hundreds of the things!"

"So why do you want to pay an exterminator if you're doing it yourself?" A good one. He laughs.

She slaps him stingingly on the arm. "You're not funny, you mean bastard!"

For an instant—just an instant, but it rushes through him like a wildfire—he almost does hit her. Things go a little bit upside-down, like when he sometimes gets up too quick, gets dizzy, and almost falls. "Don't...don't you ever do that again," he tells her, with enough of his true feelings in his voice that she backs away a few steps, like a dog trying to decide whether to bolt.

"I want those things out of here, Karl," she says, but whining now like a stuck-up kid. "They're disgusting."

"Oh, they're in the sink, isn't that too bad," he says, mocking her. "Did it ever occur to you, you lazy bitch, that all you have to do is turn on the water and wash 'em down the drain?" He does, using the rinsing hose to send all the little leggy black creatures sliding and swooshing away to watery death. "Bye-bye, you little fuckers." He turns to her. "See? Problem solved."

She's gone pale now, her face cold and hard. She hates it when he calls her "bitch"—as if it wasn't the best possible name for someone like her, someone who was pretty damn cute in high school but has long since gone fat and mouthy, just like her chain-smoking, vodka-gargling mother, but who also puts on airs like she's too good for him because she watches Oprah and reads an occasional book.

"Why are you so hateful, Karl? It's not just ants in the sink." Her voice starts to rise. "What about the ones on the floor? What about the ones on the counter, and in the damn cabinets, and in the goddamned *sugar bowl*, Karl? Huh? What about that?"

Why don't they think, he wonders. Why *can't* they think? Because all this Oprah, Dr. Phil, everything's-about-feelings bullshit clouds their minds, that's why. Not a one of them can think about things logically, make a plan, solve a problem... "Oh, Jesus, shut your mouth for just a minute, Norah—I know it's hard for you, but try—and I'll show you what to do with the goddamn sugar bowl."

The ants trek across the table in a wavering line. You have to admire their focus, if nothing else, he thinks. They're like him, in a way—small, maybe, but tough and strong and well-organized. They're carrying little grains of sugar from the bowl across the table and down onto the floor, then off to their nest or hive or whatever they have. It's kind of funny, really. If you're an ant, finding that sugar bowl must be like winning the lottery.

He put his hand under the sugar bowl to lift it. The plastic table cover is sticky and it grabs at the hairs on the back of his hand. Something hot and red flares in him again. "No wonder we got ants everywhere. This place is filthy. Now, pay attention, stupid, and I'll show you something. Ants in the sugar bowl, big problem? I don't think so." He goes to the sink and dumps out the sugar, stands for a moment, sweat on his face and his heart beating strangely as he watches the little black shapes dig out of the pile of white crystals on the floor of the basin. Then he sluices them away with the rinsing-hose.

"Empty the sugar bowl," she said. "Real clever, Karl. God, it's just like you always say, men are just *smarter.* I wonder why I never thought of it? And when I want to put sugar in my coffee, or on my cereal, why, I'll just go scrape it out of the drain. Brilliant."

He isn't going to look at her because if he does he's probably going to smack the shit out of her. He only ever did it once before, when they were first together. She came back from her mother's after two weeks and they didn't talk about it again. She hadn't seen Oprah in those days.

"Just because *you* don't use sugar doesn't mean I don't want to use it, Karl." She was still using that voice, the one that made his hairs stand on end. "They're into the sugar bag in the cabinet, too, but I'm sure you thought of that already with your superior male logical intelligence. So tell me, Mr. Spock, am I just supposed to give up sugar entirely?"

Wouldn't do you any harm, you fat bitch, he thinks. His head hurts and he doesn't really want to talk any more. He wants another beer, maybe two—shit, maybe four—and then he wants to go sit in the living room and watch the baseball game, or wrestling, or anything that means he won't have to think about any of this.

"Shut up and look," he tells her. "Just...shut up. I'm warning you." Mr. Spock, huh? Compared to the crap that fills her head, he *is* an alien genius. His teeth are clenched so hard now that it's making the headache worse. He rinses the sugar bowl, dries it off with a paper towel, then refills it from the sugar bag after flicking off a few six-legged explorers. It's the hot weather. The ground gets dry and the little bastards come in looking for water, but then find out where all the good stuff is.

Little shits. His moment of identification with the ants is long gone. Just somebody else who wants to rip him off.

When the clean, dry sugar bowl is full of clean, dry sugar, he takes it to the dishes cabinet and rummages around until he finds a bowl large enough for it to sit in comfortably. Then, with it nesting there like a small boat in a bigger boat, he fills the outer bowl with water and holds the whole arrangement out for Norah to see.

"Get it?" He points to the inch-wide span of water now ringing the sugar bowl. Karl is pleased to get the last word for once—he couldn't have proved his case against her lazy thinking more completely if he'd had a chance to prepare in advance. There's absolutely no way for her to refute this evidence. "It's like a moat around a castle, see? The ants can't get to the sugar bowl. They try to cross the water, they drown. No ants in the sugar. Get it, Norah? *Get it?*"

He's about to set the sugar bowl back on the table when he remembers the stickiness that had sucked at his arm. He wipes the sweat from his forehead. Bad enough the heat, but the whole goddamn house is sticky, too. Ants? The way she cleans, they probably have roaches... Karl puts the sugar bowl up on top of the refrigerator, then pulls the plaid cover off the kitchen table and holds it out toward her. "Go on, make yourself useful. Clean this shit up, the ants won't even *want* to get on the table. It's only because you keep this place like a pigsty..."

He picks up his ax and starts toward the garage. The headache is beginning to ease.

"You...you *bastard*!" she shrieks. "You stupid, ignorant bastard! Those damn ants are *everywhere*! What am I supposed to do, bring in the hose and just fill the house with water? Is that what you're saying?"

He's not going to argue any more. He showed her—he *shut her up*—so why won't she stay that way?

"Don't walk out on me!" She's screaming louder now, that voice like a dentist's drill—he swears he can feel it buzzing in his fillings. *"Don't you dare!"*

"Shut your damn mouth or I'll slap you silly." He tries to get the garage door open but she's blocking his path. He grabs her arm and yanks her out of the way. The garage beckons like a cave, dark and cool, quiet and safe. Then he feels her fingernails in the skin of his neck, burning, sharp, and her other hand in a rude little fist, smacking away at the back of his head.

"Don't you dare turn your back on me, Karl Eggar, you ignorant pig! Don't you dare! Don't you...!"

And suddenly something just expands inside him, a great, hot plume like the blast that leveled Hiroshima. He can feel it blaze up through the whole length of his upper body, out of his guts and up his spine and out the top of his head, rising like a mushroom cloud. He has the ax in his hand and suddenly everything has turned hot, the very air is blazing like an oven. Everything is flow, and noise, and movement, and all of it is glowing red—a single hot, moving, expanding thing with him helpless in its midst, helpless but laughing as the ax rises and falls, over and over again. Each time it strikes it makes a sound—*skutch, skutch, skutch*—as satisfying as sinking a steak knife into a thick porterhouse. He can't stop laughing. Heat and the glorious pounding—the pounding! He feels like he is hammering the world in half.

For a long time after he has finished swinging Karl only stands, the ax now hanging in his hands, heavy as an iron girder. His limbs tingle, even his scalp prickles. He is drained, as bonelessly weary as if he has just had a ten-minute orgasm. But there is a...thing...on the floor. No, many things, one big and the rest in all kinds of sizes and shapes. It's hard to make out details because the kitchen is very messy. The walls are spattered and dripping red. Red everywhere.

The exhilaration is beginning to wear off. He sinks into a crouch in the middle of one of the larger scarlet puddles. The strangest, thickest, saltiest smell is in his nose. He's trying to think, staring at what's left of his wife. Call an ambulance? No point. No ambulance in the world is going to do any good. All the king's horses and all the king's men aren't going to put...that...

He retches up what is in his stomach, a slurry of beer and less identifiable components. The smell combines with the blood and suddenly he is on his side in the warm red goo, unable to do anything further until he has emptied his stomach to its lining, until he is gagging out air and streams of mucus. Then, numb and unable to think about much of anything, he staggers to his feet, drops his shoes and clothes where he stands, then steps carefully over the abstract red splatters as he leaves the kitchen.

He stands under the shower for what seems like hours, hoping in a hopeless kind of way, like a superstitious child, that if he waits long enough and lets enough water run over him, when he goes back to the kitchen things will be...different.

But, of course, they are not. He stands shivering, looking down at the bloody meat and bone, the scatter of pieces that had seemed so inevitably connected once, but now seem as random as an emptied bowl of stew. His stomach lurches again but there is no longer anything in it to throw up.

Think, he tells himself. Think. Don't panic. That's when people make mistakes. Don't think with your emotions. Be a man. Be...logical.

First things first. The shower was a mistake. He shouldn't have left the room. The police, they have all this equipment now, special lights and chemicals to detect blood stains, even stains that are so small or so old you can hardly see them. He'll put his shoes back on and stay in the kitchen, and if he has to go anywhere else, he'll leave the shoes here so he doesn't track any blood.

But he has to leave the room almost at once because the blood is pooled everywhere across the floor, right to the baseboards. He doesn't think it will soak through the vinyl flooring, but at the edge of the floor it will definitely get into the gaps between the flooring and the walls and that will be that. So he goes to the garage and gets a big plastic tarp left over from camping and then, back in the kitchen, gingerly lifts the largest piece up onto it—it is surprisingly heavy for only part of a person—then begins piling the other decent-sized chunks onto the plastic as well. He has to stop several times to gag again, but after a while he gets used to the smell and a sort of gray haze covers his thoughts and he can work without thinking too much about what he's doing. Still, the discovery of a finger with a wedding ring still on it makes him pause for a moment. It's not that he loved her, or even gave a damn about her, but this...this is so...final. Not to mention the fact that he'll spend the rest of his life in jail if he gets caught, and that's if he's lucky. And now he's cleaning up. He's trying to hide what he did. That could get him the death penalty.

Karl pauses for a moment, then gives a sort of shrug. Too late now. The bitch drove him to it. Admitting that he did it, calling the police, going to jail—that would be giving her the last word. That would be Norah having the last laugh as he spends the rest of his life, maybe fifty years or more, suffering for what *she* did to *him*.

But how will he get it all clean? He's seen it all on television cop shows. Eventually, they'll come, and he'll be the first suspect.

Karl surprises even himself by laughing. Of course he should be the first suspect. Because he did it! He's sitting naked in his kitchen in a pool of his wife's blood!

No, think, he tells himself. Look. There are red splatters everywhere, and dozens of pieces flung all over the room still to find. And on top of everything else, ants, hundreds of the little bastards still crawling everywhere, oblivious, and if they aren't already doing it, they'll soon be tracking thousands of little bloody ant footprints everywhere. The ants are searching for food—they'll head right for the blood and bone chips and bits of meat. And even if he keeps them off the body, how will he find all the pieces of Norah and get this kitchen clean?

The idea, when it finally comes, is so good that he begins to laugh again.

You dumb bitch, he thinks. You could have watched Oprah for a hundred years and you'd still never have an idea as good as this!

He gets to work.

Once he has every visible piece collected on the plastic tarp, some of them already crawling with tiny black insect bodies, Karl begins to scrub. He concentrates on soaking up blood first, as quickly and thoroughly as possible, using paper towels and rags from the garage. It takes a couple of hours, and after a while he realizes he is dizzy with exhaustion and hunger, so he stops to stand naked in the middle of the kitchen and eat corn chips from the cupboard. While he is getting them out he notices a few random droplets of red on the cupboard door, six feet above the ground. There must be hundreds like that, he knows. Still, he has a plan.

When he has finally mopped up all the blood he can see and mopped the whole floor with rubbing alcohol to kill the traces, he takes the red rags and the ruined torso and the for-lorn, bloody pieces, even the ants climbing on them, and wraps them all together in the plastic tarp and tapes it shut. Then he sits down on the floor to wait. He has blotted up every ant he could find, mashing them into the bloody rags now wrapped inside the tarp, and for the first time today the kitchen is ant-less. Norah would be pleased, if she wasn't dead.

The sky is darkening outside and the sounds of the empty house give him the strangest feeling that he should finish up soon because his wife will be coming home from work soon—but, of course, she won't. Besides, it's Saturday. The weekend. Tomorrow's Sunday. He stares at the huge tarp swathed in duct tape. Day of rest.

His laugh, this time, is raspy and hoarse.

He opens a beer, but doesn't have to wait long. Within ten minutes the first scouts of the ant army return to the kitchen. Karl sits, sipping on his beer, and lets them walk past him—hell, they can walk over him for all he cares. He's smeared in blood again, so why wouldn't they? But he's waiting for something else. At last he sees a trail beginning, leading from the entry point in the sink cabinet, out to the wall beside the trash can, then looping back again. The trail becomes an orderly line. The ants are at work in earnest now. After a few more minutes, Karl moves the trash can. There, stuck to the wall down by the baseboard, is a sliver of something pale—bone, fat, it doesn't really matter. He wipes it up with a piece of alcohol-soaked tissue and throws the tissue into a trash bag, then goes back to watch some more.

It becomes a weird sort of sport, following the busy ants as they do his work for him, locating with their ant-senses all the body pieces and bloodspots too small or too well-hidden for him to have found on his own. They find what looks like a tiny slice of eyelid and eyelash stuck to the refrigerator door handle—how did he miss that? More shockingly, they locate an entire toe that has bounced out of the kitchen into the hallway. That would have been a bit of a giveaway, wouldn't it? Karl laughs again. He's beginning to enjoy this, despite the mute presence of the bundled tarp.

It goes on throughout the night. The blood gets sticky, dries, and when he finds hidden spots he has to scrub harder and harder to get them clean. He brings his spotlight out of the garage to help him see better. The ants themselves are repaid for their searching by being wiped up along with whatever they have found. It doesn't quite seem fair, but hell, they're only ants.

At last, sometime around ten the next morning, his eyes red and his head ringing with exhaustion, he sees that the ants are all walking aimlessly. There is nothing left to find. No pieces, no spatters, nothing. The tiny, mindless creatures have done their work. They have saved his life.

Logic, he thinks as he drags the tarp to the garage. He'll deal with the rest tonight, when it's dark. Cold, hard, logic, that's how to do things. Mr. Spock? Damn right.

Sunday has its share of struggles, too. He empties her car trunk and glove compartment, files the vehicle identification number off the engine, removes the plates, then puts what's left of its former owner in the trunk and, when night-time comes, drives it down to the salvage yard where he used to work. He certainly hadn't imagined anything like this when he copied the old man's keys before they got rid of him, but it just goes to show the quality of ideas Karl Eggar has.

As he closes the gate the dogs come at him, growling, hackles raised, but he knows them both, calls them by name, gives them the remains of his lunchtime cold pizza. They wag their tales happily as he drives the car into the crusher. The salvage yard is out by the bay, and the landfill next door is closed. Nobody to hear when he fires up the crusher except for maybe a few migrant fishermen out in their boats. No car lights coming down the bay road, either, so with rising confidence he gets into the crane and pulls out Norah's car, which looks like a wad of metal gum, then after swinging it over onto one of the piles of wrecks, drops a few of the other smashed cars on top of it so as much of her car as possible is buried. It'll all be gone to the smelters on Monday night. If not...well, since they're right beside the landfill, it's not like the place doesn't already smell like wet garbage.

He walks home, careful to keep to the shadows and enter the house through the back door. No, he thinks, we don't want surprise witnesses telling how he went out with Norah's car and came back on foot.

You the man, Mr. Spock, he thinks as he takes a well-deserved beer out of the refrigerator. He's suddenly single, the house is quiet, and with all this cleaning he's managed to drive the ants out of the kitchen, too.

Oh, yeah, you the man.

He calls them himself, of course—it doesn't make any sense to wait. Waiting is like a little kid covering his eyes and hoping he's turned invisible. Karl calls them Tuesday morning, tells them his wife hasn't come back since she drove away on Sunday night.

When he opens the door he's immediately reassured to see two young officers, the kind of square-jawed, just-out-of-the-academy types that always say "Sir," and "Ma'am," even to half-naked lunatics they're arresting for drunk and disorderly. Probably neither of these fellows has even *seen* a dead body.

"Come in, please." He tries to sound both pleased to see them and properly worried. "Thanks for coming so soon."

"No problem, Mr. Eggar," says the shorter of the two. He's freckled and has the wide-eyed look of one of those born-again Christian kids in Karl's old high school, the ones who always studied and never cheated. "Please tell us when you realized your wife was missing."

"Well," he says with a humble sort of laugh, "I'm not sure she *is* missing. To tell the truth, she was pretty pissed off at me when she left. Argument, ya know. I called her sister in Trent to see if she was there, but she hasn't heard from her." Of course she hasn't, unless she can hear all the way to the scrap heap at the salvage yard, but he called her late the previous night to make the timeline look good. Thinking, always thinking. "Hey, come on into the kitchen. I'm just making some coffee."

He leads them in, holding his breath as he does, although he knows there's nothing to see. Even a county forensics team wouldn't find anything, he's been that thorough, so what are these two bowling-leaguers from the sheriff's department going to see except a clean kitchen? And not even *too* clean: he's given it a bit of a temporary-bachelor look, cereal out, bowls unwashed. He gestures them to two of the chairs at the small table, then lifts the pitcher out of the coffee maker and pours himself a hot, black cup full. "Can I get you some?" he asks. They shake their heads.

"Tell us more about what happened Sunday," the one who hasn't spoken before says. He's tall, mustached, slightly familiar. Maybe he worked in the Safeway or something when he was a kid. That's one of the funny things about small towns, the way you keep seeing faces and features. Karl has never liked the idea of other people knowing his business, but Norah, well, you'd have thought it was her own soap opera to hear her go on all the time about everybody else's private lives.

He works his way slowly into his story about the argument, although now it's a story about a guy who just wants to drink a beer and his wife who keeps nagging him to chop some firewood.

"I told her, Jeez, it's the middle of summer, Norah, but she's all, 'It's going to be a cold winter, Karl. You always put things off to the last minute.' All I wanted to do was watch the ball-game. Anyway, I guess I sorta called her a name—the 'b' word, if you know what I mean—and went off to do it. Better than having her riding my back all day, I figured. But when I came back in the house she was gone. Figured she was just letting off some steam, but then she didn't come back. When I got up the next morning and saw she'd never been home, well, I called you guys. Do you think she's all right? I hope she's all right. It was just a stupid argument."

He can tell from their expressions, which are already glazing over, that they think this is a waste of their time. A fight, they're thinking, maybe a bit worse than he's telling. She's got a boyfriend—that's what they're also thinking—and now she's shacked up with him, deciding whether to come back to ol' Karl or not.

Oh yeah, he thinks, and almost laughs. She's shacked up, all right. But it's kind of a small apartment...

"Look," he says to Officer Born-Again while the tall one is writing the report, "you sure you won't have some coffee? I just made it."

The small, freckled one shrugs. "Sure, I guess. Been a long morning already."

"There you go." He pours it out, hands the officer a steaming cup. "How about you?" he asks the other. "Change your mind?"

The one writing the report shakes his head. "No, thanks, I'm off caffeine. Doctor's orders."

Karl nods sagely. "Yeah, it's probably not good for any of us, but I figure, hey, what's life without a few risks?" He's ready to have a good long chat, actually. He's all but in the clear and it feels good. His new life starts now. Maybe there's even a way he can collect Norah's insurance...

The smaller cop looks around absently. "Uh, sorry to bother you, but you got cream and sugar?"

"Milk, hope that's okay. It's not expired or anything." He takes it from the fridge. The sugar he can't immediately find. "Never use it myself," he explains, but just then he spots the edge of the sugar bowl. It's sitting, for some reason, up on top of the refrigerator.

TAD WILLIAMS

It is only as he grabs it and something wet slops onto his wrist that he realizes it is still sitting in the dish of water he placed it in to keep the ants out of the sugar. The bowl has been sitting up there all this time, ever since...since...

That day. The day he was right about everything—even the sugar.

Because the moat around the sugar bowl has definitely worked. The ants never got near it. Karl can see that clearly as he sets it down on the table in front of the freckled cop, because there in full view, perched on a mound that is snowy white except for the crusted bit of sugar at the top that has gone brown with dried blood, lies the severed tip of one of Norah's fingers, nail and all.